Raymond Williams (1921-1988) was born in the Black Mountains, in the village of Pandy. One of the most influential thinkers and critics of this century, he was also a distinguished novelist and all his fiction is set against the background of the beautiful border country of Wales where he grew up, and where he returned increasingly in later life. His much-admired novels include the trilogy *Border Country*, *Second Generation* and *The Fight for Manod*, as well as *The Volunteers*, *Loyalties* and the first part of *People of the Black Mountains: The Beginning*.

By the same author

RAYMOND WILLIAMS

People of the
Black Mountains

2 The Eggs of the Eagle

Paladin
An Imprint of HarperCollinsPublishers

Paladin
An Imprint of GraftonBooks
A Division of HarperCollins*Publishers*
77–85 Fulham Palace Road,
Hammersmith, London W6 8JB

Published in Paladin 1992
9 8 7 6 5 4 3 2 1

First published in Great Britain by
Chatto & Windus 1990

ISBN 0-586-09059-2

Printed in Great Britain by
HarperCollinsManufacturing Glasgow

Set in Sabon

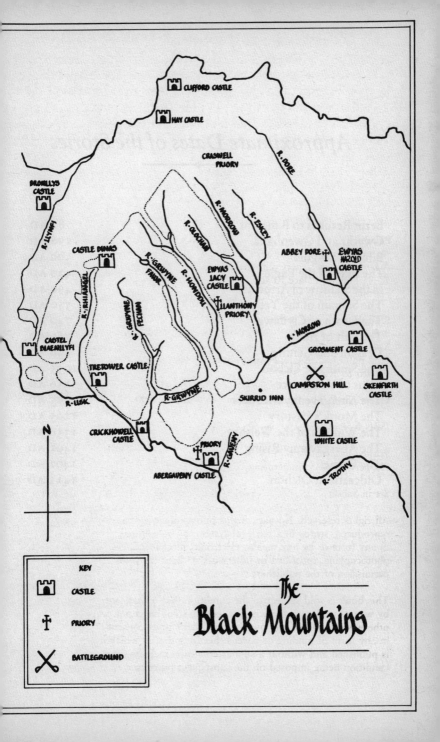

The Black Mountains

KEY

CASTLE

PRIORY

BATTLEGROUND

Approximate Dates of the Stories

◆

First

S ee this layered sandstone in the short mountain grass. Place your right hand on it, palm downward. See where the summer sun rises and where it stands at noon. Direct your index finger midway between them. Spread your fingers, not widely. You now hold this place in your hand.

The six rivers rise in the plateau towards your wrist. The first river, now called Mynwy, flows at the outside edge of your thumb. The second river, now called Olchon, flows between your thumb and the first finger, to join the Mynwy at the top of your thumb. The third river, now called Honddu, flows between your first and second fingers and then curves to join the Mynwy. The fourth river, now called Grwyne Fawr, flows between your second and third fingers and then curves the other way, south, to join the fifth river, now called Grwyne Fechan, that has been flowing between your third and your outside finger. The sixth river, now called Rhiangoll, flows at the edge of your outside finger.

This is the hand of the Black Mountains, the shape first learned. Your thumb is Crib y Gath. Your first finger is Curum and Hateral. Your second finger is Ffawyddog, with Tal y Cefn and Bal Mawr at its knuckles. Your third finger is Cadair Fawr. Your outside finger is Allt Mawr, from Llysiau to Cerrig Calch, and its nail is Crug Hywel. On the high plateau of the back of your hand are Twyn y Llech and Twympa, Rhos Dirion, Waun Fach and Y Das. You hold their shapes and their names.

Yet the fingers are long and skeletal, curving on themselves, and at their edges and in the plateau there are glaciated cwms and cross valleys, red rockfalls and steeply gouged watercourses. Beyond the hand are other heights: Troed and Llangynidr to the west, between Rhiangoll and Lake Syfaddon; Brynarw and Sugar Loaf to the south, and then the isolated Skirrid, the Holy Mountain; east, each ridge running lower, Cefn and Arthur's Seat and Merbach, before the dip to the meadows of Wye.

Beyond these outliers are two rivers to the sea. Mynwy carrying Olchon and Honddu flows to the circling Wye. Grwyne and Rhiangoll flow into the Usk. Wye and Usk, divided by Wentwood, the old Forest of Gwent, flow to the ancient seariver, the Severn Sea, where Wales now looks towards England.

The hand of the Black Mountains. From a distance, in good light, the long whaleback ridges are blue. Under cloud they are grey cloudbanks. But from within they are many colours: olive green under sunlight; darker green with the patches of summer bracken; green with a pink tinge when there are young leaves on the whinberries; dark with the heather out of flower, purple briefly in late summer; russet with autumn bracken, when at dawn after rain the eastern slopes can be red; pale gold in dead winter bracken, against the white of snow. Yet black, a cellular black, under storm cloud: a pitted honeycomb of darkness within darkness.

The valleys are always green, for the grass is bright there. Yet from the ridges they seem woodlands, with farms and fields in clearings. At midsummer, on the closely trimmed hedges, there are stands of honeysuckle and of pink and white wild roses, and on the banks beneath innumerable foxgloves. It is close looking up from the flowers to the steep bare ridges, but the contrast is sharp: above the bleak open tops, with their heather and sedge and cottongrass and peat pools, their paths which dissolve into endless sheep tracks, their sudden danger with few landmarks in low cloud and mist; and below the settled green valleys, with their network of banked lanes, their patchwork of fields, the few ploughlands above the sandstone a wet dark red or dried pink; their scattered stone houses, rough layered or ashlar, from brown or grey towards pink and green under rain. This settled and that open wild country are still within the shape of the hand.

Press your fingers close on this lichened sandstone. With this stone and this grass, with this red earth, this place was received and made and remade. Its generations are distinct but all suddenly present.

GLYN TO ELIS: EIGHT STAGES

◆

Before the time of *The Eggs of the Eagle* long ages of history had passed for the people of the Black Mountains, and many tracks had been followed in the journey of the young man, Glyn, into whose mind these stories of the past arise.

One day in the recent past, Glyn had driven his mother from London to the mountains, to stay with her father, Elis, while she recovered from an operation. Their journey was long, and as they reached the cottage at Llwyn Derw high on the hillside in the falling dusk, they could see that the windows were dark. No one was within but a note lay on the kitchen table outlining the walk which Elis had taken that day. He had planned to walk from Twyn y Gaer, in the next valley to the west, climbing past the Stone of Vengeance and the ancient stone circle of Garn Wen, across the ridges to Blaen Olchon and then along the Cat's Back to his home: fourteen miles across the mountains.

Elis had spent his life here – he knew every inch of his route, every contour and stream, every ancient place – he could not be lost, but he might be lying injured somewhere on the hillside. When he did not return Glyn set out to search for him. But as he reached the heights, moving now through patches of moonlight and blocks of shadow, thinking of the past and present of the land around him, suddenly a strange word came, distant, distinct, but not his own, 'Marod . . .', 'Marod at once awoke . . .'. A story opened, of men and their womenfolk sheltering in the caves, hunting horses before the last ice-age. And as he walked on, past the old stone graves, the circles and dolmens, scanning the ridges and gazing into the valleys below, more stories of the past related to each place arose in turn: stories of settlements and herders, of trading and marriage, of the coming of the Measurer and the mysteries of the Druids, of plague and peace and invasion through many centuries. He saw how the ways of the mountains had changed as different peoples came and lived among them, keeping their separate ways and speech, but banding together against invaders, in uneasy alliance.

All this Glyn saw and pondered as he crossed the heights, reaching at last the high ground of Tal y Cefn. To the north, above the scarp, lay the earthworks of an old British camp, perhaps the court of a lord. And he thought how, as well as the traces in the land – the arrowheads, the circles, the earthbanks – from the time of the Romans, for the first time, after ten thousand generations, came written traces, accounts which, by convention, would be called 'the beginning of history: the true, because recorded, story of the land'. In fact such records, applying the generalisations and false simplifications of a foreign empire and a different, centralised culture, had distorted the true, more complex history.

Glyn thought of the British resistance in these mountains to the Roman invaders: of the league of the Fisher Kings and the Roman victory at the Battle of Claerion, of the Roman leader Clutacos and the British slave Derco, who had disappeared from the battle, deep into the woods with his bow and spear, to remain an enduring symbol of resistance. The men of the valley spoke in deference to Clutacos when they said this dangerous slave could not be found – but Clutacos was not deceived, 'He kicked his pony angrily. He led his warriors out of the valley towards the high plateau and the long ridges to Banavint. Derco, hiding in an old oak above the track, watched them riding across the skyline.'

Berin Returns to Banavint

◆

Berin son of Clutacos walked slowly up the stony track to Banavint. The old defence banks and ramparts of the stronghold had been slighted. There was now a broad open way into the settlement.

Berin stopped and looked around. Sheep grazed across the slopes. The old zigzag track from the valley to the spur was as he remembered it. In the valley the scattered huts of Masona were occupied and busy. Men were working on timber, and children playing by the river. In the broad fenced clearings were cattle and pigs. He had avoided Masona on his way back, crossing the river Hodeni farther south and climbing through the oak wood. He did not know how he might be received in Masona. His old woollen tunic was torn and stained. His sandals were broken after his long rough walk. For two days he had followed the river Uisc and then climbed to Isgirit, the Broken Mountain, to look down at the fort of Gobanio. At first he had moved at night, under the half moon, but in his own thickly wooded country he had risked moving by day.

There were no guards or dogs at the entrance to Banavint. There were no sounds of life. He forced himself up the last and steepest part of the track, and walked into the old stronghold. His father's house, on the far side of the enclosure, with its high conical thatched roof, was as he remembered it. But the guard hut at the entrance was ruinous, and many of the other huts, across the enclosure, were neglected or deserted. Berin walked slowly along the old path to the gateway of the inner rampart. It too was open, its timbers roughly thrown down.

He waited, breathing the good air. It was the clear sweet air of his childhood, which began only at this height. He ran his fingers back through his long matted hair. It had not been dressed as it should have been since that morning of the battle above Iupania, eight long years ago. He approached his father's house, walking quietly. There was no sound from inside, but he could smell the sharp smoke of a peat fire. At the entrance he stopped and looked into the shadows.

There was a movement inside. Clutacos, now in his fifty-fourth year, had been sitting on bracken close to the smoky fire, but now he jumped up, drawing his dagger.

'Father, it is Berin.'

Clutacos stopped, peering out.

'What name? What are you doing here?'

'I am Berin, father.'

Still holding the dagger, Clutacos came forward. Berin stepped so that his face could be seen in the light. He saw astonishment, even fear, in his father's lined face, which was heavily grimed from the fire.

'You cannot be Berin. He is in the other world.'

'Not the other world, father. Though it has often seemed that I died to myself.'

'Berin was killed a brave warrior, at the battle of Iupania.'

'Not killed, father. I was taken that day by the Romani.'

'I do not believe you. My Berin would not have been taken.'

'Many thousands were taken, and I among them. The Romani made us their slaves.'

Clutacos looked around, bewildered. Then he came out of the house, still pointing the dagger. When Berin did not move, Clutacos reached out his hand and touched Berin's cheek. He put away his dagger and touched Berin's right arm. He closed his eyes for some moments and then squared his shoulders. His long hair was now grey but he still spiked it roughly with lime. His big grey moustache was stained yellow from his nose. There was a faded blue bar on his forehead.

'Is it the truth, this shame?' he asked harshly.

'It is the shame of us all,' Berin answered.

'Not all. Not all. It is the shame of Vindon and Cadi, the King Fools of the battle. And now the shame of Sisill, who has ridden down to submit.'

Berin reached out his hand and gripped his father's shoulder.

'There is much to tell. We will sit by the fire. I must rest.'

'There is no honourable rest in submission.'

'Father, I have not submitted. I have escaped and come home to you.'

Clutacos stared into his face. He began to turn away but then suddenly threw out his arms and clasped Berin close to him. They stood holding each other tightly. Berin closed his eyes.

Later, when they had eaten and drunk by the fire, Berin began the long story of all that had happened to him.

He had been born four years after the defeat of the Roman army at Claerion. In those four years, and in his own first two years of life, the Siluri and their close allies had won many victories. Ostorius Scapula, who had threatened to destroy their very name, had died during the fighting. Their only disappointment was that they had killed him by pressure instead of in battle. All over the Silurian lands, in repeated summer campaigns, the Romans had fought to establish camps and forts, and held some of them, but at Gobanio they had again been heavily defeated. In a new kind of war, the Silurian peoples used the shapes of their country to make sudden attacks in forests, in mountain passes and in swamps. They now fought, the Romans said, like bandits, with spears and bows. Under constant pressure, the Romans tried to draw them out into pitched battle, remembering their victory over Caradoc. Yet when at last this happened, a full legion under the command of Manlius Valens was defeated east of the Hsabren. The Silurian warriors rode, as in early days, through the submissive lands of the Dobuni, showing their new power. The long war began slowly to turn. The Roman forts were reinforced and held. The roads between them were improved. The Siluri, driven back west of the Hsabren, returned to harassment and sudden attacks. But now every year the forts were stronger and many warriors were lost trying to take them by storm.

Thus through the years of Berin's childhood the war settled into stalemate. The Romans had strong forts at Burro and Cicucio and had recaptured and rebuilt Gobanio. They had also, after a fierce battle in which Clutacos was wounded, retaken Claerion and built a large, heavily defended camp. Yet the land between these forts they did not control. When they moved through it, from fort to fort, in large numbers and heavily armed, they were still often ambushed and there were many running fights. Nor could they yet bring new forces, for there was other heavy fighting in the east and north of the island, and the garrisons had to rely on themselves.

So it had stayed while Berin grew and trained as a warrior. Then, when he was eighteen, news came from the coastal kingdoms that a new invasion was imminent. A Roman fleet was gathering in the estuary and a new legion from the south was encamped along the Hsabren, with many thousands of auxiliaries, Thracians and Iberians and Gauls. The High King Vindon was proclaimed War King, and his brother Cadi commanded the sea defences. The Roman commander, it was learned from prisoners, was called Julius Frontinus.

In a Council at Iupania a strategy was decided. An army was to be assembled in the lowlands below the Great Wood, to meet what was foreseen as a combined sea-borne invasion and a legionary attack from Glevum along the northern bank of the Hsabren. The princes of the mountain kingdoms argued against this strategy. The legionaries could also attack directly west from Glevum to the broad valley of the Guuy, as in earlier campaigns. And if this happened the army would be taken from behind, along the valleys of Guuy and Uisc. But Vindon was adamant. The main threat would be from the sea, and every available warrior would be needed to defeat it. Berin, with a hundred other warriors from Madrun and Iuas and Elfael, rode down to the great gathering of the army.

In the following spring the invasion came. It was much heavier than expected. There were landings at many points, as far west as Nedon. The legionaries pushed up quickly through the lightly defended valleys. At the same time, virtually without opposition, part of the new legion reached the Guuy and, marching from the camp at Claerion, fought through to the upper valley of the Uisc. Here at Cicucio they were joined by those from the sea. The whole force turned east, towards Gobanio and Burro. The main Silurian army was still not engaged, but now there was a heavy Roman push along the north bank of the Hsabren and, at the same time, a direct sea-borne assault on Iupania with more than three hundred ships. Iupania was captured and material and supplies were quickly unloaded. The wharf was under the hill where the stones of the Old Ones still stood. On the ridge above Iupania the Silurian army waited.

Vindon was entirely confident of victory, once his warriors were committed. But now the legionaries from Hsabren's north bank joined those at Iupania, and from the west, down the Uisc, the northern force was approaching. Vindon prepared for the decisive battle. It was a day, he announced, that would decide forever between liberty and slavery.

Berin, with the other mountain warriors, was on the left wing. All the Silurian warriors were brightly painted for the attack. They shouted in unison as the long trumpets sounded. But as they began their charge heavy engines unloaded at Iupania hurled metal bolts among them. The bolts fell thickly as arrows from the bowmen of Menhebog. The warriors charged fiercely, but still the bolts rained down and there was shouting from behind as horsed auxiliaries rode in from the forest. The legion, formed in wide order under its shields, advanced towards them. Some warriors, Berin among them, slashed gaps in the legion's ranks and turned to fight among them. But now the Roman javelins were being thrown and their ranks were quickly reforming. The first and bravest of the warriors were soon isolated. Berin's pony was killed under him and he fell among the feet of the legionaries. He felt a heavy blow on his helmet and lost consciousness.

When he recovered the battle was effectively over. He saw Vindon with blood streaming from his face, being marched roughly down by two legionaries. While the scattered fighting continued, the Romans, like the Siluri, were still killing, but as the victory became clear the Romans were given new orders and went round tying the wrists of their prisoners. Berin, hoping to be taken for dead, was kicked into movement and then roughly tied. He was unwounded, though there was a heavy gash in his helmet and only his gold neck torque had saved him from the blow. With hundreds of other warriors, he was marched to sit at the foot of the hill, under a guard of Thracian horsemen with big copper discs on their breastplates. A short grey-haired Roman looked over the prisoners with contempt.

That was the first moment of an unforeseen, an unimaginable condition: in this defeat Berin had become a slave. The brave rhetoric of Vindon, with its heroic contrast of liberty and slavery, was in another world from this efficient and contemptuous herding. There was now an endless waiting under orders and for orders, a slow aching realisation that for the rest of his life he would be no more than an object, an available body for others to dispose. He thought of jumping in a sudden attack on one of the strange foreign horsemen. He knew he would soon be cut down, but he was willing to die as he had been brought up to live. In defeat in his own kind of war he would, as the son of a prince, have been killed. His head would have been taken, in triumph, by his conqueror. But that was the wager of a hero, win or lose. This new dull subjection, this Roman way of taking every body for labour or for fighting, was a shock and a humiliation. To be left squatting on the ground, under the whips of alien horsemen, broke the spirit of the painted lords.

On that first day of a seemingly endless eight years he had been marched down with the others to the old royal capital of Iupania, where they were forced to carry the Roman stores that were being continually unloaded. It was then, even so early, that he had seen the full power of this Roman machine. War and trade, which in his own world had been essentially separate, were now combined in a planned and well supplied occupation. The Romans had not come for a victory but for an empire. As a slave he had become one of its available resources and supplies.

In the following days the scale of the Roman operation continued to amaze him. The old fort at Burro – a defended enclosure for the earlier landing-place up the Uisc – was being dismantled, and a new fort, nearer the mouth of the river, busily prepared. The Romans, getting as near the river-name as they could, were calling the new fort Isca. With hundreds of other prisoners Berin was sent into the great wood to fell and drag timber for walls. He was surprised to see the legionaries themselves, the foot-soldiers, doing the actual building of the walls. The non-Roman auxiliaries were used to guard the prisoners, to oversee their work, and to ride out on patrols.

There were constant rumours among the prisoners about what had happened to their kings. Vindon had disappeared. Some said that he had been killed, others that he had been taken in chains to the Roman lands of the east, or even, like Caradoc, to Rome itself. Cadi, however, was alive. He had been seen unchained, with a group of Roman officers. Soon the rumour began that he had made formal submission, in the name of the whole Silurian federation, and was being allowed to retain the title of King. Men who had previously been on raids across the Hsabren explained that this was the Roman way. One Roman had been heard to boast that they made a habit of using a people's own kings to enslave them. Yet it was hard to believe that Cadi would accept this. He had in any case no right, beyond his assigned command for the battle, to speak in the name of the twelve kingdoms. The prisoners argued this, as a relief from their heavy work, as if they were still disposing their affairs.

The first walls of Isca were quickly constructed: high stockaded earth banks with ditches. Already, within the enclosure, timber buildings were being built by the legionaries, and the demand for wood was incessant. Berin worked in the timber gangs all that summer and on through the autumn and winter. He was strong and could do the work, and there was comfort, as things settled, in being with his own people. There was even, as he noticed with surprise after several months of labour, a certain shared pride in the very construction of Isca: in the fine quality of the harbour and in the scale of the buildings inside the walls. Certainly anger also persisted, at this confident Roman possession of what had been their own lands. But in the minds of the former warriors, the dominant feeling was a continuing if unspoken sense of shame. Among the others who were now also the labour force of the Romans – the former slaves and the freemen herders and farmers – there were very different feelings. But the warriors, where they could, kept their distance from those who were not of the kin.

One day a Roman officer, stopping to watch as they were dragging heavy logs through the winter mud, called Berin to him. He could speak a little British.

'You do this work as if born to it, Briton.'

'Yet I was not born to it.'

'Yes, those who were born to it, your own British slaves, tell us much about that.'

'What do they tell you?'

'That you were harder masters than any Romans.'

'It is a lie,' Berin said.

'But why do they tell this lie? In Gaul as now in Britain we have noticed this: that your slaves are treated much worse than ours.'

'People tell lies to new masters,' Berin said, straightening his back.

'But you don't tell lies?'

'I have no masters. I was defeated in battle and now work under guard.'

'Still the old Silurian arrogance!'

'I am what I am,' Berin shouted.

The Roman smiled and rode on.

When spring came the warrior prisoners, under heavy auxiliary guard, were moved east from Isca. As they marched they were surprised to see ahead of them, on flat ground below the old stronghold of Melio, north of Iupania, what looked from a distance like another fort, with earth banks and palisades. They entered through a low defended gateway and found roads laid in a grid inside the enclosure. There were already three low rectangular buildings. They were fed and slept under the banks, but the next morning were assembled in front of one of the buildings, instead of, as before, being sent to their place of work. After they had waited for some time they were astonished to see Cadi and others of their own people coming out of the building. They were dressed in their war cloaks, though without helmets. Their ranks were painted on their foreheads. Cadi called for silence and addressed them:

'You are welcome, my brothers, to the new capital of our people. This is Venta Silurum, the city of the Siluri, the proud new capital of the people of whom it was once foolishly said that their very name would be banished from the earth. For it is as a wise man has written: neither by atrocity nor by mercy are the Siluri changed.'

The prisoners stared at him. Some began talking among themselves, but Cadi called for silence.

'Honoured warriors,' he addressed them, 'of a proud people, whose name will live in perpetual glory! Times change like the tides of our beloved Hsabren. Thus we must learn never to mistake mere rashness for bravery. For what is the truth of our situation? In our beloved island, honoured warriors, we have wasted our blood and our treasure in endless battles among ourselves. Yet Rome, that great and once feared city, has for eight hundred years, by good fortune and discipline, found a way beyond the wars of brother and brother. The power of Rome did not enter our lands for any gain to itself. It was summoned to our island by all those who were weary of the endless and fatal ambitions of those few who would be tyrants. All that Rome now asks of us, honoured warriors, is the least that is necessary to maintain the peace. For a peace between peoples cannot be maintained without armies, and armies need paying and that means taxes. Yet everything else, the fruits of our dear land, will continue to be equally shared. Is our way then not clear, honoured warriors? Should we choose the ruin that would follow revolt rather than the peace and safety of an honourable alliance: an alliance which now stands between peace and perpetual war? I have no doubt what all honourable men, who love their country as I do and who understand our situation, will answer to that. Yet, honoured warriors, I am troubled. In the poorest and most backward of our lands, and especially in the small mountain kingdoms, there are still men who see Rome not as an ally but as an enemy. While others have chosen this honourable peace they continue to fight: not as warriors but as bandits by night and in cowardly ambushes. They will never succeed against the power of Rome. But for our peace and safety they must be brought to better judgement. That is why I now address you.'

Cadi's words were listened to in absolute silence. The warriors, who for a year had been dragging timber as slaves, could not settle their own thoughts. Yet at last one spoke.

'Are you suggesting we should attack them, Cadi, men of our own blood?'

Cadi smiled.

'No, brother. The time of battles is over. I am addressing you because I know that there are among you honoured warriors from these kingdoms: Madrun, Iuas, Erdyl, Carvon, Elfael, Briganio. To all these I now make this honourable proposal. It was only during the emergency of the building of the fort of Isca, and of our own city, that you were taken to heavy labour, beyond your condition. Now, with our buildings rising, it is open to any of you who are from those kingdoms to return home, to say in honour what you have seen, and to persuade your fathers and your brothers to the better ways of peace. Those who are from the kingdoms I have named may now step forward.'

Nobody moved. The man who had asked the first question spoke again.

'You say we can go home. Would the Romani then come with us, so that we lead them into our lands?'

Cadi hesitated.

'What is your name, brother?'

'I am Bodic of Carvon.'

'I will answer your question, Bodic. A detachment of cavalry, not

Roman but auxiliary, would indeed accompany you: not to be led into your lands but to assure your own safety.'

There was again a long silence.

'Come, brothers,' Cadi called, 'it is your High King who addresses you. Step forward, on your honour, those who will now choose peace.'

The prisoners looked at each other. For some time nobody moved, but then two moved forward together and more than ten others followed them. Bodic of Carvon did not move. Berin, close beside him, stared at the ground. Cadi moved quickly among those who had stepped out. He embraced each man. As this was seen others stepped forward.

Berin knew that all in his group of prisoners were from the mountain kingdoms, since they had been together in the attack. But the old tribal markings on their faces had long since disappeared. There were now only twelve who had not moved.

'Bodic of Carvon,' Cadi called, 'follow me.'

Bodic did not move, and a guard came forward and took his arm. Berin stood ready to help Bodic, but he did not resist. He shook off the guard's hand and walked behind Cadi, who was making his way back into the building. The men who had stepped out were following him. Those who were left were surrounded by their auxiliary guards.

'You have chosen,' one of them said, in bad British. 'You have chosen to be slaves.'

The guards' whips were now drawn. The prisoners were forced close together and made to run back out of the walls of what Cadi had called the city, and on to the road to the west. For the rest of that day they were force-marched. They thought they were being returned to the timber work for the fort, but instead they were lined up for the ferry across the Uisc and then marched up its western bank. They were driven into a much narrower track, rutted by cart wheels, that led up into the hills. At last, at the end of the track, they saw huts and ditches and fires. There were Roman legionaries, fully armed, and in pits all around more than fifty men: most of them, Berin saw, of the old slaves. The auxiliaries delivered their prisoners to the legionaries and rode back down the track. A legionary who carried a dark stick looked them over. They were dismissed for the night but were not given food.

At dawn next morning they were roused. They were given bowls of sour barley porridge, and there was good water at a spring. They were led into the workings. A man they took for a Roman, though he wore no military uniform, again looked them over. Then he called up one of the earlier workers, who carried a long stick. This man explained, in good British, that they were at a lead mine. There was also silver, mixed with lead ore, but what they had mainly to deliver was the lead. 'Lead for the pipes of Isca,' he added proudly. The prisoners were given picks and shown where to dig and what to look for. Berin worked his first day in what was to be seven years' labour in the lead mine.

Within a month it was as if there had never been any other life. The work was heavy, but they were young and strong. As they could, in times of waiting when a new seam was being prepared, they built themselves wooden shelters up the line of the spring. Their food, brought up in ox-carts, improved, and they trapped hares and caught squirrels and birds. Every day the ox-carts went laden with lead down to Isca. As time passed Berin was sent, from time to time, with the loads. The track was often bad after rain, and men were needed to push the wheels.

Every time he saw Isca now he was more impressed. Great buildings were being raised, inside the enclosure, which was laid out in a grid of roads. He learned the names of some of them: the *principia* or headquarters; the *praetorium* or house of the commander of the legion; the two big *horrea* or granaries where corn was stored. Beyond these were the long wooden barracks of the legionaries and the stables of the auxiliaries. Much of the lead was delivered directly to a large bath-house, where deep conduits led in water from the river. There were also lines of latrines.

The whole order of the place was like another world. Berin had not known that there could be such buildings, yet the legionaries working on them seemed to take them for granted. He heard it said one day that this was, after all, only a rough frontier fort: 'what we have to put up with among these bloody Siluri.' He was deeply impressed by all that the Romans could do, though he still remembered Cadi, and others of his own people whom he saw mixing with the Romans, with bitter contempt. It did not make it easier that already, outside the walls, there were British huts, with men selling hides and woven cloaks and even fine jewellery. There were also huts with British girls for the legionaries to use.

It seemed impossible now that there could be any way back to the life he had lost. Yet as he learned to listen to the legionaries, picking up some of their language, he could hear how many were discontented and angry. There was talk of a mutiny and of fighting among Roman soldiers somewhere in the east. One day there was excited talk of a war between Roman generals, somewhere across the sea. There was also, later, talk of fighting still in the north, against British warriors. He heard the familiar name of the Ordovici and other names which were strange to him.

Yet that distant world, whatever was happening in it, had little connection with his own days. He did not, in these early years, think seriously of trying to escape. There was nothing to go back to. His life as a warrior was ended. Even if it were true that there was still resistance in the mountains, in sudden attack or ambush, he could not go back as a defeated warrior who had been a slave. He did not want to go back to that hidden and cowardly fighting. What his kin represented in the conduct of war made him despise all fighting except open and honourable battle. If that brave life had ended, he must make what he could of this fallen existence.

Yet finally he escaped, in a moment's decision, driven by a new danger. He knew Roman ways well enough by now to understand their obsession with order. It was of their own special kind: a constant weighing and reckoning, a making and remaking and checking of lists. On one of the visits with the carts to Isca, a British trader told him that the Roman authorities, with Cadi's assistance, were tracking down all members of the former ruling families who had not been accounted for. There were the dead, the submitted, and, now being sought, the unsure. In the daily work at the mine the slaves knew where all had come from and often spoke of their old places. If the search came close, Berin's name and place would be quickly discovered, though he had never spoken of his rank.

Late one day, seeing a group of British horsemen, finely dressed, riding up the rough track, he did not stay to take his chance. He went as if to his hut and then ran hard into the forest, up the steepest slope, well away from the hunting tracks. He ran until he was exhausted. There were no sounds of pursuit. As soon as the moon was up he struck north, keeping away from the river. By dawn he was in sight of his home country, looking across with longing at his familiar mountains.

Clutacos listened closely to Berin's story, though often angrily interrupting when he heard of the indignities heaped on his warrior son.

'Why did you not spring on them and kill them with your hands?'

He was even more angry when Cadi's speech was reported.

'That was the tongue of a Silurian but the mind of a Roman.'

'Many agreed with him, father.'

'Out of fear, that is all. No true Lord could speak in that weak way.'

'It was also a lie. Cadi said that the Romans did not come for gain, and that the taxes were only to maintain the army. But they are taking all our wealth. They are shipping our metals and selling our corn and our slaves and our hunting dogs. It is also known that rich chiefs in Rome pass great quantities of face, that they call coin, to the British princes who have submitted. The princes take these faces as honourable gifts but the rich Romans demand tribute of more faces, more coin, until the gifts are returned to them. There is no honour in that city. They loot and steal and call it government.'

Clutacos stood and stretched his thin legs. Berin saw that they were scratched and sore below the knees.

'It is known that Rome is a lower order of life,' Clutacos agreed. 'But what is much worse is that there are Lords of our kin who not only submit to it but who imitate and join it. I have told you about Sisill. He rode down to Cadi, not as an honourable parasite, in true dependence on a king, but as a parasite to a parasite who is the creature of an alien and an enemy. I heard Sisill's words, while I still attended the court. The Romani, he boasted, will show us how to become rich. When I challenged him he had the impudence to call me a barbarian: a man of the wild mountains. These were his foul words about his native people and place.'

Berin did not answer. After pouring out his own story he was now anxious about his future. His father was saying what he expected him to say, but this was no longer Clutacos Lord of Erdyl and of Iuas, in his stronghold and with his warriors and attendants around him. This was a bitter, ageing, isolated man, and then what could be the life of the son of such a father?

'I have not told you the worst of this Sisill,' Clutacos continued.

'When I challenged him in the court he ordered me back to Banavint. On the next day, while I was hunting, he came with warriors and took Guenedd, his sister and your honoured mother. He still holds her in Madrun under guard. I would have ridden at once and fought him for Guenedd, but the few warriors I still had refused me, and it was no use appealing to the farmers and the slaves. He has said that Guenedd will not be harmed while I obey and keep the peace. It breaks my soul, son, to have to submit to it.'

Berin hesitated and then put his arm across his father's shoulders. Clutacos took the comfort for a moment and then shook himself loose.

'It will be known that you are back with me,' he said, roughly. 'Someone will see you and tell him, and he will come even with Romans or the other foreign dogs to hunt you down. If they know I am not alone but have my warrior son with me they will strike at once. They leave me here as I am, only because I am old.'

'What should I do?' Berin asked.

Clutacos thought for some time, took his son's arm and led him out of the house and across the enclosure. By the old southern gatehouse there was a stretch of wall which had not been slighted. Looking anxiously around, Clutacos began to pull out stones from the centre of the wall. Behind the facing layer was a carefully made hollow and within this an object wrapped in fine red cloth. Clutacos reached in and took it in his hands.

'Do you know what this is?'

'A sacred bowl?' Berin answered, guessing from the shape.

Clutacos smiled and unwrapped the cloth. Inside it, still beautifully clean, was a helmeted skull. Berin knew it at once, from his childhood, when it had rested on the highest pole above the threshold of the house.

'Yes,' Clutacos said, smiling up into Berin's face. 'It is the Roman Lord, the Prefect, whom I killed at Claerion.'

Berin nodded, gazing at the skull.

'After the defeat of Vindon,' Clutacos continued, 'your honoured mother persuaded me to take it down from the house. She wanted it buried, but I would not agree. I will not bury my honour, or the sign of my revenge. Instead I hide it and keep it safe, for when the day of honour will come again.'

Berin reached out and touched the helmet.

'Yes, my son,' Clutacos said. 'Lay your hand on our honour. We will both lay our hands. We will swear that whatever comes we will never submit to our enemies. Swear!'

'I swear.'

Clutacos smiled and took the cloth and carefully wrapped the helmeted skull. He put it back in its hiding place and replaced the facing stones.

'But now you must go, Berin. You may already have been seen. You are the only hope of our people, and you must be kept safe.'

'I am tired, father. I will go tomorrow, though I have no idea where to go.'

'You must go now. When the herdsmen come in with the cattle it may be too late. Go down into the forest and stay through the night. Tomorrow climb to the ridge and cross the plateau to Menhebog.'

'Why Menhebog?'

Clutacos turned away. Berin, watching carefully, saw signs of struggle in his face. It was some time before he spoke.

'The hunters of Menhebog submit to no man,' Clutacos said slowly. 'It is the great shame of Iuas, for they are all born slaves.'

'I too have been a slave, father.'

'You were never by nature or condition a slave.'

'And those in Menhebog?'

Clutacos turned away and was silent.

'Is Menhebog not the place of the bandit Derco?' Berin asked, since his father would not speak.

'It is not known, my son, whether Derco lives, or indeed whether there ever was such a man. When the men of Menhebog are asked they say only that he is not here but will come. Yet what is quite certain is that they hate Sisill. They would never surrender you to him.'

'But will they take me in?'

'I do not know, Berin. They have indeed no love for me. But there is no other place for you now. When they have heard your story . . .'

'As a slave coming to slaves,' Berin said, bitterly.

Clutacos walked back to the house. He took down a sword and spear and gave them to Berin. Then, looking long into his face, he put out his arms and embraced him. They held close for some minutes.

'Now go quickly and in honour,' Clutacos said and released him.

Gwydir and Gwenliana

◆

'Liana, come quickly, come and watch them,' Ventina called from the doorway.

Gwenliana looked round, unexcited. For the second time that morning she was brushing her long auburn hair by the unshuttered window of the little wooden house. Ventina was always watching the road through the vicus. If a pig passed she would look in and shout about it.

'No, truly, Liana, there's a steer loose and in a shop and the shopman and the cowherd are fighting.'

'Let them fight, Ventina. It makes no difference to me.'

Ventina put her hands on her hips and smiled.

'It might make a difference if you came and saw the cowherd.'

Gwenliana got up.

'Why?' she asked.

Ventina was still smiling at her.

'Oh, nothing. He just looks like that boy from Madrun you were talking to last fall.'

'And if he does? I only asked him about my aunt, who lives in his village.'

'That isn't what Lucius thought.'

'How do you know?'

'Because he told Quintus. He said no man in the legion could be sure of these British-born girls, once they were out of his sight.'

Gwenliana tied up her hair.

'I expect he meant you, Ventina. You're British.'

'No I'm not. I'm Roman British. My father was a citizen.'

'Yes, and he was killed before he could legalise you. So really you're the same as the rest of us.'

Ventina looked anxiously out.

'Anyway,' she said, 'it was you Lucius meant. He'd seen you there talking, and if you can't now cross your own threshold . . .'

'Is it still going on?'

'You see,' Ventina laughed, 'you do want to know.'

Gwenliana looked down at her newly washed stola. It was white to the floor, with gold threads in the flounces and again at the wrists of the long sleeves. She had put it on out of boredom. It was almost a year since Lucius had gone, with most of the fighting soldiers of the legion, to establish the new Emperor Albinus. He had said that there would be only one battle in Gaul, against the pretender Severus, but the news was that the war was going badly, and there was even a rumour that the Emperor had been defeated. Left behind in the vicus, having little to do while Lucius was away, she had attended mainly to herself: to her hair and her clothes.

It was nearly three years since she had been given to Lucius. At twelve she had been brought down from Madrun to be an ancillula in the town house of old Darren in Venta, the prosperous city of the Siluri, with its fine roads and baths and houses. It had been like arriving in the other world: the big courtyard house, the orchard and garden, the mosaic floors and piped water, the shops in the town. And the ancillulae were treated kindly: as children they were almost like pets. Yet as she got used to Venta and saw the older British women, still servants, doing the hardest work in the kitchens, she did not want to be an ancilla. She could not go back to Madrun. After Venta there was nothing for her there. But when her father came visiting from Isca, where he worked in the legion bath-house, she listened carefully to his stories of the fine life in the fort and of the way to a good life that many British women were finding.

The Roman legionaries were not allowed to marry on active service, but after sixteen years and then four as veterans they could marry legally. Their wives became Roman citizens and the men could settle and farm on a grant of land. For the British girls, of course, this meant living without marriage until the years of service was completed. But unless the legion was moved away most of the soldiers kept their promise to marry them. There were already British women, who had been born slaves and begun their lives as servants, settled as comfortable Roman citizens and farmers' wives on the territorium along the Uisc.

Gwenliana's father Cadalus was a great admirer of all Roman ways. Everything else, to him, was just the old barbarian dirt. Left a young widower in Madrun, he had put his infant daughter into his sister's family and gone to work first in Venta and then in Isca with the legion. When she was fifteen he began telling his stories of British women living happily in the vicus at Isca. At first Gwenliana did not take much notice. She knew only that she did not want to live her whole life as an ancilla. But as she got older she was moved from personal attendance on Edina, who came down to Venta with old Darren for each quarter's council (this was now formally the Council of the Republic of the Silures), to much rougher work in the bath-house. The child pet became simply one of the many servants, yet everything she saw of life in Venta – the fine houses and clothes, the luxurious food – was being enjoyed by women less attractive than herself, and it was often their attractions rather than their birth which had got them these advantages. In Roman and Romanised society, her father regularly explained, the gifted and deserving could prosper. It was not like the old rigid caste life of the barbarian Britons.

But these were only general arguments. When Cadalus actually proposed that he should find her a legionary with whom she would go and live in the vicus at Isca, she was shocked. The legionaries were rough and foreign. The little wooden houses of the vicus, where so many British women kept bed and welcome for their legionaries, were almost as different from the fine gentry houses of Venta as the old wattle and thatch huts back in Madrun. It took more than a year of her new work in the bath-house, and the increasing nuisance of drunken grabs by old Darren's guests whenever the council met – one of them had hit her and shouted that she should know what an ancilla was for – before she began listening more carefully to her father and accepting his view that she was, after all, in a position to choose.

She did not now know, looking back, all the strands of her choice, but after hearing her father's stories she had rejected younger men and those still early in their service. Her only real attraction, she could honestly say, had been to Lucius, who was thirty-seven and had served twelve of his sixteen years of prime service. In four years he would be released and given a plot of land. She would still be only twenty, and in another four years would become a citizen.

It had not worried her that her father described Lucius as a lonely, quiet man. He had been badly wounded, and was still scarred on the forehead following a battle nine years earlier, when the legion had put down a mutiny in another legion to the north. He was still a fighting soldier as well as a skilled tiler. He wanted children for when he could realise his long ambition and become a farmer. When Cadalus took her to him, he was shy, protective and kind.

There had not yet been children. Gwenliana – Liana, as Lucius now affectionately called her – privately decided that no child would be born until he got his full release and could legally marry her. Lucius, though anxious, blamed himself, and she always affectionately reassured him. But with every year that passed she knew her decision had been right. Sometimes, in these affairs, everything went as planned. But sometimes a veteran, after many years with his woman, took money instead of a land grant and went home to Gaul or Iberia or even Italy, leaving the woman with their children and no means of support. There were also cases of older women being put out for younger, without any redress.

Gwenliana watched it all carefully, but kept to her own rule. If everything happened as it should, at the right time, she would stay with Lucius and give him children. Yet when that right time would be was becoming a problem. Some of the saddest cases, for then the men were not to blame, was when part of the legion was sent to a battle and some of the men were killed. She knew very little about these battles, but since she had first come to Venta, and overheard the talk of the lords, there had always been fighting somewhere. It was mostly far in the north or across the sea, but there were also conflicts between the great generals and claimant emperors, like this last clash between Albinus and Severus, which Lucius explained to her. If the Emperor Albinus were confirmed by defeating Severus it would go well with the legions which had supported him: all the legions in Britain, he said proudly. Yet now, after nearly a year's absence, there was a strong rumour, though it had been officially denied by the Prefect, that Severus had defeated the Emperor and that many in their own legion – the proud Second Augusta – had been killed. Gwenliana, though still anxious for Lucius, knew that she had been right to keep herself available for a quite different future.

The shouting in the street had died down.

'I suppose we might as well look,' Gwenliana said.

She followed Ventina out. It was a warm, golden autumn morning, with some mist still hanging over the river. The traffic was going through again: packhorses with hides and pots; a rich fat merchant on a black stallion which he couldn't really control; a line of carts of threshed corn. Across the river blue smoke rose from the bath-house and shouts of drilling in the distance from the parade ground. Only a small cadre had been left behind to guard the fort, mainly older men. She had hoped Lucius would be one of them but he had a reputation, from the mutiny, for bravery, so he had marched with the Emperor.

Farther up the dusty road a small herd of cattle had wandered loose towards the river. As the young women made their way through the groups of people standing talking at their doorways, they saw the black steer, the juvencus, now roped and quiet. Some way beyond it, several men were clearing the debris of a shop. It was the leather merchant's, Marodus. The whole stall front, on its posts, had collapsed. The men were pulling bags and tunics and saddles from the smashed timber. Beyond it they saw the end of the potter's stall, also badly damaged. Broken pots lay in the road and the men were trampling over them and breaking them again. The jeweller's next to the leather merchant's had not been touched, but old Silvino, the crafty one, had taken his best pieces back into his interior, away from the crowd and the fighting.

Yet what fighting had there been? There was no sign of it. The two young cowherds, easy to pick out in their rough brown woollen mountain tunics, were helping Marodus to sort out his goods. A Roman official from the saeptum stood by, watching them. Gwenliana could not see the faces of the cowherds. That she might know either of them was just Ventina's usual teasing. But then one turned and she saw that it was Elid from Madrun, skinny Elid, whose family lived right up in Menhebog. She looked more carefully at the other young man. All she could see was his freckled neck and arms and his curling sandy hair.

'Yes,' Ventina said, watching her.

'And what if it is?'

'Gwydir and Gwenliana – even the names go together,' Ventina said, laughing.

Gwenliana pushed her hard on the shoulder.

'Right, that's enough,' the official shouted. 'Leave the rest and get the cattle to the saeptum.'

'And what about this damage?' Marodus protested.

'You must take that up with his kin in Madrun.'

'You know I can't do that.'

'Then go to the principium. Make an official complaint. I can't hang about here for a few dusty bags. I've got the cattle render to see to.'

Elid stood back from the wrecked stall. The other cowherd turned and walked down, with his stick, to the cattle on the riverbank. Elid took the rope of the juvencus, which was now beaten and quiet.

The cattle were driven up from the river. Gwydir walked behind them, waving his stick. As he came level with Gwenliana and Ventina he looked briefly across at them, as if he had already known they were there. But he did not break his step. Gwenliana looked after him, while Ventina smiled.

There was quite different trouble at the saeptum, where the annual cattle render must be delivered. Gwydir and Elid got their animals into the fenced enclosure, on the riverbank below the bridge, next to the slaughterhouse. The official who had followed them down now went to his render lists and called them over.

'Fourteen. Thirteen vaccae, one juvencus.'

'That's right.'

'What do you mean it's right? The render from Madrun is twenty-three.'

Gwydir touched Elid's arm and stepped forward.

'I am to say, sir, that our herd has been stricken with disease, following the heavy rains of the winter. Many of our best animals have had to be slaughtered. These fourteen, I am to say, are the first of our render. The others will follow when we have controlled the disease.'

The official, Varius, a squat, bald man with thick black hair on the backs of his hands, looked contemptuously at Gwydir.

'You say that, cowherd, as if you had learned it by rote.'

'It is what my lord, young Darren, commanded me to say.'

'Then your young Darren is a cheat. There has been no disease in Madrun. I have the reports.'

'I drove what I was given to drive, sir.'

'And demolished the property of honest shopkeepers, as well as bringing short count.'

'I brought the fourteen I set out with.'

'Liar! Which way did you travel?'

'By our track to the road from Cicucio to Gobanio, where we stayed the first night. Then from Gobanio to Burro, where we slept and watered the cattle. Then today from dawn to Isca.'

'And which of your kin did you meet along the way, to give away Roman cattle?'

Gwydir hesitated.

'None, sir.'

Varius stared keenly at him. One of the lanii, the butchers, came up from the slaughterhouse to ask about the cattle. Varius, preparing to walk away with him, pointed to Gwydir and Elid.

'You are to wait. You will answer for this.'

Gwydir looked at Elid, and then sat in the sun. It had been hard to carry it off. It would probably get harder. But young Darren had believed Gwydir could do it:

'You look so honest, even a bit stupid.'

For of course there had been no disease in Madrun. The herd was healthy and large. But it always made sense to try to cut down on the render, or on the poll-tax. If the local procurator's officials or the beneficiarii were slack, as sometimes happened, or if general supplies were good and there was no pressure to gather in every last beast, bag and coin, the imposition might be eased.

But there were also special reasons this year. All the lords with contacts in Venta and Isca knew that most of the Roman legions had followed Albinus to Gaul. The remaining auxiliaries were more thinly spread out. In early spring there had been a successful raid on the fort at Cicucio – Butcher's Hill, as it was locally known – by horsemen who had ridden from Briganio but who had not been identified. That raid, to the others, had been rash, though there had been good booty of hides and silver. What was mainly happening, while they waited for news of Albinus, was a careful reconnaissance, easily carried out in the course of ordinary movement and trade, of all the Roman settlements in the area. Madrun took a special interest in two places: their own old site, Gofyl, up the Guuy from Claerion, where the Romans had taken over and improved the dome-furnaces for ironworking, and Gobanio, always the place of the smiths, where the Romans made and repaired their own weapons. If there were to be serious raids, these places of access to weapons would be decisive. Meanwhile, with the Roman hold weakened, they could at least try to withhold part of the renders and taxes.

It had gone on like this through the summer. Every care was taken to get the latest news from Venta and Isca. But no attempt was made to involve the British families there, for they were still by inheritance the ruling aristocracy of the Silures, and had cut themselves off in their comfortable Roman styles. 'The fat people of Venta', the mountain people called them. Yet on a visit a question could be asked, in a tone of great solicitude, concerning the fortunes of the Emperor and his courageous legions, and then the councillors of Venta, the honorati and curiales, enjoyed showing their intimate knowledge of the doings of these noble Romans with whom they were so closely allied.

From just such a question, in late summer, young Darren, (who had refused to live in Venta and had let his uncle replace him on the council), heard what sounded like a reliable account of the defeat of Albinus at Lugudon in the south of Gaul. The legions with him had suffered heavy losses.

Young Darren took his time passing on the news. He let none of it get out to the peasants and the slaves, who if they reacted at all would act wildly. Instead he rode to visit all the old mountain kingdoms, sounding out the younger men who still proudly – though as a matter more for songs than as practice – traced their descent from British warriors. He found interest but caution. Obviously the story would have to be confirmed. But as the young Lords thought it over, it began to seem quite possible that the Roman army in Britain might never return. The continual fighting in the wider empire, and the constant struggles for the imperial succession, might force them to leave Britain to its own devices, at least for many years. And if that happened there could be more than raids. There could be a successful general rising.

Five days before young Darren gave Gwydir his instructions about the cattle render to Isca, he heard confirmation from his uncle of the defeat of Albinus. It was so grave, said his uncle, that news was not being allowed to spread beyond the most trusted officers and councillors. For it might be as much as three years before any legions could return to Britain, and meanwhile nobody in Venta wanted trouble.

Young Darren consulted Cangu, the traditional Wise Man who still kept his influence, though under the Roman power his old title and functions were not openly acknowledged. Cangu smiled, for he saw the news as the fulfilment of a prophecy. By their native reckoning, which it was his duty to sustain, this was the year 700, of the twenty-fourth cycle, in which it had been said, in a dream, that the Britons would free themselves. Armed with this news, Darren rode again round the neighbouring kingdoms, and active preparations began.

Meanwhile he would not withhold all his render. He would not give the Romans warning of what was to come. He sent Gwydir with the reduced number and openly involved him in the lie. Gwydir had taken it as just the usual cheating. But now, sweating in the saeptum, waiting for the return of the macellarius, he was thinking it through again. For talk of a general rising was much more widespread than the lords supposed. Moving with the herds, and keeping their eyes open, Gwydir and his family had picked up many signs.

Elid dropped off to sleep in the warm sun. Gwydir watched as the cows were roped and led into the laniana, to be followed by the bellows of slaughtering and the familiar butchering smell. A shadow fell across him and he looked up to see Cadalus, who was making his way from the bath-house to visit his daughter. Cadalus was lean and bronzed in his Roman clothes. He organised his life around the exercises of the baths and had a reputation as a wrestler. He recognised Gwydir and Elid as coming from Madrun.

'What are you drooping here for?'

'Cadalus,' Gwydir said, getting up. 'We are ordered to wait because it is said our render is too small.'

'And is it too small? Do you still cheat up there?'

'Cadalus, it is not for me to say. I am only a stick to drive the beast to the saeptum.'

'That's them, is it?' Cadalus said, nodding towards the laniana. Gwydir said nothing.

'How many were you short?' Cadalus asked.

'Nine, it was said.'

'Then you will be punished, for certain.'

Gwydir looked away.

'Is it fair play to punish the stick?' he asked.

'It is how Roman order is kept. The stick, the arm, the head. That is the discipline of the empire.'

'It is still not fair play.'

'Fair play is a word of the barbarian, Gwydir. The better Roman word is law.'

'And the word for law is sword,' Gwydir said, looking hard into his eyes.

'The sword above the scales, it is true. That is why our life is so good.'

'And if there are other swords?'

Cadalus laughed.

'Against a legion?'

'Of course. But it is said that the legion has gone.'

'It is where it should be, with its Emperor.'

Gwydir waited for some time.

'It is the year 700, of the twenty-fourth cycle,' he said, looking carefully at Cadalus.

'You see,' Cadalus said, 'you cannot even count in those barren mountains. The year is not 700, it is the year 950 AUC. Nine hundred and fifty years, just think of it, from the foundation of Rome to this mastery of the world.'

'That is not what I heard.'

'Then you heard wrong. Until the end of time men will count their years from the foundation of the Immortal City. That is what empire means.'

'It's just what I heard,' Gwydir said. Elid had woken up.

'Whatever year it is,' he said, laughing, 'I could do with some food.'

'No, we have to wait here,' Gwydir said.

'There's food in the vicus. Let just one of you stay,' Cadalus announced, taking charge.

'You go, Elid,' Gwydir said.

Elid got up and walked away with Cadalus. Gwydir was glad to be alone. If he went with Cadalus there would be the embarrassment of seeing Gwenliana again, and he did not want to face that. They were the same age and had grown up together in the same settlement. He had not missed her much at first when she went away to Venta. It was part of growing up to be moved around like that. He had understood and even laughed at her when she had come back full of stories of the fine houses and ways of the capital. Let her enjoy it if that was her way.

It was different when she was given to Lucius: a girl like that, to an ageing Roman soldier. And of course she then changed in herself. He would have preferred to be ignored when, coming down with the previous render, she suddenly came smiling towards him and put her hand on his wrist. He had never admitted any special feeling for her, but she was so direct and engaging that he wanted to respond. It was perhaps the touch of the Roman on her: that sort of pushing at the world, reaching out and taking what you wanted. It was also, he knew, the fine clothes, the elaborate hair, the practised smile: those ways of pleasing a protector.

He had heard others talk contemptuously of the whores and kept women of Venta and Isca. He did not feel that way himself. From the condition of a slave most moves were much the same. What he resented was not that she had chosen a Roman, but that, having done so, she came to him as if nothing had happened. For what could he be expected to do? He had to drive the cattle to the saeptum, get his quittance, and make his long way back to the hills and the herd. There was no space in his life for her kind of pleasantry, even when it came with smiles and easy words. She pretended a close friendship: something they had never actually had. There was only the memory of a place and of children playing together. She may have thought she was being affectionate, but she was actually only playing and disturbing him.

Yet in the long year since that meeting something had changed. The change was in himself, though he did not want to recognise it. He kept seeing Gwenliana in his mind, and thinking about her. He had been looking out nervously for her house when he got slack with the steer and let it break loose and do all that damage. That had been a warning. Nothing but trouble could come from her. She had her life nicely planned out, with her legionary and her citizenship and her farm. That was a world away from anything possible or conceivable in his own life. Unless . . .

He turned and looked around the saeptum. The steer was being roped to be taken in for slaughter. What he was remembering, suddenly, but could hardly bear to think through, was the talk of a general rising. He had heard Darren, drunk, talking loudly with a guest. It was the usual boasting talk of how well the Lord could fight, and of what treasure they could get from a successful raid. But it was also another kind of talk, with an ugly anger near the surface, of what they would do when they had the chance, to the fat pigs of Venta and the rubbish of the Roman hangers-on. 'A few torches in their houses, and then their women running out.' They had laughed loudly at that, and put their arms round each other's shoulders, rocking with strength and excitement.

Gwydir sat and covered his eyes with his hands. He could not think of this. Yet as it pushed at his mind he remembered Gwenliana again, and what he now saw was different: not the smart girl taunting him, but a marked-out victim, her life driven this way or that by whoever, for the time, had the power.

His eyes were still closed when Elid came back.

'You missed your chance, boy,' Elid said, laughing. 'That Gwenliana had prepared fine food and drink for her father, but she soon gave plenty to me.'

'I can see you've had a drink.'

'Aye, mead too. Good Roman mead.'

'From our honey, I expect.'

'Aye, but they make it well.'

Elid lay back in the warm sunshine. After a while he lifted his head and looked across at Gwydir.

'Aren't you off then?'

'It was you said I'd missed my chance.'

'Get away, there's lots of women there. And they're lonely, with the legion off fighting.'

'Then best leave them to it.'

'We'll see about that when it's dark. But you've still got to get something to eat.'

'I'll look around,' Gwydir said, and walked away.

The vicus was quiet again. Children were playing in the road and down towards the river. A great many dogs, of all sizes, foraged around the backs of the shops and houses where the rubbish was thrown. Gwydir found a stall selling small cakes of spiced bread and pieces of goat cheese. He spent the two brass sestertii he had been carrying since the last render, when he had sold a bag of black-berries. There was an oyster stall next to the bread stall, but he could not afford both. A British girl at the stall offered him water with his bread and he drank a whole beaker. He was sitting at the side of the road, finishing the cheese, when he looked up and saw Gwenliana. She was just a few paces away, looking down at him.

'Gwydir. I thought it was you.'

'You knew it was me.'

'But what sort of insult is this, that you are buying food when you could have come to my door?'

'I've got my respect.'

'Respect! When you take no notice of hospitality? Have you all forgotten your manners in Madrun? Don't you feed your guests anymore?'

He got up and began to turn away.

'Your friend Elid wasn't too proud.'

'No, so he told me.'

'Then why didn't you come?'

'Taking my turn?'

'What does that mean?'

'You know, Gwen.'

'I know, do I? But you can still call me Gwen.'

'Well, I don't know your Roman name.'

'I don't have a Roman name.'

'Only a Roman man.'

'Yes, a good man.'

'I believe you, Gwen.'

She smiled and was moving closer when there was a sudden noise up the road. A troop of horsemen, Batavian auxiliaries, was riding full gallop through the lines of houses and shops, scattering the children and the dogs. Their horses were sweating heavily, some foaming at the mouth. The riders shouted as they passed, but the words were indistinct.

'What did they say?' Gwydir asked.

'I couldn't hear.'

Ventina came running, and caught Gwenliana's arm.

'Gobanio has been taken and the British are coming this way.'

Gwenliana was pale. She looked up at Gwydir.

'Is it true, Gwydir? Is it really a rebellion?'

'How would I know things like that?'

'We must get our stuff and move into the fort!' Ventina was crying.

'Yes,' Gwenliana said, still looking at Gwydir.

'You're afraid of what they might do to you, are you?' Gwydir said to Ventina.

'I'm afraid of what soldiers always do to women,' Ventina answered, sharply.

'Not to their own women.'

'But we aren't their women. We are Roman women.' Gwydir laughed.

'Some protector you've found!' Ventina said to Gwenliana. 'But whatever you're doing I'm getting in to the fort.'

'Yes,' Gwydir said. 'You should both go.'

People were now pouring from the houses, carrying bundles. The shops and stalls were packing up.

'The cowards come only when the legion is away,' Ventina said.

Gwenliana did not move. She was still looking intently at Gwydir.

'Go on,' he said to her. 'They have no reason to respect you.'

'But why should they hate me? Why do you hate me?'

'I don't hate you, Gwen. But I know what is said. That you are the women of our oppressor, the women of our enemy. You are the loose women, the greedy women, who turned from their own men for money.'

'Not money, Gwydir. I wasn't bought or sold.'

'It was love then, was it?'

Gwenliana looked away.

'Why do you have to be hateful to me?' she asked quietly.

'Why do I have to be anything to you, Gwen?'

'Because I know you like me. I saw it last year. And it's the same still. That's why you're pretending to be nasty.'

'I'm not pretending anything. You made your choice. And since you've made it you must go to the fort. They're your people now.'

Ventina had gone, but Gwenliana still stood dazed, watching the people stream past her towards the bridge to the high east gate.

'I'd rather go to Venta. Gwydir, will you take me to Venta?'

'What's the good of that? They're as likely to go for Venta as for the fort. There's less defence there, and as much to get hold of.'

'Then I'll go and hide in the forest.'

'No, Gwen. Go to the fort.'

She looked sadly at him. There were tears in her eyes.

'Gwydir, do you know my father?'

'Cadalus? Yes. I saw him just now.'

'He works in the baths. He gets to know what the officers say. It's being kept quiet, but the legion that was here is defeated, nearly half of them killed. And because they were following the old Emperor they'll be broken up, they won't be sent back here.'

'Is Lucius alive?'

'We don't know. We don't know any of the names, except some of the officers. And it's certain that Albinus is dead.'

'Lucius might still be alive.'

'But if he is he probably won't be sent back here. And I'm not his wife, you know that.'

'You have kept house and bed for him. In the law you are his wife.'

'Not in any law that helps me. Only while he is here.'

Gwydir looked down the road. There was crowding and shouting at the bridge. On the far bank of the river, north of the fort, auxiliary cavalry were riding out, in the direction of Gobanio.

'I still say you should go to the fort.'

'But there's nothing for me there. Nothing.'

'Gwen, there's nothing for you here.'

'You don't mean that, Gwydir.'

'Yes, I mean it. Come on, I'll take you to the bridge.'

She walked beside him, without speaking. It was difficult to see what was happening at the bridge. The crowd there was getting bigger and there was angry shouting and crying.

'What's happening?' Gwydir asked, as they got to the edge of the crowd.

'The commander has closed the gate. He will have no more Britons inside.'

Gwenliana gripped Gwydir's arm.

'You see. Now we'll have to go to Venta.'

'You'd never get there, if it's Venta they choose to attack.'

The crowd at the bridge was beginning to disperse, except for some who went on pleading and crying at the closed gate. The shout went up that they must make for Venta, and already the first groups were setting out on the road east. As people pushed around them Ventina came back to Gwenliana.

'We've got to get to Venta, Liana. It's our only chance.'

'Will you come, Gwydir?' Gwenliana asked.

'No. Not to Venta.'

'But why?'

'I came here with cattle. With any luck I can still get hold of a few of them. And I'm not afraid of this rising.'

'You'd choose the cattle?' Gwenliana said, amazed.

'They're my living, Gwen, the herd.'

Ventina pulled at Gwenliana's arm. Reluctantly, still staring at Gwydir, she let herself be pulled away. They joined the crowd streaming along to Venta.

Gwydir ran back to the saeptum, looking for Elid. The place was deserted, though several cows were still penned in their enclosures. While he was running around, looking, he heard a shout from Elid, who had gone through to the laniana.

'We'll eat good beef tonight, boy.'

He was carrying a big piece of meat wrapped in sacking.

'Didn't they take the meat to the fort?'

'They took what they could, but they were shit-scared when they heard that the gate was being closed.'

'Should we try to drive a few back then?'

'Aye. Though most of ours are meat.'

They unpenned five good heifers. They got their sticks and began driving them back towards the now deserted vicus.

'Might as well pick up a few hides on the way,' Elid said.

'Aye, why not?'

They were picking over the shop which their steer had wrecked when they heard, from the forest behind them, a long blast of a horn. Looking up they saw a troop of British horsemen galloping down towards the vicus. Most were riding their own mountain ponies, but some of the leaders were on the bigger Roman horses. They were carrying long spears, most of them Roman. The leaders were in their feast cloaks, of coloured stripes and checks, and had the blue paint of rank on their foreheads.

'What are you?' one of them shouted across.

'Cowherds from Madrun. We came on a render.'

'Then keep out of our way. Get what cattle you can and drive them back where they belong.'

'Yes, Lord,' Gwydir replied.

The troop rode on through the vicus. The last riders dismounted and found fire. They ran along the road between the houses and shops, setting them all ablaze. Gwydir and Elid hurried to drive their own cattle clear.

'Is this the only attack?' Gwydir shouted to one of the torch-bearers.

'No, they're coming down from the west on Isca, but our main body is going through the forest to Venta. We're going to finish the Romans off. All the kin are riding.'

'We'll get back then,' Gwydir said hastily.

They drove the frightened heifers up the dusty road. With their best efforts they could not move fast. Behind them a great cloud of smoke rose from the burning vicus, and Gwydir could see fires beyond that, from the saeptum and the bridge.

On each side of the road, now, were the fields and small farm-houses of the Roman veterans. There was no sign of people or animals, except for a few hens. Gwydir wondered where all the farmers had gone: probably into the forest until the fighting was over, though the men were all trained soldiers and could have been assembled to fight.

'Shall we get us a few hens and eggs?' Elid said, 'for we'll have to stay somewhere overnight.'

'We can have a look,' Gwydir agreed.

They found a farmhouse well back from the road. They approached it cautiously, but there was nobody about. Then they heard a noise from a shed at the back and looked in and found a young horse.

'He'll save our legs,' Elid said.

Gwydir did not answer. He was staring at the horse.

'Leave him for now,' Elid said. 'We'll get some eggs and eat a bit.'

Gwydir did not move.

'What is it, boy?'

Gwydir turned and looked at him. His eyes were unfocused: what Elid called the blind look.

'Seen a wonder, have you?'

'You'll be all right here,' Gwydir said, quickly, 'and if I don't get back you can manage the five heifers.'

'Get back from where? You're not making sense.'

'I'm taking the horse. I'm going to try to get Gwen.'

'Gwen, that Cadalus' daughter? She's a Roman bitch, isn't she?'

'Yes, Elid. She is.'

He untethered the young horse, and soothed it. He led it around the yard, talking quietly close to its head. Then he mounted, gently, and rode back south, following the line of the road but keeping east of it. There was still heavy smoke ahead, from the burning of the vicus, and another fire across the river, beyond the walls of the fort. He could see horsemen dismounting and flashes of weapons and shields.

He turned to stay clear of Isca and began moving east, following the edge of the great forest. He pushed the young horse harder now, until he could see the line of the road from Isca to Venta below him. On this stretch the road was empty, but soon he saw a light cloud of dust on the road ahead. As he came nearer he could see the hundreds of people who had set out for Venta. They had stopped, on a slight ridge, and many were sitting on the grass. Beyond them he could just make out the large houses of Venta, in a light haze.

He rode through the trees until he was at the nearest hidden point to the crowd of refugees. Then he tethered the horse to a young oak and moved to a clearing near the road. He came forward, walking slowly, as if from Isca. A few people looked at him, but most were sitting tired and dazed. He made his way round the edge of the crowd, looking for Gwenliana. Several times he thought he had seen her; there were many with her auburn hair. Then he found himself face to face with Marodus, whose shop the steer had wrecked.

'What are you doing here?' Marodus asked, irritably.

'Getting away from the fighting. They'd taken all my cattle.'

'It's your people from the mountains that are causing this trouble.'

'Not me,' Gwydir said. 'I'm just a herdsman.'

'And not much good even at that!'

'I know. I said I was sorry. But what's happening now?'

'There's a troop of the barbarians ahead of us. They're looting in Venta. We're just waiting to see what happens.'

'And at Isca?'

'They say there's a big native attack. They're over the walls on the north.'

As Marodus was speaking Gwydir saw Gwenliana. She was sitting with her hands stretched forward and her head bowed. Gwydir moved round until he could speak from close behind her.

'Say nothing. Just listen.'

She had jerked up her head and begun to turn, but now she stayed still.

'When you get the chance, just get up and wander away. Walk as if you were going to be private in the forest. I have a horse up there. We can get clear away.'

Gwenliana said nothing. Staring at her back, Gwydir realised that he had been giving her orders; he had not asked if she wanted to come. He had not even really put the idea to himself. His mind was entirely set on the method of escape.

'Will you do that, Gwen?'

There was still no answer. Gwydir waited. There was disturbance and shouting on the far edge of the crowd. Then Gwenliana rose and walked slowly up towards the trees. She walked as the ancillae were trained to walk, her back very straight, her head up, her paces balanced and regular. Several people gazed at her as she passed. In the fine white stola, with the neatly braided hair, she walked as if quite separate from the tiredness and confusion all around her.

Gwydir moved in a different direction, following the line of the road back to Isca. Then, when he saw his chance, he ran hard for the trees. He looked back from cover. She was still walking, as if to where he had tethered the horse.

'Here,' he called, urgently.

She glided to a change of direction as if she had not heard him. She walked slowly into the trees. She came up and briefly looked at him, but still said nothing.

'I didn't want you finding the horse and riding off on your own,' he said, staring at her.

'What do you think I am?'

'Right. Let's move.'

They walked the horse through the trees. Gwydir was looking for a track which he had seen leading deep into the forest. It was some time before he found it again.

'Do you want to ride now?' he asked, as they came to the track.

'It depends where you are taking me.'

'Elid is back on a farm by the road to Burro. But I think that's too dangerous. If this track's any good we can go north, towards Blestium, and then follow Myngui back to the mountains.'

He was walking ahead of her. When he turned he saw that she was watching him carefully. As their eyes met she smiled.

'How will you know which is north, in here among the trees?' she asked, in a soft voice.

'I always know which is north. In my head.'

'That's not possible, is it?'

'I know, so it must be possible.'

The track was now running east of north, but it was obviously best to follow it. The sky was still light, though under the trees, big oaks with heavy canopies, it was at times almost dusk.

'Can you walk faster?' he asked.

'I can do whatever you tell me.'

'You shouldn't say things like that. It's your life as much as mine.'

'Has it been?' she asked, and looked away.

They quickened their pace. There was a crossing of tracks and the trail to the northeast broadened.

'We'll ride,' Gwydir said. 'Get up behind me.'

'Am I allowed to hold on to you?'

'Don't play with me, Gwen.'

He mounted and helped her up. When the horse was used to the weight he moved to a slow trot. There was better light ahead and soon they were out of the main forest and on to a wide upland. Gwydir quickened the pace. Away to the west they could see the great dark wall of their native mountains, but still they rode north. There were now huts in a clearing ahead and they rode up the slope to avoid them. Below the huts were three large standing stones.

'The gods of the old people,' Gwydir said, pointing.

'Are they?'

She was holding very tight to his back.

A sharp descent appeared ahead of them, and beyond it the gleam of a river.

'Myngui,' Gwydir said.

There was no answer.

As the descent became steeper he dismounted and led the horse.

Gwen stayed on its back. They were now among trees again, and he could not find a track. They were almost down, over the rough ground, when Gwydir stopped abruptly. He turned and put his finger to his lips. He pointed. Behind a boulder ahead of them a man was crouching. Gwydir looked round for a loose stone and then went slowly forward.

'Are you in peace?' he called, when he was within throwing distance.

'In peace,' came a hoarse reply.

Gwydir walked forward, still holding the stone in his fist.

'We are of Madrun. We look to follow Myngui to our mountains.'

The man stood up. He was short and dark, nearer fifty than forty. His face and arms were blackened with smoke.

'It is the year 700,' he said, gazing at Gwydir.

'I have heard that.'

'It is the year of freedom, in the twenty-fourth cycle.'

'Yes, I have heard it said.'

'I am Taric.'

'I am Gwydir.'

The man was staring past Gwydir at Gwen.

'She is a Roman?'

'No. She is one of us. But she has been with Romans.'

Taric came forward and gripped Gwydir's arm.

'You must not go down into Blestium. There is heavy fighting. The old Lords want the iron of the Romans.'

'Are you an ironworker?'

'All my life and my father before me, at the furnaces of Blestium. The old Lords attacked, but then the Romans gathered and are attacking them again. They are fighting for the iron of swords.'

Gwydir looked down at the stone in his hand. He dropped it. Taric looked up at the sky.

'You can hide, as I do, but they are riding many ways. And the night will be cold.'

'There is not much time if we are to find shelter.'

'Your lady will need shelter.'

Gwydir smiled. He looked back at Gwenliana who was sitting erect and silent in her white stola with gold thread at its wrists. He could see how they would be taken for lady and groom.

'Is there any safe shelter?'

'I will take you,' Taric said. 'For the lady.'

'Where is this shelter?'

'We must first cross Myngui. I know a ford. Then there is a way I will take you to a cave that I've known since a boy. The lady will be safe there.'

Beckoning them to follow, he led the way down to the river. They crossed at some distance from Blestium, where they could see the smoke of big fires. Gwydir and Taric were wet to the waist in the river, but Gwenliana rode through dry, lifting her legs clear. Then they were climbing again, on a track through dense trees. The light was fading as the sun went into cloud above the mountains. When they reached a ridge there was again a steep descent. As they came out of the trees they saw the riverjoin of Myngui and Guuy to the south.

'One more climb,' Taric said, 'but first there is swamp. Stay very close behind me.'

They crossed a valley, full of rushes and swampy sedge, and climbed again into trees. There was no track but Taric seemed to know the way. As they reached a low hill, where the trees had been cleared and there were earth banks and ditches of an old stronghold, they saw the Guuy running in straight water to the south, its smooth surface coloured by the fading pink light. Taric pointed ahead.

'A bad swamp again, but then there, under the trees.'

He set off and they followed. Gwydir led the horse. It was very bad going across the swampy valley. Several times they were in mud and water to their knees, but there was then a stony bank and a rough track up it. Scrambling up, Taric showed them, proudly, a wide flat terrace.

'Shelter,' Taric said.

He was pointing to a bluff of limestone, stained and discoloured by rain. Young beech grew above it, and trails of ivy hung down over its face. Taric smiled and ran across. He pulled back a trail of ivy.

'The cave of the old ones. Cala.'

There was a long narrow opening and, beyond, a flat shelf of rock, which looked as if it had been worked. Gwydir climbed to the shelf and as his eyes changed to the dim light, he could see a sunken chamber, carefully smoothed, with a firm rock floor.

Taric came behind him.

'The lady can sleep in the chamber. You and I will lie in the entrance.'

Gwydir nodded. He walked back to Gwen, who had dismounted.

'As fine as anything in Venta,' he said, smiling.

She put her hand out and held his arm. She did not speak.

He tethered the horse. When he got back Taric had shown Gwen into the inner cave.

'We'd better not light a fire,' Gwydir said.

'No. There are too many soldiers about.'

Gwydir sat in the entrance and leaned his back against the rock. After the long day it was strange at last to have nothing to do. Gwen was very quiet beyond the shelf of the cave. Taric moved close to the wall and stretched out, his head on his arm. Watching the fading light, Gwydir felt his eyes heavy and closing. There was a silence everywhere as deep as the silence of the high mountains.

In the mist of first light Gwydir woke. Taric was still sleeping heavily and there was no sound from Gwen. He looked at the horse and then scrambled down the bank and through the swamp. He wanted to get to the lookhill, to see the country west to the mountains. Breathing heavily from the climb he reached a high bank of the old stronghold. There was bright sun now from the east. Beyond the mists of the near valleys stretched the long clear line of his mountains. The ridges were very dark and straight, like the lower edges of storm clouds. Between the lookhill and the ridges was the rise of Isgirit the Broken Mountain. Seen from this unfamiliar direction it was like an animal lying down. The ridge was the hard spine and there was a massive head and shoulders at the northern end. It was as if at a shout the strange beast would stir, would get up and stand free. Above it, in the mass of the mountains, there was the hump, like a shield boss, of the Great Seat of the Clouds.

Gwydir laughed. He picked up a pebble and threw it out towards the mountains, then he looked back down. There were two figures on the platform in front of the cave. Taric was walking across to the horses. Gwen, very clear in white, was staring up at the lookhill. He waved and she waved back. He shouted and ran down to her.

Bibra in Magnis

◆————————————◆

Bibra was woken by the noise of heavy cartwheels on the cobbles in front of the house. She was still looking around, dazed, as the carter shouted: 'Ostrea! Ostrea!'

As she hurried to get up she felt the stalk of the daffodil in her left fist. She looked down at it, bewildered. She could remember nothing since she had come to the door of the outhouse, after cleaning the big olla, and squatted for a moment to look at the flowers. Many years back, she had been given three bulbs by a pedlar. She had spiked them into the loose soil under the wall, around a root of heather which a cowman had brought her from the mountains. The pale, small daffodils had increased through the years, and each spring the ladies stopped to look at them as they passed. 'You are a real flower girl, Bibra,' her own lady Cocceia had said. But she had not intended to pick one today. Squatting with her back to the wall, with the warm sun on her face, she must have dropped into sleep and somehow seized the flower. She looked down at its head and lifted it to her lips. 'My sweet one,' she said under her breath.

'Hey woman, these ostrea are alive, you know.'

Bibra put down the flower and walked to the cart. The driver was a stranger: a heavy man of about fifty, with a drunkard's red face.

'They're in good seawater, aren't they?' she said sharply. She was always determined to hold her own. She looked in at the tightly packed barrels in the well of the cart. The driver was staring down at her, but she was used to this staring from strangers.

'You on your own, Mother?' he said, more kindly.

'It's my work to clean them. I'll help you with our barrels.'

'For Burros, three.'

'That's what I was told.'

'I'll get a man to help lift.'

'Do you think I can't do it?'

'I'll get a man anyway.'

He jumped down and went round the back of the main house. He had been shocked when he had looked at Bibra. She was well over sixty but in height like a child of ten. Her body was bent forward from the loins and her head was bowed forward from the shoulders, which were heavily muscled for a woman. Her bare feet were small, as were her hands, but the fingers she stretched out towards the oyster barrels were broad and strong, the skin dark. She had an old brown wool tunic, fastened by a bone pin on her shoulder. The grey hair was thin on her scalp, but she had fastened it above her ears with pins.

Yet it was when she looked up at him, challenging him about the work, that the real shock had come. It was an old woman's nutcracker face, the nose thin, the chin prominent, the pale blue eyes sunken, but something terrible had happened to it. It was as if the whole right side was not there. The right eye was dragged down, the right edge of the mouth was crooked, the cheek that should have been between them had atrophied. There were only three black stumps of teeth in her mouth.

He found a house-slave and they unloaded the three barrels.

'What is it, another feast?' he said to Bibra. He wanted to speak to her, to make some further contact. He also wanted to ask what had happened to her face, but didn't dare. She was sharp and bossy with him, telling him exactly where to put the barrels. This outhouse was her place, obviously. It was the size of a small room, with good walls and an earth floor. There was an old stained and heavily cut table near the doorway. There were lines of pots and bowls along the walls. A big rough mortar stood in the far corner. Beside it was a thick layer of straw with a light-brown hide blanket. She slept there beside her work.

'The Lord Burros is in poor health,' Bibra said. 'He is to go tomorrow, poor man, to his last hope, for the pains of his gut are beyond the skills of our healers. But he is to go to your seariver, where at Nemetobala there is a temple of healing.'

'A temple of a lot of things, from what I hear,' the carter said.

'Then you have heard wrong. It was a guest of my Lord who told him of the temple. It is a healing and sacred place.'

'For his gut, you say?'

'It is a very terrible pain.'

'Better not to have a feast then. Or is it to try to finish him off?'

'It is a family feast of prayer and hope for his healing.'

'It usually is for oysters. I've carried them all over, because our waters are the best.'

'Well don't think it's just oysters. Not in this, the best house in Magnis. You'll never have seen such food as there will be here.'

The carter went to the doorway. He turned and looked back at her. She was already plunging her hands into the seawater and turning the shells between her strong fingers.

'Try and get a few for yourself,' he said, quietly.

'Get on with your business,' she said and turned her back.

Bibra cupped her hands full of oysters and looked them over. Then she dropped them back in the barrel and went with her pail to the water cistern by the kitchen at the end of the house. The Lady Cocceia had come out to the veranda, which ran the whole length of the front of the house, facing the broad main street with the wide channel in its centre. Cocceia was stretching her arms and loosening her neck in the warm sun.

'Did I hear the oysters come?' she called.

'Yes, my lady. Three barrels.'

'Are they good ones this time?'

'They look quite good, my lady.'

Bibra filled her pail at the cistern. Cocceia watched her closely. It had been difficult to keep her on since the day Burros had seen her, her arms bloodied with the venison she was cutting, and shouted that they should send her back to the mountains. It was wrong to keep anyone so ugly around the house. But Cocceia had made her excuses. The woman was still a good rough worker and had been with them so long. She was, in any case, mostly kept away from the house. There would hardly ever be a time when he or his guests would have to look at her. Burros had hardly listened, only repeated his order to send her back to the mountains. Cocceia had managed to put that off, and since his illness had worsened he had forgotten about it. Yet it was one thing to stick to the idea of keeping Bibra and quite another, now, when she had to look plainly at the bent, ugly figure and that terrible twisted face.

'Is the Lord in any less pain?' Bibra asked.

She had stopped with her full pail at the edge of the veranda.

'I'm afraid he isn't, Bibra. But shouldn't you be seeing to those oysters?'

'They will be ready in good time, my lady.'

She walked on to her outhouse. Cocceia called after her. 'Bibra, you can bring me some of those daffodils. I would like a few in the house.'

'Yes, my lady,' Bibra said and put down the pail.

She picked seven of the best blooms and carried them to Cocceia.

'You grow them so well, Bibra.'

'No, my lady. The little bulbs grow themselves. Even at the edge of the forest they grow by themselves.'

'Yet yours are still the best.'

'If you say so, my lady.'

Cocceia turned away. She could no longer bear to look at the wretched woman, who spoke and acted as if she were still some young and pretty ancilla, polite, well trained and attractive. Cocceia herself was tall, with red hair dyed to near its original colour. She knew most things that could be done against age, to preserve face and body. But nothing could be done, could ever have been done, with this unlucky woman. She was a creature of another kind, like those women in stories who were born old and ugly but by the same token never died. They lived in mountains and forests or in the other world, and were dangerous to all humans who met them. The stories were not really to be believed, but looking at Bibra they almost seemed possible.

Bibra had indeed been born in the mountains, in the hut of her shepherd father Cottos and her mother Clouta, on the eastern scarp above Masona. She was the fourth of five children, and the third girl. Clouta had thought her, from the beginning, the prettiest of her babies. Her blue eyes were especially bright, and she seemed always to be smiling. She did not grow as strongly as the others, but she was so happy a child that she was always the joy of the family.

Bibra was six, still small but healthy and pretty, when the winter still remembered as the Great Snows came to the mountains. Cottos was out the whole time, first rescuing the sheep, digging them out from the deepest drifts that anyone had seen, and then carrying hay to feed them, though many soon died. The snow lay thick and heavy on the heather roof of the hut. At first it kept in the warmth of the big wood fire but then it had to be cleared in case it broke the roof.

The boys clambered up to sweep it off. Bibra, seeing it as a game, climbed up to join them. It was not snowing but there was a strong and bitter east wind. When the job was done the children came in, cold and wet, and drank their broth. Clouta noticed that after the meal Bibra was unusually tired, but that seemed natural after the work.

They all slept well that night, when it snowed again. Cottos had to dig out from the door to go down to the sheep. The other children were up and talking when Clouta noticed Bibra still lying on the bracken, her arm drawn up over her head, her face turned to the sticks of the wall. She went to wake her. As she turned the little body towards her she saw the change in her face. It was as if a deep line had been carved down the cheek, which had then fallen in. The mouth was twisted and the right eye was hanging down, fully opened. Clouta cried out, alarming the child, but then held her close to her breast. It was some time before she turned her and again looked down into her face.

It was like nothing she had previously seen. She knew the small twists that settled into some faces, so that one side of the mouth was always higher than the other, or there was a crease from lip to eye. Nobody knew the cause, and on many faces it became hardly noticeable. She thought of how cold and tired Bibra had been, after clearing the snow. The chill of that bitter east wind put pains all over the body. Cottos always had pains in his back in the deep cold of winter. She herself now ached in her shoulders and arms, and in the joints of her fingers. But this damage to the face, to the pretty face of her prettiest child, was very different. There seemed, for one thing, to be no pain. There was only a heavy tiredness, a numbness. Very gently, turning her fingers so that the callouses would not irritate the still delicate skin, she felt along the damaged side of the face. Bibra did not react in pain. She simply stared up at her mother, with the hanging and opened right eye very prominent. It had widened to what looked like surprise or shock, though there was no actual expression in it.

She lifted Bibra close to the fire and laid her down. She heated a bowl of broth and held it to her lips. Bibra gulped, still dazed. In a jar at the back of the hut Clouta had her stores of dried comfrey leaves. She mixed a handful, and moistened them with warm water to a poultice. Testing it against her own cheek, she gently applied the poultice and took a braid from her tunic to tie it into place. Then she set the little girl to lie on her left side, close to the fire. It was all she could do. With the deep snow outside she could not take the child to the older women, who might know what to advise.

The deep snows lay through three moons. All over Masona there were illnesses and accidents, and many deaths. With her mother's careful nursing, Bibra became well again in herself. Even the damage to her face seemed to lessen slightly, though Clouta wondered whether it was only that they were getting used to seeing it. She was always careful to hide her own shock and pity when she looked at it, and as she recovered her strength Bibra for much of the time seemed quite unaware of it, though she asked several times why she could not close her right eye, even when she slept. When the thaw at last came, with heavy floods, one of the oldest women, Brocina, who was known for healing, came and looked at the child. She had never, she said, seen so bad a case, but the only known remedy was to rub fat into the cheek. It had to be pork fat, and from a young pig. Clouta followed this instruction exactly, though Bibra disliked it, because of the smell.

As the days got warmer, Bibra recovered her whole strength and was again, as before, smiling and happy. It was only in months and years that the full effects became apparent. Her slow growth, which had been noticed before the damage to her face, became much more of a worry. None of the family were tall, but Bibra, at every stage, was behind them. Her body was strong and active, but at ten she was hardly taller than she had been at six, and at twelve, when other changes began happening, she was still a hand's width shorter than the shortest of her sisters.

Yet this mattered less than what also happened at that age, when the girls in the settlement were becoming more conscious of their appearance. Playing one day at the river, with a group of other girls, Bibra quarrelled over a toy wooden boat which Cottos had carved for her. As the words flew an older girl shouted at her: 'You'd better shut up. With only half a face you've only got half a brain.'

Crying and touching her face, Bibra ran to her mother.

'Is it true?' was all she kept asking.

'No, of course not, my love,' Clouta said. 'You've got as much brains as anyone.'

'But have I only got half a face?'

Clouta hugged her close.

For the damage had now become worse. Clouta dated it from a fever, that spring, which all the children had suffered from. In other families several children had died. Her own children had recovered, without apparent ill effects, except for Bibra, whose face now seemed to atrophy, on its whole right side. The effect was to make the earlier damage – the twisted right side of the mouth, the hanging and widened right eye – much more obvious. Clouta had taken care to avoid any chance of Bibra seeing her own reflection. There was nothing of that kind in the hut, and all Bibra had seen was distorted reflections in water. But the child could now feel with her fingers the difference between the two sides of her face, and she was aware of the numbness on the damaged side. One day, slipping away on her own, she went up to the big house of the Lord Matucenos, under the old bank in Banavint. There in a reflecting bronze shield she at last looked clearly at her face. She did not come back to the hut until after it was dark, and when Clouta spoke to her she broke down in terrible crying. She cried for many days and Clouta could not console her.

The Winter of the Deep Snows, when Bibra's face was first damaged, was in the Roman reckoning the year 993, *anno urbis conditae*. In the British reckoning it was the year 744, at the end of the twenty-fifth cycle. But this way of counting was becoming less common. The events of the year 700, when it was believed that following the withdrawal of the legions Roman power could be overthrown, and when Cicucio and Gobanio and Isca had been attacked and partly destroyed, were now only a bitter memory. For the Roman legions had come back. The leaders of the rebellion had been executed. The villages of the warriors had been burned. The faith of the lords in an eventual military victory had been weakened even in their own proud families. Among all the rest of the people it had quite disappeared.

What took its place was a developed trading economy, with regular local administration and a system of money payments, to which even the mountain peoples had now adapted. This civil life was centred on the prosperous accommodation in Venta, which was not only the capital of the Republic of the Silures but inhabited by fully Roman citizens, as all freeborn British now were. Matucenos, whose grandfather had been installed as lord after the execution of young Darren and his allies, accepted the advantages of the new order, even in the least developed regions. From his mountain territory he carried on a profitable trade in wool and hides – wool now sold at 200 denarii to the pound – and in recent years a growing trade in young horses, of the good Black Mountain breed. He no longer dealt directly with Isca and Venta, as his grandfather had done, but with a British dealer, Cintus, in the little town of Magnis just across the Guuy. Almost all supplies for the Roman army and administration were directly requisitioned, by taxes in kind, but there was still substantial trade among the Romanised Britons, especially in the towns.

Magnis had grown up around the crossroads where the north–south road from Viroconium to Isca met the east–west road from Glevum to Claerion and Cicucio. At first it was a frontier post, in the time of the old battles between Majimarus and Ostorius, and had become a posting station, with supplies and changes of horses, in a scatter of wooden buildings along the roads. With the development of trade, British and Gaulish merchants had built larger wooden houses, and labour was conscripted from the former inhabitants of Caeriddon to enclose a small walled area, later strengthened with ramparts. There was good trade in grain and pottery from the east, and in wool and hides from the uplands and mountains beyond the Guuy.

In the general rising of the British year 700, several of these houses had been burned and the merchants had fled east. But when the Roman army came back, under the governor Virius Lupus, the houses were rebuilt, on a still larger scale, and the merchants and dealers began to prosper. All the time the traffic of the old posting station increased. It was in this period, before Bibra was born, that Velacos, a lineal descendant of the old kings of Caeriddon, whose father had made peace with the Roman power, became the leading dealer in wool. In his later years he established a workshop where weavers from the Black Mountains made products in demand all over Britain and the northern empire: the traditional hooded waterproof cloak, the caeracalla – the Birrus Britannicus – which sold for as much as six thousand denarii, and the woollen rug known as the Tapete.

His sons divided his business after his death. The elder, Druto, kept the general wool trade. The younger, Perico, moved the workshop a little way upriver. Perico prospered most, and soon after the Winter of the Great Snows was able to employ craftsmen from Venta to build and furnish a small villa, with the workshop behind it. Cocceia, daughter and only child of Druto, inherited the general wool business, and in her father's old age was married to Burros, the younger son of Lleu of Eposessa. Eposessa was the famous Place of the Horses east of Magnis, where there was a flourishing business in buying and training the mountain ponies, which were in increasing demand for the post.

The general trade in wool continued, but in the early years of their marriage came the first signs of a deep and general economic disturbance. All civil trade was now in money, and, after the conflicts and invasions in Gaul, the currency had become uncertain. After the devastation of northern Gaul, increasing amounts of grain were exported, especially to the Roman legions on the Rhine. Even in the west of the island the price of grain rose dramatically, at just the time when the value of the coinage was being eroded. In 1035 AUC there was a bitter dispute over a sale of horses to Cintus, who was a supplier to Eposessa. The money offered to, among others, Matucenos of Banavint, for the annual supply of young unbroken ponies was too little to buy the expected amount of grain and pots, let alone the luxuries they had bought in their best years. While the dispute was still being argued, Matucenos and other lords from the mountains raided Magnis and Eposessa and took back their ponies. In the fighting at Magnis, Cintus was killed.

Inflation and collapsing currency brought similar outbreaks all over Britannia Superior: the denarius was worth less than a hundredth of its value at the beginning of the century. Supported by two of the legions, the commander of the Channel Fleet, Carausius, declared himself Emperor. He promised to protect Britain from the foreign influences undermining its economy. He ruled in Britain, issuing new coinage, for seven years until he was murdered by one of his officers, Allectus, who was in turn killed, after three years, when the continental Emperor Constantius invaded the island and was received in Londinium as the 'Restorer of the Eternal Light'.

The economy and the currency were again reorganised, and Magnis and the mountains, with all the southwest of the island, passed under the tighter administration of the new province Britannia Prima, with its capital at Corinium. The prosperity of the merchants began to return. A joke went the rounds, that 'we have gone from the time of the wolf' (Virius Lupus) 'to the time of the medlar' (the old British name of Corinium).

In the time of Constantius, Bibra had been a slave for fifty-four years in the household which was now that of Burros and Cocceia. It was the most prosperous house in Magnis. After the death of Cintus, Burros, with his family connection to Eposessa, had added horse dealing to his wool trade, and he was also a grain factor, importing from the east the additional supplies which the lords of the mountain kingdoms bought with the money from their ponies. Only Urbigen, the importer of pots, and Mapon, the dealer in hides, were of comparable wealth in the prosperous little town, with its views over the Guuy to the long blue wall of the mountains.

At the time of Bibra's crisis, when she saw at last the full damage to her face, there was a crisis of another sort in the household of their lord Matucenos. He had ordered plate in the expectation of a high price for his ponies, but the price fell and he also failed to meet his full supply of wool to Druto. He was forced to cover his debts with a fresh supply of slaves.

The mountain girls were especially valued for their simplicity and modesty. The girls of the local Magnis slave families, living at a busy crossroads of traders, messengers and army detachments, had a different, unacceptable estimate of themselves. Matucenos professed his sorrow, but seven unmarried girls of the slave families of Banavint and Masona must be sent to the new life. When this order of their Lord became known, several marriages were hastily arranged, including two for Bibra's elder sisters. But Bibra herself, with six others, set out one autumn morning to walk into Magnis. She was valued at thirty thousand denarii, by comparison with forty thousand denarii each for the other six. Because of her appearance she was put to work in the kitchen. She never returned to the mountains, though she saw her brothers and one of her sisters, at long intervals, when they came on business to the town.

The sickness of Burros lay heavily for some years on the household, though it did not affect the prosperity of the business. Always a heavy man, from middle age he began to put on an almost uncontrollable amount of weight. At first this did little more than accentuate the ordinary stomach ailments which were common in Magnis, but then more severe pains began and soon became chronic. The skills of the local healers, as Bibra had told the oysterman, could do little to relieve him.

One day a beneficarius from Isca, staying in the house on one of his regular journeys to inspect the trading and supply routes, recommended a visit – almost a pilgrimage – to Nemetobala on the seariver. The place had been known as sacred from before the time of the Romans, though there were different accounts of its origins. It had certainly been a grove of the High Druida of the Fisher Kings. But there was also an old story of a magic tree which grew near by: to all appearances an ordinary ash tree, but one which every seventh year bore miraculous red apples. The tree, if it ever existed, had long gone, but among the British country people the place was still remembered as the grove of the holy apples. Indeed apples were still cultivated there, on the warm southern slopes above the great river.

Nemetobala was now used exclusively by the Roman and Romano-British citizens of Isca and Venta. Several temples had been built there, and healers from far and wide had settled to take in those suffering from diseases of the lungs and stomach. People with diseases of the bones went to the warm mineral baths of Aquae Sulis. With the offering to the chosen temple and the fee to the chosen healer the pilgrimage to Nemetobala was very expensive, but Cocceia was insistent that Burros should go. Apart from everything else, she and Burros had no children and the household would pass on his death to a nephew from Eposessa, with no guarantee of her own maintenance.

Partly to renew good relations with the Eposessa family, and partly to mark the significance of what she insisted on calling the pilgrimage – they chose, for family reasons, the temple of Nudd – Cocceia had arranged the feast for which the oysters had been ordered. In the late afternoon all the guests, first the women and then the men, went to the bathhouse and then assembled, in their best Roman clothes – fine togae and stolae – on the veranda, which had doors opening to the triclinium where the feast was being laid. The ancillae, young girls from the mountains, brought beakers of honeyed wine. The wine was imported through Isca, but the honey was the fine sharp-tasting hawthorn honey which was a speciality of the mountains of Ines. The guests were all in high spirits, looking beyond the town walls and across the shining Guuy to the mountains, where the ridges were now black under a spreading yellow light. The sun was setting behind a bank of clouds, and wide rays slanted down and picked out the green of the foothills.

They did not move into the triclinium, where the bronze oil lamps were burning, throwing shadows across the mosaic floor and the tapestry hangings, until Burros was carried in, by two boy slaves, and set on his couch in the place of honour. On the low marble table oysters and pigeons' eggs were laid for the gustatio, and the beakers were refilled with honeyed wine. Before they ate and drank, Stabius, the nephew from Eposessa, invoked the blessing of Epona, Goddess of Horses, on the respected and well-loved Burros, chief citizen of honoured Magnis. Burros, obviously in pain, bowed his head in acknowledgement.

The oysters were especially fine. Cocceia was congratulated on their quality and careful preparation. Yet she remained preoccupied by the courses still to come. The boar meat she was sure of, with its sauce of honey, pepper and wine, and there could be no doubt of the beef, from the herd at Madrun, or of the tiny mountain lambs from Banavint. But the supporting dishes, including swan and duck from the Guuy, and especially the dormice stuffed with minced pork and hazelnuts, had been fiercely argued about in the kitchen. She had even, irritatingly, been called from her bath to give an opinion. Of course, to serve six main courses was beyond the ordinary ambitions of Magnis or even Eposessa, but she was determined that the occasion should be fine and long remembered. As it turned out, all the courses were good except for one of the swans, which had been overcooked. But the honeyed wine was still circulating so freely that few of the guests really noticed.

It was a long, slow, full meal. When the dishes were cleared for the mensae secundae, with the apple puddings, the honey-sweetened cakes and the bowls of walnuts in cream, the whole company spread out and relaxed. Only Burros had eaten little: a few oysters and then some chops from the little mountain lambs – what the beneficarius called burned fingers – of which he was especially fond. Stabius, on Cocceia's right hand, kept praising her hospitality, often repeating himself as the wine took effect. 'A good meal shows a good business,' he kept saying, 'and we have the well-respected Burros to thank for that.' 'It was my father's business before it was my husband's,' Cocceia at last found occasion to say. Stabius held her arm tightly and smiled. He said, through the wine, 'That will never be forgotten, any more than we could forget your beautiful hospitality.' Cocceia, still half watching the girls who were serving – often, at this stage of a meal, they were inclined to slip away – returned his smile and relaxed.

Before the company could disperse, the boys came in to carry Burros to his bed. They lifted him with difficulty, for he was both heavy and limp. As they put their arms around his waist he cried out in pain. His face was dark red and he was sweating heavily. When at last they got him up he shouted for them to stop and called Stabius across to him. Stabius approached, smiling. Burros spoke breathily, close to his ear.

'You understand this little deal tomorrow? The man from Banavint.'

'Magalos. Yes.'

'I shook hands on one brood mare and one young unbroken stallion for nine thousand five hundred denarii. It's a special delivery, since he needs emergency wheat.'

'The price of wheat is going up, of course.'

'When is it not going up? But the last delivery is still in the store. I shook hands on forty-eight modii.'

Stabius drew back slightly, but Burros grasped his arm.

'Eight wagon loads, forty-eight modii, if the quality of the ponies is standard.'

'As you say, Uncle. And he needs this wheat in emergency.'

'Yes, they don't eat much bread, those rough mountain people. But this will be enough to tide them over till harvest.'

'Very well, Uncle.'

'Look carefully, of course, at the ponies. These mountain people can be crooked, if they don't know who they're dealing with.'

'Uncle, we still have an eye for ponies in Eposessa.'

'Right. So see to it.'

The boys who were carrying Burros were now sweating as heavily as he was himself. He nodded and was carried away. The whole company stood, in respect, as he passed down the triclinium.

In the late morning of the following day Bibra was sitting in the sun, scouring the ollae after the feast. Through the west gate and along the main street came a little procession: two riders, each leading a tethered pony, and behind them four ox-carts. As they came nearer, Bibra recognised Olen, the son of her younger brother.

He was riding with Magalos, the young lord of Banavint. She jumped up excitedly and walked beside Olen, reaching her hand up to his saddle. Olen smiled down at her.

'I will come to see you, Aunt Bibra, but we must first deliver these ponies.'

'Why are you bringing ponies now? It is the wrong season.'

'There is no choice, Aunt Bibra. There is hunger in Banavint and Masona. My lord has arranged this special sale with your master.'

'But my master has gone for his sickness to the grove of the holy apples.'

'There will be someone else to deal with it.'

Bibra stood back and looked at the ponies. They were poorly fed, under their thick winter coats. The brood mare was grey, with a black mane. The young stallion was red, with a sprouting mane the colour of straw. Bibra went to the brood mare, speaking quietly and patting its neck.

Magalos had dismounted and was calling round the back of the house. The steward Eppius came out and looked the ponies over disparagingly. Yet after more words Magalos called back to Olen and told him to take the animals to the pound.

'You should really take them on to Eposessa,' Bibra heard Eppius say.

'Why Eposessa?'

'Because that's the only place you'll get your money. My master Burros is sick and it is his nephew Stabius who must pay you.'

'The deal was not for money but for wheat. We shook hands on forty-eight modii.'

'I know nothing about that. My orders were nine thousand denarii for one brood mare and one stallion in good condition.'

'Nine thousand five hundred, buying forty-eight modii of wheat.'

'It may be nine thousand five hundred. But there is still their poor condition.'

'There are none better after a winter like this.'

'That may be so, but you and I don't decide the weather. Are you afraid they wouldn't get to Eposessa?'

'I haven't the time to waste. I've got my carts waiting for the first half of the wheat. They can load twenty-four modii.'

Eppius did not answer. He walked to the pound to look again at the ponies. When he came back he seemed pleased.

'I'll tell you what I'll do, Lord Magalos. I want to oblige you. We'll ride together to Eposessa, but the ponies will stay here. Meanwhile your four wagons can be loaded with twenty-four modii.'

'Do we have to go through all that?'

'I'm afraid so. I am no master. I can only follow my orders.'

'But I shook hands with Burros.'

'It is Stabius you must deal with now.'

Magalos looked around, distracted. Then he called to Olen that they must ride on to Eposessa. Eppius smiled and gave orders for the loading of the carts. Bibra, disappointed, watched them riding away.

It was late afternoon before they returned. Eppius jumped down and went through the veranda into the house, calling for drink. Magalos and Olen did not stop but rode at full gallop down the broad main street, jumping the big ditch in its centre. They disappeared through the western gate and turned towards the river crossing. It was a long time before they came back, now riding slowly. Their mounts were very tired; Olen's smaller pony was drenched in sweat and foam.

Magalos stopped in front of the house.

'Eppius!' he shouted.

It was the ringing cry of a challenge, as at the games. There was no reply.

'Eppius, come out,' Magalos shouted again.

The steward came to the veranda. Bibra saw that he was wearing fine sandals that belonged to Burros.

'We have to finish our deal,' Magalos said, quietly.

'I make no deals. I am not a master,' Eppius replied.

'I shook hands with Burros. For one brood mare and one young stallion nine thousand five hundred denarii, being forty-eight modii of wheat.'

'You heard the terms from Stabius. Because of the poor condition of your animals, seven thousand two hundred denarii. And the price of wheat you saw posted in Eposessa: 300 denarii per modus.'

'This is an evil,' Magalos shouted. 'I shook hands with Burros for forty-eight modii. I do not run word. No honourable man runs word.'

'You have had your twenty-four modii. That is the end of the deal.'

'I have indeed had twenty-four modii. And I have ridden to see that my carts are safely beyond the river and into my land, or you thieves would have them too.'

'Then you have had your entitlement.'

'I have had no entitlement. My people are hungry. Even with forty-eight modii we would only just have managed. And I have shaken hands with Burros. There can be no running word.'

'I am sorry, Magalos. There is no more to say.'

Eppius turned to go back into the house but Magalos, drawing his dagger, ran quickly up and seized his arm.

'You will listen to me, Eppius. There is still, while we are men, fair play in the world. I will have my forty-eight modii.'

'It's no use threatening me,' Eppius said, calmly. 'It is not what you call fair play, as in the old times. It is fair trade, at a just price.'

'But it is not just. You have put your coins, your faces, between man and man. Before the time of the Emperor Carausius, when the faces were losing all value, we dealt again as men. We traded ponies for wheat, hides for pots, wool for axes and knives. We knew what we handled and we made fair exchange. It is said now that the faces can be trusted, but I shook hands with Burros on a brood mare and a stallion for forty-eight modii of wheat. Now you and this Stabius run word, offering only twenty-four. Should I not then take the further twenty-four? Is that not fair play and fair trade?'

Eppius released his arm and stood away.

'You should not do anything foolish. There is good Roman law in Britannia. And besides, Magalos, you have no waggons here to load, and I have put guards on the grain store.'

Magalos raised his dagger. He looked carefully along its edge.

'It would not be honourable to attack you,' he said, and put the dagger away. 'And indeed I have no waggons. But still I shook hands with Burros, and I now make the reckoning. For the twenty-four modii I will leave the brood mare but take back my stallion.'

'You cannot possibly do that.'

'I can, Eppius, and I will. And I will keep the stallion until Burros returns. He will understand what I have done, because I have never known him run word.'

'The stallion must stay,' Eppius said, firmly, 'and when my master returns you can discuss it with him.'

Magalos rubbed at his head. He had long reddish hair and a heavy moustache. His eyes were heavily lidded and seemed to bulge from his face.

'Olen,' he called, 'go to the pound and bring out our stallion.'

Olen moved at once but Bibra ran after him. He was ahead of her at the pound but she came up and caught his arm.

'You must not do this, Olen. This stallion is delivered to my master's house.'

'But my Lord has told me to fetch him.'

'Your Lord! The Lord of Banavint! But my master Burros is the chief citizen of Magnis. His house has the beneficarius and other great lords as its guests.'

'Aunt Bibra, what can I do? I live in Banavint.'

He took the rope tie from the gate and went into the pound. As well as the brood mare and stallion there were eight other horses and ponies. As he went towards the stallion there was a shout from the house and Eppius came running, with three men from the household.

'Thief!' Eppius shouted.

Then Magalos was running up, drawing his long dagger.

'Back!' he shouted. 'I am taking only my own.'

Eppius and the slaves stood back, watching the dagger. Magalos shouted to Olen to bring out the stallion. The young beast was nervous and seemed ready to rear at Olen, who tried to calm him.

'I've got the gate,' Magalos shouted. 'Let him out.'

Olen tried again, but as Magalos turned Eppius and the slaves rushed him. The gate swung open. Bibra, her shoulders hunched, peered up at the fighting, nervously shaking her hands. Suddenly the stallion was loose and rushing towards her. She put her hand up over her face as he swerved to try to avoid her. But as he passed her he struck her shoulder and knocked her to the ground. Magalos was free again, holding the others back with the threat of his dagger. But the gate was now wide open and the other horses and ponies rushed through and galloped down the street.

'You fool!' Magalos shouted to Eppius. 'Now you have lost them all.'

Magalos, Eppius and the slaves rushed after the frightened

animals, but Olen stayed. He bent over Bibra, who was lying quite still. After she had been knocked down by the stallion she had been trampled by others in the herd. Olen turned her body over, to see her face. There was no wound on it, only grey dust on her nose and forehead. The twisted right side of her face, which he had never before seen so close, was a dead, bloodless grey. Her eyes were wide open but there was no movement in them. He felt for her heart, through the rough tunic, and then for the pulse at her wrist. Her left hand was clenched to a fist and he straightened the rough stained fingers. When he knew that she was dead he lifted her in his arms and walked through to the street.

There were people watching from a distance but nobody near the house. Magalos and Eppius and the slaves had gone after the runaways. Olen's own pony was gone. He carried Bibra to where he had first seen her, at the doorway of the outhouse. There was a pile of oyster shells against the wall. She was hardly any weight in his arms, though with his fingers he could feel the strong muscles of her shoulders. He laid her gently down by her flowers.

Olen stayed, squatting beside the body of his kin, until as the light was fading Magalos rode back. The red stallion was tied beside his own mount. Olen looked up at him. While he had been waiting, beside Bibra, several people had come out from the other houses. They were standing at a distance, looking across.

'Get on the stallion,' Magalos ordered. 'I've got your mount safely tied on the other side of the river. Eppius and his gang are still chasing their ponies.'

'She is dead,' Olen said, staring up at him.

'The old woman?'

'She is Bibra the sister of my father.'

'I have never seen her.'

'She has worked in Magnis all her life.'

'I'm sorry,' Magalos said. 'But we must get out of town before Eppius is back. He will rouse the town and we will not get away.'

'She has to be buried,' Olen said.

'Leave that for them. She's their servant.'

'She is the sister of my father.'

Magalos stared at Olen. He jumped down.

'Get digging tools from the yard. We'll bury her where she is.'

Olen went and found two mattocks. He began digging a grave.

When they saw what he was doing, two men of the town came across and protested. Magalos drew his dagger and told them to keep their distance.

He then took the other mattock and swung it. The earth was dry and loose around the walls of the outhouse. With the two of them digging there was soon a shallow grave.

'That's enough,' Magalos ordered. As Olen hesitated, he lifted the small body himself, and laid it on its back in the grave.

'Are there no words?' Olen asked.

Bibra's eyes were still open. One of the bone pins had fallen from her thin hair. It lay across her twisted face. Olen bent down and closed her eyes. He laid the pin by her left hand. As he brushed the tunic a small coin fell in the dust. It was a minim with the face of the Emperor Carausius: the smallest of all coins. Olen left it lying beside her.

'In peace,' Magalos said, raising his right arm and spreading his fingers.

Olen reached across and picked two of the daffodils. They had been almost covered by the dug-out heap of soil. Olen put the flowers on her breast.

'In peace, lady,' he said.

He bowed his head and closed his eyes.

As soon as he had spoken Magalos began pushing the earth in again. Olen left the work to him until the body was covered, but then he joined in, smoothing and stamping the loose earth.

'Now. Fast,' Magalos ordered. 'We must get back to our own place.'

Olen gripped the stallion's sprouting yellow mane and pulled himself on. It reared, but he kicked its sides and turned it, bending low over its neck. They raced away down the street to the west gate, then swung south across the river to the mountains.

————◆————

Glyn saw the reservoir below him. The water was sparkling, its ripples from the west reflecting the moonlight. Beyond it the narrow valley of Grwyne Fawr was dark with plantations of spruce.

If he was seeing the reservoir it meant that, following what seemed a good track, he had come too far west along the ridge. He must look to move over to a track nearer Capelyfinn.

Yet the reservoir fixed his attention. Its level was high. The reflections moved unceasingly. The effect was almost hypnotic, staring and trying to follow the infinite movements. There was one broad track of direct moonlight, running at an angle towards him from the inlet of Grigws Uchaf, the smaller tributary stream, which looked back up the valley to the source of the main stream, among scattered peat pools on the western dip of Tal y Cefyn.

The big Grwyne, the Grwyne Fawr. It was strange that unlike the other rivers of the mountains it had been named backwards from its join with the river in the next valley west, beyond the Gader and Waun Fach. That Grwyne Fechan, the little Grwyne, was shorter than its brother but might still, in the old habit, have had its own name. Even the short stream here, at the northern end of the reservoir, had its valley name, Cwm Clyd. Surely not the snug but the sheltered valley. It would be a relative term, either way, on these bleak tops.

Grwyne: Guerinou in the earliest records. Yet nobody in the mountains called it the Grwyne reservoir. It was the Blaen y Cwm dam, named after the farm two miles below the wall. Its building was a major event in its time, the 1920s. 'A remote and ancient place now penetrated by modernity.'

How often, in how many turns of the times, had that kind of thing been said by the Romans, and by all those after them whose minds still moved in Roman forms of definition. The finely engineered roads, the great buildings, the aqueducts. Little of any of these had come to this military province; none at all to these mountains. Should we then compare that great empire to the twentieth-century District Council of Abertillery, which had found in these empty hills – but they had not been empty; the sheep-farms still ran along each valley – a source of plentiful water for the crowded thousands of a mining valley, south across the Usk in the coal-bearing rocks? In modern times that was the effective frontier: a change, within a few miles, from emptying rural to crowding industrial Wales. Mountain water piped to that crowded valley around Abertillery where nearly all the collieries were being shut down.

Empty hills. Empty valley. The penetration of modernity. At the mouth of Grwyne Fawr was the hamlet of Fforest Coalpit: one of the only two places in these mountains – the other above Cusop – where getting coal had been attempted but abandoned. The building of the dam was forced by the mining to the south. In that sense it was like the drive of the Roman project, piping resources from periphery to a centre. The self-described civilisation was incidental.

Yet the dam should not be blamed. Families turning their taps for this sweet Black Mountain water were of the same people as those of the mountains. Many had moved down there for work. Down from the declining rural economy that was a part, an intended part, of that later empire, the British, which the Romanising minds with all the confidence and coldness of an assumed superiority, had built and asserted. The work on the dam itself had been welcomed locally at a time of widespread unemployment. It had even sounded heroic, for first a railway had to be built, from below Crucorney through the causewayed marsh of Cwm Coed y Cerrig and up the long valley. The crumbling concrete foundations of the old construction huts lay, with more ancient traces, along the banks below the wall.

It was not the only railway to penetrate the mountains. There had been a passenger railway up the Golden Valley, beside the Dwr, or Dore, that was said, with the Normans, to have become D'Or. That was the Grain Valley of Nemet and Tami. The railway had been closed, for reasons of economy. Also closed was that larger branch from Hereford to Brecon, which followed the Roman invasion route up the banks of the Wye. From Hay there were still traces of the abandoned tram-road that preceded the railway: built to carry house-coal when the mining valleys were opening. To the south, between the Skirrid and Brynarw, was another abandoned tram-road, north from Abergavenny. Its embankment could still be traced like an old defensive earthwork. What is called Offa's Dyke path now, crosses it, though there was no Offa's Dyke in these mountains. The border then was still the Wye. The historical gap had been closed by naming a tourist path across the mountains. Some visitors already supposed, from the resonance of the name, that they were following that old battle frontier.

Penetrations of modernity. Most were already outdated and abandoned. The few survivors were ageing. Yet each had been real in its time. If the Romans had no use for these mountains, still the places they had chosen were nearby and could be seen. The walls of Isca, now Caerleon. The outlines of Venta, now Caerwent. The buried traces of Magnis under meadows in Kenchester near Hereford.

There was no sudden withdrawal of those penetrations. Magnis increased in prosperity, after the time of the death of Bibra in 300. Caerleon was heavily damaged in the rising of 196, when Gwydir rode back with Gwenliana to the mountains. The Romanised British economy, controlled from cities far beyond these mountains, prospered before and after the legions finally marched away. There was no sudden withdrawal, only the last of many ambitious reinvasions of Gaul and the Empire.

The people who mourned the slow loosening of the imperial order – people echoed through the centuries by a residual curriculum, shaping their minds – were of a distinct class: the Romanised gentry and merchants of the cities. Less is heard from those who rejoiced in the departure of an occupying power. Even less, indeed nothing, is heard from those, more numerous than either committed faction, whose conditions of life stayed the same under whatever title: nominal modernity or revival; practical breakdown or recovery. Yet there are reports of escaped slaves joining forces with the Scots and Picts whom Rome and Romanised Britain saw as enemy barbarians. Saxon mercenaries and wagemen rose in what Romanised Britain called rebellion. Brought in to defend the rich of the cities, they decided to fight at last on their own account. Within the long irruption and confusion of so many names and peoples, the slaves and bondmen of the island took what chances they could. But in raid or theft, in withdrawal of labour or in arson they broke only briefly from their long and humbled condition. Other powers, other titles, stood waiting to control and subject them.

The moon's path was now brighter across the waters of the dam. The wind had dropped. Glyn turned and checked his directions. He must move back east across the narrow ridge, though he must stick to tracks. The footing was too rough to stray far.

He stood and called into the night. No voice answered him, but there was the noise of movement away to the left. He stopped and pointed it. The noise came again. It could be a sheep or perhaps a large bird. A black cock grouse had got up as he moved down from Tal y Cefyn. Or perhaps some other large bird, though the noise was sharp and distinct.

He walked carefully towards it. It could even be a fox. There were dens in the rocks of Tarren yr Escob, above Nant y Bwch. He stopped and listened again. There was total silence. He shouted, but still there was silence. He walked into rough hummocky grass, but there was no further sound. He moved back to the track and began crossing the ridge.

The Eggs of the Eagle

◆

At the feast of the five kings, in the ruins of the fort of Govaniu, the bard Mabon told the vision of the Eggs of the Eagle. The kings had met in council of war, to secure their mountains and valleys against the wandering bands of armed men who were ravaging between Hafren and Guuy and north from Guenta and Isca. The five kings were Iddon of Ercing, Gwrfoddw of Uwch Coed, Owain of Ystraduy, Athruys of Madrun and Cinuin of Euas. In the blaze of the fire and of torches, the kings and their warriors fell silent when blind Mabon rose to speak.

'For there was an Eagle, great ones, rapacious and sharp-taloned, which through the cycles of the years had ravaged the Land of the Mighty. It was an Eagle so old that the oldest among us were not able to remember, through our dimming eyes, when its broad dark wings had failed to shadow the pastures of the Pretani.

'Yet a day came, after that long night, when men looked into the skies and the great Eagle had gone: whether dead and rotting on some bare high rock or flown to other lands beyond the narrow seas.

'Through that day and for many days following, the men of the Pretani climbed to their highest watchpoints and searched all parts of the wide sky. But in east and in west, in south and in north, there was no sight or sound of that commanding and terrible Eagle.

'Then to some, newly fearful, it was as if the sun had failed to rise, as if great Lugh had deserted them. For the Eagle, though cruel, was part of the only world they had known.

'But in others, as days passed, and there was only bright sun above the pastures, with no heavy shadow of wings, there was a rising joy, a steady quickening of the blood. As men and as kings, they learned to look at each other without casting anxious eyes to the threatening shadow of the predator.

'Yet still, as they looked at each other, they seemed to see strangers, for the memory of the shadow had darkened their eyes. And as strangers, bitterly, they fought among themselves.

'Then on a certain day, on a ledge in the rockfall of Ysgyryd, where in the oldest days the giant Orgo rested his heel, a young shepherd found the nest of the Eagle. The nest was broken and deserted, but three great eggs lay within it.

'The young shepherd, Iduerth son of Taroc, brought others of his kin to see the wonder of the eggs. While they watched, at a little distance the hot sun beat down on the rock ledge.

'There was then a sudden sound, as of the breaking of a branch, and they saw that the shells of the great eggs, which were white with many patches of brown, were beginning to crack and to splinter.

'Then Iduerth and his kin drew back, afraid. Where there had been one terrible Eagle now three would be born. They then at once sent runners to the Wise One, to my brother Rhiadaf, to hurry to see the strange sight.

'When my brother Rhiadaf came to Ysgyryd the sound of the cracking of the eggs was as the shattering of sandstone at the edges of a fire. Then as he watched, from his distance, the sound grew louder again, until at last it was the cracking of thunder and the sky above Ysgyryd was darkening.

'Now dark smoke was rising from the ruins of the nest, and coiling around the great eggs. And beneath the nest the mountain itself was shaking.

'At once my brother Rhiadaf ordered the people down to the valley. He followed them there. Watching from the distance, they could see only the great black cloud over Ysgyryd, but still they heard the shattering thunderclaps of the breaking of the shells.

'It was at this time that I, blind Mabon, came among them, drawn by the news of so great a discovery. And it was I, Mabon, who saw without eyes through the black cloud over Ysgyryd, and what I saw I tell now for a truth.

'For I saw the first egg break, at its narrowest end, and there was no ballie, no nestling, no creature within it. But as the shell shattered there poured out a river of dark blood, as fierce and fast as the Myngui in spate. And tumbling in the blood were the helpless figures of naked men, who held tiny spears and shields as the flood tossed and scattered them. Yet wherever they were thrown they seemed still to strike at each other, but uselessly, for all were tumbling like broken sticks in the torrent of blood.

'Then, as the blood still poured, the second egg was breaking, and I looked to see again a river of dark blood. Yet this egg had broken differently, at its broad end, and a creature was stirring within it, turning upon itself, and it was covered with white down to which pieces of the shell and of the membrane adhered. And I could see at last what it was: a naked infant eagle, gasping for breath and struggling to move. But as I watched, great ones, its movements became convulsive and then enfeebled. It died, as I watched, where it was born.

'Yet in its death, I now tell for a truth, it was still the hard shape of an eagle, and in its curved beak, beyond anything I have seen, a live fish was struggling, that had been inside the egg. I saw the silvery scales, the round eye, the notched tail, and it was moving, still alive though gripped by the beak of the eagle.

'Then, as I still wondered how such a thing could be, that the infant eagle should die yet the fish it had caught in its shell still live, the third and last egg was breaking, but the manner of this was different again. For a deep crack appeared in the side of the egg and became a wide crevice. Yet nothing appeared in it, though I watched very closely, until at last I saw, from the edge of the crevice, a wisp of yellow mist that slowly thickened and eddied until it was rising like smoke from a grass fire. The mist thickened again and spread out more widely, and a wind caught it, until it moved and rolled as clouds move and roll in our valleys. Its colour, as it rose to a cloud, was still yellow, a deathly yellow, and as it passed over the land I could hear the sounds of choking from people and from beasts.

'It is this now, great ones, that I tell for a truth, of the Eggs of the great Eagle that has left the Land of the Mighty: of the first egg, that poured a river of blood; of the second egg, and a dead eagle gripping a live fish; and of the third egg, from which rose the cloud of choking yellow mist. What these things may be I cannot interpret, for I say only what without eyes but in truth I have myself seen.'

There was a long silence around the fire when Mabon had finished speaking. Pasgen son of Cinuin rose from the fireside and took the old man's elbow and guided him gently back to his place among the kin of Euas. It was Iddon of Ercing, always a leading spirit, who spoke first in the hushed company.

'What Mabon has seen is to be thought upon,' he said, with authority.

'Yet it is very simple, my Lord,' said the tall Branud, chief Wise One of the land of Uwch Coed.

'It is not simple to me,' said Owain of Ystraduy.

'But consider, my Lords,' Branud said, stepping forward. 'The great Eagle, it is obvious, is the power of the legions, which have now left our land. And the Eggs are what the legions have left us, the foul progeny of Rome.'

'So much might be seen,' said Gwrfoddw of Uwch Coed, impatiently, 'but it is not the heart of the vision. If the Eggs are of the Romani, what is the meaning of the river of blood, of the live fish, of the cloud of yellow smoke?'

'These things also are simple, my Lord,' Branud said. 'For consider only the most terrible egg, with its river of blood and men with spears and shields carried along in it. Is this not what happened when the legions left the land: that the realm broke into a warring of tyrants until blood drenched the pastures?'

'Be careful, Branud, what you are saying,' Gwrfoddw answered angrily. 'What I hear in your words is the foul talk of Guenta, of those lice of the Romani. For when was there not blood, while the Eagle of the legions darkened our land? Indeed I do not see the Eagle as the Romani in Mabon's vision, as if they were one Eagle. Did they not spill each other's blood in their endless battles and rivalries, their emperors and pretenders, their tyrants who used our blood in their private wars? And did they not, in that long night, spill rivers of our own peaceful blood, as they fell on our fathers and stole and looted and punished? We did not have to wait until the legions left the land for a river of blood: those cowardly legions, unwilling to fight but ready to steal, which Rome at last became.'

'I did not mean, my Lord, what you have drawn from my words,' Branud said, hastily.

'Then you meant nothing,' Gwrfoddw replied. 'For it was no realm that broke into the warring of tyrants. In their own lands, among their own kin, the princes of the Bretani have recovered the inheritance that was cruelly wrenched from their fathers. It is in that inheritance that we now lawfully meet.'

'Yet there is still much blood,' Iddon of Ercing said, quietly. 'I agree with my brother Gwrfoddw that the river is not the blood of the kings of the Bretani, who have recovered their ancient lands. But is not that the meaning of the vision, that the blood is not of us but of what the Romani have left us?'

There was silence for some time. Many men stared into the fire and were unwilling to speak. Branud, abashed, moved back into the shadows.

'I have a suggestion to make,' old Glesni of Madrun said, rising. 'I believe that the heart of the vision is the live fish in the beak of the dead eagle, and I interpret it in this way. You have all spoken, my Lords, of Rome and the Romani, and of the Eagle as the power of their legions. Yet consider, my Lords, that through seven cycles of the years all free men of this island have been described and many have described themselves, as Roman citizens: that is to say, as Romans, though of British blood and birth. Now see what has happened since the legions, the old Eagle, have gone. These British passing as Romans wished the Roman rule to continue in their own hands. This is especially true of those who might be our neighbours, but who seek to act as our overlords: the Roman British of Guenta and Isca: those changed men who live under the title of the Republic of the Silures, which they announce not in their own but in the Roman language. Consider the ancestry of what were once the free Silures: the Fisher Kings of the Seariver, who in times long past fought the Roman invader. We then see the meaning of the dead eagle and the live fish that is still in its beak. The true Roman power has indeed died, but this petty fish still lives in its beak: a struggling creature that was once free but that is now content to live in the Roman mouth. Thus the vision, my Lords, is a warning: that the proud claims of those altered Silures of Guenta should not deceive us. For they were once the prey and are only the creature of the Roman enemy.'

Old Glesni looked around. There were many voices of agreement. Gwrfoddw rose and put his arm across the old man's shoulders.

'It is the truth you have spoken,' he said, staring around. But now Rhiadaf of Ercing was getting to his feet.

'My lords, I hesitate, after the wisdom of Glesni, but you will remember that I myself saw the great Eggs, though I did not see them breaking but saw only the dark cloud that hung over Ysgyryd.

I agree now with Glesni that the heart of the vision is the fish in the mouth of the dead eagle, but I cannot agree that this fish is an emblem of the Siluri, the Fisher Kings. For those Kings themselves caught fish. What then is the true meaning of the emblem? It is this, my Lords. Among the many customs which the Roman brought to our lands was an upstart rite, foreign to our ancient religion. This rite, they proclaimed impudently as the official religion of the Roman State. You know this petty rite, my Lords, which in Guenta and Isca and in other cities is now observed by all those who are slaves to Roman customs. It is a rite of what they call a Christ, and the sign of this Christ is a fish. Thus we see at last the truth of the vision of Mabon my brother. The power of Rome and of its legions is dead, but out of its mouth comes this falsehood, this alien superstition, which we would never have known on this island if the power of the legions had not carried it here in its beak.'

Iddon of Ercing rose to stand up by his countryman.

'This is at last clear,' he announced. 'It is the great wisdom of Rhiadaf. Yet consider, my brothers, that the effect is the same as the wisdom of Glesni. For it is indeed from the aliens of Guenta and Isca, men of our own blood who have betrayed it to be Roman in all things, that all dangers now come. The escaped slaves, the vagrant raiders, who now harass the whole island are no final threat to us. They are not warriors but looters and thieves. It is very different in the case of that Republic of the Silures that would prolong its power under a Roman title. For already they hire foreigners to defend their privileges and to fight their wars. With their Roman habits they would overawe us. With their Christ they would draw us from our true religion. Thus the agreement we have made, to help each other in defending our lands, may begin with the wandering bands but will end against the Silures. It will be against their ambition to be the hatched eggs of the Eagle.'

There was loud applause. The warriors of each kingdom stood and raised their spears. The feast was about to disperse when it was seen that Branud, who had quickly recovered from his rebuke by Gwrfoddw, was standing by the fire with his arm raised for the privilege of a voice. Impatiently, the others listened to him.

'My friends, in my own interpretation, and in the valuable interpretations by my brothers Glesni and Rhiadaf which have built on its meaning, we have together discovered the truth, or almost all the truth. Yet though I have no wish to prolong our deliberations, I am in duty bound by the oath of the Wise to remind you all that we have not yet spoken of the third egg, that is to say of the cloud of choking yellow mist.'

'What is it then?' several voices shouted.

'It is hard to be certain,' Branud continued, 'but I believe it is to be a warning of fire. For you will remember that Mabon spoke of it as both mist and smoke, yet if it choked men and beasts it could be no ordinary mist. Thus I conclude that it warns us of fire, of a great fire that might consume our lands.'

'The smoke or mist was yellow, my brother,' Rhiadaf observed.

'It is very uncertain,' Glesni added. 'And it is for this reason that I think it is not an emblem, as the fish is an emblem. It is a vagueness, a shifting, an uncertainty, an obscuring. It is an unseen, unseeable, future of our lives, when the Eagle has died and none of its eggs has given live young.'

The others waited, but there was little wish to say more. The climax reached in the speech of Iddon of Ercing left all other talk uncertain, even superfluous.

'We will think further of all these matters,' Iddon said with an authority that was meant to bring the talk to an end.

Pasgen, son of Cinuin, who had led the blind Mabon back to his place, spoke respectfully to Iddon but could not resist adding: 'In all the interpretations, my Lords, we have not asked for guidance from the Wise One who saw this vision and who might then best help us. Should we not, before we go, ask help from wise Mabon?'

There were a few voices of agreement, though almost all now wanted to leave. Iddon sighed, staring at Pasgen, but then turned to look where Mabon was sitting, among the kin of Euas. As he looked more closely he laughed, for Mabon's head was lying back and his mouth was open. For some time, through all the talk, he had been fast asleep.

In the Shadow of Artorius

◆

'When the teyrn feels the frost, he remembers the taeog.'
Caran looked up, sweating from his work on the skep, as his father Tarac spoke. Following his direction, but keeping his hands firmly on the bottom panel of the skep, he saw what had prompted the words: the line of horsemen riding slowly up the track in Cwm Bedd.

'The lords are early. There is little they can take,' he said, returning to his work.

'Yet they will take whatever there is,' Tarac said, continuing to look down at the slow-moving file, which was skirting the bottom wood. He could hear the voices of the horsemen as they called to each other in the still, sharp air.

The bond tref of Crugader, in which Tarac and his fathers had been born, lay along the upper banks of the stream Nant y Bedd, below the old defended hill village of Crouco. The stream was named from the ancient grave which had once been the Long House of the family of White Cap, now known as Cerrig Calch. It was said in the stories of the people that the lords themselves had once lived in Crouco, but had left it with the coming of the Romani. They and their kin now lived in the broad fields cleared from the woods of the valley of the Uisc. The fathers of Tarac, who had been their herdsmen around Crouco, had stayed where they were, on the higher land, building and rebuilding their huts along Nant y Bedd, before and after the time which was remembered as the day of Guenyn.

Many stories were told of Guenyn, the wise hero of Crugader, who had so great an understanding of the wild bees of the woods that he was never driven away by their stings, but could bring them together where he had planted a grove of apples, in land cleared of other trees. The grove lay open above the Uisc to the sun of the south. The frosts of spring rolled through its slopes to the valley fields below. Since the time of Guenyn the people of Crugader, though they had sheep for summer pasture over Cerrig Calch towards Allt Mawr, and pigs in the oak woods below Old Crouco, made a large part of their living from the honey of the Afalon of Guenyn, which was now a wide grove containing more than a hundred straw skeps of the bees he had brought together.

The summer had been hot. The open pastures away from the springs were a dry light brown. There had been none of the usual gales and storms at the equinox, but now the frosts were early and were already colouring the leaves in the woods. The yield of apples was low but the stores of honey were heavy. When the usual dawnbwydd, the winter food-render for the teyrn, had been set aside, there was still enough to make good bragget, their famous honeyed ale, though they then also made less cider. The dry pastures and poor hay crops meant that they would have to dispose of more yearling sheep to the freemen of the floodfields along the Uisc. But, properly bargained, they would also get more oats for their winter baking.

It was this way in any year, Tarac reflected. The mix of all that they tended and grew had different yields in its different parts but generally balanced to a living for the families. The only thing that was likely to destroy the balance, except in rare years of exceptional weather, occurring once or twice in a lifetime, was war or the effects of neighbouring wars, as their lords asserted and disputed boundaries and supremacies.

Ystradwy, the bro to which Crugader had been assigned, had been relatively peaceful through most of Tarac's lifetime, though in the time of his father there had been fighting with the lords of Uwch Coed to its east. Morudd, the young teyrn of Ystradwy, who liked to describe himself with the old title of brorig, king of the homeland, was the son of Onbraust, daughter of the king of Uwch Coed. That marriage had settled the old fighting, and Morudd had himself married into the Uwch Coed ruling kin, accepted the seniority and supervision of that more populous and powerful kingdom.

In Crugader none of these matters was known for a certainty. Indeed none concerned them unless some dispute led to blood and then to heavier exactions.

Tarac saw, looking down, that Morudd himself was among the horsemen riding slowly up Cwm Bedd. This was not a good sign, for it was still a moon to the end of the year and the payment of dawnbwydd at Samain. What was worse was that all their produce still lay open to the eye. Among the huts the apples were piled in their shining heaps, beside the open cider presses. The extra bragget, fortunately, had been stored in barrels deep in the groves. But most of the comb for raw honey was still stacked by the troughs, where the women were kneading and separating the wax and collecting the slow-dripping honey. Even most of the heather honey, from the skeps carried to the mountain, was back at the huts. Its extraction was done separately because it crystallised so soon after separation from the wax.

'At least there's one empty skep to show them,' Tarac said, dropping his voice.

Caran was working on a skep where there were signs of disease. The foul smell meant that the wax was black and most of the working bees dead. He had wanted to burn it without opening it, but Tarac insisted on it being opened and examined. Much was still to be learned of this sickness.

'I could drop it as they arrived,' Caran said.

'There might be enough still alive to give them a warm welcome.'

'It will do better as a disease,' Tarac answered, 'for they know little about honey except its taste.'

There was a shout from below. One of the riders, the chief huntsman, was galloping towards them. He reined his pony in close to them: a familiar intimidation. Tarac looked calmly at the pony: one of the herd of charcoal grey with long black manes that were so numerous on Allt Mawr.

'Honour to the brorig the Lord Morudd,' the huntsman shouted. Tarac smiled up at him.

'Honour to the teyrn and to all uchelwyr,' he replied, politely.

'Your name,' the huntsman demanded.

'Tarac son of Anailo of the tref of Crugader.'

'And this?'

'My son Caran, my first-born.'

Morudd rode up and smiled around. A tall, fair young man, barely twenty, he had an easy, friendly, even informal manner.

'Using your skill on the little devils?' he said, as he dismounted and walked over to Caran.

'I would keep away, high one,' Caran said quickly, moving the bottom panel of the skep.

'Are you saying they are dangerous? Though I suppose you fellows are used to getting stung.'

'Something of that sort, high one,' Caran said, and opened the skep. A mass of blackened wax and dead bees fell to the grass.

'Great Gods, what a stench!' Morudd shouted, stepping back. 'Is that the best sort of honey you can raise in Crugader?'

'It is a disease, high one,' Tarac said.

'I can smell that it is a disease. You will be telling me next, I suppose, that all your bees are sick, and all your apples rotten with grubs, to escape your dawnbwydd. Come, we will talk to the rest of your people.'

Caran put down the skep. Tarac took his knife and cut several stalks of green bracken. He carefully covered the mess of wax, to examine it properly later. He then led the way up the old track to the big clearing among the huts. All the people who were working there wiped their hands and gathered round. Morudd stood at a little distance and addressed them.

'You are honest people in Crugader. You have a good and even a famous tref. Your honey is of the finest and your cider is excellent, though you somehow never make enough good bragget for the court.'

Several of the people were now smiling, though the faces of the younger men were harshly set.

'We have never had cause to complain of your dawnbwydd. Except in the odd year when your cider has been as sour as an old witch's milk.'

Some of his listeners laughed.

'So that what I now have to say is not between your lord and your duties. You have been, I must tell you, faithful in these. But there is a whole world beyond this peaceful little spot of Crugader. It is beyond even our own peaceful and beloved bro of Ystradwy. There are great matters in it, high matters. You must listen while I explain them.'

There was a general silence, except for the angry barking of a dog tethered by one of the huts. A girl slipped away and released it. It came in, sniffing curiously around the legs of the strangers.

'In the far east of this honoured Island of the Mighty there is a great court, which can trace its authority to the power of the legions, the high power of Rome. The legions have long left us, but there, in the East, there are Britons, once of our lineage, who keep alive in all their ways the old power and honour of Rome. There are among them great warlords, who defend the Island, but in their own ways, which are different from our ways.'

Morudd paused and looked around. 'You may think that what I am saying is of little concern to you. But it is what now makes me come among you. For indeed those great kings have many foreign enemies. There are the old Britons of the North, whom they call the Picti, the Painted Ones. There are the Scotti, who sail across our western sea and both settle and steal among our neighbours in the west. And then, above all, there are the Saesneg, who are coming in great numbers across the eastern sea and invading the lands of these kings.'

'Are they still far from us, these enemies, high one?' one of the elders asked.

'It is a good question,' Morudd said, smiling. 'For in truth I have to tell you that these foreign enemies are still far from us. Only the Scotti, from Erne, are within three days' ride of our bro. But I am speaking of high matters, and in high matters nothing is simple. For in years long past, one of these kings, the Gwrtheyrn or Vortigern that many now curse, himself brought into Saesneg fighters for his wars against the Scotti and the Picti. Yet, he brought in so many that at last they turned against him, and against all these Romish Britons who had hired them, and they took much of the land for themselves. It is against these Saesneg, above all, that the great kings of the East, of the lowlands, now fight.'

'Yet they are still far from us?'

'Very far. You need not fear them. For in many battles the Emperor Ambrosius pushed them back. And now in a decisive battle the warlord Artorius has so defeated them that they have run far back to the east.'

'All is safe from the Saesneg. But now follow me carefully. For in his great victory Artorius saw a vision: that the Island of the Mighty would again, as in the days of the legions, be a single Brittania: a realm of a single rule. And to secure this realm he now wars against all who dispute it, foreign enemies and Britons alike.'

'Is he not a Briton himself?'

Morudd smiled. 'I will tell you something of that, in its turn. The name we know him by, Artorius, is Roman.'

'Have the Romani then returned? The legions of the Eagle?'

'Not the Romani. Their legions are defeated and scattered. But in their place, in the very centre of the Island there is now this ameraudur, this emperor, who would rule and govern the whole land of Brittania.'

The men of Crugader looked at each other. They shifted their feet.

'But is the bro of Ystradwy within this Brittania?' a second elder asked.

Morudd smiled. 'That is yet to be seen. But now listen. For Artorius, as I told you, is fighting many battles, to our east and to our north and to our south. In his latest wars he moved west from Guenta, which admits his authority, along the coast of the searriver towards Demetia, where the Scotti were settled in great numbers. To our north, along the Guuy, one of his generals, the Goth Theodoric, drove west to link up with him. On his route, this Theodoric lost many men against the archers of Euas. Then the horsemen of Artorius, riding north towards Cicuti, were seen by our brothers of Madrun as a warband. Two of their highest men were killed. Artorius, in a fury, charged the prince of Madrun with unlawful killing. There was trial and arbitration at Guenta, and Artorius was awarded galanas. But the amount was disputed. Some awarded a hundred cattle for each high man, others as few as three. It was finally agreed that galanas of a hundred cattle should be paid for both deaths. The bro of Madrun was thus charged.'

Morudd paused. He could see, looking around, that the people of Crugader were listening only as if to a legendary story, interesting enough in itself, but not of their own time or place. He lifted his right hand and asked them for patience, lowering his eyes and chopping lightly with the edge of his hand. As the people shifted their feet, acknowledging an uncertainty, he spread his hands on each side of his waist, and, pushing back his head, laughed suddenly. His listeners looked up, surprised but also curious.

'The ways of men,' he said easily, 'make the gods laugh. For now listen. The elders of Madrun took a hundred cattle as galanas. Artorius at first accepted them. But then as he looked them over he rejected them for they were of the wrong colour.'

Several men laughed. 'There had been no word of colour in the formal arbitration. But now Artorius raged. He said he would have no cattle except red and white. And as he said this he had his whole army around him. The elders of Madrun had to agree. They drove away the first cattle. With great difficulty, searching their whole land, found a hundred red and white. These they drove again to Artorius. When he saw them he smiled. He then gave an order . . .'

Morudd broke off and laughed. His audience waited, curiously. 'One of you asked me if this Artorius was indeed a Briton. This is hard to say, for his lineage is both British and Roman, and his name is Roman. It is said that in his court, like all the high men of the East, he speaks only the Roman tongue. Yet in his demands and challenges he can speak our British language. But not, as you will hear, speak it well. As the fine red and white cattle were being delivered there was a great storm. The whole business had to be hurried. Artorius shouted his command that they should be taken at once to the high fort. But, in the hearing of all those who were witnessing the judgement, his actual words were different. In his imperfect knowledge he confused what he was saying. He used a feminine noun as a masculine, so that what he actually ordered was that the cattle should be taken at once to the tall bracken.'

There was loud laughter.

'The storm was very heavy,' Morudd continued, laughing, 'and Artorius rode away, believing his orders would be quickly obeyed. As indeed they were, for the elders of Madrun at once drove the cattle back where they had come from, into the tall bracken of their own mountains.'

Everyone was now laughing. Many were repeating the joke of the words to each other.

'So he was no true Briton,' an old man shouted. Morudd held up his hand.

'You must judge that for yourselves. But Briton or not, he has a powerful and terrible army. Did he not defeat the Saesneg at Badon? Did he not win victory after victory in north and south, until the whole island east of Guuy now obeys him? Is this the kind of man who would rest in his own error? A man who would smile and say "My friends, it was all an amazing mistake"?'

The listeners went quiet.

'Anyone who believes that doesn't know this Artorius. He has the old Roman style, that his word is law. Even a feminine as a masculine is still, in his mouth, a lawful command. For what makes it lawful is his army, which he has now brought in great strength to the Uisc below Burrio. He is demanding not only the original galanas but sarhad as compensation for this new insult of disobedience. If he is not obeyed, the five kingdoms will be ravaged: not Madrun alone but its allies Uwch Coed, Ercing, Euas, Ystraduy.'

There was now a grave silence. But while the older men looked uncertainly at each other, the younger were staring with open suspicion at Morudd.

'It is under this threat I now come to you,' Morudd continued. 'For while the galanas is still only the charge of Madrun, the charge of the sarhad is on us all.'

'But that's not right,' one of the young men, Carfor, shouted angrily.

'The sarhad also should be on Madrun,' another voice shouted, 'since it was they took back the cattle.'

'In our law it is so,' Morudd at once agreed. 'But this is the stronger law of the ameraudur. It is the sharp law of the Eagle. I have ridden with my brothers of the five kingdoms to see the army of Artorius, which is camped across the Uisc below Burrio. I have to tell you that against them we would be as the shrew to the kite. Many have tried to intercede, learned men of the religion of Artorius, which they call Christian. But he is not to be dissuaded, he will have his demands. If the mistake in his words is now mentioned it only makes him more angry. He has even threatened cruelty to the holy interceders, learned and harmless men.' Morudd paused. No one was now willing to question him. 'I am sorry,' he continued. 'I am even ashamed, to come thus to Crugader. You have been loving and faithful in your dawnbwydd. With your sweet bees in your afalon you are living as if in that other island, beyond the death of men. The island of the happy, of all sweetness and of blessing.' He paused again.

Their lips were compressed.

'I am sorry, I am even ashamed,' Morudd repeated. 'It is not fair to you. It is not fair to any of us.'

The silence was now openly challenging.

'We have made the reckoning,' Morudd at last said. 'Ten sesters of honey, eight yearling ewes, twelve barrels of new cider.'

Nobody moved. Then at last Tarac stepped forward.

'This is in addition, high one, to the render of the dawnbwydd?'

'Sadly it must be so.'

'It is not possible, high one. The dawnbwydd itself is due in one moon. If we render what you ask we shall go hungry this winter. But not only us men, women and children. To get the honey you demand we must empty more store skeps. Yet our very springtime depends on them. When the sun returns there will be few bees. It is not only the honey that will then be short, for ourselves and for the dawnbwydd. It is also the fruits of the bro, that the bees will not suck in the flower. If you take so much, high one, the fruit will be barren and the honey will be scarce. But there will still be demands.'

Morudd nodded, as if in agreement. 'I know this is true. But it is not I, your brorig, who demands this sacrifice. It is the army of Artorius. If we do not pay him the whole bro will be ravaged. Many will be killed and many huts burned. All our stores will be seized or destroyed. And is not that, I ask, even worse?'

Tarac hung his head. 'He is to be cursed, this Artorius,' he said quietly.

'Perhaps,' Morudd said. 'But, if so, only secretly. To stand and curse any man with so great an army is simply to turn a knife on ourselves. In all the lands where he has ridden, with his horsemen and his victories, there may indeed be curses, but none are heard. What is heard, instead, is the high shout of triumph. What is heard is applause of the High Saviour, the Protector, the Redeemer of his country!'

'And do you join in such applause, high one?'

Morudd flushed, angrily. 'We submit only to get him to leave us, to take his army away. This Artorius will pass, as others have passed. We will be patient and look to our own lives, until this heavy shadow is lifted. Our only oath, before our fathers, is to defend the bro.'

Tarac stepped back. Morudd, calling to his attendants, walked across to his horse.

'I will leave my exactor,' he shouted, but the word was not understood.

'What is exactor?' Tarac asked the chief huntsman. Morudd was riding away with all but three of his troop.

'It is a word of Artorius's,' the huntsman replied. 'It is a word of the Romani. It means only, in our tongue, collector.'

'Why then did the teyrn use it?'

'The brorig chooses his own words,' the huntsman said sharply. 'Who are you to pick and choose what words he may use? You just get your people together, and we'll arrange this render.'

'It would be easier just to give you all the bees,' Caran said.

'No insolence,' the huntsman commanded. 'And no tricks. I know all your tricks.'

Slowly, still dazed, the elders of Crugader came together. They sat close, shoulders touching, in the clearing. They began discussing how they might manage this new and heavy demand.

In an interval of the talk, which would probably continue all day, Carfor, standing impatiently with the younger men, turned to Caran beside him.

'Do you believe in this Artorius?' he asked.

'What do you mean, believe in him?'

'I mean believe that he exists. That there is a real Artorius, a flesh-and-blood Artorius, who behaves as they say.'

Caran stared at him. 'Why should we not believe it? There are always kings and lords. Why should there not be an Artorius?'

'Because the teyrn says so?'

'He said so. He also said that he came here in shame.'

'Shame is a word. He came here for honey and cider and ewes.'

Caran hesitated. 'Only to give to Artorius.'

'If there is an Artorius!'

'We shall see,' Caran said, 'we shall see if we hear of him again.' He lifted his hands to his face. There was still the smell of foul brood. He stooped and rubbed his hands on the grass.

The Samain of the Yellow Death

◆

Gord was first to see the barricade, on the old road of the legion between Gobanio and Burrio. They had heard distant shouting as they rode out of the oak grove. Now they could see many people gathered around the barricade of carts. It was guarded by archers and spearmen and by men holding flaming torches, in the light of the late autumn morning. Beyond the barricade was a crowd of men, women and children, heavily burdened with goods. There were laden packhorses and waggons. The noise came equally from the cries beyond the barricade and the angry commands of the armed men guarding it.

'Stay back, master,' Gord said. 'I will go and ask the reason.'

Nyr hesitated. At fifteen he was just beginning to want to give orders. For ten years, in everyday matters, he had always done what Gord, his slave guardian, had decided. He saw that Gord, strong and active in his thirties, had loosened the dagger at his waist and touched his bow. But any danger was not on this side. There were armed men of Uwch Coed, allies of Ercing and Euas.

Gord rode quickly forward. Nyr followed, more slowly. This journey was important to him. After ten years in the class of Dyfrig at Custenhin he was to join the community of the church in Guenta. He had spent the summer in Banavint with his sister Galaes, in a worldly life which was very strange to him. He had counted the days to this ride to the south, the place of so many saints.

Gord had finished talking to the armed men on the barricade as Nyr rode up. When Gord turned and saw his young master, he shouted angrily.

'Get back. Get away from here.'

'You must not order me like that,' Nyr replied.

'It is plague,' Gord shouted. 'The plague that is stronger than teyrn or taeog.'

Nyr's face reddened under his freckles. He pushed his fingers back through his loose, fine, sandy hair.

'Where are all these people from?' he asked, looking beyond the carts.

'Guenta, Isca, I don't know. There's plague all along the seariver.'

Nyr looked at the harassed guards. 'Who's in charge here?' he called.

A black-haired knight of Uwch Coed, his sword raised, rode across to him.

'Who are you?' he challenged, harshly.

'I am Nyr son of Erb, brorig of Ercing.'

'And your business?'

'I am on my way to the church of Teilo in Guenta.'

'Then you can spare your pony. Teilo is already gone, across the sea to Armorica. Most of the priests have gone there: old Samson, Paul Aurelian, and some say Gildas.'

'But there's been plague before.'

'Not as bad as this. A black death came in with rats from the ships, and many hundreds died. But what has come now is a yellow death. In the harbours and along the coast there are already more dead than the living can bury.'

'What is this yellow death?'

'It is not known. There is great shivering and fever as in the black death. But there are no buboes on the body, only a racking cough and spume of spitting. It kills, it is said, in three or four days.'

'Then we must pray to be spared it.'

'Pray if you like. We're blocking our roads. All who can move from the coast are running this way, carrying their bloody spume to infect us. We shall hold them back. We shall kill them if we have to.'

Nyr looked at Gord, who had been listening carefully.

'Let's get back to Banavint, high one,' Gord said.

'Yes, perhaps we should.'

As he spoke there was a great crying beyond the barricade. A young woman in her twenties, with two small children clinging to her, was trying to climb the barricade. She was screaming for mercy.

The spearmen, embarrassed, were holding her back with their shafts.

'For pity,' she cried, 'will you not let me save my children.'

'Nobody passes,' the knight ordered.

'My lord,' she shouted, 'one of these children, I admit, is my own. But the other is the son of a nephew of Lord Honorius.'

'Of old Ynyr's kin, is he? Then let Ynyr look to his own. It is Ynyr who trades with these foreign ships, from the sea he calls the centre of the world. It is Ynyr who wants his wine, his fine pottery, his foreign ornaments. Well he has got his wine and the rest, but he has also got the rats, and the rats are killing his people. We will not let them kill ours.'

'This is not a plague of the rats, high one. You can look at these children's bodies, there is not a mark on them.'

'Yes and while I am looking they will cough their death in my face.'

'For pity, high one,' the young woman pleaded.

He looked down at her, hesitating. There was a loud shouting away to the left, where a strip of stubble ran beside the road. A young man with long fair hair was riding a white stallion at a gallop over the stubble, passing the barricade.

'Kill him,' the knight shouted.

Two arrows flew at once. As they hit the rider he seemed to stop in mid air, while the stallion galloped from under him. A third arrow went into his chest as he tumbled to the ground.

'You see that we mean what we say,' the knight shouted.

The young woman was now weeping. The two little boys were very pale and still at her side.

'Push her down,' the knight ordered.

The spearmen pushed with their shafts, but she turned and hurried down herself. She sat on the road, sobbing. The crowd beyond her began putting down their bundles. There was a deep silence.

Gord turned his pony.

'Let's go,' he said to Nyr.

'Yes, we must take the news,' Nyr replied. 'But there is just one more thing.'

He rode across to the knight.

'We are going back. What is the honour of your name?'

'I am Idwerth son of Rhys of Uwch Coed.'

'If I give the news, in Ercing and Euas, I shall be asked why this plague is called the yellow death. Do you know this, Idwerth son of Rhys?'

'I do not know it. It is said that what kills is a yellow mist, a yellow smoke, as in the legend of the Eggs of the Eagle. There have been many mists along the coast, where the death is at its worst. But others say that the yellow is the colour of the dead, where they lie in the roads, too many for the living to bury.'

'I give you honour, Idwerth son of Rhys.'

'Honour to you, Nyr son of Erb.'

Nyr turned and galloped away. It took some time for Gord to catch up with him. Nyr's pony was a Black Mountain stallion, a gift from Gwrfan brorig of Euas, who had married Nyr's older sister Galaes. Nyr's visit to Banavint had been a further move in the new policy of the dynasty of Ercing, to repair the old alliance with Euas. There had been a split during the childhood of Nyr's father Erb, when Ercing, Uwch Coed and Ystradwy had moved into closer relations with Guenta. In this change the ruling familes had taken the Christian sacrament.

The change was especially significant in Ercing, where Dyfrig of Madle, through the influence of his mother, became one of the most famous priests of the land. In Guenta, under his Roman name Dubricius, his authority in the Church was second to none. It had been natural to put Nyr under the authority of Dyfrig, but the beliefs of the neighbouring kingdoms remained uncertain. In Uwch Coed one part of the ruling family had turned against the Christians, seeing them as 'the left arm of the power of Guenta'. The mountain kingdoms of Euas and Madrun also rejected the Christians. It was only two years since Gwrfan, the new young brorig of Euas, had agreed to resume the old alliance with Ercing, by his marriage to Galaes. And it was only this summer, while Nyr was in Banavint, that Gwrfan, encouraged by Galaes, had at last banished the Wise Man Glesni. Nyr had watched the formal rejection. He had been disturbed by it, in ways he could not interpret. He knew, from his education under the rule of Dyfrig, that the old order of the Wise Ones was an order of falsehood, a barbarous and stubborn opposition to the truth of the Lord Christ. He had copied in class the decisive words of the holy Gildas:

I will not list the devilish monstrosities of my own land, some of which we can see today, stark as ever, inside or outside deserted city walls: outlines still ugly, faces still grim. I will not name the mountains and hills and rivers, once so pernicious, now useful for human needs, on which, in those days, a blind people heaped divine honours.

It was a class joke that the holy father had listed them while saying that he would not. And this, without doubt, was the evil order to which Glesni belonged.

Yet the old man had been so gentle, so willing to listen to the testimony of the truth of Christ, that Nyr found himself uncertain. In manner and in conduct, for all his false faith, old Glesni could be mistaken for the best of Christian priests. Guiltily, as his curiosity overcame him, Nyr had attended the ceremony of the water, where the rivers Myngui and Ondi joined below Banavint. Glesni spoke in old words, which Nyr could not always follow, of the sweetness of the water and the sweetness of the grass on the mountains from which the water sprang. Then he sang in words which Nyr could not understand at all. He cast a shining sword into the brown pool where the mountain streams swirled as they joined. He turned to the people crowding round and gave what seemed a blessing, though in strange, false words:

From the death to the life, from the blood to the water, from the pride to the prayer. Now from the child to the holy mother.

All the people, quietly, repeated his words.

'You'd better let him rest,' Gord now called across, looking down at Nyr's pony.

'Why? He can take it.'

'It's not only today. It's tomorrow. It's the care of the creature.'

Nyr slowed and dismounted. They were above Gofanio. They walked their ponies down to a brook and rested. Nyr lay looking up at the wide sky, a pale blue of autumn. He saw yellow smoke drifting across it from the south. He rubbed his eyes and sat up. The sky was a clear pale blue. He was again reminded of Glesni. When Nyr had sought him out he had spoken, gently and sadly, of the visions of the old ones. Among them was the story of the Eggs of the

Eagle. 'It is still said among us,' Glesni explained, 'that the live fish in the mouth of the dead eagle is the sign of your Roman faith.' Nyr considered the sign. The sacred mark of the fish was indeed holy. But from the third egg came a yellow smoke. Nyr remembered Idwerth's strange words about the yellow death.

'Before we go to Banavint . . .' he said, getting up.

Gord looked at him, waiting.

'Before we take the news, I must speak to old Glesni.'

Gord stood, surprised.

'He is driven away, high one. The lord Gwrfan has renounced him.'

'But I know where he has gone. It is to the cell of Sulis, by the bank of Myngui where Euas marches with Uwch Coed.'

'It is a holy place, high one.'

'It is not a holy place. It is a retreat by the river.'

'As you say, high one. But it is named for Sulis, who is the goddess of healing.'

'Goddess! What nonsense is that? There is only one true god.'

'As you say, high one. But it is what she is called by the people.'

'And by you, I suppose?'

'I am your servant, high one. I do not touch these mysteries.'

Nyr caught his pony and walked it for some distance.

'I have a question for Glesni. About the signs of the yellow death.'

'I will take you there,' Gord agreed.

The cell of Sulis was in an oak grove between the brooks of Greitiaul and Gualon as they flowed to the Myngui. Approaching along the Uwch Coed bank, they saw thin woodsmoke rising among the trees. They found a wide sandbank where Myngui curved. Great leaves of butterbur were growing at the edge of the sand. There was creeping buttercup among the litter of smoothed pebbles. The water of Myngui was deep brown but clear. There were many shapes and colours in the small stones of its bed. On the far bank, in Euas, were two large stumps of oak.

'This is the place of the Stubs,' Gord said, lowering his voice.

'Is it used in some ceremony?'

'It is said, high one.'

They rode slowly through the river and up the far bank. The smoke was coming from a hearth within low dry-stone walls. At one corner of the hearth was a carved sandstone head. Its features were blurred with age, but there were still the unmistakable signs of the sacred head: the grim face denounced by Gildas. The prominent eyes were balled. The mouth was a slash. Spikes of hair lined the scalp. A full moustache curved down from the lip. On the layered block which supported the head, a thick-spoked wheel was also a rayed sun.

Nyr looked at it suspiciously. Gord stood quietly beside him. There was no sign of Glesni.

Gord dismounted and walked through the trees to a rough hut. It had low stone walls and a roof of hazel branches and bracken. There was a low porch at its entrance, with bunches of herbs and flowers hanging from its rafters. Gord stooped and looked inside. In the far corner, on a bed of bracken, old Glesni was asleep. Gord went in and touched his shoulder. At once the old man opened his eyes.

'Wise One, the lord Nyr is here to question you.'

Glesni sat up, looking curiously at Gord.

'Nyr? The young brother of the lady Galaes?'

'The same.'

Glesni eased himself from the bed. He brushed down his rough brown tunic.

'I will go to him. He is young.'

Gord led the way out. They walked to where Nyr stood waiting at a little distance from the hearth.

'Nyr, my son,' Glesni said, raising his hand.

'My father,' Nyr replied.

He then seemed to doubt his own words.

'You have matters to question,' Glesni said, and sat beside the hearth.

Nyr squatted opposite him.

'There is one great matter. I was journeying to the church of Teilo in Guenta. But beyond Gofanio there was an armed barricade, against the many who flee north from the plague. I could not go on to my church.'

'I understand, my son.'

'This terrible new plague is not the black death but the yellow.'

Glesni narrowed his eyes.

'I remembered what you told me of the third egg of the eagle: the yellow smoke that none could explain.'

'Indeed none can explain it, my Lord.'

Nyr hesitated. He looked around, nervously.

'Might it have been a sign of this plague, Father?'

'A sign? I cannot say.'

'Yet there were signs, in your beliefs, as there are signs among us of the true God?'

'There are many known signs of this world, and of the other world. But I know no sign of a yellow death.'

Nyr rubbed the back of his thumb along his teeth.

'The holy Teilo, it is said, has left for Armorica. Many other holy fathers are also leaving our land.'

'They have their reasons, my son, without doubt.'

'To escape the plague? Is that what you are saying?'

'I do not know their reasons. I can say nothing.'

Nyr clenched his fists. 'Yet are they not shepherds, who should stay with their flocks?'

'They have no sheep, my son. But they have their estates and their lands.'

'Only the lands of the true Church. Yet there are still our people, a grieving and terrified people, as this yellow death comes among them.'

Glesni smiled. 'Who knows, my son, if so evil a plague can be healed?'

Nyr jumped up, swinging his arms.

'But if we cannot live we should die together, in Christ. It is the great truth of our faith that our Lord gives us life everlasting.'

'A life not of this life, my son?'

'An eternal life. That is why he died for us.'

'And you die to this life for that other life of your Christ?'

'It is our way, Father.'

Glesni raised his hands and closed his palms.

'It is an idea that interests me. With us also there is another life, after what is called death. But it is not different in kind from the life we live here. It is only another form of it.'

'Then you are limited to this world. To this corrupt world, from which only Christ can redeem us.'

'To this world of both sweetness and corruption, my son.'

Nyr looked away. He walked towards his pony, which was grazing the fine grass among the trees. Then he turned back, and threw up his hand. When he spoke his voice was agitated. The higher tones of a boy edged the deeper broken voice.

'You speak of lands and estates. It is true, my Father. There are saints of the Church who have many slaves and possessions. The holy Cadoc, it is said, keeps a hundred men at arms.'

'I have heard this, my son.'

'But there are others, Father, who live quietly and humbly. They are called the watermen, for they take only water and bread. They also renounce the company of women. They fast, standing day and night, in the honour of Christ, until in their vigils they come to see the heavenly glory.'

'It is their way, my son.'

'Their way, but which is the true way? To be both a lord of the world and a servant of Christ? Or to renounce the world for that higher life which is promised us?'

'It is for them to choose, my son.'

'But which is the true way, Father? Which is right for them to choose?'

'How can I tell you, my son? I do not know your Christ.'

'You can tell me which you think is the better life.'

Glesni hesitated. He looked under his eyebrows at Gord. Gord, holding the look, nodded almost imperceptibly.

'I am old and uncertain,' Glesni said, slowly. 'But neither way to me is a holy life.'

'Neither way? But what other way is there?'

'To live by power and by possessions cannot be sacred. It is against the grain of our earth, of which we are children, not masters. But then to enter some starving frenzy, some cruel rite of renunciation, that also is not sacred. It denies all the sweetness of the life of the world.'

'There is not only sweetness, my Father. There is the yellow death.'

'You have told me, my son. There was the black death before it. Your holy Gildas said the plague was a punishment for the sins of the people.'

'It must indeed be a punishment, for there is a loving God.'

'It need not be a punishment. It is a corruption of life, from rat or from flea, which we must learn to understand and to heal.'

'You are not denying there were sins?'

'There have been many wrongs. I do not know your word sin. I have heard your teachers say that all men are born sinful, even as they cry from the womb. But I have also heard it denied, by men of your faith. They say both grace and error are what men actually do.'

'No, that was the heresy of Pelagius. It was false teaching.'

'Some said Pelagius. Among us, in the old times, he was known as Morcan. What he said, though in Christ, we could more clearly understand.'

'So this plague is what men have done?'

'It has come among us, it seems, in what some men have done.'

Nyr looked around, greatly agitated. He then pointed to the hearth.

'What is that carved head?'

'It is old.'

'And that wheel beneath it?'

'It is said it is of the sun.'

'You do not say so yourself?'

'It is of the old ones, my son.'

'And Sulis? Is she here? Your goddess of healing?'

'She is where there is sweet water. Sweet water that eases the body.'

'Then she is a pagan falsehood. An idol.'

'Pagan indeed, my son. For that is a word of the Romani, to mean the country people. People like us of this land.'

'It is a word of the Church, to mark out falsehood.'

'We cannot change that, my son. For we are of this land and only of this land.'

Nyr hurried across to his pony.

'Gord,' he shouted.

'Yes, high one,' the older man answered, following him.

Nyr swung to his saddle.

'I knew I would not get an answer,' he shouted back at Glesni. 'But I wanted to put the question.'

Glesni raised his hand, spreading his fingers.

'Until we learn to answer it, go in peace and safety, my son.'

Nyr looked away. He dug his heels into the pony and hurried back to the river. Gord followed but waved back to Glesni, who stood by his hearth, hand still raised.

They rode to the gates of Banavint. A group of larger huts had been built down the slope from the old hill camp, towards the dispersed farm huts of Masona along the river. Nyr cantered past the guard and hurried to find Gwrfan. He was in the yard beyond the huts, watching young ponies brought down from the mountain to be broken.

'Back already, Nyr? Couldn't you face it?' Gwrfan called.

'Gwrfan, you must listen. There is . . .'

'Later, boy. Can't you see these ponies?'

'There is great danger, Gwrfan. You must listen to me now.'

Gwrfan put his hand to his dagger and looked out across the valley.

'What danger? What are you talking about?'

Struggling for his words, still disturbed by the encounter with Glesni, Nyr told all he knew of the barricade and the plague. Gwrfan's face darkened as he listened.

'They will not hold them in Uwch Coed,' he shouted when Nyr had finished. 'Not with some simple barricade on the road.'

'Then what can be done?'

'I will call the elders. And then we must talk to Madrun.'

He began shouting orders. Messengers ran in several directions to bring the elders of the kin. When they were at last assembled, in the feastyard before the large huts, Nyr had again to tell his story. Then Gord was called and had to say what he had seen. There were many questions, before Gwrfan at last gave his orders.

'We will ring our mountains with fire,' he called. 'On every road and track, at every ford of our rivers, there will be archers. Nothing will move into our mountains. I shall ride now to Madrun and Ystraduy, to complete the ring. While I am gone make the fires ready. All other work is to stop. Warn the archers of each tref for their own roads and fords. Elid, ride to Maenhebog. All their archers are to come as a reserve for the ring. Now move.'

Nyr, on a fresh pony, followed Gwrfan as he rode over the mountain to Ystraduy and the court of old Hywel son of Morudd. Hywel was hard to persuade. Nyr had to tell his story twice and submit to hard questioning. Even then Hywel would do nothing until he had sent a kinsman into Uwch Coed, to the barricade beyond Gofanio, to see if the story was true.

Gwrfan and Nyr slept that night under Hywel's roof. In the morning, when the kinsman had still not returned, they rode on along the old green road into Madrun. They passed under the ramparts of Dinas Rhiangoll, the old Dunon Osniu, and into the court at Llys Maturn. The brorig Tewdwr ap Rhys was away, on a visit to the north. Gwrfan spoke to the elders and Nyr had to tell his story again. The elders of Madrun, the most withdrawn of the mountain kingdoms, quickly agreed to the plan of defence.

Gwrfan and Nyr rode back to Hywel, whose kinsman had now returned. Hywel agreed to the plan of guarding all roads, tracks and fords. But the ring of fire, he insisted, should be kept in reserve. What good would it do, if the roads were well guarded?

'We do not know this yellow death, lord Hywel,' Gwrfan said. 'Yet the black death was carried by fleas on the rats of the ships. When the rats died the fleas left them for other animals. They have been seen on squirrels, tree rats that scurry through our woods. Only fire, in the end, can defend us against them.'

'There will be fire at Samain. It is not long to wait.'

'It may be too long. We shall build our fires in any case. We shall cut bracken and pile it, and add brush and thorn. We shall then watch and wait. We shall hope not to burn along the ridges where our two bros march.'

'That would be a danger to our cattle and sheep.'

'There will be no danger to your animals if you build your own fires, on the outer ring of the mountains.'

'We will consider it,' Hywel said, and could be brought no further.

Gwrfan and Nyr returned to Banavint. Preparations for the defences were well under way. Nyr went in to talk to his sister, Galaes, who was alarmed by news of the plague. She was talking of returning to their father's court in Ercing. Nyr argued with her. It might be less safe in Ercing, if the flight of refugees from the coast continued. Many, undoubtedly, would come by boat up the Guuy. Galaes accepted his advice, but she was still uneasy in Euas. It was a hard, rough life in the mountain kingdom, after the more polite and prosperous Ercing. She was envious of Nyr when Gwrfan sent him with a message to their father Erb and their elder brother Peibio, telling them of their plans against the plague. Gwrfan asked for the ring of fire to be extended beyond the Dwr, which was the boundary of Euas and Ercing, to the last heights above the Guuy. Nyr took Gord on his journey. They were warmly welcomed. Erb agreed to the extension of the ring of fire. Peibio, who would rule after him, rode west to order it. Erb had already received his own reports on the plague. The Guuy and the frontier with Uwch Coed along the Myngui were heavily guarded.

Nyr and Gord returned to Banavint. There were now more reports from Uwch Coed, and Gwrfan's assessment was confirmed. The refugees were still coming in great numbers. The spread of the yellow death was very rapid, and many were ill and dying as they set out north. Others were already too ill to move, and their families stayed with them, but sent their children towards the mountains. All roads north were now barricaded, but it was easy to avoid them by moving at night or through the western hills. There were other reports of dead squirrels covered with fleas, as in the black death. It was still not known whether the yellow plague was spread through animals, but nobody was willing to take a chance. Even old Hywel of Ystraduy had been persuaded by his sons to join the plan for the ring of fire. All that remained to be decided was the time of the burning.

There was pressure from the older men to wait for the night of Samain. For they were looking to the fire as more than a physical obstacle. It would be a purification, indeed an offering, as always in its history. In Ystraduy, as now in Euas, there was formal adherence to Christian beliefs, among the ruling family. But even among them, and everywhere among the people they ruled, the old festivals were still more important, shaping the living year. In Madrun and in the mountains west of Ercing, the old religion was undisturbed.

Samain was the true time, within the old beliefs. It was the beginning of the year, as marked through fifty generations. It was the time of sacrifice, to keep all evil at bay. Through its night, in all darkness, forces beyond human strength were loose in the land. The other world itself might be seen.

Physical arguments also supported it. By the night of Samain, almost all the leaves would be gone from the trees. The bracken would have turned to its golden brown. The time of burning and cleansing, in which the festival had begun, would lie ready around them.

In the end only a few, including Gwrfan, wanted the fire earlier. Gwrfan was little concerned with such beliefs, old or new. In one argument, in Ystraduy, he offended most of his hearers, saying that only priests and women could be taken in by such stories, and that there was really nothing to choose between the Wise Men and the Christians. Indeed the Christians, he said scornfully, were busy trying to turn Samain into a festival of their own, calling it the Night of All Saints or All Souls. But it scarcely mattered what any of them called it. It was the time of the dead growth, that must be burned away. With the plague threatening them, the fire would burn a broad strip across which no animals or people, or for that matter spirits, could pass. It was agreed that he was talking recklessly. Wiser heads must prevail, in the choice of Samain.

So the time of burning was settled. Gwrfan got his way to the extent that the archers and other armed men were sent out at once, not only to the roads and tracks and fords, but to the long stretches of open country between them. There was much to arrange. The people and animals of the settlements bordering the mountains had to be moved inside the ring of the set fires. They went into the cross-valleys and along the lower spurs. One old woman of Masona refused to leave her hut. She cried wildly of the time of the Black Stranger, who lived in the mountains and spread a choking death. Her neighbours tried to explain that it was different now, and that the mountains would be safe. But she struggled and fought against them and in the end was forcibly moved.

The fires were set in broad strips along the outer ridges and spurs. At intervals, on the old beacon points, larger fires were prepared, to blaze first as signals for the whole ring to be set alight. Meanwhile all their animals – sheep, cattle and ponies on the uplands, pigs and goats in the inner valleys – were driven far inside the ring.

The night of Samain was clear but hazy. There were a few faint stars but no moon. It had passed its last quarter. As darkness gathered none of the people went to their beds. All were waiting, in upland and valley, for what they were already calling the Great Samain. It would be more than the beginning of another year. When the mountains flared, another time, another world, could be expected to be opened.

It was agreed that the first beacon would be lit on Ysgyryd. When the flames rose there, Nyr shouted excitedly. Gwrfan himself lit the beacon high on Banavint. Soon all the points of the beacons, north and south, were visible. To the south there were the flares of Penyfal and Crouco, to the north the spreading fires on the ridge beyond the

Dwr. There was an especially high beacon at the old Long House above the Guuy. Further west and north, unseen from Banavint, a line of beacons ran from Maen y Bard to Maenhebog, to the heights above Llys Maturn, across to Dinas Rhiangoll and to Troed and Alt Lwyd and Buchlit. Southwards, above the Uisc, beacons flared on Trumau and Alt Mawr and Cerric Calch, and blazed across to complete the ring at Deri below Penyfal.

Now trumpets sounded along the line of the fires. New flames and smoke lit the lower sky. There were strange shapes in the air as the leaping flames danced in the smoke. There were excited shouts as these shapes were seen. Young men on ponies rode inside the long lines of the fires. Many were riding bareback and shouting as they raced. The trumpets were blown repeatedly, as the thrill of the fire mounted.

Gwrfan, his face shining, put his arm across Nyr's shoulders. He was drinking from a beaker of bragget, a gift from Crugader in Ystradwy.

'To the safety of our mountains,' he shouted. 'To the safety for ever of our own Black Mountains.'

GLYN TO ELIS: 10

◆

G lyn had reached the outcrop of Gofeinion, where the ridge track rose again to the height of Chwarel y Fan. Gofeinion: perhaps the Blacksmith's Anvil, as it already appeared on some maps. Then the name would be a metaphor, unusually for this land where so many of the place names were narrowly literal; repetitive physical descriptions of ridge or valley, summit or hollow, swamp or field. Yet relate Gofeinion and old Gofanio, the Roman Gobannium, the modern Abergavenny. That was now the mouth of the little river Gavenny, flowing from under Brynarw to the Usk. But perhaps before the Romans it was also the place of the smiths, below those southern limestone heights where a modern iron-working had begun the history of industrial South Wales.

A line of boundary stones ran northeast from the outcrop towards the steep scarp of the Honddu valley near Capelyffin. The line followed no features, yet it marked both a modern and a very old border. Now between Gwent and Powys. Recently between Monmouthshire and Breconshire, and thus in one version between England and Wales. In the past, over many centuries, between the local homelands of these mountains: the kingdom, the bro, the cantref, the cwmmwt, the lordship: the tangled yet surprisingly persistent divisions of this land.

For this outcrop had been marked as a border, a frontier, between the old homelands of Euas and Madrun, Euias and Talgarth, Gwent and Brycheiniog, the lordship of Ewyas and the lordship of Hay, long before the English imposition of the boundaries of shires. There was also, here, a disputed diocesan border, between the Bishoprics of Llandaff and St David's. The names in the old list were only intermittently identifiable but they gave a general line.

Truyuisc dycilydris dyr all lwyd dy lech buchlit dy cecyn y
pennypyn march diguornoid dy ritnant dy hanher din march-
lithan dy ol gabr dy bron cateir neveni dy latguerionou dyguar-
thhaf buch dyr vuncyl dyr brydell dy hal ruma dy main y bard
yulycat nant y bard nihyt yr guairet hyt pan discynn yn
dour . . .

The marker stones on this bleak top, now made little sense. Yet this was because they were being seen, as in the far past, from the mountains outward. If they were seen as they were marked, by much later orders, they made more sense. For it was not the mountains and their valleys which had come to be marked. The old staged grazing areas indicated by the dolmens, the long houses, of the first shepherds, and then following them the metal people, with their intensive use of the uplands, were inner, internal traces. The real homelands were within the high country. After the change to a wetter climate, and the long spread of blanket peat over the high tops, the markers had shifted to settlements on the periphery of the mountains. Their boundary areas then ran back into the highlands, in broad and often arbitrary divisions. The only feature they acknowledged was the run of a river.

Wealth and power were now on this periphery. It had been so in the valley courts of Euas and Madrun and Ystradwy, each with its area of mountain grazing above it. Yet none of these small king-doms, bordering the mountains, could compare in population or production with the new lands being cleared in Erging and Uwch Coed or the rich meadows and grainfields along the Wye. Thus Gwent, from its base along the Severn, had grown until Uwch Coed, above the wood, and Is Coed, below the wood, were a single kingdom. This new Gwent pressed closely on a relatively prosper-ous Erging. Madrun in the west, became part of the extending kingdom of Brycheiniog, with its rich lands from the upper Wye and the Lake to the upper Usk. The smaller homelands of Euas and Ystradwy were always under pressure from these larger powers of the lowlands. Dynasties shifted. Powers passed. Yet for fifteen hundred years the old boundary lines were followed, even when their names were almost forgotten.

It was in many ways an ending, that night of the Great Samain when fires circled these mountains in the crisis of the plague. After severe bubonic plague, came 'the yellow sickness', reaching a peak in 549. The deaths were many and the effects were longlasting. In many places there were too many dead for the living to bury. The infection followed the old trade routes that had survived the Roman empire. Starting from the Mediterranean, it came in ships to those parts of Britain which most closely continued their old Roman connections. By contrast the invading Saxons, now firmly established in the east of the island, were much less affected. They had little interest in the old Roman patterns of trade. They followed their own bearings. And so, in the generation after the plague, to the decisive battle of Dyrham in 577, the Saxon power made its restless way westward to the Severn. The old British kingdoms of the Cotswolds passed under English rule.

In 584, the Saxon leader Ceawlin drives west across the Severn, but his army is crushed at Tintern by the army of Meurig of Gwent. Twenty-six years later the warriors of Iddon of Gwent defeat an invading Saxon force between Abergavenny and Monmouth. West of the Severn, and especially west of the Wye, the old British kingdoms, though weakened by the plague, still hold their lands. But north of the Wye, and pressing on Erging, the English settlers begin moving into lands still being cleared from the forest, where the main population had been British.

Glyn cast his mind back over that distant history. From 650 this region, running north to the Wrekin is ruled by Merewalh, son of the Mercian king Penda, a friend of the British kings, often in alliance against other Saxon forces, both north and south. After Merewalh comes his son Mildfrith, who in 693 founds his cathedral at Hereford. (Its bishop owed allegiance back east to Canterbury.) Mildfrith is buried in the cathedral he had founded.

In the next century, under the Mercian king Ethelbald, who claimed sovereignty over all southern England, pressure on the British lands resumes. The relative independence of the Magonsaete of Mildfrith, in peaceful relations with their British neighbours south and west, is overridden by more centralised control from the Mercian high king and his ealdormen. The English armies press west, and in 743 an English force crosses the Wye at Hereford, ravaging south into Erging and North Gwent.

Glyn touched an old boundary stone. His search for Elis, across these wastes of high plateau was now inseparable from what Elis had shown and told him. It was a history and a landscape that still in some sense informed his identity. Much of the history was disputed. Much of the topography was overlaid by late and arbitrary names. Yet a structure of feeling was still tangible: the body of a land and of a people. It was an invaded land and a mixed people, but it inscribed an identity, or offered to inscribe it. His immediate search for Elis came through as this inscription.

'To the safety of our own black mountains!'

'Taid! Taid!'

The Death of Clydawg

◆

O len touched Iddic's arm and pointed without speaking. Iddic
followed his direction and smiled, shaking his head.

'They are coming,' Olen insisted.

'Yes, they are coming.'

They were looking southwest to the high mountain wall of
Cwrwm between Wern y Cwm and Pant. The old track which ran at
the foot of the scarp was hidden among trees but Olen had seen
sheep scattering on the slope. A pair of magpies had risen suddenly
and were flying down towards the valley.

'Should we tell him?' Iddic asked, nodding towards Cynwg of
Alarun, who was standing with an obvious sense of importance on
the threshold of the burned-out oratory. Cynwg had been there
from first light, pacing the fence of the circular enclosure. He was
wearing his finest cloak, of wool trimmed with fox fur, although the
morning air was sunny and mild. It was to an anxious Cynwg that
the message had been sent, that the royal party would be arriving
and the people must be assembled. He had passed the order to his
household and slaves in Alarun. But the peasants of Trineint and of
Ferdun, and of the old lands above Tir Mynach, were not under his
orders. The message from Lord Gronw, the old brorig now teyrn of
Banavint, was simply passed on. Cynwg always insisted on his title
of breyr of Alarun, but Olen and Iddic and the others had their
direct bonded settlement, under the Lord Gronw.

The Mynwy, flowing noisily behind them, was swollen with
spring rains. Above the ford, it had the familiar milky-brown colour
of spate. The men of Ferdun stood close beyond it, on the rutted
track beside the sacred well. In their steep wooded uplands they had
learned to keep their distance.

'The High King Ithael will now be old,' Iddic said.

'In his sixty-ninth year.'

'Yet the victory was won in his name.'

'It was won,' Olen said.

He was still looking intently up the track that passed Cwmcoched. The sun was shining on the young bronze leaves of the oaks. The magpies had settled again.

It was not often that such power came into their valley. Yet since the fighting anything could be expected. When the Saxons had invaded, south from Ferleg, that they called Hereford, it had seemed safe here. The looting and burning were along the Guormoi and the eastern Mynwy. But then, one terrible day, a troop that had been ravaging along the Dwr valley crossed Ferdun, burning as they rode, and came down on Alarun. Cynwg and his few warriors fought for some hours between Mynwy and Olchon, but then fell back north to Parc y Meirch. The peasants of the valley, seeing the fires on Ferdun, immediately took themselves and their animals up past Lech Luit on to Cwrwm. They watched from the mountain as the hall and huts of Alarun were burned. They were slow to come down again. They waited three days, even after news came that the High King Ithael of Glevissig had driven the Saxons back north across the river Gwy and, through the Bishop Berthgwyn, made a peace with Ethelbald, the High King of the English.

There had been no fighting in this valley through more than four lifetimes. The sudden invasion and devastation dislocated their peaceful sense of life. While they stayed on the mountain, they appealed to Olen Cyfarwyd, the storyteller, for stories that would begin to make sense of these terrible events. But he was unable to offer them any. His preferred stories were of much older times.

The first horsemen were now coming into view, above Cwmcoched. They were breaking into a gallop, down the old track towards the river. Watching them as they rode, Olen remembered the enemy troop which he had seen riding fiercely down from Ferdun. The new riders, he had to remind himself, were of their own British king.

The horsemen did not slow as they approached the burned church and the people crowded in its enclosure. The men quickly stepped back, and the women pulled back their children, as the first seven of the British warriors rode through the gate into the clearing. At once they formed a circle facing outwards. Their horses sweated and pawed from the gallop. They were young men, their hair falling to their shoulders, their faces shaven except for the long moustaches curling around their mouths. They wore sleeved leather jerkins with wire facings, and tight black woollen trousers tucked into high boots. Their large helmets were slung by straps on their left shoulders. Each warrior, as he looked out at the waiting crowd, had his hand on the hilt of his long sword.

Cynwg, as chief landholder, moved forward to speak to them. But the nearest warrior drew his sword from its scabbard. Cynwg hurriedly stepped back.

'We are honoured to welcome the High King,' Cynwg called in his deepest voice.

None of the warriors answered or even appeared to hear him.

Now, riding more slowly, the main body of horsemen came in sight. The waiting families looked up towards them. They were again warriors. Seven riders carried raised spears in the front of the column. Behind them was an old, very small man, with thin white hair cropped close to his skull. The enamelled hilt of his sword, the plumed helmet on his shoulder, the finely decorated harness, shone brightly in the sun. Behind him rode two middle-aged men, black-haired with heavy moustaches, their swordhilts and helmets shining. A long procession followed: two younger men, one wearing his burnished helmet; an old lean man, tonsured, in a black gown dropping to his ankles; seven men of various ages, all tonsured and wearing the same black gowns, and finally a troop of sworded warriors led by a tall, fair young man in his thirties. The people could now recognise some of the faces. Gronw teyrn of Banavint was the older of the middle-aged men. His son Mabsu rode at the head of the spearmen. Helygwydd, the old priest of the burned church, was towards the back of the clerics. The whole company rode inside the circle which the warriors had cleared. Cynwg again stepped forward, but Mabsu gestured him back.

Gronw turned in his saddle and raised his voice.

'Honour to the High King Ithael! Honour in the land which he has freed and now protects.'

Led by the warriors, the company shouted the name of Ithael. The old man, frowning, dismounted. He looked uncertainly around. Gronw beckoned to the priest Helygwydd, who dropped clumsily from his pony and hurried forward.

'They burned the church,' Ithael said, staring unbelievingly at the debris of charred timbers.

'As I reported, High One,' Gronw anxiously replied.

'Yet they are Christian men.'

'It was a frenzy, High One,' Gronw said nervously.

'It was their ignorance of the martyr,' Helygwydd said, with more conviction.

Ithael looked around. 'Where is the martyr buried?'

'In the mound between church and river, High One.'

'And his stone?'

'It has fallen, High One.'

Ithael looked angrily around. 'This has been badly done, Gronw. Badly done.'

'As you say, High One.'

All the company now dismounted, except the first ring of warriors, who still guarded the cleared space. The old, lean, tonsured man came forward.

'It was right, my Lord King, to wait for the new consecration.'

'You may think so, Bishop Berthgwyn. But it is still badly done. Is the stone not sacred? Is it not an evil omen that it is fallen?'

'It is sacred when it is blessed, my Lord King.'

'And has it not been blessed?'

'It was blessed but is now defiled. It must be blessed again.'

'Is it this your Church teaches, Bishop? That the stone may lose its holiness?'

'It is what the Church teaches, my Lord King. For it is not the stone, but the blessing of the stone.'

Ithael looked at the mound and at the fallen stone. He then looked across the river where the men of Ferdun were standing.

'Who are those across the river?'

'They are of Ferdun, High One,' Gronw said anxiously.

'Why will they not cross?'

'They will cross, High One.'

Gronw shouted to Mabsu to bring the men of Ferdun across the river. Mabsu went to the ford and, drawing his sword, shouted angrily. The men moved together, in front of their women and children, and without looking at Mabsu began crossing on the stepping stones.

'Where is the holy well of the martyr?' Ithael asked.

'It is across the river, High One, beyond the ford,' Helygwydd explained.

'Is that why they were standing there, beside their holy well?'

'It is the well of the martyr, High One.'

'Perhaps they do not think so. Is its water sweet?'

'It is of the sweetest, High One. And its supply is as unfailing as the mercy of Lord Christ.'

Ithael nodded. He turned to the Bishop.

'We are wasting time, Berthgwyn. Let us do what we have to.'

'It is for you, my King, to renew the sacred grant.'

Ithael frowned. Bishop Berthgwyn whispered to the priest Helygwydd to fetch a bowl of water from the well. Ithael drew his sword. There was a sharp intake of breath from the people watching him. For as he raised the blade into the sunlight there was a ripple of lights along its surface, a moving pattern of colour and brilliance like the shining skin of a snake.

Ithael turned the blade downwards. He spread his fingers under the hilt, which was bright red with many garnets. He advanced to the low mound and knelt with some difficulty. Holding the sword in front of him he kissed the blade. He then laid it at the edge of the mound.

'In thanksgiving and in reverence, and by my soul in Holy Church, this gift of land is renewed.'

Berthgwyn now stood behind him. He held out a leather-covered book of the gospels. Ithael placed it on the stone and joined his hands over it.

'As an island placed in the sea, so is this land of the Holy Church.'

Bishop Berthgwyn received the bowl from Helygwydd. He sprinkled water on the head of the stone. Ithael eased himself back and, lifting his sword, stood slowly. He replaced the sword in its scabbard. Berthgwyn now called forward the reader Ili. Ili turned to the people and read loudly from a scroll.

'Ithael son of Morgan, King of Glevissig, with the approbation of his sons and heirs, Ffernfael and Meurig, and the consent of their heirs, Ithael and Ffrewddyfr, sacrificed to God, and to Saint Dyfrig, Saint Teilo, and Saint Oudoc, and to Clydawg the martyr, and to Bishop Berthgwyn, all the territory of Merthyr Clydawg as it was better given to Clydawg the martyr and the three hermits, Libiau, Gwrwan and Cynwr, with all its liberty and commonage in fields and in woods, in water and in pastures, and without any payment, great or small, to any mortal man beside to the Holy Church, and as an island placed in the sea free from every service and without an inheritor unless with the wish and for the benefit of Holy Church, and with refuge according to the will of the refugee, without limit, and as long as he should choose to remain be safe within its protection. Amen.'

The other priests and the nobles repeated *Amen*. As they did so old Ithael was already walking to his horse. His grandson Ffreddyfr helped him to the saddle. The warriors of the ring closed around him and they rode slowly out of the clearing. The company of spearmen followed. All heads were bowed as the High King passed.

The rest of the company now relaxed. When Ithael and his guard had ridden out of sight, Gronw of Banavint shouted for silence. Bishop Berthgwyn stood by the gravemound. He raised his hand, with fingers spread.

'It is fitting that we should remember this day the holy martyr Clydawg son of Clydwyn, who in the time of our fathers was here in his kingdom, enjoying peace and administering justice. It was in this very place that he received his crown of glory. He stood waiting, here on Mynwy, for a meeting of hunters, and his mind was filled with sacred devotion. Yet one of his companions had very different thoughts. For there was a maiden who loved Clydawg and told all who sought her that she would marry none but this holy prince. But the companion, hearing this, and himself desiring her, was filled with an evil spirit, and in the malignity of rashness and the malice of lust he struck down and killed the holy Clydawg, who stood innocent as a lamb to the blow.'

Bishop Berthgwyn paused. He raised his arm and pointed over the river.

'The holy Clydawg breathed his last by the well which he made holy. When his friends went to his body it was of an uncommon lightness, as if it would rise from the earth. They lifted the body to a carriage that was harnessed to oxen and they began to carry it to the house of his kingly family. But in this ford that you now see the yokes of the oxen began to break. New chains and new ropes were again broken to pieces. For now the body which had been light was exceedingly heavy. It could not be carried through the ford. Though his friends angrily goaded the oxen, they could not draw the carriage by as much as a step. As they stood wondering, it was as if a ball of fire held them back. Then at last they knew the sign, from the great heaviness of the body, that the martyr must stay in this place, which God had prepared for him. And when this was known to them, they prepared a grave, and they placed there the body of Clydawg, and they covered the grave with a mound and with a stone. And in the night following the burial, while they watched, still wondering at all that had happened, a column of fire rose from the stone into the night sky. Thus, seeing his holiness, and the clear will of God, they sought the counsel of Holy Church. An oratory was built by the mound and was consecrated. Through generations since that time this place has been venerated, by all of this bro of Euas and by pilgrims from lands beyond it. In the holy memory of the martyr they have found God's peace and forgiveness.'

Berthgwyn stepped away from the mound. He coughed, clearing his throat. Standing in the crowd, Iddic touched Olen's elbow and whispered.

'He is a holy cyfarwyd.'

'He is a bishop,' Olen said, gravely.

The ceremony seemed to be over, and the families were ready to move away. But Gronw again shouted for silence and Berthgwyn called the reader Ili.

'The boundaries of the land granted to Holy Church by King Ithael son of Morgan.'

Ili's voice was loud and clear but there was now no need to raise it. All the people were silent and straining forward to hear. Ili read very slowly and paused on each name.

'From the stone in the freckled moor along the ridge of Cwrwm to the stone on the summit and along to the stone above the brooks of Trineint. Along Trineint downwards into the Olchon and along the Olchon downwards to Ynys Alarun. Then upwards to Maen Tyllawg . . .'

There was an angry shout from Cynwg.

'You are saying our Hole Stone in Alarun?'

'Maen Tyllawg indeed is Hole Stone.'

'But that is impossible.'

Ili looked at Bishop Berthgwyn, who waved him to continue.

'. . . upward to Maen Tyllawg to the burial mound, to the second burial mound, and so to the Mynwy.'

Cynwg pushed forward.

'This is impossible,' he shouted to Gronw. 'You told me nothing about this new boundary.'

'Is it a new boundary?' Gronw asked, quietly.

'What he has read takes half of my hereditary land.'

'Which you hold by my leave and by the leave of the High King.'

'Which I hold from my fathers,' Cynwg shouted.

Young Mabsu stepped between them. He had his hand on his sword.

'But which you could not defend, Cynwg. Which you ran from before the Saxons. Which is no longer any man's land except by the power of the army of Ithael the High King.'

'This isn't right,' Cynwg protested. 'I fought the Saxons for as long as was possible.'

'But not long enough,' Mabsu answered.

He emphasised each of his words with a slap on his sword hilt.

'I will ride after the High King. I will put my case before him,' Cynwg shouted.

'Stay where you are,' Mabsu ordered. 'The land has been sworn and dedicated. There is no more to say.'

Cynwg turned angrily away. Few were willing to meet his eyes. But one of his slaves, Gord, for some reason was smiling. Cynwg hit him with his stick across his eyes. Gronw, Mabsu and Berthgwyn watched, calmly.

'Ili, continue,' Berthgwyn ordered.

'From Mynmy,' Ili read, 'through to the influx of Nant Cwm Cireith, along that brook to Ferdun mountain, along the ridge of Ferdun to the pool, from the pool to the source of Hilin, along Hilin to Mynwy, along Mynwy downwards to the influx of Bist . . .'

There was another cry from the crowd. Ili continued steadily.

'. . . along Bist to its source, from its source to the ridge, and so directly upwards to the stone in the freckled moor, from where the boundary began. Whoever will keep this, God keep him. Whoever will separate it from Holy Church, may he be cursed.'

There was anxious talk among the families. Many of the men were arguing about the names they had heard. Some were unfamiliar as Ili had pronounced them. Mabsu called for silence and Gronw spoke.

'My beloved heir, my gwrthrych Mabsu, will now ride the holy bounds. The priest Helygwydd and the reader Ili will accompany him. One man from each holding and each household is now ordered to go with them, so that all can see where the boundary has been set and there will be an end to all disputes.'

Cynwg stepped forward again.

'This new boundary, my Lord . . .'

'I have told you, Cynwg.'

'But my Lord, it is known among all the people of this valley that the land of the martyr Clydawg, as confirmed to Libiau and Gwrwan and Cynwr, and through the generations to the heirs of Cynwr, was of a very different and much smaller extent. It was simply of land along each bank of the Mynwy, below Alarun.'

'Cynwg, you have heard the land newly given by the High King.'

'But it cannot be right, my Lord. For as the holy reader pronounced the gift he said, very clearly: "as it was better given to the hermits Libiau and Gwrwan and Cynwr." And that is the old boundary.'

'Did you read those words, Ili?' Gronw asked.

'As it was better given to Clydawg the martyr and the three hermits Libiau, Gwrwan and Cynwr,' Ili read again.

'Yet nothing,' Cynwg protested, 'was given to Clydawg. He was already King of this place. You heard the Bishop say so. The grant that governed this place was to the hermits.'

'You have heard the new boundary, in the name of the High King,' Mabsu said, and again touched his sword.

'It is not only a part of Alarun that is newly enclosed,' Cynwg persisted. 'It is also the old lands of Trineint and of upland Ferdun and above the old Tir Mynach to Cwrwm.'

'All lands of Euas from Banavint,' Gronw said sharply.

'Yet not only so, my Lord, as some of these can tell you. For the old land of the hermits was passed, by inheritance, to the sons of Cynwr, and is divided now in five parts.'

'If it was so it is now redeemed,' Bishop Berthgwyn said firmly.

Cynwg shook his head in despair. He looked around at the families, but they were avoiding his eyes.

'We've heard enough,' Gronw said. 'You will now all, as ordered, travel the boundary.'

Mabsu went to his horse. Helygwydd and Ili went to their ponies. Of the others that were to follow, most were on foot. But Cynwg, who began on foot, soon sent a slave to fetch his best stallion. They began by moving up the left bank of the Mynwy to the ford below Alarun, towards Ynys Escil. They then traced the boundary west. At this point, and throughout the tracing in Alarun, from the two mounds to the Hole Stone, the talk was exclusively between Cynwg and Mabsu. Cynwg protested at every mark, but Mabsu made Ili read the words again and then dismissed all Cynwg's objections.

They moved downhill to the left bank of the Olchon and followed it to the junction with Trineint. Olen, walking with Iddic and his other neighbours, saw that a young priest, Ieuan, had joined them. He was scarcely more than a boy. His temples and neck were disfigured by red swellings below his rough sandy tonsure. He seemed to want to be with them and talk, avoiding the dignity of the head of the column. They were nervous of talking openly with him. They did not know him and he was a vowed priest. But in the waiting at each mark, while details were being argued, they began to talk more freely.

'Even Cynwg is right sometimes,' Iddic said. 'This is not the old boundary.'

'Cynwg has most to lose,' old Kavan said. 'It isn't only part of his land in Alarun. It's also that part of the old monkland which he inherited through the generations from the eldest son of Cynwr. All that is now vowed to the Church.'

'Do you not also lose?' the young priest asked, in a blurting, half-broken voice.

The others looked at him carefully. Iddic risked a reply.

'To teyrn or to Church, to breyr or to Christian brother, is for us as one.'

'You mean you pay the same either way.'

'We render as we must by the law,' Olen said, carefully.

'Yet because you must. Only because you must.'

Olen looked at him again.

'We honour the King and Holy Church,' he said steadily.

The young priest laughed.

The column was moving again and they walked some distance in silence. Then Ieuan said, impulsively:

'Yours is a very beautiful land. Is it not made more beautiful as the place of the holy Clydawg?'

There was no answer.

'It is a sacred and beautiful story, as the good bishop told it,' Ieuan declared, trying again.

There was again no answer.

'You still use that ford,' he continued. 'Did you find it difficult to believe that oxen with chains could not pull the body of a single man?'

'That was the miracle, the sign,' old Kavan replied.

'Which you truly believe?'

'Which we are told by those who have authority to know.'

Ieuan laughed, rubbing his bristled scalp. 'But do you have no memories of Clydawg yourselves? You are after all the descendants of those who lived in his time.'

There was no answer.

'In my bro, below Gwy, we have our own memories. We have also our remembrancers.'

The others looked at Olen. He shook his head but Ieuan was watching.

'Are you the cyfarwyd?' he asked Olen directly.

Olen hesitated.

'In a poor way, sir,' he at last replied. 'We are a very small people. We are not as the great courts, with their famous storytellers and bards.'

'Yet you have stories?'

'Of a rough kind, sir. They are not worth repeating when there are greater stories to hear.'

'Stories of Clydawg?'

'There are plenty of stories,' Iddic said, intervening. 'There is a story of the name of this place, that it is from the old goddess Clota, who was the spirit of fast-flowing rivers. The place of washing, by the ford, was known as the place of Clota.'

'And you believe that?'

'It is a story. There is another story of a hermit, Clitauc, who lived at the holy well and was murdered. There is yet another story that a king at the time of the legions, Clutacos of Euas, who had fallen into disgrace, was buried secretly by his friends near the sacred well.'

'All these stories cannot be true.'

'Perhaps none are true. But the well, for a fact, is from the oldest times. And above it still, in the steep woods from Mynwy to Ferdun, there are three cairns of the oldest of our peoples, who were called the Black Shepherds.'

Ieuan thought for some time.

'You are saying, are you, that this place was already sacred, with its well and its cairns, before the time of the knowledge of Christ?'

'By the stories it may be so,' Iddic answered.

Olen and the others were now worried by the way he was talking. They tried to change the subject but Ieuan, still boyishly eager, would not let the matter go.

'What you say, my friend, could be true. For it is the wisdom of Holy Church to seek out places considered sacred by the old beliefs and to claim and redeem them for Christ. Have you not seen our Christian churches raised on the very mounds of the pagans and within their enclosures? Have you not seen the old pagan stones marked anew with the cross?'

'We have heard this,' Iddic said.

'It is no secret, my friends. To act thus is the duty of Holy Church.'

'To redeem them,' Kavan said.

'Indeed to redeem them. But then consider also that this may have happened to the stories and the memories. That they too, in their turn, have been redeemed for Christ.'

'Yet they would then not be true,' Iddic said.

'My friend, they might still save souls.'

The column was climbing now along the course of Trineint, where three brooks joined. The mountain above them was full of colours in the sunlight. The first green of young bracken showed among the pale golden brown of the old; the first yellow flowers of the gorse; the pink haze of the young leaves of whinberry. To their right the high crag above the rockfall of Lechluit was black and grey where the light touched its fissures.

At a place where the brooks divided, arguments started about the main stream to follow as the boundary. Slowly the whole column halted. It was obvious that the dispute would last for some time. Olen and Iddic sat to rest in the sun. The others gathered around them. Ieuan sat easily in their midst.

'There is indeed a story of Clydawg,' Olen at last said.

'Then let us hear it,' Ieuan invited.

'It is different from the story of your bishop.'

'But no worse, under God, for that.'

Olen shrugged his shoulders. He raised his right hand and spread his fingers. When he spoke again it was in the cyfarwyd voice, pitched sharper and higher.

'Clydawg son of Clydwyn was a Prince of the Kingdom of Brecheniauc, beyond these mountains. In the Kingdom of Brecheniauc lived the High King Brachan, who was the father of Clydwyn. And beside Clydwyn, Brachan had ten other sons and more than twenty daughters. The sons of Brachan gained kingdoms and the daughters of Brachan married kings, so that their power extended over land and sea.

'It was then proposed by Clydwyn son of Brachan that his son Prince Clydawg should marry Aranwen daughter of King Gwyddgi of Euas, for this was in his time. Yet King Gwyddgi had a nephew, the son of his sister, and this nephew was Pascen, a famous huntsman and breaker of horses. King Gwyddgi had no sons, and it was expected by Pascen that he would inherit the kingdom of Euas. Yet for this he must marry the maiden Aranwen.

'This Pascen was ill-favoured, though of great strength. The whole upper part of his body, not only his chest but his shoulders and back, was covered with thick black hair. He could lift stones which the strongest among all other men could scarcely move from their place, and the distance of his arrows was a wonder to all who watched him. For it is said in Banavint that he once shot an arrow from the ridge of Cwrwm into the woods of Ferdun above Mynwy, and that it killed a stag there.

'The prince Clydawg son of Clydwyn was tall and handsome. His skin was pale like milk and his long hair was bright red. Aranwen first saw him when his father Clydwyn brought him to meet with Gwyddgi, on the frontier of their lands by the pass of Fincul. And this Aranwen was not herself beautiful, though pure and obedient in her life.

'When Clydwyn and Gwyddgi had spoken, Gwyddgi returned to his court to seek advice from his kin. Many were doubtful of the wisdom of the marriage thus proposed, for it was seen as a spreading of the power of the sons of Brachan. Yet others were fearful that if they did not agree to it, there would be war from Brecheniauc, and Euas could not stand against them. Aranwen, too young to give her own word, wished only that the marriage could be quickly agreed, for she had loved Clydawg from the moment of their meeting.

'Pascen at this time was away on a hunt, beyond the young Gwy. When he returned with many trophies, he heard the news of the betrothal, and he raged before Gwyddgi. "Is it not enough," he said, "that you meet with these foreigners, these Hibernians, these Gwidelig, who would take our land as they have taken so many others? Must you also be deceived by this trick of a marriage, which is offered only to take Euas from its true kin and lineage?" And when Gwyddgi sought to answer, Pascen shouted over him, and Gwyddgi ordered him from the court. But this Pascen would not leave. He took his hunting glove and threw it between them. He taunted the king crying, "Gwyddgi Gwidelig," as to a foreigner.

'None could reason with Pascen, and none dared to challenge him. But his mother, the sister of the King, brought him back at last to renew his allegiance, and Pascen was then quiet. And Gwyddgi met again with Clydwyn and Clydawg, and it was agreed that Clydawg should visit the court of Euas and be entertained in the manner of his rank.

'Now it must be told that in Ferdun, where there is deep forest, there lived hunters who acknowledged the rule of Euas but who avoided all company of shepherds and herdsmen and lived their own separate lives. And among these hunters there was a cult of the horned god Amaethon, who in other places is known as Cernunnos. Under the steepest slope of the forest of Ferdun, on the bank of Mynwy, a sacred well was known as the well of Amaethon, and it was beside the ford. And none from Euas would approach the hunters of Ferdun, save Pascen who was afraid of no man and who was himself a great hunter.

'When Prince Clydawg came to the court of Euas there was great honour and ceremony in his welcome, and among those who most warmly received him was Pascen, who brought a gift of a fine white mare. There was feasting in the hall, and singing and storytelling, and at the feasts Aranwen sat close beside Clydawg, on the right hand of King Gwyddgi. And as the weather was fine it was arranged that there would be a hunt in the forest of Caer Gwaled, which lies across the broad valley below Banavint, where Mynwy and Hodoni run together. This hunt, as was customary, was to be led by Pascen, who promised Clydawg the first honour of the kill.'

Shouting broke out at the head of the column. Mabsu was impatient with the dispute about the brooks of Trineint, and was trying to impose a solution, taking the boundary as the northern stream. But others resisted this, arguing that the true source, by name, was always that with the greatest flow.

'Your story, Olen,' the young priest said, looking up with the others at the knot of arguing men, 'is in fact very close to that of the holy Bishop Berthgwyn.'

'Except for the rivalry of the kingdoms and the ambitions of Brecheniauc,' Iddic said, quickly.

'But that is a very small matter. Come, Olen, finish the story.'

Olen had locked his hands together. The fingers were pressing until the knuckles were white. He stared down through his arms at the rough grass. At last he again raised his hand and spread his fingers.

'The hunt rode across the valley to the forest of Caer Gwaled, where there were always fine stags. And they had chosen Caer Gwaled because they would not enter the forest of Ferdun, where the hunters of Amaethon welcomed no man. The prince Clydawg was riding on the fine white mare which he had been given by Pascen, and Pascen rode amiably beside him. And indeed in Caer Gwaled they roused a fine stag, bigger than any Clydawg had seen, and he rode shouting in its pursuit and Pascen beside him. And the stag was swift, as swift as his pursuers, and he bounded north like the wind, towards the forest of Ferdun.

'Now in the forest of Ferdun, Clydawg and Pascen thought they would lose the stag, for it was beginning to outpace them. But as they still rode furiously, glimpsing their quarry among the trees, they saw that it was limping, in its right hind leg, and they were now quickly overtaking it. And as they reached it Pascen drew back, leaving Clydawg the honour of the kill. And Clydawg killed the stag, and jumped down from his mare in his excitement. And Pascen praised his skill, and helped him to cut the great trophy of the antlers. And Clydawg in his excitement embraced Pascen, and thanked him for all he had done.

'And the body of the stag was left for the followers, and Clydawg and Pascen rode down from Ferdun, to the ford by the holy well. And Clydawg was carrying the trophy of the antlers before him on his white mare, and his own skin was white, under the bright red of the hair of his head. And at the ford he dismounted, leading the mare by the bridle through the waters of Mynwy. And Pascen had already crossed, and was riding ahead of him.'

Olen paused. He looked across, directly, into the face of the young priest, who urged him to continue. Olen closed his eyes.

'And the hunters of Ferdun were among the trees at the ford, beside the well sacred to Amaethon. And the sun was glittering on the rapid waters of Mynwy, and the light through the trees was dazzling all eyes as the breeze shook the leaves. And now in the eyes of the hunters of Ferdun the shape was shifted. In the waters of the ford there was a great white stag, and its antlers proud above it, and they knew that this was the quarry of the god Amaethon, which he pursued through all his days. And then the hunters of Ferdun drew their bows and shot the white stag, and it fell in the ford, its blood staining the water, and over the body of the stag lay a beautiful young man, with white skin and long red hair, as Amaethon himself would appear to men.'

Olen again paused. The column ahead was beginning to go on, but none who were listening wished to move.

'Pascen, as I have said, riding ahead of Clydawg, heard a cry from behind him. He turned and rode back to the ford, where he found Prince Clydawg and his mare lying dead in the water. And there were seven arrows in the body of Clydawg, in a cluster around the heart. And Pascen raised a great cry, and the followers joined him. And while all stared in shock and in grief, Pascen commanded the followers to seek out the evil hunters and they searched in the woods but none of the hunters of Ferdun could be seen. And Pascen, in grief, commanded the body of the man and the body of the horse to be dragged to the bank of the river, and he left two men to guard them while he rode fiercely to the court, to give the awful news, and to fetch an ox-cart to bring back the body of noble Clydawg.'

The whole column was now moving, beginning the ascent of the rhiw to the ridge. Olen and Ieuan and the others got up and moved with them, but they still clustered around Olen as he approached the end of his story.

'Pascen returned to the ford, with King Gwyddgi and others, and with the priest whose church was in the enclosure of Banavint. And their shock was still great as they approached the body of Clydawg. And as they came beside it there was a great cry from Gwyddgi, for the head of Clydawg had been struck from the body and was nowhere to be seen, and the two who had been guarding it had altogether disappeared. And they stared in disbelief at the headless body and Gwyddgi said piteously: "how can we return this body of the prince to his father Clydwyn, when the head has been savagely severed?" And Pascen, raging, swore vengeance on the hunters of Ferdun, though the priest still looked at him strangely. And while Gwyddgi could decide nothing, for the shock had been too great, news came that the ox-cart which they were bringing for the body had broken its wheel, on the track below Wern Cwm.'

They had reached the angle of the rhiw, where it turned in zigzag south towards Cwrwm. Olen paused to gain his breath. Before he resumed, he again looked directly into Ieuan's face. The young priest was eager for his words. His face was sweating with the climb and the red blotches on his temples and neck stood out angrily.

'And the priest of the church of the enclosure of Banavint spoke earnestly to Gwyddgi, beyond the hearing of the others, and together they looked at Pascen, who was now standing by the well on the other side of the river and was calling and challenging the hunters of Ferdun, though none were to be seen, but only the thick green shade of the forest. And Gwyddgi then spoke and commanded that the body of Clydawg should be at once buried, on the spot where he lay, and a grave was dug, and lined with fine stones from the bank of Mynwy, and prayers were said over the grave before the capstone was laid over it and the earth heaped above it. And Pascen, reverently, stood with the others at the grave, and vowed to raise a memorial that would mark it for all time. And on the third day after the burial, Pascen brought the fine stone, and it was raised on the mound, and the stone was sprinkled with water from the well. Yet that night, while vigil was being kept, a fire sprang up suddenly, beside the stone on the mound, and in the light of its flames all looked across the river and there, standing with bows drawn, at the edge of the trees, were the hunters of Ferdun, and the antlers of the stag, a little raised from the earth, were laid beside the well of Amaethon.'

Olen walked on, without speaking, as his story ended. On the steeper path none spoke for some time. Ieuan walked close to Olen, among the dead bracken at the edge of the track.

'Thus he was indeed a martyr, and a Christian martyr,' the young priest Ieuan said, finally. 'For he was killed, in his innocence, by heathen men.'

Olen met his eyes but said nothing.

'Yet was Pascen not suspected?' Ieuan went on to ask.

'It is not told. Yet he married Aranwen.'

'But was there no vengeance from Brecheniauc, for the slaying of their prince?'

'It is not told. Yet Pascen inherited Euas.'

'There would have been galanas paid,' Iddic insisted.

'By the hunters of Ferdun?'

'By Gwyddgi,' Iddic said, 'for it was within his kingdom and he did not want war.'

'Yet the hunters of Ferdun,' the priest persisted, 'did they still look to their god Amaethon?'

There was a tension among those around him. Nobody dared to speak. Ieuan looked closely at them, his eyes bright and searching. At last Olen met his eyes.

'Was not your church burned?' Olen asked, quietly.

The Gift of Acha

◆

Acha the Saxon slave-woman climbed the stile and reached the path along the bank of the river. The shade of the alders was welcome, after the burning sun. The Mynwy was very low, its pools a deep brown, almost black, among the flat stones. The moss was still bright green at the edges of the stones, where it trailed in the running water, but on the dry tops it was brown and shrinking. The big pool where her Lord Idwallon made his catches of eels was still and shallow. Swarms of flies danced above it. Near the far bank, by the bole of the big oak, pretty damsel flies were darting between light and shade.

Acha took off her sandals to bathe her feet in the slow-running water. Looking quickly around to make sure she was alone, she pulled the skirts of her long tunic up to her waist. As she felt the cool air on her skin a kingfisher darted from the bank just below her. She saw the flash of blue and emerald as he swooped downriver for minnows. It was as if in some way she had released the lovely bird, as if it had flown from herself. Yet that, she thought, settling, and dipping her feet in the cold water, was only a fancy from the past.

She was heavy and tired. Each year she was more tired. The fieldwork, always hard, was already too much for her, though she could not afford to admit it. She had no other future. At least now, between cutting the hay meadows and the coming oat and barley harvest, she had been given the lighter job of collecting herbs and willowbark. She had taken her chance to walk further from the neuadd and the yards, to be by herself. After a time the other voices would fade and she would hear her own words: words of her own language, childhood words. The forgotten songs, happy and sad, came back. She seemed already to be hearing them.

'When leaf is loosed and rides the stream
It bears away the summer's dream.
When seed is shed the waters bring
New promises of leaf in spring.'

In the nineteen years since she had been sold to Idwallon, among the bargains after the heavy fighting by Hereford, she had remained Saxon and was always treated as a Saxon, even by the other slaves who were all British. She had learned their language and adapted to their customs, but she was still the Saxon woman, the foreigner.

Inside her head she kept her own language, and she was careful to teach it to her daughter Hilda, though, born among the British, the girl had learned to speak among the other children, and thought their language her own. Hilda would speak English with Acha, when they were alone together, but often reluctantly, as if humouring her mother. In this, as in more important ways, she had never accepted her mother's idea of her: an idea of a quite other future, in freedom. Yet this was now just as well, in the disappointment of Acha's second appeal and the support Idwallon had been given by the priest.

The British words of that ruling drowned the song. Yet as she stood, distracted, pushed on to her work, Acha sang the remembered song – carrying, carrying – at first hesitantly under her breath, but then voiced and full-voiced, for she was alone by the river. The herbs and bark would be quickly gathered. There were several big white willows with good two-to-three-year-old bark, and the banks were heavy with meadowsweet. There was comfrey and elder, and just along the path a little stand of feverfew. She stooped and picked the pretty white flowerheads of the feverfew, and put them in the leather bag which was slung on her chest. As she stood, putting her hand on an ache in her back, a dragonfly almost brushed her face. She saw the big jewelled eyes and the sheen of colour on its wings. She moved to see it, as it seemed to stop above the meadowsweet, but then it darted again, bright against the alder leaves. Its body was like the narrow dark male catkins of the tree. In the hot summer the green female catkins were already unusually large.

'Asleep and remembering
Carrying, carrying . . .'

Acha broke off her song. There had been a sudden sharp noise, as of a breaking stick. She pulled down her tunic and looked anxiously around. Far across the river, in Gwent, there were men with a cart, but the sound had been much closer. On her own bank, in Euas, there was nobody to be seen. She shifted her bag and walked across to get the comfrey leaves. But before she had reached them she distinctly heard a voice.

She stood very still. Her face was suddenly cold. Then the voice came again, high-pitched, even crying. She pin-pointed it now. There was a clump of sallywillow, that the British called helyg, twenty yards further along the bank.

She narrowed her eyes, looking into its base, and walked cautiously forward. As she came closer she saw a quick movement and a glint of light blue. She pulled her knife from her belt.

The voice came again. It was high and disjointed. She could make out no words. But then suddenly some words were distinct and they were English words. She stared in astonishment, but then English words came again. There was a cry for water and a strange muffled complaint that the moon was failing. Acha shook her head to clear it. The words were repeated. *The moon is failing.*

She moved very slowly around the sallies, holding her knife ready to strike. She could now look in through a gap in the trees, opening towards the river. A young man was lying there. He was on his back but rolling uneasily on his shoulders. His light blue tunic was darkly stained with blood. There was dried blood on his long yellow hair, which was tied with a blue braid. Across his thighs his right hand still gripped his sharp-bladed handsax. His leather sandals were caked with red mud.

Acha moved slowly towards him. As she saw his face she recognised the sweat of high fever. He was still talking about the moon, but his words, now certainly English, were disjointed. She was afraid to move closer. Then he rolled on his shoulders and opened his eyes. They were a bright pale blue. She felt a pull of feeling towards him, but he had seen her and was trying to raise himself, lifting the long knife.

'It is safe, I am a friend,' she said quickly, in English.

He stared up at her.

'You are sick and need help. I can help you,' she said.

'English?' he muttered, still puzzled, closing his eyes and opening them again.

'Yes, English. I am Acha.'

He struggled to raise himself to his elbows.

'Acha? English? Am I then home across the Wye?'

'No. This is the Mynwy. We are among the Welsh.'

He fell back again. He closed his eyes.

'You are wounded. Let me help you,' Acha said gently. He did not answer. She emptied the herbs from her bag and fetched water from the river. She kneeled beside him and pulled a handful of grass to wipe his face. He lifted his head suddenly and asked to drink from the bag. The water spilled down his chin to his tunic. Acha looked at its weave. It was a fine cloth, and the leather belt at his waist was closely decorated with silver. When he had drunk she bathed his face and then ran her fingers over his wounded shoulder. There was still wet blood under the stiffened cloth.

'Acha,' he said, staring up at her.

'Yes?'

'How are you here, among the Welsh?'

'I was sold, my lord, I am caeth, a field slave.'

He released the handsax and gripped her arm.

'Is it far to the Wye?'

'I cannot reckon it, my lord. It was a heavy day's walk when I was brought here.'

'But you will help me, Acha?'

'I am helping you, my Lord.'

'Why do you call me Lord?'

'Are you not lord?'

'No, but my father Wihtred is gesith in Geardcylle. I am his second son.'

'And your name, Lord?'

'I am not Lord. I am Hicel.'

Acha gazed down at him. The drink and the bathing had soothed him, but the fever was still high. She moved away and gathered the discarded herbs. She emptied the bag of all but a little water. She waited. He had dropped into sleep.

It would not be a good infusion, but it was all she could now manage. She waited until he stirred again and then put her fingers between his lips and poured the liquid into his mouth. He coughed but got some of it down. Then he looked up and gripped her arm.

'The Welsh will kill me if they find me.'

'Why should they kill you?'

He stared at her, frowning. 'Even you must know of the fighting.'

'There is often fighting.'

'We raided south to Guorbo. We drove them before us. Then there were horsemen from the east and they slashed us down.'

There were new beads of sweat on his forehead as he tried to explain. She dried the sweat, lifting the hem of her tunic.

'There are no horsemen now,' she said, gently.

'I lost my sword and ran,' Hicel said, his breathing becoming rough. 'As I ran I fell. I think a rib is broken. But I managed to hide and then by night I started back. Yet it was the last of the moon and it failed me.'

'You are safe now. But I must dress the wound on your shoulder.'

'What do you know of wounds?'

'I know that I must clean it and dress it.'

'No, I have to get back. I must get back across the Wye.'

'You will get nowhere until you are well.'

'Will you come with me, Acha? You know this country.'

'Why should I come with you? I do not know this country. I know only this estate.'

'Where you are a slave of the Welsh.'

'Where I was sold to, Lord Hicel.'

He stared into her face. 'You do not look a kind woman,' he said, surprising her.

'My life has not been kind,' she managed to say.

'Yet you are helping me, Acha.'

'Because you are wounded.'

'And because I am English?'

'English, Welsh, there is no difference in that.'

'Yes, there is a difference, Acha.'

She did not answer. She got up and stood away from him. He tried to raise himself, gripping his handsax.

'Put your knife away,' she said contemptuously. 'I am going back to the neuadd. I shall get cloth and ointment, and I shall get bread and meat.'

'If you bring the Welsh down on me . . .'

'What? With your broken rib and your wound?'

He made an effort to be calm, looking curiously up at her. 'There is so much I could give you, Acha, if we got back to our own people.'

'It's too soon to be thinking about that.'

'But you are already thinking about it.'

'I am thinking only of my daughter.'

'You have a daughter?'

'A grown daughter. Hilda. She is a house-slave of Idwallon.'

'Then she could come along with us.'

Acha reslung her bag on her neck.

'None of us is going anywhere. You must first be made well.'

She turned and walked out of the trees and along the bank of the river. She did not hurry. She knew that she must fill her bag before she could safely go back. She found feverfew, and dandelion, and picked the big leaves of comfrey. She took her knife and peeled long strips of white willowbark. At last, walking slowly, she reached the fence of the estate and went into the compound. There was hardly anyone about. Iddic the old groom was sitting by the stable, with a bowl of some mixture in front of him. But he was not working. The dogs were stretched out in the shade of the long barn. The sun had the drowsy heat of late afternoon.

She took her bag to the stillroom. Gwenda was sleeping at the table, still holding her knife on the chopping board. She stirred and looked up at Acha.

'You've taken your time.'

'I haven't been . . .' Acha started, and then realised she was speaking in English.

'I had a long way to go, for the best bark,' she corrected herself, quickly.

'All right. Leave it. I know you field-women.'

'What do you mean?'

'Some man, I expect. Some nice man by the river.'

'There is no man by the river,' Acha said, fiercely.

'All right, all right, don't sound so disappointed. Though I bet you looked out for one.'

'No, Gwenda. I am past caring for men.'

'Then you are unlucky, Saxon. You might have got a bit of life for a change.'

Acha pretended to laugh. Gwenda slapped the table, laughing

heartily, and got up and walked out to the yard. Acha watched her cross to the privy and then hurried to the shelves. She found an empty box and filled it with sphagnum and with chamomile ointment from the big wooden bowls. Then she slipped out and hurried to her own hut. She tore cloth from her second shift and concealed it in her breast. Then she crossed to the big house, the neuadd, and found her daughter. She asked her for food.

'Are you so hungry you can't wait?' Hilda said, irritably.

Acha touched her daughter's hand. She looked up into her face, which was young and pretty. The cropped hair that marked the slave was in tight fair curls above the smooth, light skin.

'It is for a special reason,' Acha said, hoarsely.

'There's always some reason.'

'It could be for your future.'

'My future!' Hilda said. 'Are you still thinking about that old nonsense?'

'This is different, I swear it. Now fetch me the food.'

Hilda sulkily obeyed.

Acha went out again, concealing the food in her bag. She was careful to follow an indirect route to the river. When she was in sight of the clump of sallies she waited, looking in all directions, until she was sure she was unobserved. As she went in among the trees she saw that Hicel was sleeping. His face was very pale but relaxed. She bent over him and put his handsax out of reach. As she moved he opened his watery blue eyes.

'It is Acha,' she said. 'Rest.'

'Acha,' he said, and smiled.

'Here is mutton and oatcake. Then I must dress your wound.'

He raised himself and began to eat hungrily, but soon his mouth stopped chewing.

'I can't take much yet.'

'It will come.'

She took her knife and began cutting through the stained patch of tunic. He cried in pain as the cloth which had been stuck to the skin came away. She looked down at the long, ugly wound. She took her bag and fetched water and began carefully bathing it. As she worked he looked up into her face.

'You have had children, Acha?'

'One daughter, as I told you.'

'Of what age?'

'She is eighteen, nearly nineteen.'

'Her father is a Welshman?'

'Indeed not. He was an Englishman, Cenwalh.'

'That sounds a Welsh name.'

'He was English, I tell you. We were together on the estate of Cerdic at Magon, before I was sold.'

'You were bearing your daughter when you were sold?' he exclaimed, gripping her arm.

'Lie still. Let me see to this.'

'But don't you know, Acha? If you were pregnant when you were sold the child was born free?'

She had cleaned the wound and was beginning to spread the ointment with the tips of her broad fingers.

'I knew it,' she said, dully. 'I expected it and claimed it. But I was told in Welsh law it is not the case.'

'Then they were lying, Acha.'

'I don't know. My master Idwallon was quite certain, and the priest supported him.'

'Then your daughter is still a slave?'

'A house slave.'

He lay back and rested his head. She had to lift him again to bind the cloth round his shoulder.

'When you were sold, Acha . . .' he began again.

'Be still now.'

'When you were sold, how long had you been with child?'

'It was the second month.'

'They did not try to argue that she was conceived after you came here?'

'Some of them tried. The women. They were jealous that I'd go with their men. But the child was English. Everyone could see from her colour.'

Hicel smiled. 'Is that easy?' he asked, looking up through the branches at the distant sky, where white clouds were now gathering.

'She is your colour,' Acha said. 'Your yellow hair, your blue eyes. You could be taken for brother and sister.'

'But there is great mixing now, Acha, among the Magonsaete and the Hwicce. There are English and Welsh wives and husbands. There are names that are of both.'

'Not Hilda,' Acha said.

She had finished the dressing. She poured a cup of water, and again offered the meat. He drank but hardly ate.

'I must go, I shall be missed,' she said, getting up.

'But you will come again?'

'I will try to come tomorrow.'

'When I have got my strength I shall get back across the Wye. And you must come with me, so that your daughter can be free.'

'I can't do it for that. I've heard too many promises.'

'I would swear to you, Acha. I would swear on my life.'

She gazed down into his face. She said nothing. She collected her things and hurried away.

It was late afternoon on the next day before she could again go to Hicel. As she approached the sallies she saw him standing behind the branches. He was holding his handsax ready.

'I've brought you this,' she said, and held out an old, worn brown tunic, which she had found hanging in the barn.

He took it and ran his fingers over it. He held it to his nose.

'I'll wash it through in the river,' she said quickly.

'No, I can do that.'

'You!'

She took apples from her bag, and soft cheese wrapped in leaves.

'Are they cruel to you, these Welsh?' he asked, watching her.

'Not especially cruel. It is the ordinary life of a slave.'

'They don't flog you?'

'They flog all slaves who offend. As all masters do.'

'But you do not offend?'

'I work. I work hard.'

'And your daughter? Is she abused?'

'She is not. The penalties for that are very heavy.'

'But she will go, in her time, to one of the Welsh slaves.'

'If she is still here,' Acha said.

Hicel looked at her again. Her features were hard. The mouth was a tight line and the eyes were cold. The skin of her face and neck was rough under the slave's cropped hair, which was bristled grey and light brown.

'You have been thinking of my offer?' Hicel said.

'No, my Lord, I cannot come with you. There is nothing for me, I should still be a slave. Any English lord could return me as a runaway. There are terrible punishments for that.'

'But I would not let that happen.'

'You could not stop it. You are not above the law.'

'What would they do to you?'

Acha closed her eyes. 'A slave in Cornou who had tried to escape had his right hand severed. His woman and his children were sold across the sea.'

Hicel shifted his legs and lay down. He kept his hands behind his head.

'Cornou, you say? Where is that?'

'It is two settlements south. Masonu then Cornou.'

'And this place?'

'This is Suluiu. It is an old place of one of their saints.'

'And the mountains back there?'

'They are the Black Mountains. This river rises among them.'

'What lies to the north?'

'Elchon. Where the Mynwy turns east.'

'And beyond that?'

'I don't know. But the Wye is north, by Ferleg.'

'Ferleg? Where is that?'

'Ferleg that the English call Hereford.'

Hicel looked down at his body.

'The rib is still very painful,' he said, as if to himself. 'But I could rest often. I could walk by night.'

Acha was now watching every movement of his face. He seemed for some time to forget her, and she turned to go.

'No, don't go,' he said quickly.

'Why should I stay?'

'Why should you have helped me at all?'

She thought for some time, and then squatted at his shoulder. 'Your father, you said, is gesith in Geardcylle?'

'Yes.'

'Where is Geardcylle?'

'On the river From. East of Hereford.'

'You are the second son?'

'Yes, Haefer is eldest. My father Wihtred was made gesith under the new High King Offa. With good service his land will go down to Haefer.'

'And you will get nothing?'

'I have to serve the High King or an ealdorman. If I give good service I may be given land.'

'Army service?'

'Of course.'

'Then there would be little you could do for her. There might even be nothing.'

Hicel turned, sharply. He winced as the pain shot through his wound.

'For her? I don't understand you.'

'I cannot come with you. But my daughter Hilda could come.'

'Your daughter? But you and she can't be separated.'

Acha moved her tongue, contemptuously. 'You understand so little, you lords. There is nothing for me if I go back across the Wye. Only the same hard life of a slave. At worst they would send me back and I would be punished or sold again. But, as you say, there is the law, there is the English law. My daughter was born free. You could make her free.'

Hicel stared at her, surprised. He thought for some time. 'But Acha, unless you come, there will be no one to tell of her birth.'

'You can swear it. They will believe you.'

'It would be better if you came.'

'Or Cenwalh might still be alive, in Magon. He could swear it.'

Hicel touched his handsax. 'I should be believed,' he said, firmly.

'You would have to swear it to me,' Acha said, her voice rough. 'Two oaths, do you understand? That you would swear for her freedom. And that while she was with you, you would do nothing to harm her.'

'I would not think of harming her.'

Acha frowned. She turned away and spat.

'Have I said something to offend you?'

Acha rubbed her hand over her cropped hair. 'If she were free,' she said, 'she could marry. She could marry a ceorl in Geardcylle.'

'That's jumping ahead.'

'Yes, it is. But unless we jump ahead I shall fetch the Welsh.'

Hicel's mouth dropped open. He could not understand her.

'You would do all this for your daughter? And perhaps never see her again?'

'It is her right, by law.'

'I will think about it, Acha.'

She got up angrily. 'They would be glad, you know, the Welsh,' she said roughly. 'They would have the right to kill you, because you came burning into their country. Or they could hold you and get payment, from the ealdorman of the king.'

'There's no need to threaten me, woman.'

'Isn't there?' she said.

She got up and walked back to the neuadd.

Late that night she went to the big house. Hilda was asleep with the other girl slaves, in the outhouse behind the kitchen.

'I am ill, I need your help, come with me,' she whispered, as the other girls were stirring. Hilda followed as Acha dragged her hand. They went quietly through the compound to the shadow of the stables.

A pony, disturbed, kicked his stall. Acha drew Hilda down beside her and told her, still whispering, of her discovery of Hicel and of the plan they were considering. Hilda, half asleep, was at first barely interested, but the idea at last got through.

'You mean you would send me with that soldier into enemy country?'

'Keep your voice down. It isn't enemy country. It's English. It is your own people.'

'But I still wouldn't know them. All the people I know are round here.'

'But you can speak English. I took good care of that. And you would be free, just think of it. You could marry a freeman.'

'Some warrior who comes here burning and would sooner or later get killed.'

'Not a warrior. What are you thinking of? Your birth would not allow it. But when you are free you could marry a ceorl, perhaps even one renting his own land.'

'A stranger, mother.'

'A stranger now. But what will happen to you here? Some Welsh slave will take you, and you will have his children and grow old.'

'They are all my friends here, mother. They are the people I've grown up with.'

'And they are all slaves. If Idwallon has a bad harvest, or when he dies and that Guruth succeeds him, you could be sold off in a day. And not just to Cornou or Elchon. There are ships all the time up the

Severn Sea and they sail away heavy with slaves. Talk of strangers then, girl! You would be with foreign men who cared nothing for any of you.'

'Mother, why are you trying to frighten me?'

'Because I am my age and you are your age. Because I know the world and you don't.'

'They are decent people here. They would never sell me. And I couldn't bear to leave my friends.'

Acha gripped her shoulder until it hurt. 'Where is your father now, tell me,' she said, angrily. 'Where is Cenwalh who said he loved me, and my brothers Edric and Imma, and all those loved ones of Magon whose faces I still think I see?'

'Yes, it happened to you, Mother. But that was the fighting.'

'There is still fighting. Haven't I told you this Hicel is wounded?'

Hilda shivered. The night air was cold. 'If he is wounded, mother, he will wait.'

'Of course. But not more than two days. He could be found at any time.'

Hilda did not answer. Acha, waiting, drew her slowly towards her breast. Hilda rested there for some minutes, until Acha pushed her away. She told her, roughly, to go back to the others.

On the next day, having waited till evening, Acha went again to Hicel. He greeted her warmly and fell on the food and drink she had brought: mutton and oatcake and cider. When he had finished eating she bathed his wound and put on a poultice of comfrey leaves. He smiled and put his hand on her shoulder.

'Mother Acha, are you coming across the Wye?'

'I told you. I cannot come.'

'And your daughter?'

'She will come. She is afraid but I will persuade her.'

Hicel smiled again. 'Very well. I will take her.'

Acha shook off his hand. 'Not like that you won't,' she said roughly.

'What do you mean, like that?'

'Get your handsax,' Acha ordered.

He drew the long knife from its loop on the decorated belt. He had been sharpening it on a stone from the river. Its edge and its long point gleamed.

'Swear,' Acha said.

He tightened his fingers on the handle and laid the blade flat across his chest.

'No,' Acha said. She put her fingers on the blade, on its unsharpened edge, and lifted and turned it until the narrow point was at his throat. As she was moving it he gripped her arm, to control it.

'Now put both hands on the hilt, fingers locked.'

'Acha, this is . . .'

'Do it,' she said angrily.

He held the handsax firmly, with the point just touching his throat.

'That you swear for her freedom, and assure it.'

'I swear I will witness until your daughter is free.'

'And on the journey you will not harm her.'

'I swear to respect her and to keep her safe.'

Acha put her large rough hands over his. As she pressed he could feel the prick of the bladepoint. 'By your life, Hicel! Swear!'

'By my life!' He was staring close into her eyes. There was a wildness in them now, and he was suddenly afraid of her. She kept her hands on his for so long that he thought his own hands would tremble, but hers were hard and unshaking. At last she released him.

'I will bring her late tomorrow, when it is just getting dark.'

'And food for the journey?'

She looked at him contemptuously. She turned and went away. As she walked along the bank she saw the kingfisher again. Its bright colours were gone in a moment.

Next morning, early, she made a chance to get Hilda alone.

'You will go with him tonight.'

'Tonight! No, that's impossible.'

'Keep your silly voice quiet.'

'But mother, I can't.'

'Leave it for now. I'll tell you it all later.'

At mid-afternoon Hilda had a break in her work. She went out to find her mother, who was with other field slaves cutting fern. They walked away to talk safely.

'Mother, I am not going,' Hilda said, firmly.

'Yes, my girl, you are going.'

'But you are just giving me away to this man.'

'No, he has sworn to respect you. And he has sworn to make you free.'

Hilda said nothing for some time.

'What is he like, this Hicel?' she then asked.

'Think nothing about that,' Acha said, roughly.

'I mean what age, what kind of man?'

'He could be your brother. Perhaps five years older.'

'And he is the son of what did you say, a gesith?'

'It is the rank of Idwallon. It is a landed rank, under the king. Hicel is a second son. His position will get him believed.'

'Is he gentle?' Hilda asked.

Acha slapped her bare arm. 'Think nothing about that,' she said again.

Hilda looked away. It seemed to Acha that she was smiling to herself. Acha was about to upbraid her again when she moved close and whispered. 'I got talking to Cargen. He came to see Elen. I knew he'd been with lords, to the Guuy.'

'You fool!' Acha said.

'No, he didn't know what I wanted. He just likes to brag about everywhere he's been. But I know it now. Along the Mynwy to the join of the Dwr, along Dwr to the join of Guormo, along Guormo to its source and then from a ridge the Guuy is in sight; by Ferleg.'

Acha stared at her.

'Cargen said they are all fools, the Saxons. They have good land along their rivers but still their kings order them to go off and fight. They are like dogs, he said, they all lick the feet of their masters. And all they think of is their beer and their bread.'

'Cargen knows them better than I do, I suppose?'

'It's all right, mother. He says they make a good living.'

'You are going for your freedom,' Acha said, sternly.

'Oh that, yes. Do you know, when Cargen was talking, Elen got so angry with him. Well at least she made out she was angry. She said the Saxons were just animals, with nothing better to do than come and burn and steal from us. And Cargen said it wasn't so, here was a pretty Saxon girl listening to us, and he pointed to me. And Elen said that wasn't true, I was as British as any of them. But Cargen just laughed.'

Acha drew away to look at Hilda more clearly. The girl was now happy and smiling.

'Do you know what you will be doing?' Acha said roughly. 'Do you know how dangerous this journey will be?'

'Well, you're sending me, mother. But this Hicel will keep me safe.'

'When we spoke at first you said you wouldn't think of going.'

Hilda laughed. 'Well I thought it over and I decided you were right. I shall be glad to be free, and when I am free, mother, I shall come back for you. Or I shall get Lord Hicel to come back for you.'

Acha did not trust herself to speak. There was a shout from the other women and Acha looked back at them.

'Be ready from dusk,' she said quickly. 'And no more talking to anyone.'

'Can I not even tell Elen? I will have to say goodbye to her.'

'Tell no one. Say nothing. Or you will be caught and flogged.'

'You are very hard with me, mother.'

Through the long evening, waiting for the light to fade, Acha sat quietly by herself, under a tree beyond the compound. She had concealed a bag of food for Hicel and Hilda to take. At last, seeing the torches being lit in the neuadd, she went to find her daughter.

'I have hidden my cloak by the stables,' Hilda whispered.

'Then come. Come quickly.'

They fetched the cloak, and Acha retrieved the bag of food. As they were leaving the compound two figures rose ahead of them. Acha froze, but Hilda went forward.

'You two again!' Acha heard her say.

'Aye, come on, Saxon, you come too,' a man's voice answered.

'In the dark with you, Cargen? Not likely.'

'He'll go and fetch Bran, if you like,' a girl's voice said.

'No, Elen. No thanks. I've got a job to do for my mother.'

'Is that her there behind you?' the girl asked.

'No. Now you two just go on.'

Acha watched the shadowy figures move away. She hurried to Hilda and gripped her arm. She guided her along the roundabout route to the river, which she had previously followed. As they got nearer the water there was a little more light, but Hilda could still only find her way by holding Acha's hand. Acha went forward to the clump of sallies. She waited, but nobody came. At last she went in among the trees, but there was no sign of Hicel. She went back to Hilda, looking everywhere around.

'Here,' a quiet voice came. It sounded across the river. 'Here,' the voice repeated.

Acha stared across. Then, leaving Hilda, she walked through the river. Hicel heard her coming and was ready to help her up the bank.

'What have you come across here for?' she asked staring up at him.

'They may send dogs. It will be safer across the water.'

'But it is Gwent on this bank. It is another kingdom.'

'All the better for that.'

Acha stared helplessly. She could not properly see his face, only his looming shape.

'Is she with you?' Hicel asked.

'She is waiting across the river.'

'Then bring her over.'

Acha waited.

'Will you fetch her or not?' Hicel said, sharply. 'Or shall I go on alone?'

Acha again waited. 'You will remember what you have sworn,' she said fiercely.

'I remember. Now fetch her.'

Acha slithered down the bank. She waded through the Mynwy. The water was cold. 'He is waiting. Come,' she said, taking Hilda's hand.

Hilda held back for a moment and then let Acha lead her across. Hicel stooped to help them both up, but Hilda avoided his hand. As they stood on the bank, Acha gripped Hicel's arm.

'I give my daughter into your oath.'

'On my honour,' Hicel answered.

Hilda turned to her mother and embraced her. Acha held her close and let her kiss her cheek.

'All safety to you both,' Acha said, releasing her.

'And my thanks to you, Acha,' Hicel said formally. 'I shall never forget you.'

'We will come back for you, mother,' Hilda said, now crying.

'Go,' Acha said.

Hicel reached for Hilda's hand but she again avoided it. He led the way, moving quickly, along the track beside the alders. Acha, straining her eyes, saw them disappear into the darkness.

She sat wearily on the grass, rubbing her wet legs against the cold. She stayed listening, for a very long time, until she could be certain they were beyond her hearing. The night was very quiet, though there was a dog barking, far away towards Elchon. She waited for the barking to stop and then walked slowly back across the river into Euas.

Acha heard nothing more of her daughter. But it is known that Hicel took her safely across the Wye and that she was eventually given her freedom, although it was a complicated case, long argued. Hilda was married in Geardcylle to a freedman who was settled on new arable land. She had a daughter and two sons. The sons were becoming young men when Offa of Mercia confirmed the Welsh frontier with his Dyke. No part of the dyke was built along the Wye facing Erging, because a separate settlement, an independent but subordinate alliance by Erging, was agreed, with the river as frontier.

Hicel continued to serve the king, in the hope of land. In 777 he was killed on the Upper Wye, where Offa had marched against the Irish, who were still pushing from the west. Acha continued to live in Suluiu beyond the year of his death, still a slave of Guruth son of Idwallon. She was never suspected of complicity in her daughter's disappearance, since it was obvious to everyone that she would never willingly have let her daughter leave her: she was a Saxon caeth and an alien, who had only her daughter, of her own blood, to live for.

Dragon and Gentile

◆

Caran was resting above Cochyd, beside the Stones of the Old People. His sheep were grazing along the western spur of Troed. The summer day was warm and quiet. The lake, far below, shone like silver. On the cranog, close to the northern shore, a woman was moving along the outer walkway. Caran could not tell, from this distance, whether it was his mother Gwen or his sister Olwen: they were of the same height.

Caran smiled thinking of them. His mother was from a family living high on Cefyn Moel. She still complained about living on the little artificial island, especially in the damp mists of winter. Yet she had come when Iddic had asked her, and had always managed their lives well.

There was always extra work on the cranog, repairing or replacing the outer ring of round piles, or the steps and rails on the walkways. But the hut and barn were large. The safety of the cranog allowed more to be passed on, from fathers to sons, than the more exposed huts along the valley and at the edges of the lake. So the family was respected for living on the cranog, and the story was told that in the old times, before the loss of the sunken land, it had been the place of a king.

Certainly the old work was solid: beds of stone to the depth of a man beginning six paces in from the present summer edge of the lake; huge black oak piles holding them and old transverse beams making platforms. There was now a narrow walkway to the shore but the old dugout boats were still kept for fishing and for winter when the walkway was flooded. Since the time of the rule of Elgist, through six generations, the family of the cranog had common grazing rights on Troed. Caran knew, looking over it, that the life he was born into was unusually well provided for.

There had been black smoke, all day, to the south beyond Alt Luid. It had been a whole summer of fires and rumours. In the spring there was the alarm over an army of Black Gentiles, riding and burning along the Gwy from distant Hereford. There was fighting at Llyswen, but the enemy army turned north towards Buellt and the lands around Llyn Syfaddon were left undisturbed. Later there were repeated reports that a much larger army of the Gentiles was ravaging in Gwent and Glywysing, but that was still far enough away.

For as long as Caran could remember there had been stories of raids by the Gentiles, along the coasts and up the rivers. But, three summers earlier, King Elisedd had announced at the render that there had been a great victory of the British and the English, fighting in alliance, against a huge Gentile army near the mouth of the Gwy. The *micel here* of Haesten had been reduced to eating their own horses. They had been killed and scattered. It would be the end of them, Elisedd had foretold. But still, this summer they were back, striking south and west from their winter base on the river Hafren, against the British lands.

Caran called his dogs and began walking down. As he approached Cochyd he could hear strange noises from the south, beyond Blaenllynfi. There was a distant clang of metal, as in the hammering of the smiths in the forges at Gwernyfed. There was also a distant, echoing clamour of voices. Caran ran to a viewpoint and looked out towards the source.

Two horsemen were galloping from Bwlch down the track past Blaenllynfi. Other horsemen rode behind them: three; five; nine. Behind these more riders were galloping into a wide line, several spurring to the higher ground. The shouts were louder now, and the warriors on the hillside were halting and firing arrows at the first group of horses. Caran saw two fall, and other pursuers rode up and speared their fallen riders.

Still the chase continued. Caran lay and concealed himself. There had been eleven and were now nine of the pursued. Along the line of pursuers one rider was carrying a thin green flag on his raised spear. Caran then knew that they were of Brecheniauc, and that the pursued were the enemy. These enemies were now riding towards him, but on lower ground. He looked hard at the two leading riders, big men, on unusually large black horses. They wore short tunics of mail, and their helmets were of a kind he had not seen: wide-brimmed above their bearded faces, and crested on the crown. One of the two was wounded in the arm. He was riding precariously with only one guiding hand. The others still galloped behind.

There was a trumpet call from the north. From the edge of the forest a new line of horsemen galloped towards the pursued. They were shouting wildly. Caran knew them immediately. This was the personal troop, the teulu, of Tewdwr son of Elisedd: the troop known throughout the kingdom as the Dragon. They were now almost upon the leading enemy riders, who, seeing this new danger, began swerving down towards the lake. Caught between the two troops, several of the later riders halted. They moved closer together and prepared to fight. Caran saw two of them go down, slashed with swords from their mounts. Two of the Dragons also fell. The troop from Blaenllynfi was now up and joining the fighting. At last the enemy broke off and followed their comrades down to the lake. Caran heard Tewdwr shout to get after them.

Caran had been watching the fighting from the safety of concealment, but now he stood, differently roused. For the leading riders of the enemy had reached the edge of the lake and were galloping west along it. He watched, cold with a new fear, as they splashed through Nant Cui and towards the walkway from the cranog. He shouted and began to run but he was too far away. The pursuers had stopped, briefly. Tewdwr was talking to the leader of the first troop. But meanwhile, as Caran ran, the first two enemy warriors had jumped from their horses and were crossing the walkway to the cranog. Their swords were drawn.

Caran came to where four had fallen. One of the Dragons called for water. 'What are they?' Caran shouted.

'Water,' the young Dragon repeated.

'They are attacking our place on the cranog.'

'Water, brother, for the love of God!'

Caran looked around. A helmet had rolled loose from one of the dead enemies. He snatched it up, still anxiously watching the huge man who had worn it. He was lying on his back with blood around his mouth. Caran ran to the brook and filled the helmet. Its leather straps were black with sweat. The crest on the crown was a wrought boar. Above the forehead arch was a red-painted snake. He raised the Dragon's head and helped him to gulp the water. Then he again asked his question.

'What are they?'

The young Dragon was weak. Caran had to ask again.

'Normanyeit duon.'

'What is that?'

'Black Gentiles. Northmen. Of the warband of Agnar.'

'They have gone in with swords to our cranog,' Caran shouted.

The young Dragon closed his eyes. He was too weak to go on talking. Caran threw down the helmet and ran on towards the lake. His dogs, excited, ran barking and leaping beside him. He was out of breath when he got to Nant Cui, where Tewdwr and the others had dismounted and were watering their ponies. He made to run past them but Tewdwr shouted for him to stop.

Caran hesitated.

'Here,' Tewdwr ordered.

Caran walked across. He had never been so close to the king's son. Tewdwr was short, with very broad shoulders. His pale red hair was tightly curled. His face and arms were heavily freckled.

'Your name?'

'Caran, High One.'

'Of what place?'

'We live on the cranog, High One. My father is Iddic.'

Tewdwr looked round at his troop. He was smiling.

'How many of you are there?'

'There are my father and mother, High One, my sister Olwen and my younger brother Ifor.'

'The Black Ones have cut down the walkway to the bank.'

'I see that, High One.'

'Yet they cannot escape our vengeance. We shall wait.'

Caran wiped the sweat from his eyes. He turned to run on.

'Are there beasts on your little island?' Tewdwr called.

'Two oxen, High One, and five goats.'

'And grain?'

'None till the new harvest, High One.'

'Seven of them got across. Black Agnar himself is among them.'

'I know nothing of the enemies, High One.'

'Because we protect you from them, Caran son of Iddic.'

Caran looked away.

'You have boats on your island?' Tewdwr asked sharply.

'Two small boats, High One, for the fishing.'

'Where are they?'

'Tied on the southern walkway.'

'The Gentiles will not get away. We shall leave a guard here.'

'But my mother and father, High One? My sister . . .'

'Do you want to swim across and join them?' Tewdwr interrupted and laughed.

'I will do what I must,' Caran said.

'You will do what you can, which is very little. These are warriors, Caran. These are the last warbands of the Great Army of Haesten. They are from the two hundred ships which ravaged Lloegre. They were defeated on Hafren by our British kings and the Saxon Alfred, but they then raised new blood from their lands in the east and now fall on the Cymry. They are fierce and terrible warriors. In Gâl, in Iwerddon, in Lloegr, they have soaked all our peoples in blood. But the last few of them now are at the edge of our swords.'

'They are called Black Gentiles, High One?'

'Black Northmen. Normanyeit duon. Their name for themselves is Vikings.'

Tewdwr smiled and turned to his warriors. Caran meanwhile looked across at the cranog. There was no sign of movement around the buildings. The main walkway to the bank had been axed to pieces. His dogs were looking up at him, wondering why he did not go on home. He crouched and rubbed their heads.

Tewdwr remounted and rode away with half his troop. The other troop, which had pursued from Bwlch where they had ambushed the warband, were also preparing to leave. Ten of the Dragon warriors were left, to guard the cranog. Tewdwr was sending a troop of bowmen to keep up the siege. One of the Dragons, an older man, now in command, came over and sat beside Caran. He put his arm across his shoulders.

'I know how it is, lad. We'll do all we can.'

'Will they harm them, do you think?'

'We don't know, lad. Would your father try to stop them?'

'Yes, he fights off thieves. He stands with his slasher at the end of the walkway.'

'How old is your brother?'

'Ifor? He is fourteen.'

The Dragon got up. He looked across at the cranog.

'I am Morcan,' he said. 'Stay close to me, lad.'

'I have to stay close.'

'You have a sister, did you say?'

'Yes. Olwen.'

'How old is she?'

'Nineteen.'

Morcan sighed.

In the fading light the troop of bowmen arrived. Morcan sent them to their places along a wide stretch of the bank. The outliers could cover the far side of the island. They lay waiting in the shelter of low banks and bushes. The Dragons then moved back, to the slightly higher ground. They had rounded up the big horses which the Vikings had abandoned. They tethered them with their own ponies, collected wood and lit a fire. Morcan came for Caran and led him to the fireside.

'We have to wait, lad,' he said. 'It is all we can do.'

After dark an ox-cart came, with mutton and ale. In the back of the cart lay the wounded Dragon who had asked Caran for water. He was pale and delirious. The carters were taking him to the neuadd at Bronllys.

After the meal the guards were posted. The other warriors slept by the fire. Caran, bitterly cold even though very close to the fire, could not fall into sleep. He watched the cranog with heavy eyes. His dogs lay close to him. After some hours of darkness there was a small fire on the island, on the yard by the open lake. He heard only one high shout, but otherwise all was silence.

Morcan was woken by the guards at first light. The Dragons belted on their swords and stood to. There was a light mist around the island and across the lake. Waterbirds were rising in the far bank, but there were no other signs of movement. Morcan went off to visit the bowmen. They had nothing to report.

When the sun was well up Tewdwr came back with the rest of his troop. Riding with him was a young woman with shining black hair. She wore a white tunic embroidered with gold thread and there were gold bracelets and rings on her arms and hands. One of the Dragons told Caran that the lady was Marcela, only daughter of the King of Buellt. She was laughing with Tewdwr as they rode and looked across at the cranog. Then Tewdwr sent her back and rode down to the edge of the lake, by the broken walkway.

'Agnar!' he shouted. 'Black Agnar! Show yourself!'

There was no movement on the cranog. Tewdwr shouted again. Then a man appeared from behind the barn. He was in mail to his waist. His helmet shone in the sun. He was holding a long sword above his head.

'Who calls for Agnar the Black?' The words were Cymreig, but with a strange sound.

Tewdwr laughed. 'I am Tewdwr, Dragon of Brecheniauc, son of Elisedd.'

Agnar pointed his sword and shouted back. 'What insolence will you offer, Little Dragon, to Agnar the Black?'

'Your blood in the lake, Agnar. Your black heart to the depths of the Sunken Land.'

'That is a man's work, Cymro, not a boy's.'

'I have heard of your battles, Agnar. How you fought with Haesten in defeat at Buttingtune. How you fought for Anarawd, selling your sword for gold, when like a kite he swooped from Gwynedd and threatened this land. They are famous battles but they are old battles. You have little blood left.'

Agnar lowered his sword. 'There is blood enough,' he shouted. 'But now hear me, Dragon. We did not come to the land of the Cymry to burn and destroy. We are warriors who have sailed many seas, but have at last come to land. We wish now to settle, to live peacefully, to grow and to trade.'

'On our land, stranger, which you came first to conquer?'

'It was so,' Agnar called. 'But you are brave fighters. We shall not overcome you. We now ask only that you allow us to settle and live peacefully. Give us the status of alltud under the power of your king. We will obey and serve him.'

Tewdwr hesitated. He looked round at his warriors and bowmen.

'Why should I give you anything, Gentile?' he called at last.

'Because you are an honourable prince.'

'An honourable prince puts all invaders to the sword.'

'Even when they would serve him?'

Tewdwr again hesitated.

'I do not trust you, Gentile.'

'Yet we are as we are, High One. You cannot come and take our lives without deaths of your own people. Not only your warriors but these peasants we now hold.'

'It is not honourable, Agnar, to trade for the lives of peasants. These are matters between the well-born.'

'We would have it so, Dragon. Give us some small corner of your land and we will settle in peace.'

'As you have settled in Lloegre!' Tewdwr shouted, recovering his confidence. 'As you have taken half Lloegre from the Saxons and still assault them for the rest.'

'Yet those warriors are now at peace in their homes in the east of the island. What the Saxons once conquered is now conquered from them, but the peace has been made and the solemn treaties will hold.'

Tewdwr turned away. He walked up and down along the edge of the lake. His hands were joined behind his back as he walked, head down.

'Only his father the king can decide such a matter,' Morcan said, quietly.

But Tewdwr had now made up his mind. He returned and called to Agnar.

'You will get none of our land, Gentile, except to be buried in. Whether we kill you or wait till you starve, you are finished. But I will still accept your surrender on no terms. You have been defeated in battle. By the law of all nations you will become our slaves.'

'Warriors as slaves, do you say, Dragon?'

'It cannot be strange to you, Gentile. Haven't your ships raided our coasts and our rivers and carried away British slaves? Men and women living free in their own lands? You have sold them in Gâl and in Iwerddon. You have carried them in triumph to your own nests. Is it not now your own turn for the yoke?'

Agnar shouted in strange words, and turned angrily away. He disappeared behind the buildings into the centre of the island. When at last he appeared again he was with another warrior. Each held a woman in front of him, with a knife at her throat.

Caran, who had been watching from a distance, broke away and ran forward. Black Agnar was holding his mother, the younger warrior his sister. Olwen's face was very pale and her eyes were closed.

Gwen saw her son and shouted: 'Keep away, Caran. There is nothing you can do.'

Tewdwr looked between them.

'That is your mother?'

'Yes, High One.'

'Do as she says. Keep away.'

'I cannot, High One.'

The blood rushed to Tewdwr's face, darkening the heavy freckles. He stepped quickly to Caran and struck him with his fist to the ground. Caran lay staring up at him.

'You see you cannot frighten us,' Tewdwr shouted across to Agnar.

Agnar hesitated, then with a nod to his companion released Gwen. The young warrior led her and Olwen back out of sight. Agnar came forward to the very edge of the sunken walkway.

'There is one last solution, young Dragon, if you are as brave as you say.'

'No escape, Gentile,' Tewdwr shouted.

'I do not speak of escape. Among honourable warriors, in final dispute, there is only the trial of combat, man to man. We call it Holmganga.'

Tewdwr stared across at him.

'The combat is governed by law,' Agnar called. 'Each champion has his weapon and three shields. He is seconded by a companion. A space is marked out, four paces each way, and a great cloak is spread and pegged on it. Outside the cloak are three further squares, each at the distance of a foot. There are then four hoslurs, hazel posts. The warriors stand on the cloak and exchange their blows. The warrior who is challenged strikes first. When the three shields are useless the warriors must fight on the cloak. If blood falls on the cloak the wounded man may end the combat. But if he retreats beyond the poles, outside the Hazelled Field, he is beaten. The price is then paid.'

Tewdwr stared at Agnar in silence.

'I am challenging you, Dragon. I, Agnar the Black, call you to this combat. If I am killed or, worse, wounded we are all your slaves. But if I gain the victory you pay Holmslausn and you let us leave your land in peace.'

Tewdwr still said nothing. Then he called to Agnar.

'What weapons?'

'Each of our choice.'

Tewdwr looked down at Caran, who still lay on the ground. Caran avoided his eyes.

'I accept,' Tewdwr shouted. 'It will make a quick end of it.'

'Then be prepared,' Agnar called back.

Tewdwr, now excited, returned to his warriors. Caran waited, looking across at the cranog. There was now nothing to be seen but the familiar shapes of the buildings and the walkways, with the water lapping gently at their edges. He looked up at Troed, where the sheep were grazing along the hill. Then he looked beyond the lake to the peaks of the Beacons. They were blue and peaceful under the sun.

As he moved to walk back, two of the foreign warriors were on the far walkway, where the boats were tied. They got into the little boats and paddled out in the lake, calling and laughing to each other. The bowmen along the bank stood drawn on them. But they went only a little way and then paddled back to the island.

Caran hurried back to the soldiers, looking over his shoulder. There was excited talk in the troop as Tewdwr put on his helmet and mail and selected three shields. Morcan stood close beside him, holding Tewdwr's long sword. Then Morcan walked down to the lake and called for Agnar. He did not appear, but two Vikings went to the boats and paddled slowly to the shore. They walked with Morcan to choose the place of the combat. When this was agreed they paced it out and Morcan fetched a great cloak to cover the fighting area. It took time and some argument to cut and place the hazel poles and make the whole site ready.

One of the Vikings took a boat to the island and returned with Agnar. Morcan looked at the dressed warrior, in his ring mail and his helmet with its painted boar. He was as tall as Morcan himself, and of about the same age, above forty. There were white hairs in his full brown beard.

'Has the little Dragon sent you to fight for him?' Agnar asked contemptuously.

'My lord Tewdwr comes to your challenge,' Morcan replied.

'Then let us hope he can fight better than you people build boats,' Agnar laughed. 'These logs are the dugouts of savages, while our great ships sail the oceans.'

'The difference,' Morcan said, 'is that we stay in our own lands. Because we have a land worth staying in.'

Agnar laughed.

'You are the little Dragon's companion? You will hold his following shields?'

'As my lord orders me.'

'I have no wish to humble him. He refused all other ways.'

'You will not humble him, Gentile.'

Agnar laughed again. 'It would be a better fight if you were the champion.'

'I serve my Lord,' Morcan answered.

There were shouts from behind them. Tewdwr was riding down to the square. The lady Marcela rode beside him, and the rest of the troop were in open order behind them.

'He's bringing help,' Agnar called laughing.

Tewdwr halted and dismounted. He came forward to stand at the edge of the square, holding his sword and first shield, with its painted dragon. Morcan stood beside him, where the other shields lay on the grass.

'You are still waiting?' Tewdwr shouted.

Agnar turned and picked up his sword. He drew it from its scabbard. Morcan's eyes narrowed as he saw it. It was pattern-welded along the blade, in the design of a broad weave. Morcan had heard of such swords, with their intricate patterns. It was said that the design was fashioned to be filled in with blood.

'Ready,' Tewdwr shouted. He had only glanced at the sword.

Agnar, still outside the square, now lifted his sword above his head. He raised his face towards it, and called in a deep formal voice. 'Torch of the Blood I now hold in my hand! This torch will burn the flesh of my enemy! This torch will light the depths of his wounds! In its shining blade is the blood warp. Its weave waits for the blood of my enemy. I salute and bear you, Torch of the Blood!'

Tewdwr was looking across at him angrily. The warrior seconding Agnar repeated the cry. Tewdwr looked round at Marcela and then stepped forward into the Hazelled Field. He lifted his sword in his mailed glove.

'The sword of the Dragon of the Cymry,' he shouted.

'Is that all?' Agnar asked, stepping into the square.

'It is enough.'

Agnar stood with raised shield to receive the first blow. Tewdwr slashed with his sword, jumping to make the blow heavier. Agnar's shield was cut to its centre. He threw it down and took another.

He raised his own sword. Tewdwr's shield moved just before the blow. Its edge was sliced through. Morcan quickly replaced it.

Tewdwr struck the next blow. Agnar's shield was undamaged, and with his own next blow he sliced Tewdwr's second shield. Tewdwr wiped his forehead and struck again. Agnar's second shield was badly damaged and was replaced. With his third blow Agnar made Tewdwr's third shield useless. The edge of his long sword was still exceptionally sharp. After blows as heavy as these most swords were blunted.

Tewdwr, now unshielded, looked up at Agnar. The Viking was laughing, waiting for victory. Crouching and circling, Tewdwr kept the bigger man moving. He then sprang suddenly, slashing down at the turning shield. Agnar grunted as he took the shock of the blow along his arm. He threw down his shield and put both hands on the sword's leather hilt. He stamped forward, swinging the long sword horizontally. Tewdwr, jumping clear, put one foot beyond the cloak but then quickly regained his ground. They now moved to strike and parry, Agnar advancing relentlessly and Tewdwr darting to turn and strike.

Both were sweating heavily. Agnar, though stronger and with the better sword, was beginning to show fatigue. His heavy broad slashes came at longer intervals. Then suddenly, gathering his strength, he screamed and rushed forward, slashing low at Tewdwr's thighs. Tewdwr jumped from the slash and Agnar stumbled, unbalanced. Tewdwr could not raise his sword but he cut with a short blow across Agnar's forearm. Blood spurted and fell on the cloak. Tewdwr rushed in to exploit his advantage, but Agnar lowered his sword and stepped back.

'My blood claims the right to rest,' he said, breathing heavily.

'What new rule is that?' Tewdwr shouted contemptuously.

'I do not end the combat,' Agnar answered, proudly. 'I rest to bind my wound, and we fight again at dawn.'

Tewdwr looked round uncertainly. Marcela was smiling happily.

'I grant your petition, Gentile,' Tewdwr said, stepping back. 'You have your freedom till dawn.'

Agnar and his companions walked back to the boats. Tewdwr,

surrounded by his Dragons, was laughing and talking excitedly. Morcan watched the Vikings cross and then spoke to the bowmen. As he returned to the horses he saw Caran sitting beyond them. He went over and sat by him.

'It will finish in the morning.'

Caran did not answer.

'We have all to learn to wait, lad. It is the trial of war.'

Caran looked up at him. Morcan was shocked to see the pain on the narrow, bony face. The eyes were rimmed with the dark of strain and fatigue.

'How can they do it, Morcan?'

'Do what, lad? fight?'

'No, I understand fighting. But they have turned it into a game, a play.'

'It is a law of combat, among the bonheddig of the Gentiles.'

Caran looked away.

'I know how it must be for you, waiting,' Morcan said, quietly.

'Yes, but does my lord Tewdwr know it?'

'It is only to release your family, lad. The Lord Tewdwr is risking his own blood.'

'It is not to release my family. He could have said to release them before the combat was agreed. He could have made that condition.'

'These are matters of lordship, lad. You must trust your Prince.'

Caran looked away.

'Through another night, with those savages holding them?'

Morcan hardened his voice. 'Do nothing foolish, lad. Do nothing on your own.'

'Do nothing? Is that all my life is good for?'

'You have your own life, Caran. It is not the life of fighting. The Gentiles are skilled warriors. It is all they are raised to be.'

Caran got up, stretching his arms.

'You don't understand me, Morcan. You are kind, but you don't understand me.'

Morcan shook his head. 'Take care,' he said, putting his hand on Caran's shoulder.

The fire was being remade. The ox-cart came again, with cider and mutton. Tewdwr and Marcela had ridden back to Bronllys.

Morcan persuaded Caran to eat, and, as darkness fell, smiled to see that he had fallen asleep, curled near the edge of the fire. The guards were set, and at last the camp slept.

It was cold when Caran was wakened by a hand pressing his shoulder. He looked up in the glow from the fire to see his young brother Ifor. He sat up quickly. Ifor put his fingers to his lips.

'How did you get here?' Caran whispered.

Ifor bent close. 'They shut me in the barn, but there's that old loose plank by the woodpile. I worked it and slipped through and swam to the bank.'

Caran felt the dripping wet tunic. 'You must get that off. But where are the rest of the family?'

Ifor stood and stripped off his tunic. His shoulders and arms were very thin.

'Where?' Caran asked, gripping his knee.

Ifor crouched beside him. He was shivering. 'They killed father when they first came,' he whispered. 'He stood against them on the walkway.'

'And Mother and Olwen?'

'They took them to the house.'

'Have they harmed them?'

'I don't know. I saw nothing from the barn.'

Caran stripped his own tunic and put it over Ifor's shoulders. He went across to the horses and found a saddle rug to wear himself. As he was returning the guard challenged him.

'What's that you're stealing?'

Caran explained. The guard came to look at Ifor.

'You got past the Gentiles and the bowman and then past us?'

'I was careful,' Ifor said, shivering.

'Pull that tunic on, boy. Get close to the fire.'

He left the brothers and went to wake Morcan, who came across and heard the story again. He then put on an extra guard and stayed with the brothers, though he would not talk with them further. It was a long wait till at last there was a faint first light above Troed. The guards woke the troop and they ate. Morcan walked to look across at the island.

The Vikings had already lit their fire. He could hear their strange voices. He walked along the shore, talking to the bowmen. On the far side of the lake there was heavy mist, with a gap above the lightly rippled water. A heron was flying from the lake up the little wooded valley to Blaenllynfi.

As he turned back there was a boat on the lake. Agnar was sitting in it, and his companion was paddling. Morcan walked to where they landed.

'Have you changed your mind?' Agnar challenged him. 'Will you take the sword yourself, and replace your little dragon?'

Morcan did not answer. He was looking at the sword, which Agnar had drawn from its scabbard. It was not the same as that of yesterday, the pattern-welded Torch of Blood. This was lighter and differently formed, tapering more sharply away from the hilt. Instead of the welded iron strips, which were used to strengthen the longsword, this was of a single piece, with a different look to the metal.

'You have noticed it, Cymro?'

'I am not Cymro. I hold no land. I am a soldier of my lord.'

'But you have noticed it, soldier?'

'I have seen the new sword.'

Agnar laughed and whirled it around his head. It moved with a springy lightness.

'Meet the Serpent of the Wound,' Agnar shouted, mock-slashing towards Morcan.

Morcan did not move.

'It was made by your smiths?'

'Not by ours,' Agnar said. 'It is new. It is of the Franks of the Rhine. I took it in battle.'

'A heavier sword will crush it.'

'In my hand, perhaps,' Agnar said, and turned away.

His right hand was heavily bandaged, but he seemed to have recovered all his strength. He walked to the place of the combat and began shouting for the Dragon. It was some time before Tewdwr rode down. He had put on a long white linen tunic, embroidered with red threads. He jumped down, not looking at Agnar. The troop gathered round. Morcan moved and spoke quietly to Tewdwr, telling him about the new sword. Tewdwr nodded, but took little notice.

Facing each other, the fighters stepped into the Hazelled Field. Agnar waited as Tewdwr rushed. He parried. For some time Tewdwr made all the first moves. Agnar turned and took the slashes on his blade. Then he began to move forward, slashing as before. Tewdwr parried without difficulty.

'You think you are brave, little Dragon,' he mocked. Tewdwr rushed him again.

What now happened was so sudden that only Morcan, partly prepared, could follow it. Agnar stepped forward to slash, and Tewdwr lifted his sword to parry. Then with a quick turn of the wrist Agnar changed the downward slash to a thrust from below. The blade went under Tewdwr's guard and wounded his side. Putting one hand quickly to the blood, which was staining the linen tunic, Tewdwr shouted and slashed forward. Agnar parried and, turning his wrist, thrust again and pierced Tewdwr's shoulder. Tewdwr, hardly knowing what was happening, rushed forward, slashing wildly, but Agnar stepped back.

'Wait, Dragon,' he shouted. 'The next will be death.'

'No death,' Tewdwr shouted. The pain and the flow of blood, which was now heavy from his shoulder, had roused him to a frenzy.

'Soldier!' Agnar shouted to Morcan. 'Save your Prince.'

Tewdwr still rushed towards Agnar, who now easily evaded him. Morcan stood undecided, but then quickly stepped forward and put his arm on Tewdwr's shoulders. Tewdwr flailed at him, cursing, but Morcan tightened his grip.

'The Serpent wins our leave,' Agnar said raising the new sword.

Morcan led Tewdwr from the field and laid him gently on the ground. He bent over him and ripped the cut linen to see the wounds.

'He will live,' Agnar said, 'I had no wish to kill him.'

Morcan ordered boughs for a stretcher. He sent one of the troop for the ox-cart.

'We now leave in honour,' Agnar said walking across to them. Tewdwr would not look up at him. He was very pale, though Morcan had stemmed the flow of blood with strips from the tunic.

'Only the King or the Prince can release you,' Morcan said.

Agnar shouted angrily. 'Are you without honour in this country? Did not everyone hear the price of the combat?'

Morcan stood and faced him.

'Or will you taste my Serpent?' Agnar shouted into his face.

Morcan did not move.

'I must see to my Lord,' he said quietly. 'You can bring your men to the shore and we will ride to the Old King.'

'To keep the little Dragon's word?'

'To keep the High One's word.'

Agnar laughed. He ordered his companions to fetch the other Vikings from the island. As the ox-cart was arriving they were paddling across. With Agnar they were seven. Four were very young men, tall in their boar helmets and ring mail. On Morcan's order, their horses were returned, but the troop of Dragons moved to ride in a circle around them. The bowmen came up from the lake and joined them. When Tewdwr had been laid in the ox-cart they moved off towards Bronllys.

All went except Caran and Ifor, who had kept away from the soldiers. When the column was out of sight they went to their dugout canoes. Taking a boat each they paddled to the cranog. Caran was ahead as they rushed from the walkway. His father Iddic lay facedown in the yard. The whole left side of his neck was gaping and crusted with blood. One of the dogs was lying beside him, its head stretched on its paws. It looked up with old milky eyes, but did not move.

Caran ran to the round house. A low fire still burned by its doorway. He looked in and the place seemed empty. Then he saw his mother and Olwen sitting close under a stall. They seemed not to see him until he spoke. He rushed across to them. His mother lifted her arms and hung round his neck. Olwen did not move.

'Are you hurt, Mam?'

Gwen said nothing. He took her wrists and pushed her back so that he could look into her face. There was a swelling dark bruise over her left eye and a long red weal down her cheek. She stared.

'Olwen,' Caran said.

The girl turned away her face, which was pale but unmarked.

'Do not ask, Caran,' Gwen said, and struggled to her feet. She staggered slightly as the weight came on her cramped legs.

'Olwen,' he said again.

His mother took his arm and led him to the doorway.

'We must wash your father and bury him.'

Caran looked round the yard. By the barn an ox had been roughly slaughtered. Joints had been hacked from its haunches, but the rest of the carcass lay in a pool of thick, stinking blood, under a swarm of flies.

'That is for you and Olwen,' he said. 'Ifor will stay with you. I shall soon be back.'

'From where?' Ifor asked.

Caran looked again round the yard. He went to the barn and fetched his hunting bow and arrows.

'No, Caran,' Gwen cried.

Caran put his hand on her shoulder.

'The high one, uchalwyr, has had his combat. Now I will have mine.'

'You can't fight warriors,' Ifor said, hoarsely.

'No, but I have hunted boar.'

He went to the walkway and paddled the dugout across. The low ground by the lake was empty again. The square of hazel wands still marked the place of the fighting. He ran hard for the high ground and into the trees. He made his way by forest tracks until he could look down on the court at Bronllys.

Many people were moving in the big yard, and others were working around the barns and stalls within the high palisade. There was no sign of the Normanyeit. Then he recognised three of their horses, tethered on the fence below the guardhouse. Blue wood-smoke was rising from the open kitchen at the end of the lord's hall. He waited and watched.

It was well after noon before the Normanyeit appeared. Their horses were brought by grooms and they mounted. Caran watched closely as Awst, the younger brother of Tewdwr, rode from the courtyard with his own armed troop. The Normanyeit rode behind him. Awst turned for the road to Claerau.

Caran at once set off, running, along the track at the edge of the forest. Awst's direction must mean that they were riding to Mercia. Caran feared that they would gallop or canter and outpace him. But they were riding slowly, in the pleasant midday air, talking easily as they went.

It was hard to keep up with them while remaining unseen, though there was plenty of good cover in the woods. He almost lost them where they turned to ford the Gwy, among the open meadows, but he got through to the forest on the north, and then the upper track above Liuesi. He could now keep pace and observe them more closely. Awst was riding at the head of the column beside Agnar the Black. They were talking in what looked an easy, friendly way.

Caran caught his breath. It was almost unbelievable, a young prince of the Cymry at ease with the Black Northman who had drawn the blood of his brother. Was this how the uchelwyr really saw the alien invader, as lord to lord? If so, they must go their own ways. There were different obligations, in blood, for a father and a sister.

The column passed through Claerau and entered the forest track. Caran climbed away from the track and ran with all his strength to get ahead of them. He looked down, at one point, and saw the frontier huts, with their guards. The forest continued without mark, but there was now another danger, for this was Saxon country. Moving with great care, he worked his way down to the edge of the rutted track. He was looking for a hunting position, and at last he found what he wanted: a big oak, with broad forks, that commanded a view of the track. He slung his bow and climbed and concealed himself in the branches.

He expected a long wait. There would be long talk at the frontier: that talk of boundaries and lordships, of customs which uchelwyr alone understood. This forest, by that talk, was now Saxon. Yet these Normanyeit, who had fought both Saxon and British, would soon be riding into it, under the kind of agreement these different lords made. Caran waited only for the killers to come.

He heard them before he saw them. There was a loud laugh and then an excited shout. He took his bow and fixed his best arrow: the one with the barbed iron tip that he had traded for at Gwernyfed.

They were very close to him now. The youngest were riding ahead, talking loudly, with their helmets slung on their shoulders. There were four and then two, and at the rear of the column Black Agnar. Unlike the others he was wearing his helmet. His short tunic of mail came below his ribs.

In the brief seconds in which Agnar was exposed to the arrow, Caran's mind raced. He had thought to shout 'Dial! Revenge!' as he let the arrow fly. But that was a lord's shout. Only lords had time for it.

There was only one place he could shoot, directly down into the face. As he took the tension of the bow, bracing his leg against the trunk, he was cold and silent. He could see the small painted figure of the boar on Agnar's shining helmet. He aimed below it, into the mouth.

As the arrow hit he looked only briefly. He was then down the tree and racing for the depth of the forest. There had been no cry as the arrow struck, but as he ran he heard loud shouting voices. He took the steepest slopes and the roughest ground as he ran for the long journey home. Towards the ridge, through sharp breaths, he realised with surprise that he was himself shouting.

GLYN TO ELIS: 11

◆

Glyn shouted, cupping his hands, as the cloud-bank covered the moon. Intent on the way ahead, he had been slow to see the cloud building. It loomed now, heavy and black, in a great arc from west to south. It was flat and sharply outlined along its edge – a front moving in. As he looked more closely he saw small upward swellings from the dark mass. They were like the shapes of trees against the light on a skyline. The whole front now closely resembled one of the long black ridges of these mountains. It was high in the sky, at about thirty degrees. It could be seen as another range, raised above these heights on which he was standing, with trees and another watcher on its summit.

The rest of the sky was still clear and relatively light. Starlight and reflected moonlight kept his own country visible. Yet as he looked at the ground, in the maze of narrow tracks, he saw how much more difficult his walking would now be, and how much harder it would be, except by sound, to discover Elis. As he slowly accepted this, he cupped his hands and turned in every direction and shouted again and again.

'Taid! Taid!'

He walked slowly on. The shapes of the Skirrid and the Sugar Loaf, darker now in the altered sky, were still his best distant markers. His way lay in bisecting the arc between their peaks. He was now on Chwarel y Fan. Ahead lay Bal Mawr and beyond it Garn Wen and the Stone of Revenge. Sharply, bloodily, along this ridge, the history had moved.

It was a history more tangled, more impenetrable, than this maze of sheeptracks. Tracks never found, trodden ways not recorded or pursued were necessary to define it. Other tracks had been covered and altered, or consciously avoided. An evil king, Bede had implied, could be abolished by omitting his name from the kinglists. Bede the Saxon priest, who, when seen from this direction, was not venerable. But if the suggestion were taken seriously there would be too few names to make a list.

One of the names, Hywel, was qualified as 'the Good'. Hywel, friend of the English but patron of a consolidation of traditional Welsh laws. Yet the problem is not in the assigned names: 'the Good', 'the Evil' or 'the Bald'. It is in the seeing past them to an indecipherable scramble of rulers and kingdoms. It is in seeing under this starlight the crowded history of unrecorded and anonymous men and women, through generations of repression and war.

But then one thing this history is not – the traditional resonant clash of unitary peoples: Welsh and English, or Viking and Norman. The different peoples grouped as Cymry or Saeson were in real ways distinct – in language and culture, in customs and law. The long westward pressure of those who called themselves English changed the land and its local frontiers. Yet, within what is now accounted the clash of two nations, the real actions were more tangled. Look closer. Saxon kings and kingdoms, and rival lineages within them. Brother murders and dispossesses brother. Iago son of Idwal the Bald imprisons and dispossesses his brother Ieuaf. Ieuaf's son Hywel imprisons and dispossesses Iago . . . In Gwent, beyond Sugar Loaf and Skirrid, Arthfail son of Noe murders his brother Elise. The sons of Elise come to rule until displaced by the Saxon-sounding Edwin son of Einon. Edwin is dispossessed and blinded by Meurig ap Hywel.

A gallant people fighting an alien invader? Somewhere, somehow, it must often have been so, but always through this tangle of bloody feuding amongst warlords.

It is even harsher as the alliances for battles are traced. The kings of south Wales go to the English King Alfred for military assistance against the Welsh of Gwynedd. Fighting Danes, the *micel here* of Black Gentiles under Haesten, invade and harry both Welsh and English. Cymry and Saeson combine under Alfred to defeat these latest aliens, at Buttingtune. Other Danes, raiding from Brittany into Erging, capture a bishop, Cyfeiliog, and he is ransomed by the English King Edward the Elder.

It is now the tenth century of Christ. The ransom of the lord bishop is recorded. The rest is no more than a word: *vastatio* (devastation, ravaging). Mareddud king of Dyfed and Gwynedd pays Danish warriors to attack the Welsh king of Morgannwg. Warriors attack warriors, but the overthrow of a king is the burning and looting of settlements, the destruction of lands and crops. In tribute these are his power. But they are also the lives and livelihoods of all the free and unfree obscured behind his name.

Warlords can breed in a single people, disputing title and tribute. But now there are warlords of diverse peoples, harrying the same land, competing with each other under the resonant titles of race. In the eleventh century of Christ this becomes along this frontier, in the shadow of these mountains, a frenzy.

The long pressure of Saxon Mercia against Erging and Elfael has reached relative stability. The frontier of Mercia is now across the Wye to Dore. There are English homesteads in Grain Valley, now known as Stradle. Across the slow brown river, Welsh and English herdsmen and farmers live within sight of each other. Erging has negotiated a treaty with the English, by which it retains Welsh habits and laws but acknowledges Mercian rulers as overlords. Euas and Ystradwy, Gwent and Brycheiniog are still wholly Welsh. The smallest districts, Euas and Ystradwy, more than half the Black Mountains, are pulled between the kingdoms of east and west. Gwent describes them as 'the sleeves of Gwent'. Brycheiniog as 'the shoulders of Brycheiniog'. Into this long tension, the frenzy now irrupts.

'From the fury of the Normans, deliver us,' the monks of the Welsh often prayed. But those Normans were the Danes – Black Gentiles, Vikings – sailing to raid from Scandinavia or as often from Ireland or France. Far in the east of the island the Danes are settled in wide areas, fighting the Saxons, but also intermarrying with their rulers. Other Northmen have settled in France, in Normandie – so close to the old emigration of the British in Brittany. These fight and intermarry and claim title in their turn. To an English kingdom, under the mixed rule of Saxons, Normans and Danes, comes a Norman given the title of conqueror. Yet before William the Bastard lands at Pevensey there are already Normans from France within sight of the Black Mountains.

In 1043 an earldom of Hereford is carved from Mercian lands. The Earl is the Saxon Sweyn Godwinson. In alliance with the North Welsh Gruffydd ap Llewellyn he attacks the land of the South Welsh

Gruffydd ap Rhys. They contend in battle and devastation for the title of Wales. Then in 1046 Earl Sweyn is banished, for murdering his cousin Beorn and for abducting and wishing to marry the abbess of Leominster. The English King Edward the Confessor, whose mother is Norman, now gives the Earldom of Hereford to his Norman nephew Ralph. The French, it is said, have come to the Wye.

In 1049 Gruffydd of the South is attacked by Danish invaders. He makes a deal, and joins them to fight east, for slaves and plunder, against Cadwgan of Gwent. Gwent Iscoed – Gwent below the Great Wood – is devastated: *vastatio*. Welsh and Danes strike over the Wye against the English manor of Tidenham, formerly Buttingtune, where in 893 English and Welsh had defeated the Danes. Thirty-six pirate ships, each with forty men and eight horse, sail up the Usk. Welsh levies raised to resist them go over to the banner of Gruffydd of the South. The green lands east of the Black Mountains are occupied and devastated; *vastatio, vastatio*.

South from Hereford along the Worm to the Dore, Earl Ralph sends one of his Norman knights. His name is Osbern Pentecost. In the village of Elchon on the Dore, where Welsh and English farmers and herdsmen live in uncontested settlement, and where in 915, after the Danish raid which captured Bishop Cyfeiliog, they built a mound for their defence, he conscripts labour to build a castle. It is across the Dore, within the boundary of Euas. Meanwhile, his period of banishment ended, the Saxon Sweyn Godwinson returns to the Earldom of Hereford. The implantation of Norman castles is now widely opposed. The Saxon clan of the Godwins of Wessex challenge the Normans but lose. During this struggle between Norman and Saxon, the Welsh army of Gruffydd of the North strikes towards Hereford. In 1052, near Leominster, it defeats a mixed English and Norman force. Recovering their power the Saxon Godwins now press against the Normans in their castles. Formally banished, the Normans keep to their strongholds, but the castle in Elchon is eventually destroyed. Osbern Pentecost leaves to take service in Scotland, under King Macbeth. His nephew Alured keeps title to his lands. Ralph the Norman, known as Ralph the Timid, has survived as Earl of Hereford.

In the fall of 1055 comes the fiercest battle. An army under Gruffydd ap Llewellyn marches through Erging and Euas against the Norman Earl of Hereford. Gruffydd's principal ally is Saxon Aelfgar of Mercia, bitter rival of the Saxon Godwins of Wessex. Accused of treason and outlawed, Aelfgar has hired eighteen longships of Vikings from Ireland. With these and Irish mercenaries and his own Saxon soldiers he joins the Welsh king. They are united by family: Gruffydd has married Ealdgyth daughter of Alefgar and they have a daughter, Nest.

Patriots and plunderers, levies and looters, warriors and warlords, the mixed army moves towards Hereford. The Norman Earl hurries his defence. To the east the most powerful of the Godwins, Harold, who will be king of England, prepares to march west towards the Wye and the mountains. The storm cloud hangs in the sky.

The Smithy of Elchon

◆

Idwal heard the carts splash through the river. He hurried to the front of his forge. He was reassured to see the familiar stooped figure of Iddic of Ferdun, bringing an ox-cart laden with fresh charcoal. He could not see the man on the second cart.

'Iddic, I didn't expect you.'

'It's our regular time.'

'What's regular these days?'

Iddic halted the ox. Idwal now saw the stranger leading the second cart. He was a blackhaired young man with a stout elm bow.

'Who is he, Iddic?'

'He is Gord from Maenhebog. He has good charcoal.'

'He hasn't come to me before.'

'No, he usually goes to the smiths at Gwernyfed. But since the new war began he has changed.'

'Since the new war began we have all changed.'

Gord stopped his cart beside Iddic's. He did not look at the smith. He was staring over the good flat land between the Dulas and the Dore. Idwal's thatched house and barn were at some distance from the forge. Two red and white cows were grazing in one of the bright green water meadows, and there were goats and geese near the barn. A long stretch of burned stubble lay beyond the house.

'He is Saxon?' Gord asked, frowning at the smith and looking suspiciously at Iddic.

Iddic went close and held his arm. 'He is Idwal son of the freeman Garudd, who was also smith before him. There are many good Welsh in this valley. When the Saxons came to settle there was an Edwin from Geardcylle, beyond Ferleg. Garudd married Edith the daughter of Edwin, and Idwal has now both farm and forge.'

'And speaks good Welsh and good Saxon,' Idwal called,

laughing. 'To understand any who come.' He was looking at the charcoal in the carts. 'What do you want then? The usual repairs?'

Before Iddic could answer, Gord stepped forward. 'Repairs but also four axes,' he said, threateningly.

'Four? I can't do it. I have so little iron. There is none now from Turlestane and only a little from Y Fenni. It is all gone into swords and into fighting axes, and into the many horseshoes of the warriors.'

'Four axes,' Gord repeated.

'I can do the repairs,' Idwal said, turning away. 'Get out what you've brought.'

Iddic began unwrapping the old hooks and harness rings, and a few large arrowheads, which he had brought from Ferdun. Gord pushed past him and grabbed Idwal's arm.

'Axes,' he said, loudly.

'Have you brought old ones?'

'Three. But we need new.'

'I'll repair the three. Then we'll look at what we've got.'

Gord still glared into his face, but there was now the sound of a horse, galloping along the forest track behind them. All three men swung round. Gord quickly took his bow and fitted an arrow.

'It's all right, it's the radman,' Idwal said quickly. The horseman galloped up to them. He was a fair, blue-eyed Saxon. Gord lowered his bow, but kept the arrow in place.

'Wulfred,' Idwal called.

The radman was trying to recover his breath. A villein with a holding in Clehonger, he owed riding service to the Earl of Hereford. He had been sent south to Culan, on the frontier with Gwent, to collect messages from the Earl Ralph's scouts. He now poured out his story, in English, to Idwal. Iddic and Gord heard the words but caught only a few names. When Idwal turned his face was hard.

'We can forget our quarrel about axes. It has come again.'

'What has come?' Iddic asked.

'It is again King Gruffydd ap Llewellyn and the ships of the Black Gentiles. It is six years since last time, but all Gwent is still waste from them. Now there are eighteen Viking ships up the Usk, and the Welsh army has marched from Deheubarth, where Gruffydd of the South has been killed. There are also Saxons marching with them, under the Earl Aelfgar. They are north of Y Fenni and coming this way.'

Wulfred spoke to Idwal again. He had dismounted and watered his horse and was getting ready to ride on.

'The first horsemen are already at Crug Cornau,' Idwal said.

Wulfred remounted and rode on towards Hereford.

'Little brothers,' Idwal said, 'go home now while you can.'

Iddic began unloading his cart. Gord waited stubbornly.

'This is some Saxon trick,' he said angrily to Iddic.

'No trick,' Iddic said. 'If they are already at Crug Cornau we shall be lucky to get back.'

'And leave the charcoal here for nothing?'

'You can trust me, little brothers,' Idwal said, impatiently. He was looking at his red and white cows by the river.

'When the fighting has passed, come again. I give you my hand in fair play for my debt. I have never run word.'

Gord stood undecided. He pushed back his long hair. 'I will unload our charcoal,' he said at last. 'But I will take your two cows for the debt.'

Idwal smiled. 'Do you expect me to argue, little brother? With that army coming the cows would in any case be killed and eaten by tomorrow. Take them, in God's name, though I doubt you will get them back.'

Gord laughed. He ran to his cart and began unloading. 'How many are this army?' he shouted across.

'The report is five thousand.'

'What is thousand?'

'Thousand is two for every man, woman and child that now live in Euas. And then five for each two, little brother.'

Gord finished unloading. His face and arms were black from the charcoal. Iddic was still unloading, more carefully.

'They do not frighten us, these armies,' Gord said, taking his bow. 'We watch them moving through the valleys, and we go with our beasts to our mountains. They do not follow us there. They want easier pickings.'

'On your road back to Ferdun you will meet them, Gord. You will be the easy pickings.'

Gord frowned. He looked back towards his mountains, five miles to the west, beyond Dulas and Esclay and Mynwy.

'What's up the Dore, if we go that way?' Iddic asked.

'The Saxon homestead at Beccetune. Big homesteads further up, at Manetune and Mafurn.'

'We can avoid Beccetune. We can follow the forest ridge north towards Gord's country.'

'What is his country?'

'The highlands above Maenhebog.'

Idwal stared at Gord, his eyes troubled. 'If you are to go you must go quickly. I have my family to see to.'

Gord ran for the cows. He drove them, lowing, back to the river. He and Iddic tied them behind the ox-carts, then whipped the oxen through the ford. Idwal was already running to his house.

The first troop of horsemen rode in before sunset. They were Welsh knights, lightly armoured, on small mountain ponies. They carried long pennanted lances. They lit a big fire by Idwal's barn and fed on his geese. They sang and drank around the fire before sleeping in the barn.

Idwal greeted them warmly. Some of the ponies needed reshoeing, and he promised the work for next morning. One of the knights, Owain, an older man, came across, late, and stood by his fire.

'You have had French here?' Owain asked.

'Yes, they built a wooden castle on our mound. When they were banished by the Witan they walled themselves in. None of the people were let inside, it was only for them.'

'It is the way of the French. The Black Gentiles loot and go off. The French build and stay.'

'Yet you still bring Vikings with you. You even bring Saxons.'

'Only to kill the French and to drive them from Hereford. These French lords are the toehold of that foreign king.'

Idwal looked away.

'You are doubtful, smith? You think we shall not kill them?'

'Kill as many French as you like. They are the worst of all lords. But . . .'

'Go on. Speak freely.'

Idwal pulled a white-hot shoe from the furnace.

'Sir, you know the triad of the destroyers of the Island of Britain?'

Owain laughed.

'I know it. I know also that it has different names for the destroyers, in different cantrefs and different times.'

'That is true, sir, of course.'

'Only Arthur,' Owain said, 'is regularly the sting in the tail. Where the three destroyers marched, the land was waste for a year. But where Arthur marched it was waste for *seven*.'

'Sir,' Idwal said, 'it is the year of our Lord 1055. And by my reckoning, it has been already six years of battle and waste.'

Owain looked away.

'And will now be seven, smith, are you saying?'

'I am saying nothing. I keep to my work.'

'Aye, I'll believe you, smith. You'll shoe horses for Saxon or French, Black Gentile or good Welshman.'

Idwal took up his hammer.

'For a good Welshman now, sir,' he said, and began hammering the soft iron.

The Welsh troop mounted and rode north as soon as it was light. They were hardly out of view when the first column of marching men came down the steep track through the forest, under the spreading oaks. They were Welsh pikemen in leather tunics. Behind them, in green and white caps, was a large company of bowmen. They marched through the ford and on north without stopping.

Then came more horsemen. Idwal had seen none like them before. They were big, bearded men on black horses, with heavy mail tunics and wide-brimmed helmets. They carried long shining swords. They did not look around but rode silently and steadily north. When the next Welsh soldiers arrived Idwal asked about the horsemen. He was told that they were Vikings from Dublin.

Behind this marching company rode a large well-dressed troop, on horses and ponies. Riding together, surrounded by their knights, were Gruffydd ap Llewellyn, High King of all Wales, and the Saxon Earl Aelfgar. Aelfgar was short for a Saxon and clean shaven. He wore a heavy gold-brown cloak over his mailed tunic. King Gruffydd was hard and narrow faced, with deep-set eyes. He looked piercingly at Idwal as he rode by the forge. Idwal bowed, with his hand on his heart.

Following the riders came marching Saxon footmen, each carrying a double-headed battleaxe. The column stretched on and on. There were foot-soldier Vikings, in their distinctive wide helmets.

There were more Welsh companies, under different emblems, among them the red dragon of Brycheiniog. There was a long line of dark-bearded Irishmen, who called out as they passed, though Idwal could not understand them.

In the next troop of horsemen there were several who wanted their mounts reshoed. Idwal got to work as the army continued to stream past. It had become uncountable. It was the greatest force of armed men he had seen. When he had finished the shoeing, by mid-afternoon, footmen were still marching through. A troop of light cavalry rode behind them, spreading out and guarding every join of the tracks. There were still stragglers going through as the grey October light faded.

Three miles outside Hereford, Earl Ralph had assembled his defending army. There were Norman and Saxon knights, but the main body were Saxon levies, from the heavily populated villages along the north bank of the Wye and the fertile valley of the Frome. Many were on foot, but the Earl, following the Norman manner of fighting, had commanded all freemen to bring their plough horses and to mount them for battle. The Saxon freemen, used only to fighting on foot, were awkward and uneasy. When they sighted the first company of Welsh knights they prepared to defend themselves, but the Welsh halted, on a ridge overlooking them, and began lighting fires. Through the rest of the day the defenders watched as the great army came up and spread along the ridge. Fires burned all that night, in each of the camps.

At dawn there was movement along the ridge. Companies of horsemen galloped in each direction. Through their lines, behind drums, marched three companies of bowmen, who advanced to two hundred yards of the enemy. Now over the ridge, on a wide front, came the massed foot soldiers. They walked steadily down. They passed through the bowmen and came forward to within a hundred yards. Earl Ralph shouted and ordered the charge of his knights. The freemen followed on their plough horses. The Welsh bowmen stood and rained arrows on them. The foot soldiers shouted and charged. There was hand-to-hand fighting. And then, from opposite ends of the ridge, the Welsh and Viking horsemen were riding. They galloped savagely in behind the defenders' cavalry. The Welsh rode with set lances. The Vikings slashed with long swords. Almost at once the defenders broke. Many fled towards the river. But now the

Welsh and Viking horsemen were galloping to the ford and across it. Hereford, with its castle and cathedral, and its cluster of town houses, lay undefended ahead of them. They rode in, shouting. Other horsemen, Welsh and Saxon, were whipping their mounts across the ford to share in the capture of the city.

The first Welsh troop, under Bleddyn, rode hard for the castle. The Vikings diverged and rode for the cathedral. Black-gowned canons and priests were kneeling in the cathedral porch, blocking the heavy oak door. The Viking chief, Agnar, rode forward and looked down at them. All kept their heads bowed, their hands pressed in prayer, except the Norman canon Raoul, a big white-haired man, who stood and looked steadily up at the Viking.

'Out of our way,' Agnar ordered.

'We are in no man's way. This is the House of God.'

'It is the house of your treasure. It is your treasure you are protecting.'

'The treasure is not ours. It is our trust for the glory of God.'

Agnar laughed. The other Viking horsemen pressed close behind him. Beyond the heavy door Agnar saw men lifting a reinforced bar to its brackets.

'You play at praying,' he shouted, 'but still your servants bar the door.' He slashed his sword down across Raoul's face. He urged his horse forward, through the kneeling priests. He jumped down and went in with his sword, killing the men at the bar. The other Vikings dismounted and attacked the kneeling priests. Seven were killed; five others were wounded. Inside the cathedral Agnar hurried to the altar. There were jewelled crosses and silver communion chalices. A young priest ran in front of the altar.

'Out of my way,' Agnar shouted.

'No, Gentile. For these are the vessels of God. If your hands touch them you are cursed.'

Agnar put away his sword. He clenched his fist and hit the young priest on the temple. The priest fell.

Agnar stepped up and looked at the crosses. He turned them in his hands to examine the workmanship. His face softened and became attentive, delighted by the beauty of the work.

Other Vikings crowded round him. Saddlebags were fetched, and the crosses and cups were stowed away. The whole building was searched. Gilded staves and heavy gowns were found and taken. A large jar of wine stood in a recess beside the altar. The silver cups were taken out again and the Vikings drank, sitting laughing on the steps of the chancel.

Meanwhile Bleddyn had reached the castle. Servants ran around the gatehouse, but the Welsh rode past them. Then they dismounted and ran for the hall. As they pushed the heavy door, a company of women and older men were still sitting at a meal, at the long scrubbed oak table.

'What are you?' Bleddyn demanded.

'We are English, my Lord,' an older woman answered, in Welsh.

'All English? No French?'

There was no reply.

Bleddyn walked around the table, speaking to each in turn. 'Of what birth?' he asked, in English. Several replied with their parentage, but others, women and several men, only stared.

'Take the French,' Bleddyn ordered.

The warriors seized and tied those who had not answered. Those who were not taken sat quietly looking down.

'And now take the Saxons,' Bleddyn shouted in Welsh.

The warriors laughed and seized them. One middle-aged man drew a dagger. He was at once overpowered and killed. All the captives, Norman and Saxon, were pushed to stand by the wall. The warriors sat at the table and finished the meal.

The rest of the army was now entering the city. The burgesses — traders and craftsmen — kept to their houses, which lined the way between castle and cathedral, but all the men were seized and bound. Their women and children were not bound but were driven to sit in the street. Bleddyn, when he had eaten, walked across to the cathedral. He found Gruffydd and Aelfgar before the high altar. Agnar, bigger than either, stood with them.

'It is mine to burn,' Gruffydd was saying, sharply. Agnar laughed.

'Yet as I recover this land,' Aelfgar started. He stopped as he saw Gruffydd's face. The deep-set, grey-blue eyes were bloodshot. The hard narrow face was like stone.

'It is no longer the Church of Christ,' Gruffydd said. 'It is the church of thieves. Our British churches were taken from us. Our priests were driven out. The names of the British saints were given to oblivion. But now the time of vengeance has come.'

'It'll burn like a campfire,' Agnar laughed, 'if you let us fire it. None of you Welsh and English know how to burn stone.'

'Who can burn stone?' Bleddyn said.

'It is our power,' Agnar said. 'We of the Blood are close to fire. From ship to stone we carry our secret, to burn all that any enemy has made.'

'The whole thief house must be destroyed,' Gruffydd exclaimed, harshly. Without taking leave he walked out. Bleddyn followed him to the castle.

The fire of the sacking of Hereford was seen from the whole country around. Gord and Iddic, high and safe in the Black Mountains saw the great smoke by day and the glow of the firest by night. From the lower ground of Elchon the fire and smoke were less visible, but Idwal knew what had happened. All he now hoped was that after their victory most of the army would march in some other direction. Yet the Vikings, the Black Gentiles, were certain to come back through Elchon, to return to their ships on the Usk.

He made what preparations he could. His wife and two sons went with the other women and children into the forest of the Dore. The Saxon homestead at Beccetune was already deserted, and farther up the valley the other Saxon settlers were getting ready to leave. The goats of Elchon were led out and tethered in the deep oak woods. The pigs were driven out and turned loose. Idwal collected pots and tools and buried them in the river bank. He kept his ironworking tools and and scrap in the forge. If he had nothing to offer when they called him to work it would be even more dangerous.

The Viking horsemen under Agnar were the first to come back, riding down through the ash grove. Idwal kept out of the way behind the forge, but they rode through, fast, without stopping. Some hours later came the Viking foot soldiers, singing as they marched in two groups at the head and tail of a long column of walking prisoners. These were the Hereford burgesses and their families and more than a hundred Saxon men of the levies. They were being taken down to the Usk to be sold in the slave trade to Ireland or France.

Idwal kept out of sight. The column of fresh slaves, the men with their wrists tied, the women walking with their children, did not look around. Idwal saw how indifferently they walked through the river, barely lifting their feet. The women's tunics were wet and stained. The children took small steps, holding their mothers' hands. On the slow brown water, yellow leaves were drifting. A birch leaf stuck to a child's leg.

Idwal watched them out of sight. There was now some hope of avoiding any further disturbance. No more soldiers came that day. Then, in the following late afternoon, a mixed company of Welsh and Irish foot soldiers came shouting down through the ash grove and across the Dore. Many had picked bunches of red rowan berries, and were wearing them stuck in their tunics. When they saw the house and barn they ran shouting across to it. Many went inside. Idwal could hear furniture thrown around. He had left no food, but the soldiers would still have supplies from the city. Some of them walked to the river to drink. As they settled for the night he sat in the forge, watching.

He did not mean to sleep, but he woke, suddenly, to see three soldiers standing over him. It was just getting light.

'What are you? The smith?' one asked in Welsh.

'I am Idwal son of Garudd. I am the smith. Can I help you?'

'No thank you, brother. The lords, you see, don't give us anything to ride.'

'Not even some old donkey,' another laughed.

Idwal got up and shook their hands.

'You've killed the French in Ferleg?' he asked, approvingly.

'Whoever they were and wherever it was,' the first soldier laughed.

'There was a French Earl,' Idwal said, 'in what the Saxons call Hereford.'

'Aye, so some of them were saying. But they all come the same to us.' They sat by the low fire. Idwal fetched flat bake and cheese and divided it among them. They sat talking of their homes in the western mountains.

'That farmer across there,' one of the soldiers said. 'He's a Saxon, I suppose?'

Idwal looked across at his house and barn. A mist rose from the river across the empty water meadows. A big fire burned in the yard, and the Welsh and Irish soldiers stood around it.

'Aye, they pushed as far as this valley,' Idwal said.

'He's gone, anyhow. He's run for his life. You won't see him back, or any more of the damned Saxons.'

'I don't suppose I will,' Idwal agreed, smiling.

There was the blast of a horn, along the track from the north. Several riders were galloping down to the ford. When they saw the forge and the fire at the house they reined in. The soldiers with Idwal jumped to their feet.

Idwal at once recognised King Gruffydd ap Llewellyn. He now wore a heavy scarlet gown, and there was a big silver cross at his neck. His face was pinched and drawn with fatigue.

The soldiers stood stiffly below him. Idwal stood and bowed.

'What iron have you, smith?'

'Too little, my lord. A few axes and hooks that were brought for repair.'

'We will take them with us. There are better furnaces at Gilwern.'

'I will get them, my Lord.' He collected the axes and hooks which Iddic and Gord had brought, and some other scrap he had been saving. Gruffydd looked it over and ordered a groom to pack it.

'What are that house and barn? Are they Saxon?' Gruffydd asked.

'Yes, my Lord,' one of the soldiers hurried to say. 'We slept there last night.'

'Burn them as you leave. We burn all these Saxon sties.' He pointed forward. The troop rode through the river and up the steep track through the forest. Shouts of command rang out from the house. The soldiers shook Idwal's hand and hurried to rejoin their company.

Idwal watched them form up. At the blast of a horn the long line marched towards the ford. When only a few were left, at the house and barn, Idwal watched as they took burning branches from the fire and set them to the thatch. The flames quickly took hold. White smoke and dark smuts began rising above the mist. Idwal stood quietly in front of his forge. He waved repeatedly, as the long column passed. By the time they were out of sight his house and barn had burned down to the walls. He turned and went to the forest.

There were still golden leaves on the oaks. But the yellow ash and hawthorn leaves were falling and the leaves of the hazel were shrivelled. It was a much colder day. The wind had turned towards north and was rising. He found his family with the other families of Elchon along a stream through Tump Wood. They had made rough shelters of hides and branches, but had not dared to light fires. They were a mixture of Welsh and Saxons. They kept to their family groups, but still lived within sight of each other.

Through eight generations this had been the custom of the Dore. Welsh and Saxon retained their own languages and customs, but they followed the example of their neighbours to the east, the Dunsaete, also a mixed settlement, who had agreed a formal ordinance, supervised by each group of elders, which set rules for any cases of theft or homicide or disputed boundaries. In this valley these were known, by the Saxon settlers, as the laws of the Dorsaete.

Idwal went round the families to report what happened.

'We must stay in the forest for seven days or more, until we can be sure the army is gone.'

The families agreed. They had some food and could hunt. The hazel crop was heavy and the children were already busy picking. Those who had goats milked them. Almost all the pigs were lost in the forest, but some were near and would be found.

'We've done it before,' Idwal said. 'We can do it again.'

They stayed ten days in the forest. The men went back to the village first. All the houses, huts and barns had been burned. Only the forge still stood by the river. Idwal dug out his tools and relighted his furnace.

The days were now cold with driving rain. But the axes were sharpened and timber and firing were cut from the woods. Some families built in their old places, but many built huts close together, between the ford and the old mound. A few days later the women and children came down. They were all glad of the settlement after the cold of the forest. Most of the winter supplies of grain had been lost in the fires but several of the pigs had been found, and with hunting they could get through the winter. By late November there were frosts and they kept big fires day and night.

In early December, while they worked around the village, a boy came running.

'Soldiers,' he shouted.

He was pointing back along the main track from Hereford. Everyone came from their work and the huts. They stood together near the ford. Down the open track a troop of armed horsemen rode slowly, looking around. The families watched them come nearer.

At the head of the troop was a small, fair, cleanshaven man. He wore a big gold star at his throat, and a red jewelled brooch pinned his black cloak.

'What are you?' he called in English.

'We are of Elchon, Lord,' Idwal answered.

'No Welsh?'

'There are Welsh among our neighbours, my Lord. They give us no trouble.'

'Welsh and give no trouble?' the lord laughed. He turned to enjoy his joke with the troop.

'Under what lord are you?' an older man asked sternly.

'Of Hereford,' Idwal replied.

'You have paid your dues and your render?'

'Not since the late fighting, my Lord. For we have had no word.'

'Must you wait for word before you render your service? It is your duty to attend on your Lord.'

'We were not sure, my Lord, of his rule, since the city was burned.'

'You take leave to doubt your true Lord? You would prefer, no doubt, to render to the Welsh? Or to keep all things, grossly, to yourselves?'

Idwal looked up at the younger lord. 'We have little enough left, honoured lord, since the army passed.'

The younger lord looked around. His eyes rested for a moment on Idwal's burned-out house and barn.

'Yes,' he said, smiling, 'you whine. We hear nothing but your whining. Yet all the time you are supplying the Welsh.'

'No, honoured lord, the Welsh army has gone. And the Gentiles with them.'

'That at least is true. We cannot find these invaders and punish them as they deserve. But in the name of the King I now command you: resume your duties to Hereford.' He rode down to the ford. He looked across at the old mound. 'What structure is that?' he called back.

Idwal hurried and stood below him. 'It was the defence of our fathers, honoured Lord, against the Black Gentiles of the old time. A few years ago a castle was built but it is now, as you see, broken down.'

'What castle? Who built it?'

'The lord's name was Osbern. Osbern of Pentecost.'

'A Frenchman?'

'We understood so, my Lord.'

'And you served him faithfully?'

'We cut timber for his castle. And we rendered our dues, by the laws.'

'The laws of Osbern of Pentecost? Can none of you tell the difference between true lords and false? Do you realise, any of you, that to serve a false lord is to be traitors to the King?'

'These are very high matters for us, my Lord.'

'They are low matters. Base matters. All you do and think is quite base.'

Idwal looked away. The older lord had dismounted and was calling the people around him. His English had a strange nasal sound. 'We are come to restore peace, in the king's name. We shall bind the Welsh with iron into their own lands. You, honest Englishmen, will now renew your oaths of allegiance, before my lord the earl.'

The younger lord turned his horse and trotted back. The families looked up at him.

'I am Harold Godwinson, Earl of Wessex. I speak for King Edward. Kneel.'

The families knelt on the muddy ground. The Welsh among them, who had not understood all the talking, watched their neighbours and then knelt. One of the children cried and was hushed.

'I grant you your lives,' Harold Godwinson said. 'I grant you your lives but on a short lease. If ever again you supply or harbour the Welsh, or if you fail to resist them by all means in your power, you will feel the edge of my sword.' He drew his long sword and pushed his horse forward until it was in the front rank of the kneeling men.

'Swear.'

'We swear.'

Idwal was the first to answer. As they heard him the others spoke up loudly. Earl Harold smiled.

'Get up,' the older lord commanded.

They got to their feet. Earl Harold smiled, looking again at the broken-down castle. 'I have heard of that Osbern,' he said. 'Like all the French of Normandie he had a taste for this country of Hereford. They find it as sweet as their own land. It was from the violence of the Welsh that a few found a place here. But they abused it as petty tyrants, and now they are banished.'

Idwal listened carefully.

'They are gone,' Harold said. 'You need fear these Normans no more.'

Signs of a Vengeance

◆

In the cold bright April morning, the black twigs of the heather
and the grey upper branches of the beech wood shone in drops
from the overnight rain. On the lower branches, as the wood spread
down to the valley, new buds, tightly folded in fawn, curved to push
away the brittle bronze leaves of the old season.

The grass track from Bal Mawr was sodden, after the heavy
winter rains. Iorwerth ap Owain, riding south, heard the squelch of
his pony's hooves even at this soft pace. He looked ahead to the dark
patch where the track from Ystradwy rose steeply through the
trees. It was the only significant beech wood of the mountains:
Ffawyddog, trailing south from Coed Euas.

In any spring, in the island, eyes widen, still dazed from the dark
storms of winter. The new light dazzles and the traveller's eyes are
restless, for there is too little growth to absorb the lengthening days.

Iorwerth, touching his reins, tried to shift his mind forward from
the extraordinary winter just ended: a winter still dark and active in
memory, which this spring light scoured.

Henry King of England had died in France, on the first day of
December, 1135. Before the news reached Wales heavy rainstorms
rushed in, on wild gales from the west. A dammed lake in Elfael burst
its banks and flooded a village. Along the valley of the Wye all the
meadows were flooded. New highwater marks were recorded in the
churches. Through Christmas and into the new year the relentless
rains continued. Only the people of the upland villages and settlements could stay in their houses. From the lower villages strag-
gling families and their animals moved up to the nearest high
ground.

Within the chaos of dislocation, and while more fierce rainstorms
still swept the mountains, the news of the distant death of a king

might have passed unnoticed. But it was found that on the very day that Henry died the first great storm had drenched Wales. Now this foreign king's corpse, wrapped in bullock skins against its deliquescence, was being transported back to a memorial in England. The heavy rains and the dissolution of a feared and hated body were then known to be signs.

Iorwerth halted and called the greyhaired bard Gwalchmai forward. They looked along the spur to the rise of the old British camp. Beyond it, to the right, rose the great slope of Penyfal, and to the left, beyond Brynarw, the tawny body of Ysgyryd, that strong animal ready to rise. Iorwerth had eleven knights and more than a hundred footmen. His elder brother Morgan had a larger force, more than five hundred men, in the valley of the Usk, blocking the old Roman road from Abergavenny to the West.

The whole country had now risen, as if Ysgyryd had moved. On the news of Henry's death, Hywel ap Maredudd led an army from western Brycheiniog into the plains of Gower. On New Year's Day more than five hundred Normans and the English under their protection were killed. Gruffydd ap Rhys rode north to Gwynedd, to persuade the sons of Gruffydd ap Cynan to bring their armies south and drive out the last of the foreigners. Without waiting for his return, his wife Gwenllian with her sons Morgan and Malegwyn rode to attack the Norman castle of Cydweli, but she was defeated by Maurice of London. Gwenllian and Morgan were killed, and Malegwn captured. Yet the other Welsh armies were still in the field. Iorwerth and Morgan, established in the mountains, looked to their kin lands of Gwent, seized by the Norman Clares, with the best hope of recovery they had known in their lifetimes.

Iorwerth pointed along the spur to the old stone circle of Garn Wen. Squatting inside it, facing inwards, their backs resting on the stones, were the company of the bowmen of Euas. They had suddenly appeared above the pass as Iorwerth led in his troop. When they were told that the troop was marching only against the French, they had agreed to go along. Yet they kept to themselves and to their own tracks. Iorwerth had spotted them from time to time: small, dark-bearded, active men, in rough linen tunics and dark woven cloaks, barefoot and carrying their rough elm bows. They now squatted in silence, looking down at the beech wood.

'Why have they chosen that place?' Iorwerth asked Gwalchmai.

'It is the stone ring, my Lord, of the Old People. Perhaps it is sacred to them.'

'Are they not Christians like ourselves?'

'They are not often seen so they are not often asked.'

'But if they were asked?'

'They seem to have accepted the sign of the floods. That may be enough for them.'

Iorwerth shook his head. When he was tense he had a habit of pushing out his lips and working them in and out. It gave his broad, open face a look of sulky defiance, very different from his usual goodwill. His brown hair and moustache were closely shorn and clipped. He had vowed not to grow his hair until the kinlands of Gwent were retaken and he could again proudly display the long braided hair and flowing moustache of the warrior.

Gwalchmai had teased him about the shorn hair. It was really only to keep out the wet in these hellish rains. Iorwerth had made an effort to laugh. He knew that he depended on Gwalchmai to keep his spirits up.

'They are simple men,' Iorwerth said, looking down at the saethyddion, the bowmen. 'Yet are we less simple, to take a flood as the sign of our freedom?'

'I have explained this to you, my Lord. There are signs of this world and signs of the other world. We do not always know the difference.'

'But why should we need any sign? Isn't the cause of this war very clear, to anyone's eyes?'

'Because the Normans have stolen our country? Yet that has been constant, for seventy years. Men seek a sign, not for war but for success. The death of Henry was such a sign, whether or not there were floods. For now the Normans will fight with each other, disputing the throne.'

'Are you a sceptic then, Gwalchmai? Should we not simply be glad that so many of our people accept this sign, as the dam breaks and the valleys flood.'

'Accept it on these terms, my Lord, since other men believe it. But I could tell you many riddles of the reading of signs.'

Iorwerth looked round at his troop. They had reached the old watchtower of Euas. The bowmen, below them, squatted unmoving and silent in their ring of stones.

'Then tell us, Gwalchmai, while we wait for our spies.' He ordered the troop to gather round. The knights dismounted. The footmen sat close below the tower. Gwalchmai climbed and spread his fingers. He pitched his voice to a bardic formality.

'There are signs of this world and there are signs of the other world. Below us, as we rode, you saw the Lake Syfaddon. You heard stories, perhaps, of its abundance of fish: of its great pike, its fine trout, its many tench and eels. Yet the lake is a wonder for more than its fish. For there is an island in the lake, an island known as a cranog, that was made not by God but by men, in the time of the Old Ones. And standing one day on this island the noble Gwestin Gwestiniog heard voices of women below the grey waters, and the voices spoke of himself. "If he had come when the moon was full," one of the voices said, "he would surely have caught us." And Gwestin departed, but at the full of the moon he returned secretly, and he watched the borders of the lake. And soon five young women rose from the grey waters and swam to the shore, and there they began dancing in the moonlight among the reeds. Gwestin watched, amazed by their origin and by their beauty. As the dance was ending he rushed forward and seized the most beautiful. She turned to him and smiled. "Since I am in your arms, Gwestin Gwestiniog, I will live with you and bear you children. But if you go again to war I will at once disappear and our children with me. For we shall then belong only to the Lake." Gwestin took her and lived many years in happiness. Three sons were born to them. But as the sons grew Gwestin looked for new lands to endow them. Forgetting the young woman's words, he rode to the war that then raged in Brycheiniog. He killed and gained new lands. But when he returned to the lake, rejoicing in his victory, there was no sign of his wife or of his three sons. Even the house he had built for them had disappeared. The very marks of the posts had vanished from the grass. And now Gwestin raged in his grief. Each day he went again to the cranog that was made by the Old Ones. But though he called for the woman and for his three sons there was never an answer. No more voices were heard from the waters of the lake. Gwestin watched through moon after moon, neglecting his crops and his animals. In the end, it is told, he died mad and poor.'

Iorwerth clapped his hands and laughed.

'That should happen to any man, Gwalchmai, who takes his signs from women.'

'You are sure, my Lord?' Gwalchmai answered. He raised his arm and resumed his formality.

'Gwestin, as I have told you, heard voices from the lake. But that is nothing to what is believed by those who live around it. For they say that the broad waters cover an ancient city, which in its time was of a splendour that rivalled Caerleon. And they tell that in certain seasons this flooded city rises, like a marvel, to the surface of the water. They look out from the bank and see fine houses and gardens. They hear the cries of traders and the hammering of goldsmiths. And whenever the city rises there is a change of power in the land.'

'Is it rising now?' Iorwerth called.

'My Lord, as we rode and looked down on it, it had only flooded its banks to nearly double its size. The great rains had moved the earth until the waters were dark and obscure.'

'It is no place for signs then.'

'It is indeed a place for signs. When the skies are clear it reflects the whole world. I will tell you of such a reflection. King Gruffydd ap Llewellyn greatly loved and was greatly jealous of his beautiful queen Ealdgyth. And it was reported to him that a young lord, Awst ap Tewdwr, had one night dreamed that he lay and loved with this beautiful young woman. Gruffydd at once raged and demanded the young lord's death. But the kin of Awst stood for his surety, and prevented immediate execution. Gruffydd's complaint was heard before many tribunals, which gave judgment now on this side, now on that. Awst had dreamed of dishonouring the queen. He had not actually dishonoured her. So the arguments swung to and fro. Then at last there was agreement to submit the quarrel to the judgment of Cynan, who was skilled above all others in the great laws of Hywel Dda. Cynan heard the evidence and gave judgment in these words:

We must, even in pain, obey the laws of our land. It is an iron law that the fine of sarhad must be paid for insult. The outrage of his queen is indeed a great insult to Gruffydd. Its fine is fixed at one hundred cattle for each cantref. Thus the sarhad due from Awst is one thousand cattle. He must bring his thousand cattle to the banks of Lake Syfaddon, and range them in the sunlight by its waters. Yet the outrage, the violation, was in a dream only, and a dream is but a reflection of the truth. King Gruffydd will then by law receive his sarhad. The reflections of the cattle in the waters of the lake will be his and his alone.'

There was a loud shout of laughter.

'Gwalchmai,' Iorwerth said, smiling, 'you seem not to believe these stories you tell us.'

Gwalchmai raised his arm.

'There are signs of this world and there are signs of the other world. In times of war, when the lake is frozen, there are great shouts and clashes of the splintering ice. And when much blood has been spilled, the waters of the lake change from grey to green, and this green is seen also in the river that flows from it. When the noble Rhys ap Tewdwr was killed in these mountains, by the Norman invader, at a place known from old and new times as Twyn y Beddau, the Headland of the Graves, below the Pass of the Holy Gospel, the lake again changed colour, with red threads like veins spreading over its surface, and the great pike multiplied in the depths.'

'These were signs without a doubt,' Iorwerth said.

'Perhaps, my Lord. But of this world or the next? For those battles had already occurred when the waters changed their colour. Yet if we look for signs as prophecies, there is one more story of the lake. You shall hear it and judge. It is from nine years past. The noble Gruffydd son of Rhys, safely returned to the lands of his murdered father, but still without power to challenge the Norman rule, rode one day by Lake Syfaddon with two Norman lords: Milo Earl of Hereford, now imposed as Lord of Brycheiniog, and Pain Fitzjohn, Lord of Euas.'

Iorwerth had turned away. At the mention of Gruffydd ap Rhys his lips had jutted forward and were pushing uneasily in and out. His hand was on the hilt of his sword.

'Do you want the story, my Lord?' Gwalchmai called.

Iorwerth did not answer, but the company shouted for Gwalchmai to continue. He raised his arm and waited for silence.

'The season was winter, the waters were swollen. In the brown broken reeds the wind spoke as voices. Geese of the ice lands, swans of the great rivers, green-necked mallard and countless bobbing tern, sailed on the hammered silver, before the eyes of the warriors. The Earl Milo spoke. "It is said in your country, Gruffydd, that for a true prince of this country the birds of this lake will rise up and sing." Gruffydd, hearing him, looked long at the birds of the water. The songbirds of the woods were now far from the lake. "Then as lord of this land," he said cunningly to Milo, "now command them to sing." Milo, laughing, stepped from his horse. Clapping his hands he called, "Sing, sing now for your prince." Swans and geese, mallard and tern, moved silently on the wide water. "Now you, my lord," Gruffydd said to Pain, "for often Euas has claimed this country." Pain shook his arms and called. The waterbirds sailed undisturbed in the ripples of the wind. Gruffydd now dismounted. He raised his arm to the ridge of the mountains. He lay, face downward, his head to the east. "In your name," he cried, his eyes turning to the lake. And as he spoke a wind seemed to rise, across the grey waters. But it was not a wind of the earth. It was a wind of the birds rising and of their wings beating the water, and the air was full of their cries.'

As Gwalchmai ended there was silence. He spread his arms.

'It is a truth?' he called loudly.

'It is a truth,' the company shouted together.

Iorwerth took his hand from his sword.

'It is no truth,' he said, 'for Milo is still Lord.'

'A sign of the truth that should be,' Gwalchmai said, 'not of the truth that is.'

Iorwerth turned away. Gwalchmai came down from the watchtower and followed him. 'Are you angry, my Lord?' he asked quietly.

'No, why should I be?'

'I saw your face when I spoke of Gruffydd ap Rhys.'

Iorwerth pushed out his lips.

'He is still a hero in this country,' Gwalchmai said, 'from when he returned from Ireland and raised the revolt.'

Iorwerth walked on.

'There was only one truth in your story,' he at last said.

'It was when you spoke of Gruffydd as cunning.'

'I meant it as a compliment.'

'I took it as an insult. An insult he deserves. That affair at the lake was some trick. He had a hunter concealed in the reeds, to raise the birds when he was ready. That is what I would expect. For if he is such a hero why is he not now with us, here in the south, breaking the Norman hold? What hero would ride away to the safety of the north, leaving his wife to lead the warband.'

'The memory still burns,' Gwalchmai said.

Iorwerth turned and put his hand on the bard's shoulder.

'It burns, indeed, that he killed Owain my father. Yet it is a thread in the strangeness of the times. For my father was defending a Norman castle, as an ally. Gruffydd rose against him for his country. As a son I remember it, but I am prouder to be a grandson. It is the great Caradog who must now guide my sword.'

Gwalchmai looked away. 'Caradog's is a story not of signs but of actions.'

'Yes,' Iorwerth said. 'That is my true inheritance. My arm still rises when I think of Porthskywyt. Imagine it again. The Saxon Harold Godwinson had at last defeated the great King Gruffydd ap Llewellyn. That royal head was sent, on a stake, to the English court. Yet my grandfather Caradog was king of Gwent and Gwynllwg. The arrogant Saxon, Harold, thinking to please that King Edward from whom he hoped to inherit, built a hunting lodge at Porthskywyt, among the very stones of the Old Ones. He filled it with fine food, from all the country round, to feast and flatter holy Edward. But Caradog laughed. Choosing his day, he rode on the lodge. He killed the Saxon servants. He carried home his people's food. They had their own feast. And Harold Godwinson vowed that he would put Caradog's head beside Llewellyn's, but the year of our Lord . . .' Iorwerth broke off, laughing. He pushed his head forward, trying to control his laughter and recover his voice. 'The year of our Lord was 1065. Harold set out against us, but the Old Ones were protecting Caradog. The weak King Edward died. Harold Godwinson had only a contested throne to defend. At once, from every direction his enemies fell on him: Saxon and Dane, good Welsh and evil Norman. He never got to feast at Porthskywyt, or holy Edward either!'

Gwalchmai smiled. 'Young oaks from the grove,' he sang quietly, 'draw my foot from its chain.'

'We shall do it once more,' Iorwerth said, happily. 'We shall do it to those Clares who have stolen our land.'

'There is more now, my Lord, than a hunting lodge. There are strong castles to protect them.'

'Castles certainly. But they have still to ride between them.' Iorwerth called for his pony. It was run up to him. He jumped to the saddle and, shouting, rode away down the track to the beech wood. The bowmen of Euas, still squatting in their circle, turned and watched as he rode by. They then stood together, lifting their bows, as another horseman appeared in the opening from the woods. Iorwerth halted.

'In peace, lord,' the horseman called, raising his arm to show he had no weapons.

'Come,' Iorwerth ordered.

The bowmen now trained their arrows on the stranger.

'I have news, lord,' the stranger shouted. 'Richard de Clare has come to the castle.'

Richard de Clare, Lord of Ceredigion, was guest of the Breton Brian Fitzcount, lord of the castle of Abergavenny. Hard by the site of the Roman fort of Gobannium – now identified in Welsh legend as the castle of Cadwaladwr Fendigaid on the ancient stronghold of the giant Orgo – a wooden tower had been built on a high motte, above a palisaded bailey, by the order of Brian's uncle, Hamelin de Ballon, who had first conquered Gwent Uwch Coed. The Welsh tref on the ridge was destroyed, and the surviving families moved by force across the Usk.

Richard had arrived from Oxford. He had a small company of seven knights and squires, with their grooms and a young minstrel. Brian welcomed him warmly, for he was eager for news of the succession to Henry. There was already division, among the Barons and the Lords of the March, between the claims of Stephen and of the Empress Matilda. Stephen, in possession and crowned, had been holding court in Oxford.

But Richard de Clare, tall and florid in his forties, was in an evil temper when he arrived. He had ridden to offer his allegiance to Stephen, in return for confirmation of his claim to the lordship of Pembroke, to adjoin his lands of Ceredigion. Stephen had been cold and indifferent.

'What you have in Wales, Clare, all that any of you have, is what you can hold.'

'But my claim, Lord . . .'

'Do not bother me with it. What are any of your titles and claims in that wild land? Did not King Henry say that, by the death of Christ, though we rule them by the sword they are still its lawful inheritors?'

'Yet King Henry managed and ruled them, my Lord. And he rewarded his loyal servants, who must live close among them.'

'Clare, let me remind you. The loyalty comes first, before the reward.'

Brian stretched out his legs to the fire. His left foot brushed the shoulder of the largest of his hounds. It turned, looking up at him.

'Then you will have to come in with the rest of us, Richard. All the Lords of the March are declaring for Matilda.'

'Declaring against Stephen, you mean. But they are right. Stephen is right. What we have is only what we can hold.'

'Yet that may be the difficulty. The Welsh are superstitious, and they have taken Henry's death as a sign. They say that since he died in France, where all Normans really belong, it is a sign that we shall all soon return there.'

'I have no worries about the Welsh. They are braggart boys, shouting in the mists of their fathers. But yes, I will join the defiance of the March. And I will take Stephen at his word. I will ride to Ceredigion and prepare to take Pembroke.'

Brian moved his foot along the hound's back. 'I wonder, Richard, which way you will ride to Ceredigion. Within four miles of this castle Morgan ap Owain has five hundred men, along the road by the Usk. They have felled trees across the road and put bowmen and spearmen behind them. Along all the other main roads to the west other Welsh princes are armed and ready. Only our castles are still secure.'

Richard jumped up, angrily. 'How do you expect to hold a country if you shiver in your castles? The Welsh are a beaten people. Like dogs they may bark while you are still at a distance but if you walk boldly up they will squirm at your feet.'

'You think so, Richard? You will try that?'

'There is a route to Talgarth through the mountains. I have

travelled it before. While Morgan lurks, a shouting boy on the Usk, I will go round and past him.'

'That may be possible, though I don't advise it. But if you insist I'll come with you, with a decent troop.'

'I don't want your troop. These people are afraid of their lords. If I meet them in the mountains they will bow their heads for me to pass.'

Brian stood and looked sceptically into Richard's face. 'This is your pride talking. The pride that was wounded by Stephen's indifference.'

'Well, and if it is? I live by my pride. But now I must sleep.'

Brian watched Richard walk busily away. Left to himself, he put his hand across his eyes. The simplicity of Clare's pride was like a boy's bragging. He seemed to know nothing of the actual darkness of the world. Brian himself, by long habit, revealed none of his own deeper feelings. What could a man like Clare understand of his own fate, to have gained this lordship, and to wish to hold it for his sons, only for both sons, *both*, to have become lepers. They would be sleeping now, in isolation in the Priory, just a hundred yards away. It was a bitter and hopeless conclusion to his own pride. He struggled, every day, to conceal his grief, which so often turned to rage. Nobody guessed how often his hand moved to strike out and destroy, in this world in which God had deceived him. Two sons, two heirs, two lepers. Yet always, this far, he had restrained his savage revenge. He cared for his lordship, treated rationally with his neighbours. And to the Clares, especially, as the most powerful family of his region, he showed only prudent attention and service.

Next morning, as he dressed, Richard saw a troop of forty armed horsemen gathered outside the western gate. He went to the head of the flight of wooden steps to the bailey. Brian, already armoured, looked up and waved.

'You are going on some attack?' Richard called.

'We may go to look at Morgan. But if you meant what you said, and are going through the mountains, we shall ride with you to Talgarth.'

Richard finished dressing and hurried down the steps.

Brian put out his hand. 'I told you, Breton, I don't need you. I intend to ride as I am.' Brian looked up at him. The florid face, with its wide grey eyes and firm nose, was still handsome, though the jowls and neck were thickening. But even by the standards of the March his pride was remarkable. His absolute confidence in his lordship seemed to smooth his way through impassable dangers. In battle what seemed arrogance was a fierce and overmastering confidence in victory.

'I cannot command you, Richard. Yet in honour I must ride with you, while you are within my lordship.'

'How far is your border?'

'By the Usk, towards Crug Hywel. It is there that Morgan is waiting. Then through the mountains, by the Gwryne, to where the river turns below the great beech wood.'

'That's the way I am going. Ride with me if you like.'

'And beyond, in Euas? Should we not wait for Pain to take you through?'

'I told you. I don't need your help. I have my friends and my minstrel. I shall go singing into Wales.'

Brian turned away. His mind had stopped at the mention of the minstrel. One of his own leper boys, Rafe, had a sweet singing voice and had learned many songs. He waited for Richard to collect his companions. They rode quietly out together.

When they were on the move, in the bright April sunlight, Richard's mood changed. He begun telling stories of the intrigues at Oxford: of the studied politeness to Stephen, a politeness always with a price on it; of the whispered soundings and indirections during walks between palace and castle; of the more direct, though still cautious, approaches when Robert of Gloucester had arrived with news of Matilda.

'It is a pretty game to watch,' Richard laughed. 'But with a Stephen on the throne we are like some creature of the tide – hard shell, soft centre.'

'We will try to keep the shell hard,' Brian said.

They were riding on the track above the broad river. They could see, ahead of them, the smoke of the Welsh fires in their camp up the Usk. Richard laughed as they turned away on the side track up the valley of the Gwryne. The country was now heavily wooded, with steep slopes rising to the mountains on both sides. The river was fast and stony, its sound close and soothing.

'Why should these Welsh dogs want this country?' Richard asked, looking around. 'What use could they make of it?'

'It isn't this country Morgan wants. It's the good rich land by Usk and Caerleon, which your brother is holding.'

'Well, since they're beaten they should take what we leave them. Let them have their mountains, we'll stay on better ground.'

The track was winding through dense oaks, where the sunlight darted. Beyond the oaks there was a long grove of holly, where it was suddenly almost dark.

'You called me Breton back in the castle,' Brian said, suddenly. 'Was there some meaning in that?'

'Only the obvious meaning, that you are Fitzcount and so Breton. And by that title you belong in this country. It was the noblest of the Britons who crossed to Gaul.'

'A very long time ago.'

'It is still the true history. In Oxford we heard a Black Canon. He has written the whole story of the kings of this island, from Brutus to King Arthur and beyond. We heard him reading from his book, and it was suddenly clear. The heathen Saxons broke in to interrupt the true inheritance. Now the island is being cleared again. We resume the legacy of Arthur.'

'Do you think the Welsh will believe such a story?'

'But this canon comes from Wales. He is half-Welsh, half-Breton, and bred in this country. He tells this true story of the great King Arthur, his castles and his knights. We have only to look at ourselves to see their true successors.'

'What is he called, this Black Canon?'

'I don't remember. Galfridus, I think. The first reading was in Latin. But someone said he came from Monmouth. And he certainly knows Caerleon, where King Arthur had his court.'

'I haven't heard of him. I could ask the Black Canons in our own priory, but they think little enough of history, at least when they are talking to me. Renders, depredations, abuses of privileges, are for them as common stock as the mass. Though my uncle founded them they blame me because Llanthony in Euas has outshone them. Llanthony, by the way, is not far from our route. If there's trouble it has walls we could quickly secure.'

'There will be no trouble. But perhaps, to make certain, we should bring this Galfridus to Wales. Let these barefoot dogs learn their real history. Let them learn that their only enemies are the

Saxons, and that we, Bretons and Normans, are their true friends and lords.'

Brian Fitzcount smiled, but as he turned away he covered his eyes.

Iorwerth shouted impatiently at Owain. His young brother, just thirteen, was having trouble with his pony as they rode across the ridge.

'You ride no better than your little sister Dyddgu.'

Gwalchmai leaned over to hold the young pony's bridle.

'He's never fair to me, Gwalchmai,' Owain complained. His voice was still high and unbroken.

'Yet he brought you with the troop.'

'Only because I begged Morgan. Morgan said I would be safer up here.'

'And if the Normans come this way?'

'I can use my bow. I've been practising.'

Gwalchmai laughed, and they rode to overtake Iorwerth, who had slowed and was looking down into the next valley.

'That is the Hodeni?' he asked.

'Hodeni, Honddu, I have heard both.'

'And that smoke?'

'The Black Canons. It is the abbey of the Lacys.'

They rode north along the ridge until they could see the abbey church, and the barns and dormitories around it. The stone was a fine light grey. The marks of its quarrying were still raw on the scarp. There was a wide clearing with fenced pastures around the buildings, but no sign of animals or movement.

'It's big,' Iorwerth said.

Gwalchmai dismounted. 'It was our Llandewi Nanthodeni,' he said. 'A small church dedicated to the Saint stood there for many centuries. Then some thirty years ago a knight William, of the kin of the Lacys, hunting this valley, came upon our church, which had been deserted in the wars. He was deeply moved by the place. He laid his sword in the water and he renounced the world. Yet the world would not leave him alone. The English queen's chaplain, the priest Ernisius, sought him out, persuasively. Within five years the Norman lords were making gifts of land and labour, to build a new church. They renamed it for John the Baptist of the wilderness. Two bishops consecrated it, but still the world pressed closer. The hermit

William could not resist. Within another ten years it was a large priory, with forty Black Canons. Queen Maud herself visited it. It became famous over all England. An archbishop who saw it said it had the finest cloisters, to the glory of God, that could be seen in the whole island. By cloisters he meant these high mountains of Euas.'

Iorwerth was frowning and his lips were pushed forward.

'It is still like that?'

'The fine buildings are as you see them. But most of the canons have gone. The people of the valley never wanted such an abbey. Their produce was taken to support it, and the gifts to God of many villages around, which were vowed to their own churches, were now harshly drawn in to support the French monks. Even the fish of Lake Syfaddon, and wide pasturage through the country, were given now to the Black Canons. To the queen and the archbishop it was a remote and holy place, away from the world. But to these people of Euas it was the place of their living, in the only world they had. While it was prosperous they resisted it, and the canons called them barbarians. But the more trouble they made the more the Normans stressed its importance, this seat of canons who would preach into Wales. The end then came quickly. While Pain of Euas was in England, all roads and tracks to the abbey were blocked. The whole foundation was put under siege. As food got scarce, most of the canons left. They are now sheltering in Hereford. Only two or three remain. They live now like the hermit from whom the place began.'

'It is another good sign,' Iorwerth said.

'But it was once a sign of laying the sword in the water.'

'They did not keep to it,' Iorwerth said, angrily. He put his hand on the hilt of his own sword. A rider was galloping towards them across the ridge. Gwalchmai remounted quickly.

'Quickly, my lord,' the rider was shouting. 'The Normans have been seen. They are coming this way.'

Iorwerth sat at the head of his troop on the northern edge of the beech wood, commanding the track where it climbed from the river through the trees to the ridge. After the scout's report, the disposition of the ambush was quickly made. Iorwerth took Gwalchmai to speak to the Euas bowmen, who still made him uneasy. Gwalchmai surprised him by speaking to them first about the fine buildings of the abbey.

'Who dug and carted the stone?' a bowman answered, fiercely.

'The French brought their masons.'

'The last edge of the work, that is all.'

'Did you not learn from them about building with stone?' There was a general laugh. 'It is very finely built,' Gwalchmai said.

One of the bowmen, an elderly man, stepped forward. He was smiling. 'Do you know the story, my lord, of the French house of Alarun? Its stones are finely dressed. There is a wall that seems not built of layers of stone but of a single great slab, as it might rise from the grass of the mountain. And Iddic of Ferdun went one day to the house. No water was given for his feet. No food was offered to him. "Is it not finely built, this house?" the French lord asked him. "It is indeed finely built," Iddic at once replied, "for its walls are so strong that a man might shout here for ever and still be offered nothing."'

Gwalchmai joined in the laughter. 'You are not of Ferdun?' he asked.

There was no reply.

'What is your place?' Iorwerth asked, impatiently.

'We are of Maenhebog, Lord.'

Gwalchmai signalled to Iorwerth to wait.

'There is a Derco, is there not, of Maenhebog?' he asked. There was no reply.

'What's the matter? Can't you answer? I have heard of this Derco.'

The bowmen waited. It was at last the elderly man who spoke. 'He is not yet here,' he said. 'But he will come.'

Gwalchmai turned to Iorwerth. Iorwerth lifted his sword and gave orders.

'The French will come by the track through the beech wood. We shall attack them on the ridge. I want you, saethyddion, to go now into the trees and conceal yourselves in their branches. I want you to let the French pass beneath you. Only when they have passed come down to the track, to cut off their retreat. Do you agree, saethyddion?'

'They will not see us, Lord.'

They ran, barefoot, to the wood, and disappeared among the trees. Iorwerth rode to the wood's edge until he could look into the valley where the Normans were riding. At last he saw the head of the column, its armour glinting in the sun. He watched the column closely through a break in the trees. He counted more than fifty horsemen. He ordered his foot soldiers back to the shelter of the ridge. He reserved for his own troop of horsemen the honour of the attack.

Brian and Richard rode up to the head of their column, as it halted at the ford. The line of the river now turned north, into a steep valley between the mountains.

'This is my border with Euas,' Brian announced. 'I would expect Pain to have watchmen, but as you see it is empty.'

Richard looked around. Above the heavily wooded slopes the tops of the mountains were fawn with dead bracken and black with dormant heather. The trees near the river were full of singing birds. Among the stones around the ford a dipper moved from pool to pool.

'There is nothing to watch,' Richard said. 'It is a defeated country, and barren.'

Beyond the ford, in the broad valley running east, was a wide marsh, covered with dark broken reeds, and with willows and alders at its edges. There was a rough hut beside a group of alders, and cut white blocks and peeled bark strewn around it.

'Some clogman, I suppose,' Brian said. He ordered one of his troop to ride across and inspect it.

'Nobody here,' the man shouted back. 'And the hearth is cold.'

Richard pulled himself higher in his saddle. 'We go on,' he said, offering his hand to take leave.

'Let us ride with you, Richard. At least to sight of Talgarth. You are so very few for that open mountain.'

Richard smiled. 'You are kind, Fitzcount, but it is a matter of honour. I am a lord of this land, and must ride it without fear.'

Brian shook his head. 'That is the kind of talk you heard in Oxford, from your Black Canon. A story of knights and chivalry, within strong castle walls. In this fierce place it is no more than a song.'

'Then let there be a song,' Richard answered, and called forward his minstrel, the young Breton Gawen, who carried his plucking crwth slung on his shoulder.

Leading his knights and grooms, Richard crossed the ford and rode quietly up the narrow track through the beech wood. Brian and his troop watched them go. Before they were out of sight there was the sweet high sound of the minstrel singing.

It was a song newly learned in Oxford, of the image of the Virgin Mary which adorned the shield of King Arthur, and was now borne again by a noble knight.

> Sur un cheval munta mult bel
> E fort e curant e isnel
> Pridwen, sun escu a son col,
> Ne sembla pas cuart ne fol
> Dedenz l'escu fu par maistrie
> De ma dame Sainte Marie
> Purtrait e peinte la semblance
> Pur enur e pur remembrance.

Richard smiled happily in the pleasure of the song. He glanced down at his own shield, bright yellow with three red chevrons.

Where the beech trees came closer, above the oak and ash and thorn of the valley, the rough track was steeper. Yet the ground was more open, without undergrowth, and with a thick wet layer of fallen brown leaves. The scent of the air was different in the beech wood. The minstrel sang again of a knight in the forest, remembering the vows of his quest and repeating them aloud to squirrels and birds.

Richard de Clare rode easily, at times closing his eyes. His knights attempted to follow his mood, but the grooms were looking anxiously around as they rode, staring into the higher branches of the trees. There was no sign of any danger. But they could hardly wait to be out of the wood on to the open mountain.

After the steep, slippery climb, the track broadened and flattened. Richard saw the bright arch of the last trees, and the dark skyline through it. The minstrel sang again: a lively hunting song.

They were out of the trees on the pale mountain grass when there was a shout from their left. Richard, swinging round, saw a horseman with cropped hair, wearing a brown and yellow checked cloak.

'What are you?' he shouted, as his knights and grooms closed around him.

'I am Iorwerth son of Owain son of Caradoc.'

'Then good day to you,' Richard said, easily. 'I am Richard, Lord of Ceredigion. I am riding in peace to the west.'

'You are Clare,' the horseman answered, 'and there is no peace for you in Wales.'

Richard looked around and smiled.

'Shall we disarm him, my Lord,' one of the knights offered.

'No, leave him. He can stay on this mountain, as these Welsh like to do, shouting the names of their fathers until they echo back to Brutus.'

Iorwerth raised his arm. The horsemen of his troop galloped out from the trees. They formed a line on either side of him. The Norman knights at once spread to face them, drawing their swords.

'What insolence is this?' Richard shouted. 'Do you dare to face one of your lords in arms?'

'It is for you I have waited,' Iorwerth replied. 'You of the brood of Clares, who are thieves in this country. You will not get to Ceredigion, to what you falsely call your lordship. Its true princes are already recovering it. I could spare your own empty life, but your brood still sits in the ancient lands of my kin. For we are of Gwent, from Mynwy to Severn Sea. We have read the signs, and Gwent will be ours again.'

Richard looked carefully around. With his grooms, who would fight, the troops were fairly equal in numbers. Yet he could still not believe that it would come to fighting.

'You heard us, Welshman, as we rode through the beech wood. My minstrel was singing, for we were riding in peace.'

'I am Iorwerth son of Owain son of Caradoc,' was the only reply.

'Very well, but now we will pass. We have no duties here. This is the land of the Lord Pain of Euas. If you have some complaint, pursue it with him.'

Iorwerth drew his sword. 'You refuse to understand me, Richard de Clare. I have been waiting here to kill you.'

Richard looked around and laughed. 'But why should you want to kill me? I am riding in peace.'

Iorwerth lifted his sword.

'Is there peace?' Gwalchmai called, on the sign.

'There is no peace,' the troop shouted in answer. As the shout echoed the footmen along the ridge stood and shouted in turn.

'My lord,' said Ranulf, Richard's foster-son, 'we must ride quickly back while we can.'

Richard smiled. 'Show no fear,' he said quietly. 'They may threaten, but they dare not attack. They have too much respect for their lords.'

Ranulph turned, impatiently, looking back down the track through the wood. A company of bowmen, barefoot in dark linen tunics, now stood across it, bows drawn. They stood in pairs, back to back, facing up and down hill. He swung round on Richard, pointing the full ambush. His foster-father's face was now deeply flushed, though his lips were still smiling.

'Come forward, Clare, alone,' Iorwerth called. 'It is between the two of us.'

Richard hesitated, but then slowly rode forward. He had still not drawn his sword.

'Whether you defend yourself or not, Richard de Clare, I will in any case kill you.'

'You cannot think of such a thing,' Richard answered, calmly.

Iorwerth hesitated. Richard continued to stare into his eyes, as if to command him. Ranulf, seeing a bare chance, drew his sword and rode hard at Iorwerth. The Welsh troop moved at once. The contending troops fought from their horses and ponies, around Iorwerth and Richard who still silently faced each other. Three of the Welsh and five of the Normans fell.

'Enough,' Richard shouted, and drew his sword and rode at Iorwerth. Iorwerth, waiting for him, slashed him across his thick neck. As Richard fell the other Normans broke and wheeled. They galloped back down the track. But now arrows flew in great numbers and men and horses were brought down. Ranulf, wearing armour, was confident that he could ride through these country archers. But two arrows pierced his breastplate as if it had been a cloth tunic. He was dead before he fell.

The Welsh foot soldiers now ran down, shouting, to finish off the wounded. In the confusion Gwalchmai, who had drawn his own sword, saw the young minstrel Gawen by the bare grey trunk of a beech tree. The boy's back was turned to the fighting. His face was pressed against the smooth bark. A big pikeman was running forward to kill him.

'Wait,' Gwalchmai shouted.

The pikeman did not hear him, but Gwalchmai rode above him and grabbed his shaft.

'Let the singing boy live.'

'He's a Frenchie, Lord, like the rest.'

'He will sing songs for us, if we ask him,' Gwalchmai said.

He dismounted and touched Gawen's shoulders. The minstrel looked round, alarmed. His face was very thin, under the long fair hair. His eyes were wide and frightened as he stared at greyhaired Gwalchmai and the pikeman. His fingers had closed convulsively over the strings of the crwth.

From among the dead and dying Iorwerth called loudly for Gwalchmai. As he turned to go, the bard ordered the pikeman to keep the minstrel safe.

'Well, it is done,' Iorwerth said. He was standing by Richard's body, with its gaping wound in the neck.

'Yes, this is done,' Gwalchmai answered.

'It was his stupid pride killed him. He seemed to think he was more than a man.'

'It is the fashion of our time,' Gwalchmai said.

Iorwerth looked away. The boy Owain was watching them, holding his small bow.

'There will be songs of this, Gwalchmai.'

'Yes, there will be songs: *After battle, bitter brooding*.' The bard knelt and looked into Richard's dead face.

'You say pride. I see that. But even more I see greed. He is fed to surfeit. The richness of his living bred his habit of command.'

'He was slow,' Iorwerth said, 'his shoulders were fat.'

Gwalchmai stood.

'In our most ancient times a warrior who became fat was heavily punished. It is different now. We have no choice but to be meagre, with what they have left us.'

'It will be different soon,' Iorwerth said. 'What has happened here today will sound through all Wales. The greatest Norman lord of the west lies dead on this mountain. Like a stone thrown into your Lake of Syfaddon his overthrow will spread to our farthest shores. The princes of Gwynedd and Deheubarth will sweep their lands clear. With their power at our backs we shall recover Gwent. While the Normans dispute their throne, Wales will at last be free again. I, Iorwerth son of Owain son of Caradoc, have thrown the stone and made this certain.'

Gwalchmai looked down again at the heavy body. 'You have made your own victory song,' he said, and turned away.

Iorwerth pushed his lips forward. He stood hesitantly looking around. 'We shall join Morgan,' he said at last. 'We shall ride on Abergavenny and then Usk and Caerleon.'

'By the lake?' Gwalchmai asked.

'Yes, by the lake. It has been a true sign. And you will see, Gwalchmai, as we pass, the birds of the lake will rise and sing for us.'

The Abergavenny Murders

◆

As Cadwgan at last appeared, on the rimed wooden steps of the neuadd, his long black hair still wet from washing and his deep blue eyes dark from lack of sleep, Tomos shouted loudly to fetch the lord's horse. It was already within yards of him, and had been saddled for nearly an hour. But as cais of Crug Cornau Tomos believed in constant discipline. The boy holding the horse might have to wait until his bones ached but when the lord appeared there must be instant readiness, and his own loud voice of command to mark the dutiful moment.

Cadwgan slipped on the frosted steps. It was a bitterly cold morning, though the sun was bright above Ysgyryd. The dazzling snow above the tree line was given an edge of colour by the pale blue December sky. Two women watching from the door of the church cried out as Cadwgan slipped. There was no danger of injury, but they were accustomed to watch for signs.

Tomos took little notice. It was no part of his duties to keep his lord to the mark. His job was to deal with defaulters and thieves — few enough, he could boast, since his appointment. The general order of the settlement — order and propriety — was his entire and unremitting concern. He knew little of political relations beyond Crug Cornau. If his lord was due to visit the new lord of Abergavenny it was only orderly preparation for his departure that mattered. What happened next was some other man's duty.

Cadwgan mounted and they rode together, along the track that followed the ridge of the moraine. Cadwgan's little grey mare was much smaller than the heavy black horse, traded from Hereford, which Tomos habitually rode. He had his weight to consider, he always explained. There was no man so tall and heavy within a day's ride. The boy Olen, on a young pony, rode after them, since when Cadwgan entered the castle he would be needed to look after the horses.

In the brisk cold air Cadwgan, slowly, came fully awake. He began looking around at the snow-covered mountains. He pointed to the ice over the pool and the reeds of what old people still called Lake Triley.

'Some good fowling there, sir,' Tomos observed, briskly.

'Yes, Tomos. Yes. We must think about that.'

Cadwgan withdrew to his own thoughts. They were past Blaengavenny, on the high road, before he spoke again.

'If this new Lord William had not come . . .' he began.

'Yes, sir?' Tomos answered, as Cadwgan still hesitated.

'For a whole year, Tomos, I have been looking forward to going to Aberteifi. The Arglwydd Rhys has summoned a great Christmas assembly of bards and musicians. I would still give anything to hear them.'

Tomos looked away. He knew his young lord's weakness for rhymes and fiddlers. It was harmless in itself, but he never seemed to recognise that most of that breed were little better than vagrants – at least those that came through Crug Cornau. Wasn't it recorded that when the new inn was built, between the mill and the neuadd, to serve travellers on the road from Abergavenny to Hereford, the first man hanged in it was a fiddler, a cwrthwr? He had seen the old entry: John Crowther, hanged for sheep stealing, August 1110. His brother James was gaoled for robbery with violence. There was still a story in the village that they were honest entertainers who had been cheated of their commorth of a ewe and had then secretly taken it. But Tomos had heard too many excuses like that. It was sixty-five years back, but they were the same today: wandering men, looking for easy pickings; deserving what they got if Tomos Cais laid hands on them.

'They are coming,' Cadwgan said, 'from all Wales and as far as Ireland. There will be wonderful performances. The Lord Iorwerth of Caerleon is sending his minstrel Gawen and his bard Peryf ap Gwalchmai. From all the lands of the Cymry the finest men will be there.'

Tomos hesitated.

'Other duties here, sir.'

Cadwgan smiled.

'The Lord William thinks so, Tomos. But then he is a Norman.'

'You have met him, sir?'

'No. But I knew his uncle Mahel, who was killed in the spring at Bronllys. William inherits through Bertha his mother, who is sister to Mahel.'

'His first lordship then, sir. He will want to get it in order.'

'No, Tomos, not his first lordship. Indeed quite the contrary. He first followed his father as lord of Radnor and Buellt. Through his mother he now gains Abergavenny and Brycheiniog. It is like a whole kingdom he now offers to rule.'

'Yes, sir. I understand. One of the greatest Lords of the March.'

'We shall see, Tomos. He may make changes. But his invitation to all the gentlemen of his lordship, the uchelwyrion, was very courteously and piously delivered. We are to meet under God to discuss our affairs.'

'Very proper, sir. Since he is an experienced lord.'

Cadwgan nodded. They were riding on the dip of the road at Pantygelli. Within the high banks the road was still icy. Cadwgan dismounted, but Tomos still rode beside him, tightly controlling his big horse.

'The question is,' Cadwgan said as he remounted, 'whether Seisyll is invited.'

'Which Seisyll is that, sir?'

'Seisyll ap Dyfnwall, of Castel Arnallt. Though it may all have been settled by now. There was a disputed mill when Henry of Hereford was lord. Henry objected to Seisyll keeping his own mill. All grain was to be sent to the mill at the castle. Seisyll appealed to ancient custom. The mill was one of *tri tlws cenedl*, the three jewels of the kin.'

'And very true that is, sir. As in our own case.'

'Henry took a troop to destroy Seisyll's mill. Seisyll counter-attacked. There was fighting and Henry was killed.'

Tomos did not speak but tightened his hands on the reins.

'It's a difficult history, Tomos. There were four sons of the great Miles of Gloucester: Roger, Walter, Henry and Mahel. Roger, who was Earl of Hereford and through his wife inherited Euas, died twenty years ago. And from then the whole family seemed cursed. Miles was shot by accident while hunting beyond the Wye. Walter was killed, it is said by treachery. Of the surviving brothers, Henry was killed in this fighting at Castel Arnallt and Mahel at Bronllys had a stone from the tower fall and crush him. It's a curious series of killings and accidents. If they were accidents.'

'There's a lot of carelessness, sir. If you don't look after . . .'

'A death from an arrow while hunting? A stone falling from a tower?'

'Accidents through lack of supervision, sir.'

'You think so, Tomos? Some have taken them for signs. Yet, however that may be, only the sisters still lived. That is how our lord William has inherited. And I think it hardly likely that he has forgotten the killing of Henry. All the French, of course, blamed Seisyll.'

The slope of Deri, with the white peak of Penyfal rising glittering beyond it, now bordered the road. The long back of Ysgyryd shone blue and white in the sun. Across the broad valley the clefted curved hill of Blorenge was shadowy white. On a mound on the bank across the wide water meadows of the Usk, the castle of Abergavenny stood out clearly.

Tomos held his reins close.

'A difficult situation, sir. It will need putting in order.'

The fire in the centre of the hall burned brightly in split ash blocks. In the spaces between the oak pillars, which ran in two lines the full length of the hall, square tables were set with drinking cups and large central mess plates. Small open windows were set in the two gable ends. Through the southern square a shaft of sunlight caught wisps of the blue smoke that hung below the rafters. At an oblong table set directly below this window, so that he could see down the length of the hall, William de Braose sat alone, receiving each guest as he came forward to announce his name, lineage and place.

The guests had been received at the doorway by the constable of the castle, wearing his ceremonial keys and sword. Each guest, by custom, laid down his weapons and his cloak, before joining the file to go forward to the lord. Cadwgan warmly greeted his neighbours, Iddon of Arwallt and Tewdwr of Llancadog. But their attention was focused on Seisyll ap Dyfnwal, three ahead of them in line.

'It will really be a new start,' Iddon whispered, 'if Seisyll is welcomed.'

'I wonder he dared come,' Tewdwr said, looking away.

Two big hounds lay sprawled between the fire and the high table. The guests had left their own dogs and horses with their attendants, outside the palisade. All were conscious of the strict laws of hospitality and courtesy. They were determined, in this change of the lordship, to get every detail of ceremony right.

Old Gwrfoddw, of Cressenniau, was calling his name, title and lineage. His deep voice filled the hall. Lord William, exceptionally, rose and leaned across the table to shake the old man's hand. As he stood Cadwgan saw that he was short for a Norman. He was in his early twenties, with smooth fair hair and a clipped beard on the line of his chin. His teeth were small and regular in an attractive smile. His skin was unusually rosy and clear, almost translucent as he rose in the shaft of sunlight.

Gwrfoddw walked back, smiling. Arnallt of Ynysgynffraidd succeeded him, and it was then Seisyll's turn. Lord William did not rise but held Seisyll's hands between his own for an unusually long time. He seemed to be speaking earnestly beyond the expected formalities.

The knights of the lord's household, who were ranged in waiting along the eastern wall, had turned to watch as William greeted Seisyll. Then, as Iddon's turn came, and Tewdwr and Cadwgan prepared themselves, the senior French knight stepped forward and began showing the guests who had already been presented to their tables. Cadwgan watched the arrangement. Welsh custom was being followed. Three to a table: two Welsh and one Norman. Tewdwr also watched the arrangement and now nodded his approval.

When Cadwgan's turn came he was surprised by the coldness of Lord William's hands as they enclosed his own. But the smile was open and friendly, and the formal words were pleasantly spoken. He was shown to his table, two below the fire, where he joined Tewdwr and a young Norman knight, Robert FitzPain. Robert had no Welsh, but he bowed and smiled to them.

The last presentations were being made. As they ended William rose and signalled to the constable. A black-gowned priest, the prior of Abergavenny, entered and walked to the High Table. The company stood as he intoned a long Latin grace. When he had finished the prior sat by Lord William, on his right hand. William signalled again and the constable admitted a long line of servants, carrying drink and food.

Cadwgan observed the servants curiously. They were French in appearance. They wore brown belted tunics to their knees. They served stewed venison into the central mess dishes, and placed bread before each guest. They filled the pewter cups with red wine. As the feast began three minstrels entered, and played and sang as they walked between the low tables.

Cadwgan and Tewdwr drank and ate heartily, dipping their bread and then their hands in the mess plate. Robert FitzPain, watching them, made some joke in French, which they did not understand. When he repeated it more slowly Tewdwr understood and laughed.

'He says the Welsh only eat when they are not fighting, but then they are as fierce at one as at the other.'

Cadwgan smiled. Down the length of the hall, past the rising smoke of the fire, he was watching William de Braose. The lord was eating very little though he was drinking heavily. He was spending most of his time talking earnestly and repeatedly to the elderly prior, who sat morosely over his food.

Cadwgan wished that he could hear this intent, earnest talk, which looked like some kind of persuasion. But in the general noise of the feast, and through the music of the minstrels, he could see only the moving lips. It was William's youth that most struck him. For all the luck of inheritance, such youth was surprising, in the great resonance of his titles. The powerful lord of Radnor and Buellt, of Abergavenny and Upper Gwent and all eastern Brycheiniog, looked simply a raw youth: neat and small and fresh-faced. Yet he leaned to the Black Prior with a concentrated, settled intensity.

The food and wine were replenished. The guests ate, drank and relaxed. At a signal from the Constable the minstrels ended their music. They bowed low and left. The servants were now lined along the walls. The fire began to die down.

Lord William rose. The company eased into silence.

'In God's name peace to all here,' he called.

His voice was loud and clear. The guests appreciated the compliment that he addressed them in good Welsh.

'Under God,' he continued, 'I have good Welsh blood in my veins. For my great-grandmother Nest was grand-daughter of the noble Gruffydd ap Llewellyn, whom the Saxon Harold killed. The Lady

Nest was given in marriage to the valiant conqueror Bernard of Newmarch, and already in those years Philip de Braose was the Lord of Radnor and Buellt. The lineage is clear, my dear friends. I am as proud of mine as you in this country are of yours.'

Gwrfoddw of Cressenniau clapped his hands.

'By God,' William said sharply, 'we have at last finished with those clods of Saxons. We are well set, my dear friends, for a lasting peace. You do not yet know me, but you will come to know me. My whole life, under God, is the keeping of peace.'

He turned to the Black Prior, as if inviting his support. The prior's head was bowed, as were some others of the guests, after the heavy meal. The prior did not look up at William but only stared, unmoving, at his hands on the table.

'By God,' William said, looking back at the company, 'there is true ground for peace in this lawful and honourable succession. All who keep this peace are my brothers. With the blessing of Holy Church, the good laws of our peace will be strictly and lovingly observed.'

He again turned to the prior. The old man did not look up.

'By God,' William said, 'I have the authority of the King himself, and of Ranulf Lord Sheriff of Hereford, to keep our good peace in this country. No title of lordship remains in dispute. What we have now to fear is not claim or policy but only a different lawlessness. The petty lawlessness of banditry.'

Cadwgan looked across at Tewdwr. Robert FitzPain was watching them, smiling.

'By God,' William cried, striking his hand on the table, 'and by the direct ordinance of King Henry himself, you are here, each one of you, to swear a solemn oath. The words of the oath will be read by the constable.'

The constable spoke from the doorway.

'I swear by God,' he read, 'and on peril of my body, that no travellers in this country shall bear any bow, or any other unlawful weapon.'

The whole company was suddenly silent. William, looking intently round the hall, spoke again.

'You have heard the oath, which your King and your lord require you to swear. You will now, in the order in which you were presented to me, come to swear this oath, on your body, before this holy prior.'

There was a long silence. Then Gwrfoddw of Cressenniau rose.

'My Lord, you have received us kindly. We also came in kindness and friendship. We offered our loyalty, and you graciously received it. But this oath you now ask of us is a very different matter. It strikes, my Lord, at our hearts.'

'At your hearts, Gwrfoddw? By Christ, do you understand nothing? The bow in this country is the very weapon of treason. No lord or gentleman relies on the bow. We have swords and lances, which are the weapons of honour. The rough bow is the weapon of the peasant behind the hedge, or of the outlaw hunter in the forest, or of the bandit and enemy of the peace. Is it such wretches, Gwrfoddw, you hold in your hearts?'

Gwrfoddw remained standing.

'You are new to this country, my Lord. Though in Radnor and Buellt you might have learned it, the bow, my Lord, is the arm of this country. Yes, it is drawn by peasants and hunters. But in all the wars of our freedom, our defence has come first from the bowmen of Gwent. They are not enemies, my Lord. They are the arms of our peace.'

William stared at Gwrfoddw, but did not immediately answer. He looked across at the long lines of servants, who remained close and unmoving by the walls.

'By God,' he then shouted, 'this is not a matter for argument between us. It is an ordinance of the King which you are required to swear.'

Gwrfoddw remained standing.

'All who will swear now stand,' William ordered.

None of the Welsh lords rose. Gwrfoddw stayed on his feet, but his neighbour whispered to him and he quickly sat down.

'You are right, I am new to this country,' William said, calmly. 'But I am not new to its crimes. Sitting among you, accepting my peace, is the man who murdered my uncle. Seisyll ap Dyfnwal, do you hear me?'

'I hear you, William de Braose. I killed a thief who was attacking the mill of my kin.'

'Seisyll ap Dyfnwal, you will now swear the oath that the King has commanded.'

Seisyll got up. He turned towards the doorway. The Norman knight of his table at once got up and blocked his way.

'By God,' William shouted, 'this is the last chance for any of you. All who refuse to swear are guilty of treason, for this is King Henry's command. Any refusal is a choice of immediate death.'

Several of the Welsh now jumped to their feet. The Norman knights of their tables rose with them. But Iddon of Arwallt had raised his fist and was shouting.

'You cannot threaten us, Frenchman. We are your guests and unarmed.'

'By God, a thief on the gallows is unarmed,' William shouted back.

'You call on God, Frenchman,' Iddon shouted again. 'It seems that His name is never out of your mouth. But as Christians we have shared your bread and your wine. We have laid our swords at the entrance to your hall. We have come in fair play, and we have listened in fair play. We will discuss anything you wish, but we will not be threatened.'

There was a loud cry of assent from the other Welsh lords. William stood staring down the hall. The square of sunlight above his head had faded. His young face, which had been angry, seemed to smooth and settle into acceptance.

'By God, it is no threat,' he said quietly.

He nodded to the constable. At once the men who had been acting as servants drew daggers from under their tunics. Rushing forward in line from each side of the hall they attacked the Welsh guests. Several were quick to defend themselves, but the knights at the tables now joined in the attack. Cadwgan fell among the first, stabbed to the heart.

Tewdwr, breaking free, threw a jar of wine at the dying fire. The liquid hissed in the embers, sending up acrid smoke. Lifting a stool, and moving back to back with Iddon of Arwallt, Tewdwr fought his way towards the door, to recover the Welsh swords. But now a line of mailed soldiers guarded the doorway and the weapons. Down the hall, in the smoke and the shouting, more Welshmen were falling in the savage assault. Swinging the stool in front of him, Tewdwr broke through the line of soldiers, into the cold air of the bailey. He shouted for help to the attendants beyond the palisade. But the footbridge was now barred and heavily guarded. The attendants, already confused by the shouting, had no real chance to help.

Tomos, among them, drew his dagger and ran to the bridge. But already Norman lances were projecting above the heavy wooden barrier. Tewdwr, still shouting, was attacked from behind. He fell with two soldiers on top of him. From inside the hall the loud shouts and cries were continuing, but no other Welshman got out. Among the acrid smoke and the debris of overturned tables, among the scattered remains of the feast, fourteen lords of the kin of Upper Gwent lay dead or dying.

'By God,' William de Braose concluded, picking his way through the bodies and the debris, 'this is indeed the day of dialedd, the day of the vengeance of the Lord.'

The sky had clouded over and there was a keen wind from the east. Standing together for protection, the sergeants and grooms and their boys looked anxiously into the castle. They had seen the killing of Tewdwr, but many still expected to see their own lords reappear. Though ready to ride they were prepared to wait, as they had so often waited.

There was a movement at the bridge. The barrier was pulled aside and a troop of armed horsemen galloped out. Tomos jumped forward, lifting his dagger. Others drew their bows. But the troop did not ride towards them. It wheeled to the track, which ran east towards Usk, galloping furiously. On the footbridge the heavy barrier was pushed back into place.

At Castel Arnallt, five miles down the Usk valley, Gwladus, second wife of Seisyll ap Dyfnwal, was awaiting her husband's return. She had with her their son Cadwaladr, a boy of seven.

Seisyll's first marriage was to Dyddgu, sister of Lord Iorwerth of Caerleon. Gwladus had also been married before, to Caradog ap Iestyn who was murdered in Morgannwg. As a daughter of the hero Gruffydd ap Rhys, the Lady Gwladus, now in her forties, had known every phase of changing power in the March. She had supported Seisyll in his resistance to Henry of Hereford, during the attack on the mill. But she did not fear the coming of William de Braose to Abergavenny. She was secure in the protection of her brother Rhys, Yr Arglwydd, who was all powerful in South Wales. Even as she now waited, Yr Argylwydd was host to the great

Christmas festival of music and verse in Aberteifi. In the lesser
lordships there was often dispute and uncertainty, but the high
French Lords of the March knew the value of the friendship of
Yr Arglwydd Rhys. The affair of the mill would be settled, as so
often before, by some form of compensation. William's friendly
invitation of Seisyll to Abergavenny confirmed that.

Wearing a heavy red-and-black coat against the cold air from the
river, Gwladus sat with her bondwoman Megan in the open doorway of the ystafell, the private room beside the small wooden
neuadd. They were watching their cais, Ifor, showing Cadwaladr
how to use a small bow he had made for him. It was not of elm, like
the fighting bows of the country, but of hazel, which the boy's arms
could draw.

Ifor had been a fighting bowman before taking service with
Seisyll. He was very proud of his new position, though he irritated
Seisyll by preferring to call it *serjeant*, in the French fashion, or by
adopting the French pronunciation *keys*. Like many others of his
kind he was both hostile to the French and impressed, overawed,
by their capacity in weapons, in building, and in the manners
of lordship. 'A Norman castle,' he often said, 'is as far above
a Welsh one as a good lowland manor above a rough tract in
the hills.' He was in favour of those Welsh lords, and especially
of his Lady's brother, Yr Arglwydd Rhys, who were develop-
ing power and establishment in the still independent Welsh
courts.

Gwladus laughed as Cadwaladr succeeded in drawing the bow,
his face stiff with concentration, but then failed to let go of the
arrow as he released the tension. Ifor did not laugh. He took the
arrow and settled the boy's small fingers on its shaft.

'Each hand,' Gwladus heard him explaining, 'each hand must be
its own master. But though each is its own master they must then
move together.'

Cadwaladr said nothing. He wanted no further instruction. He
believed he could get it right by himself. Gwladus and Megan
watched as he again drew the bow, his feet planted sideways, the
string drawn back to his shoulder. The feathered arrow flew high
but not far. Cadwaladr ran after it to shoot it again.

There was the sound of horses galloping along the track from the
north. Ifor, looking down over Cadwaladr's head, saw a troop

come out of the trees and ride hard for the castle. Gwladus jumped up.

'Is it my Lord?' she called to Ifor.

'No, my Lady, these are French.'

Gwladus ran forward to see more clearly. The horsemen were mailed and helmeted. The knight at their head had a big red cross on white on his shield. They were already through the open gatehouse and into the small bailey. Gwladus ran and picked up Cadwaladr. Holding the boy in her arms she ran to the ystafell. Megan stayed close beside her. Ifor, still holding Cadwaladr's small bow, walked confidently across to the troop, which had halted.

'Which is the Lady Gwladus?' the leading knight demanded.

Ifor did not answer. He was looking, surprised, into the knight's face.

'Will you oppose us with that toy?' the knight shouted down at him.

'Oppose you, my Lord? We are the servants of the Lord Seisyll and at peace.'

The knight dismounted. He had now seen Gwladus and Megan and the boy. He walked across to them. He was a tall, red-haired young man, with narrow features and pink mottled skin.

'The Lady Gwladus, wife of Seisyll ap Dyfnwal?' he asked with a slight bow.

'I am the Lady Gwladus, and sister of Yr Arglwydd Rhys.'

'Is this boy your son?'

'He is my youngest son Cadwaladr.'

The knight looked round at his troop before stepping closer.

'You must give me the boy, my Lady.'

Gwladus held Cadwaladr more tightly.

'He is a male heir,' the knight continued, 'of the traitor Seisyll ap Dyfnwal. He is now under the protection of Lord William de Braose.'

'Who are you to say this?' Gwladus cried. 'My husband is no traitor.'

'Your husband is dead, my Lady. We are now taking his male heirs.'

'The Lord Seisyll cannot be dead. He is a guest of Lord William.'

The knight did not answer, but reached for the boy. The

bondwoman Megan at once pushed between them, but he struck her aside.

'You will do better to let me have him.'

'Never.'

'In that event I have a further order.'

Gwladus looked at him over her boy's shoulder. With her right hand she smoothed his fine hair.

'Is it the honour of a French knight to ride and seize children?'

'The children of a traitor, my Lady.'

'My husband is no traitor, and my brother is Lord Rhys, Yr Arglwydd Rhys, the King of Deheubarth, of South Wales.'

The Knight turned and called two men forward. As they advanced they drew their swords. Ifor, bewildered, now ran to stand in their way. The first soldier drove his sword into Ifor's stomach. Ifor fell.

'For the last time, my Lady,' the knight now said.

'No, you will not have my child.'

'Then no one shall have him,' the knight shouted. He drew his dagger and stabbed the boy in the neck.

Gwladus, still holding the bleeding child, screamed and turned to run. The soldiers overtook her and, pushing Megan aside, tried to pull the boy from her arms. As she resisted she fell, with Cadwaladr on top of her. He was still alive but blood was spurting from his neck. His mouth hung open.

The soldiers knelt and pinioned her arms. She kicked out violently. The knight bent and lifted the boy. He held the fine dark hair at the crown and quickly cut the boy's throat. Gwladus screamed repeatedly but the soldiers dragged her up and bound her wrists.

'Can you kill only children? Kill me,' she screamed.

'We are to hold you unharmed, my Lady.'

'When you have killed my child on my breast? So little a boy, just a child?'

'We have our orders, my Lady.'

Since she had been pushed aside, Megan had disappeared inside the ystafell. She now came running out, holding a long kitchen knife. She attacked the soldiers who held Gwladus. The nearer reached for her wrist to disarm her but the sharp blade slashed his palm.

'Be cursed,' Megan cried. 'All who ride to this evil are cursed.'

'Get the bitch,' the knight shouted, as Gwladus struggled from his arms.

Megan again raised the knife.

'By the blood of this innocent, cursed!' she screamed. 'And cursed beyond all the devil who sent you! He will lose his land and he will die starving. The seed of his body will rot in the dark!'

The second soldier lifted his sword and struck the knife from her hand. As she threw herself at him he thrust his blade into her stomach. Gwladus screamed again as the knight overpowered her.

The second soldier, now seeing that Megan was dying, lifted the body of the child. It was so light that he could hold it under his left arm. He carried it and bound it behind his saddle. Gwladus was forced across and her ankles were tied before she was lifted to lie across one of the larger horses.

The knight shouted a new order. Several men dismounted and went to the kitchen hearth. They came out with torches and began setting fire to the wooden buildings. The neuadd and ystafell were soon blazing, and they went on to every hut, stable and watchtower in the bailey. The servants of the castle ran away from the sword and the fire.

As the black smoke rose and drifted, westerly in the cold air, the troop remounted and rode to the settlement by the river below the castle. They found the place deserted. Seeing the fire from the castle, the families had fled into the woods. Every hut and barn was now set afire. The disputed mill was thoroughly broken down and its big grindstone was wheeled to the river and sunk. The winter granary beside it was burned. The troop then rode to each tref on Seisyll's estate. At each place they burned the huts and barns, and the pigs in their sties. As they left each tref, the knight stood in the saddle and shouted, though no one appeared to hear him.

'After treason, starvation! Learn and obey!'

When the last village on the border of Seisyll's territory had been ransacked and burned, the troop reassembled in close order. Gwladus, bound on horseback, was unconscious but still alive. The knight raised his shield with the red cross. They rode steadily north, beside the Usk, the report their success to William de Braose.

'He is said among all the French to be a most godly man,' Hywel ap Cadwgan repeated to Tomos.

'He killed your father,' Tomos answered, stubbornly.

'I have not forgotten,' Hywel said. 'But it is now known that the killings had been ordered by the king and the sheriff.'

'Then they are all guilty, sir. Innocent blood is not to be forgotten.'

'I am not forgetting it, Tomos. But we must understand this man. The name of God is present in every sentence he speaks. If he sees a child by the way he stops and speaks to him of Christ. Indeed he begs the child's hand on his own, to be blessed by his innocence.'

'Then he is a blasphemer as well as a murderer.'

'You are blunt, Tomos. Is he not still our liege lord?'

'Until boys grow to men,' Tomos said, staring at him.

Hywel looked back, smiling. Tomos's huge body had stiffened but was still very powerful. At the belt of his black tunic the dagger and keys marked his office. In the seven years since his father was killed in the Abergavenny massacre, Hywel had relied on Tomos for all his dealings with the men of the manor, though his mother still made all the larger decisions. Now, grown to nineteen, he continued to rely on him, though he found him increasingly narrow, obstinate, and morose.

'Come back here, Tomos,' he called, as the cais walked away.

Tomos turned.

'Can't you see what's in front of your face? That boys have indeed grown to men?'

'Men are what they do,' Tomos answered.

Hywel hesitated, then went forward and gripped the big man's hand. 'I have news, Tomos.'

Tomos did not respond.

'The Lord Morgan ap Caradog has returned from Cernow. He had called the sons and grandsons of all those murdered by William de Braose to ride in an attack on his castle.'

Tomos looked into Hywel's face. The young man was very like his murdered father Cadwgan, with the same dark, tired eyes and weakness of will. Like Cadwgan also, he thought more of music and poetry than of power and order on the estate.

'Yes, Tomos,' Hywel said, as if he had heard his thoughts, 'I shall ride. William has gone east, with half his soldiers, to help the sheriff of Hereford build a new castle. It is the perfect moment to attack.'

Tomos grunted.

'You don't think so, Tomos?'

'No, I don't. What's the point of attacking the den when the beast is away?'

'To destroy his castle, Tomos, and his goods. To strike at the base of his power.'

'That is no revenge for the death of a father.'

Hywel frowned.

'You don't understand these affairs, Tomos. By the laws of compensation for homicide . . .'

'This would be no compensation. It would be only looting and destruction of property. It is the man himself who should pay, in blood.'

'No, Tomos, that is barbarism. To kill in war is honourable, but in civil offences . . .'

'Civil offences, sir! I stood with your father's little grey while he went in as a guest, laying his weapons at the door. I waited, in good order, for the lords to complete their affairs. I then heard the screams as that beast murdered them, slack and heavy with meat and with wine. Nothing now, sir, will answer to my duty, but the blood of the murderer.'

'It is not for you to decide, Tomos. The lords of the country arrange such matters.'

Tomos looked away. 'I will do my duty, sir. But I am experienced in managing men. And I know that justice must be direct, or there is no possibility of order. William de Braose abused his great lordship, in betraying its lawful duties. If that is not punished, what order can there be, down to the lowest assailant or thief?'

'I have told you, Tomos. We shall ride to destroy his castle.'

'To burn a few buildings, while the murderer is away.'

'I have told you, Tomos.'

Tomos clenched his fists.

'I will ride with you, sir, as I rode with your father.'

'Thank you, Tomos.'

They rode that afternoon. From all the districts of Upper Gwent the Welsh rode into Abergavenny. They assembled west of the castle. There were horsemen with lances and four companies of bowmen. From Castel Arnallt, Morgan ap Caradog had brought scaling ladders.

In early evening they rode openly to within bowshot of the castle.

Morgan himself, with Ifor ap Gwrfoddw, Maredudd ap Tewdwr and Sitsyl ap Eudaf rode up to the palisade. The great gate was already closed. They rode round the high timber walls, above the solid earth bank. They stopped with particular interest at the southwest corner. While they were staring and pointing at this place the constable of the castle appeared on the parapet. Beside him, tall and gaunt, with cropped white hair, was the Welshman Adda ap Ynyr, who had entered the service of William de Braose.

'You are here against the law,' the constable shouted down.

'No, no,' Sitsyl called. 'Just looking it over.'

'With lancers and bowmen in call?'

'It's a lovely day for some exercise,' Morgan shouted.

'You'll get plenty of exercise if you dare come near us,' Adda called, in his thin, high voice.

'Go back to your praying, Adda,' Sitsyl shouted. 'Or have you forgotten the Welsh for God?'

The constable moved impatiently. He turned and beckoned below him. A line of armed soldiers climbed to the parapet beside him.

'Go now,' he shouted down. 'Go back to your homes.'

Maredudd ap Tewdwr jumped from his horse. He went to the edge of the ditch and pointed to the bank and parapet.

'We shall come in by here tonight,' he said, cupping his hands.

The constable and Adda ap Ynyr stared down at him.

'Just giving you fair notice,' Maredudd said.

He turned and walked slowly to his horse. His companions laughed as they wheeled and rode away.

As darkness came the Welsh lit fires in their camp. In the castle also there were the lights of many fires. Soldiers with torches were patrolling the parapet.

Tomos followed Hywel to the fire where the leaders were gathered. They were talking and laughing about the renegade Adda.

'You watch,' Ifor was saying, 'the first sign of life tomorrow will be Adda stripped naked and praying in the mud.'

'Shan't we be in by then?'

'No, no, he gets up at first cock. Then he goes out bare as a skeleton and presses his forehead in the dirt. He prays something dreadful, they reckon. "Evil," they hear him shouting, over and over. "Evil, Evil."'

'In Welsh still?'

'Aye. Drwg, Drwg! That old barncock don't know what he's started, raising his own bit of pride on his dunghill. Just the one harmless crow and this naked madman comes out. Drwg, drwg, in the mud! Even the cock wonders how he keeps skin and bone together. He touches no meat or wine, he'll have only bread and water. More a ghost than a man, they all say in the castle. But then wait till there's a fight. This naked madman takes his sword and fights like the devil himself. Fierce and fearing nothing, and his temper and language as foul as sin.'

'When he's killed his fill,' Morgan said, 'he can go back to shouting drwg with a conscience.'

'No, that would be a reason. In Adda there's only madness,' Hywel shyly suggested.

'Don't get too serious about him,' Ifor laughed. 'Let the old cock have his crow and then we'll have ours.'

'They're expecting us in the dark,' Hywel said.

'Aye, aren't they?' Maredudd said. 'Since I told them so nicely. So let them wear their bloody eyes out.'

The main company laughed. Only Tomos frowned.

In the heaviest darkness the bowmen began crawling forward. There were bushes and scattered undergrowth above the ditch in the southwest corner, where Maredudd had said they would attack. The bowmen hid in the bushes and settled to sleep. The next movement forward was the men with the scaling ladders. They had to stop, often, when the patrols on the parapet were looking their way. They could hear regular shouts in the castle. The whole garrison was awake and alert. At last the laddermen also were in position and settled to sleep.

The cockcrow came before first light.

'Now he'll be up and shouting,' Ifor said.

He was standing with his troop of lancers, who would go in when the bridge had been captured. In the cold darkness nobody laughed. Ifor pretended to listen for the loud cries of 'Evil'. But there was only the general noise of the defenders, as they stood prepared for the night assault.

Grey turned to pale yellow in the east above Ysgyryd. Then yellow faded to grey again. Along the river a low mist was rising. A thin daylight steadily increased.

'Right, we ride,' Ifor ordered.

His troop mounted, noisily, and rode away from the castle. Around them the other horsemen were also up and moving away. They took care to be seen from the parapet. When they were out of sight, behind trees, they halted. Morgan ap Caradog and Sitsyl ap Eudaf had crawled forward with the laddermen. They now watched the parapet. After a while the torches were put out. The constable came up and looked carefully around. It was now full daylight. There was no sign of Adda. After a further wait the constable gave his orders. The patrols stood down.

Morgan held up five fingers. As he lowered each finger in turn the laddermen and the bowmen made ready. When he at last clenched his fist the laddermen ran for the ditch and the bank. The bowmen stood with arrows drawn. The first ladder went up to the parapet unseen by the defenders. As the second ladder went up there was a shout from the keep. The bowmen aimed high, over the parapet into the bailey. The laddermen were now scaling the wall, holding daggers. As they reached the parapet the bowmen ran forward. They rushed up the ladders and spread out. Overlooking the bailey they began rapid fire. Every man in each company could fit and shoot five arrows a minute. The tired soldiers running from the huts took this hail of iron-tipped arrows. The daggermen ran above the hall to the gatehouse, where they killed the guards and opened the gate. From the wood beyond, the lancers were now galloping.

Sitsyl, on the wall, saw the constable running with his wife from the ystafell. Calling to the bowmen, he ran to intercept them. The constable immediately surrendered. Sitsyl forced him to his knees.

'Where is mad Adda?' he shouted.

'I don't know. I don't know.'

The bailey was now filled with the triumphant horsemen. Only the keep, on its mound, was uncaptured. The bowmen were ordered to shoot at its window slits and at its heavy door. Sitsyl was preparing a direct assault, up the long flight of steps, when the first building in the bailey was suddenly fired. It was the hall in which William de Braose had murdered his guests.

'Wait,' Sitsyl shouted, 'we must take the keep.'

'Wait if you like,' Maredudd shouted back, 'but I came to burn this place of blood.'

'In good time, in good time,' Sitsyl shouted.

The excitement of the burning was taking hold as fast as the flames. Everywhere, now, the wooden buildings of the bailey were being set to the torch. The lancers began pulling their frightened horses away.

'Who is in the keep?' Morgan shouted to the constable, trying to retain command.

'There is no one of importance. The Lord William is away.'

'At Llandinegat?'

The constable did not answer. Morgan kicked him in the stomach.

'He is with the Lord Sheriff,' the constable gasped.

'At Llandinegat?'

'At what you call Llandinegat. The name of the place is Dynastow.'

'Take them and keep them close,' Morgan ordered.

The constable and his wife, with more than twenty other prisoners who had run from the buildings, were marched outside. The bowmen were still shooting at the keep, but now Morgan ordered them back.

'We will ride to Llandinegat,' he shouted to the lancers, 'and finish the job.'

Tomos heard the command. He had not entered the castle. In the rush of horsemen to the gate he had at first followed Hywel. But they were among the last of the converging troops. When they reached the bridge the bailey was full. Tomos dismounted and waited for orders. He was only a few yards from where he had waited for Cadwgan and heard the cries of murder. As flames broke through the thatched roof of the hall he watched steadily, but he did not cheer with the others. He was waiting for young Hywel to return.

'We told you we'd come in by there,' Ifor mocked, riding across and grinning at the manacled constable.

Tomos gazed at the flaunting young lord.

'Only we were a bit late, unfortunately,' Ifor laughed. 'It was the fault of that mad Adda. We were relying on him stripping and shouting "Evil" to wake us up.'

The constable stared at the ground.

'Where did he get to, that Adda?' Ifor mocked. 'The great praying man, and he didn't pray. The great fighting man, and he didn't fight. Was he safely locked up in your keep with the women?'

'Adda ap Ynyr,' the constable said with dignity, 'would not stay behind barred doors if it was his duty to fight.'

'Then where did he get to?' Ifor asked, letting his horse step forward so that it was pushing the constable's legs. 'Did he show himself at last a true ghost and slip away through the mist?'

Morgan was now shouting for the horse troops to assemble. Hywel, flushed with excitement, rode back. Tomos at once mounted and followed him. The prisoners were left with one company of bowmen. The other bowmen were ordered to follow to Llandinegat. The horsemen moved out east, singing, along the track below Ysgyryd Fach.

William de Braose woke early. It had been a cold night, wrapped in a brychan under the half-built timber wall of the new castle. Ranulf Poer, Lord Sheriff, and the other noblemen of Hereford still slept beside their swords within a ring of their soldiers. The many peasants who had been conscripted for digging and hauling were also asleep, huddled close to each other within the deep ditch.

No news of the storming of his castle had reached William. The Welsh horsemen under Morgan, learning from their countrywomen the size of the Norman force, had halted to wait for the bowmen. But they took care to set guards on the tracks from Abergavenny. Before dark they captured two English burgesses, Fletcher and Skinner, who after the burning of the castle had set out to warn their Norman lord. The bowmen eventually arrived, late in the day. Everything was made ready for a dawn attack.

William climbed the rough scaffolding of the wall. He looked over the surrounding country. The land in this valley of the Troddi, running east to the Wye, was attractive and potentially very rich. Its yield, like that of the whole lordship of Monmouth, was already much higher than in any of his own extensive lordships, which contained so much mountainous land. Moreover it was relatively easy to hold. By granting Welsh rights of succession and custom, an effective peace had been secured very early.

Yet all that had come of it, William thought irritably, was a concentration of Bretons, like these weakling Baderons. All Bretons were insufferable, in their claims to be better able by descent to manage the Welsh. But while King Henry was still alive, and that damned justiciar Ranulf de Glanville, sitting comfortably in Monmouth, there was no chance of turning them out. Later, and especially if Prince John gained more influence, something appropriate might be done. It would be a natural continuation from his lands of Abergavenny.

William looked across at Ysgyryd, that damned hogback mountain that the Welsh called Holy. By God, they were still mostly pagans and wild men, setting mountains and rivers before the name of their Saviour! He froze on the thought, for by a wood at a mile's distance there were bowmen marching. As he looked more closely, he saw horsemen with lances following a treelined track.

He jumped from the scaffolding and ran through the muddy bailey. He kicked the trumpeter awake. He shouted his own alarm. The soldiers were slow out of sleep. The old Hereford noblemen were merely bewildered. But William was at once on the wall, shouting orders against the attack. The peasants in the ditch, hearing the trumpet alarm, were gathering up their tools and running away up the valley.

William looked out, coldly, as the full Welsh force came slowly into sight. There were three companies of bowmen and at least four troops of horse. He ran for his squire and sent him riding hard to Monmouth, to rouse the justiciar Ranulf to bring reinforcements. He went back to resume command, but now Ranulf Poer had taken over. The sheriff had sent his own troops forward to the ditch, and, like a fool, was himself going down there. William shouted a warning but the sheriff, brusquely, told him to keep to his place. William formed up his own troop, inside the bailey and the half-finished wall. He found a position commanding the main entrance. He mounted and drew his sword to guard it.

The attack came in very fast. The hail of arrows was heavy, but most were being aimed at the troops in the ditch. There was then a high wild cry of the charge of the lancers. William waited, braced to meet them, but as they reached the track to the gatehouse they rode left and right into the ditch itself, their lances thrusting down on the foot soldiers lying there.

William rode slowly forward. The ditch was already bloody with death. He saw Ranulf Poer stuck like a pig. An elderly official was trying to run along the ditch, but he was ridden down. The Welsh bowmen were now regrouping and shooting into the bailey. William saw a chance to bring his own troop forward and get in behind them. He turned to signal them forward. In the same moment a crushing weight fell on his back. He pitched forward into the ditch.

Tomos had stayed close to Hywel in the charge. But as the others spread to the ditch he jumped from his horse and scrambled up the wall. He wanted to see what was happening inside.

He was crouched, looking in, when he saw a smooth-haired Norman, obviously a lord, ride slowly forward to look down at the fighting. Squatting above him, Tomos judged his distance. Then he jumped on him. He wanted to pin him on the ground but as the horse shifted the Norman's body pitched forward and rolled into the ditch. There was a shout from the bailey, and Norman horsemen were riding forward.

'Lord William,' one of them shouted.

Tomos stood looking down. The body was inert. Another body had already fallen across it.

'Lord William,' the horseman had shouted. Tomos caught his breath. Was this short, smooth-haired creature the murderer William de Braose? He drew his knife and started down the ditch. But the Norman horsemen from the bailey were already streaming through the gateway. Tomos, slipping in the mud, saw a sword raised above him. With a shout he threw his whole weight into the flanks of the sweating horse. But he could not avoid the blow. There was a sharp pain along the side of his skull. He saw darkness before he fell.

The battle went on around him. The Welsh continued to dominate it. After the heavy killing in the ditch they rode out to meet the challenge of the Norman cavalry. Much of the fighting moved well away from the castle, in scattered charges. Then the Normans withdrew behind the wall. Morgan collected his cavalry and ordered the bowmen to assemble. But many of the men were now tired and he decided to rest them.

They were still resting when Norman reinforcements, led by Ranulf the justiciar, rode in from Monmouth. After a brief engagement, in which they set the gatehouse and another tower on fire,

Morgan decided to withdraw. The day had been theirs, with so many Normans killed. There would be another day.

The old man sitting on the bench by the mounting block of the neuadd of Crug Cornau could feel the warm sun on his face and hands.

'Tomos,' a voice called.

Tomos shook his head. It seemed to be the voice of the young Lord Owain ap Hywel. The voice had only lately broken. Tomos put his hands to the bench and lifted himself to his feet.

'No, Tomos, don't get up,' Owain said. 'But I have someone here who can give you news of your hero.'

'What hero is that, sir?'

Owain smiled to his companion. They looked together, smiling, at the old, blind man.

'Perhaps I shouldn't have said hero,' Owain said, still amused. 'But everyone knows that you have this man on your mind.'

Tomos clenched his fists. 'What man would that be, sir?'

'William de Braose, of course. For thirty years, my mother tells me, you have thought of hardly anyone else.'

Tomos loosened his fingers. He reached down to feel the edge of the bench. Owain stepped quickly forward and helped him to sit again.

'I'm sorry, Tomos. I shouldn't have made a joke of it.'

'It is not thirty years,' Tomos said, turning his blind eyes upward. 'It is thirty-seven, by my count, since your grandfather Cadwgan was killed by that devil.'

'In the massacre at the castle?' the companion asked.

Tomos turned towards the new voice.

'This is Iestyn ap Madog,' Owain said. 'He is riding with messages from the Middle March to his Lord Rhys Gryg. And he has news of William de Braose.'

'What news could there be?' Tomos said, sadly. 'William de Braose is not of the world of men, or I am not of it. The Saviour of Men, who is so often on his lips, is not my Saviour, or that man would not have lived so long in so great a sin.'

'You will not believe my news then?' Iestyn asked.

'Sir,' Tomos said, 'since that winter day when I stood by my horse, waiting for my unarmed lord who was never to reappear, I have had little enough cause to believe in anything. For a time I believed in the justice of revenge, but that slipped away. Just seven years after the murder of my lord I had the murderer's body lying open before me, and I then still had my eyes. But his Saviour still guarded him. If I had only drawn my knife as I jumped from the wall . . .'

'Now, Tomos, you are blaming yourself, not our Saviour,' Owain said.

'His body slipped from my hands, sir. I would have followed and killed him but the saving blow fell. My sight was taken from me so that I could not find him again.'

'You acted in honour,' Iestyn said. 'Even your blindness now honours you.'

'No sir, forgive me. It is only a darkness. It leaves me blind and helpless while for thirty-seven years that murderer has lorded our country.'

Iestyn stepped forward. He kneeled before Tomos and took his hands between his own. 'It is ended, Tomos,' he said, quietly. 'William de Braose is dead. He starved in exile in France. It is true that he lived long to profit by his murders. But no story is known till its end. In cruelty and intrigue he came indeed to seem immortal. After more than twenty years of lordship his crimes were still astonishing. He still killed his guests. In his castle above Llyn Syfaddon he seized my kinsman Trahaearn Fychan and bound him by the feet to his horse's tail. He dragged him to Brecon and cut off his head and hanged his body.'

'If I had only drawn my knife . . .' Tomos said.

'There are many knives,' Iestyn said, earnestly. 'William was very close to the evil King John. They were together in Normandie when the boy Arthur, the true heir, was secretly murdered. We do not know by whose knife. But later, when John and William had quarrelled, William's wife Maud said rashly that she knew this bloody secret. In that moment our vengeance was sealed.'

'Those are other places, sir, and other victims. Our vengeance did not come.'

Iestyn held the old hands more firmly as they tried to pull away. He looked into the wrinkled face. There were folds of heavy reddened flesh on the thick neck.

'Even the killer wolf, Tomos, at last meets a stronger. It is happening now to all these brute Normans. With his secret at risk, King John hunted William de Braose. The hunt raged through the islands like the Wild Hunt of the Twrch Trwyth, of the legend. Through Wales and through Ireland and Scotland the King hunted William and his family. At last he captured and imprisoned his wife and son, and demanded a great ransom to release them. William could not pay and escaped to France. The King put the woman and her son into chains. He threw them into a deep dungeon, with a little bacon and water. They lived in that darkness until they starved. It is said that Maud, mad with hunger, tried to eat the body of her dead son.'

'They were, after all, the King's guests, Tomos,' Owain said.

The old man said nothing.

'Hearing this news in France,' Iestyn continued, 'William de Braose starved himself. He is dead, Tomos, and as the curse of Megan said he would die.'

Tomos pulled away his hands. Iestyn was surprised by the strength of his arms.

'It is the end of the story,' Iestyn said. 'A just end.'

'You think so, sir?' Tomos said, getting up.

'It was a bitter end for so proud a man.'

'But with his last breath,' Tomos said, 'he would have called on his Saviour.'

'He would not have been heard. He would have been dragged down to Hell.'

'I think not, sir. I think Lord William de Braose was loved by the Lord.'

'What are you saying, Tomos?' Owain asked, anxiously.

Tomos got up. He walked past the two young men.

'Is there sun still on Ysgyryd?' he asked, in his old deep voice.

'Yes,' Owain said. 'But there is also the shadow of a cloud, moving across the face.'

'I see it as you speak, sir. When we attacked the castle at Abergavenny we expected to meet a Welsh lord, Adda ap Ynyr, who fought with William de Braose. We did not find him, although it is known that he was there.'

'I have heard the name,' Iestyn said. 'He still served with William de Braose, long after the attack.'

'He would rise naked at cockcrow and cry "Evil" into the darkness around him. Everyone said that he was mad.'

'He sounds mad enough.'

'He was a traitor, but not mad,' Tomos said, and lifted his arm towards the mountain. 'He was crying to his Lord, who protected him. As they have all been protected. The power of men is very small against that evil tribe, which can call on the name of its Lord.'

'No, Tomos,' Iestyn said. 'Even the worst of those men has now fallen.'

Tomos turned towards the voice.

'Sir, I was trained to order and to serve order. In its service my very sight was taken from me. But still the evil order flourishes, the greater over the lesser. In my darkness I cannot say with the prophet: now I die in peace. For there is no peace and no Saviour. I die in darkness.'

Owain hesitated. He moved to go forward, to take the old man's arm. But Iestyn stepped in front of him, shaking his head. They turned together and walked away.

GLYN TO ELIS: 12

$\blacklozenge$

'By this incident I demonstrate to you the faith of the Welsh. While you hold the sword they will submit, when they hold it they will command.'

Staring into the darkness, under the extending cloud, Glyn remembered these apparently straightforward but surely cynical words of Walter Map, 'a dweller on the Marches of Wales', in reply to a question from the great Chancellor Thomas à Becket: 'It is a reproach to a son that his father died without a wound. For which reason few grow grey. There is a Welsh proverb, Dead young man or Poor old man, meaning that a man should brave death early rather than beg when he is old.'

The heavy cloud reached over almost the whole sky. Even the guiding shapes of Skirrid and Sugar Loaf were barely discernable. It was now difficult to move at all. Though his eyes had adjusted to the darkness, the path was narrow and uncertain. When he stumbled on a stone and almost fell, Glyn knew that, not only for himself but for Elis, he must wait until by some clearing of cloud or in the still distant dawn he could walk safely and search usefully. He found a low bank rubbed bare by sheep. There were innumerable scraps of torn and matted wool, lying on the red earth like a parody of a quilt. He shone his torch over them. He could pick out particular objects but that was different, in this country, from finding his way.

It was not Map but his hard words that had first come to mind. Yet in the century of blood, which is reckoned as the twelfth after Christ, all the writers of this border are memorable. Map himself and Gerald the Welshman, and, in a different way Geoffrey of Monmouth belong in their essence to this bitterly fought frontier. Within and through the fighting, there is intricate contact between the diverse and hostile cultures. The vigorous hybrid that grows in this blood-drenched soil is different from the cultures, east and west, where the endless conflicts are mounted. In its dislocated time it is a culture which reads and prefigures a changing world. In its running together of distant sources, the swirls and eddies of its joining of diverse springs, what emerges, beyond foreseeing, in the country within sight of these mountains, now flows strongly, with its own force, into the mainstream of Europe.

It is easy to return its elements to the separate, more powerful cultures, which have the intellectual advantage of an identity of State. Free Welsh and Anglo-Norman are simpler, more plausible, more persuasive entities. Yet the growing point in this century is the difficult traffic between them. Within this long tension, the writers of the border find something different from both yet more influential than either. Here at the edges of intrigue and devastation, of repression and revolt, new voices find new words.

The poetry of the Welsh is honoured and long-standing. Yet in the wars of the independent kingdoms, against foreign invaders, but also against each other, the verse of honour often becomes bombast:

> The wounded heaped from that lord's red spear,
> And the musters of England, and combat against them
> And their destruction in wild disarray,
> And the rising to fame of that bitter sword
> In seven score languages, long in his praise.

The formal rules are strict and intricate, but the perspective, the substance, narrows: 'Our histories are written not by schoolmasters or monks or apprentices, or any base persons, but by noble bards, nobly descended barons, and fellows to lords and princes.' The predominant tone is elevated but strained:

> Sons of Gruffydd, valour in battle,
> Your violence long, dragon of Euas,
> For your fullness of rank I praise you,
> Everyone praises you, kingdom's head.

Endlessly harping on battle, it can admit only the blood of its enemies:

> I saw their ruin, three hundred dead,
> I saw, battle done, bowels on thorns.

As the honour of a people becomes the rant of a prince, the intricate history of these mutually destructive battles slips away under the stilted meters.

There is other verse, less highly regarded, both east and west of the March. There are lovesongs and cradlesongs, choruses of drinking and hunting, poems of landscape, but still in the West the battlesongs override them. In the East meanwhile, such songs are the entertainments of leisure, gracenotes before and after relentless killing, cruel management of men and of land. One scholar accounts the main literary achievements of this Norman order as the first great lawbook. *Tractatus de Legibus et Consuetudinibus Regni Angliae*, attributed to that Ranulf de Glanville who led the force to rescue William de Braose in the Welsh attack on Llandinegat, and the detailed account of the management of the King's Exchequer, the *Dialogus de Scaccario* of Richard Fitzneale. It is a simplification but it catches the drift of the time, whose energy flows into detailed and exhaustive management of property, through repeated military conquest. It is in the line of descent from the Doomsday accounting of William the Bastard. In the West against it, stand only the savage formalities of a proud and desperate resistance.

Soon sadness intervenes ever there.

> I have often had gold and brocade
> From mortal lords for singing their praise,
> And the gift of song gone, powers failing,
> Stripped of wealth my tongue fell silent.

So it is that the ravaged March, where the enemies confront but also talk and deal with each other, new strains come through. In the courts of the many lordships there are now professional translators and interpreters. Beyond their necessary business, of power and property, old and diverse sources converge and change. From the West itself, as the shock is absorbed, the formalities of the Beirdd y Tywysogion, the Poets of the Princes, are overtaken by an older and richer vernacular tradition, which now passed from word of mouth into writing. The oldest legends of the kin, from a distant world in which the other world is close, in which magic and shapeshifting are historic modes of action and revelation, are collected into script but also altered and rewritten. The distant gods and heroes are half translated into kings.

The Four Branches, the *Pedair Cainc y Mabinogi*, interweave the myths of the kin with stories of a wider provenance. The ancient tale of the young hero Culhwch, seeking to marry Olwen daughter of the giant Ysbaddaden, is spliced with a story of King Arthur and his knights, who carry out the necessary impossible tasks, among them the hunt of the Great Boar, Twrch Trwyth.

'I will pursue him no further,' Arthur said, 'but I will join with him life for life.' And by his counsel a body of horsemen was sent, and the dogs of the Island with them, as far as Euas . . .

Thus the Artorius remembered in earlier Welsh refrence as a tyrant and destroyer becomes, by mutation, the magical fighting hero. He will soon, to the world, be the King of Honour and Freedom.

And now Galfridus Monemutensis, the Black Canon overheard by Richard de Clare in Oxford, appears as Geoffrey of Monmouth, of Breton descent. As a young man in Gwent he has access to the records being collected at Landaff in its long boundary dispute with the diocese of Hereford, a boundary running across these Black Mountains and settling, still disputed, on the Dore. Land grants to churches by the old native kings, including the grant of Merthyr Clitauc, are recovered from the records. They are also in some cases forged. Geoffrey, writing in Oxford, claims to have been given, for his *Historia regum Britanniae*, 'a certain very ancient book written in the British language'. This book is not known, and may not have existed. But the stories exist, not only from old Gildas or the collection attributed to Nennius: many stories, stories retold and adapted, stories newly shaped, stories imagined or forged. A renaissance begins, in its usual mixed, retrospective and original, creditable and discreditable, serious and boldly invented forms.

The central figure of the mediation is King Arthur. William of Malmesbury declares him 'a man clearly worthy to be proclaimed in true histories', as distinct from the popular stories that are told from mouth to mouth. Yet this prefers a doubtful true history to the fable that becomes historically effective. It is Geoffrey, in Oxford from Gwent, who projects the phenomenal king. Geoffrey's own second name, or that of his father, is Arthur, a Breton name. But the hero he fashions has a European resonance. He is the King of Britain, defeating Saxons, Irish and Picts, but he also crosses the sea to conquer Gaul and march on Rome. He is restrained only by the treason of Mordred and the adultery of Guinevere. In little neighbouring Caerleon, down the Usk, a fabled golden city receives the submission of all the princes of Northern Europe. Honour is absolute, with this small land as its centre. Yet, as the story is told, the land is known as lost. A magician is summoned from the darkness of the legends to prophesy general ruin, through the 'twelve mansions of the stars'. Ancient triumph and future disaster intertwine like the Dragons, Red and White, which contend for the mastery of the island. The Usk runs boiling hot for seven months.

Thus the shape of the invention traces the blood of the frontier. But then in turn its romance is appropriated. Arthur's famous sword Caledfwlch becomes Caliburnus and then Excalibur. Before the end of the century the Norman King Richard, on his way to crusade, presents the very sword to Tancred of Sicily. It has been dug up just in time at Glastonbury.

Myrddin, who lost his reason after a vision during a battle, becomes the prophet Merlinus and then Merlin the magician. The Norman writer Wace adapts Geoffrey into his own language, and introduces the Round Table. In neighbouring Worcestershire the English Layamon rhymes the tale to a different conclusion. Chrétien de Troyes expands the cast, adding Lancelot, Perceval, Tristram and Iseult. What may have been a magic cauldron becomes the churched Holy Grail.

In this swirling of romance other, more concrete, links are forged. The bodies of a tall man and woman are disinterred at Glastonbury. It is fifty-five years after Geoffrey's story. They are ceremonially reinterred as Arthur and Guinevere. A Norman king, fighting both Scots and Welsh, claims them as noble predecessors in the recovered Kingdom of Britain. His Anglicised successors see Arthur as the once and future King of an enclosing and dominant England.

So an ambiguous romance, which is also a tragedy, becomes a myth of sovereign power. But when it is being written what matters is a resonant loss of identity. Geoffrey is a Breton in Gwent. What descent, what identity, is that? Gerald de Barri is the son of a Norman lord and a Welsh lady, Angharad, grand-daughter of Yr Arglwydd Rhys. Walter Map of Erging has a Norman father and a Welsh mother. The blood lines cross and eddy.

Gerald and Walter are very different from Geoffrey. The

handsome and popular Gerald becomes court chaplain to Henry the Second. He negotiates for him, along the contested frontier, with the Welsh princes of his family connection. He travels through Wales with Archbishop Baldwin, raising recruits for the Crusade. At Abergavenny he sees the iron-tipped Welsh arrows, which pierced the great oak door of the keep, during the attack on the castle of William de Braose. At Caerleon he sees the ruins, not of an Arthurian capital but of a Roman legionary fort. He hears also of a prophet of the neighbourhood, not Merlin but Merlinus, to whom horned spirits appear, hunting souls. He reports slily, that when these evil spirits oppress Meler too heavily, a gospel is laid on his body and they vanish like birds. But if the *Historia regum Britanniae*, by Geoffrey of Monmouth, is laid there instead, they instantly reappear in much greater numbers.

But this sceptical, mobile and wordly man ends his life fighting as Gerald the Welshman, Geraldus Cambrensis, for the right of the Welsh to an independent bishop of their choice – himself. He wants the Pope of Rome to restore the lost identity of the old British Church. In his famous *Description of Wales* these shifts of perspective are written deep into the matter. The Welsh are 'more quick and cunning than other inhabitants of a western clime'. Their sweet music charms and delights. Their rhetoric is subtle and ingenious. Their confidence in speaking contrasts with the 'inward coldness of disposition' of the English. At the same time they have no respect for truth or for the sacredness of oaths. They live by plunder and theft and by moving boundary ditches. They are severe in attack, but cannot bear a repulse. This way and that the perspective moves. The stance, the identity, engages and withdraws. Still he concludes that the English fight for power, the Welsh for liberty.

Walter Map, sceptical and worldly like Gerald, a wit and collector of tales, an itinerant judge and later archdeacon, never identifies so closely. But again a double vision is evident.

My compatriots the Welsh, though wholly unfaithful to every-body – to each other as well as to strangers – are *probi*. I do not mean morally good or especially strong, but in the fierceness of their assault and the keenness of their resistance, only *probi* in *improbitas*, prodigal of life, greedy of liberty, neglectors of peace, warlike and skilled in arms, eager for vengeance; most liberal of all goods, very sparing of food to themselves and lavish of it to others, so that everyone's food is everyone else's and none among them asks for bread . . .

Probing and shifting, praising and denouncing, identifying and alienating, these voices of the border express their true time, at the only level which has left written traces. Gathering stories and embroidering them, in Gerald and Walter, finding stories and heightening and vastly projecting them – a Lear as well as an Arthur – in Geoffrey, they move through a mobile, unidentified, intense and cruel land, of which Merlin has prophesied that the mountains and valleys will be levelled and the streams in its valleys run with blood.

The towering romance projects the double vision. The cool chronicles record it. The language is Latin, still the *lingua franca* of these men of many languages, living in a border country where Welsh, Norman French, English and Breton are spoken within sight of these mountains. Geoffrey's romance makes secular and pseudo-historical the legendary but still moving and mysterious vernacular. Gerald and Walter write a cool, observing prose, picked up in movement from place to place and story to retold story. Theirs is a detachment from attachments which are always newly perceived and negotiated. They are all writers of a border, who can move either way.

Glyn shifted and stretched his legs. In the west, perhaps, the cloud was now thinning, but there was still little enough light. A fragment of matted wool had stuck to his hand. He shone his torch into its fibres.

Augustine says: 'in time I am and of time I speak, and what time is I know not.' With like wonderment I may say that in the Court I am and of the Court I speak, and what it is I understand not. Hell, they say, is a place of punishment. So too the Court is a place, but is it one of punishment? Of a truth it is, and only in this respect milder than hell, in that those whom it torments are able to die.

Walter Map in his least common but most emphatic voice.

I know however that the Court is not time. Temporal indeed it is, unstable and various, stationary and wandering, and in the diversity of its composition often unlike itself. When we leave it we know it thoroughly. If we stand out of it for a year, a new face meets us on our return and we ourselves are new. We find natives ousted by strangers and masters by their servants. The Court indeed is the same, but the members of it are changed.

See this layered sandstone, in the short mountain grass.

The Monk's History

◆

The high, sharp call was like the cry of a bird. Conan heard it as a sound before he made out his own name. He walked to the edge of the tower roof. He had come into the summer sunlight to read the old charter in its difficult Welsh hand. Far below, on the grass of the bailey, Eirwen was calling him again. Her face was turned up to him, inside the broad white cap. He smiled and waved, but she only swung her arm, impatiently, for him to come down. Beyond her, near the gateway, Rhodri was standing with Hywel. Rhodri was looking steadily across at his mother. He did not look up at the tower.

'I'm coming, cariad,' Conan called. His deep, hoarse voice surprised him, in the still air. He looked down past the wall to the ripples and currents of the rushing Rhiangoll. Several women and girls were kneeling at the washing-place, with its broad flat sandstones. A line was stretched between three ash trees, in a surprisingly regular triangle, and white and brown washed tunics stirred in the light breeze. Beyond the washing he could see the broad green valley of the Usk, taking in the bright Rhiangoll. There was a cloud of blue smoke on the hillside above Crug Hywel. Conan followed its rising towards the high ridge of Pen Cerrig Calch. His eyes moved back along the tops to the green rise of Pen Allt Mawr and the spur of Pen Gloch y Pibwr.

He turned from the sweet air to go down by the narrow and dusty stone spiral. Eirwen would not have called him while he was working unless something important must be decided. It was obvious, from the roof, that it concerned Rhodri.

He gripped the rolled document as he watched his feet down the narrow steps between the dusty walls. The charter seemed genuine enough: a grant of lands confirmed by Genillin – in that curious spelling – to the churches of Llanbedr, Llanfihangel Cwmdu and Merthyr Issui. It was the name Issui that had caught his attention, following the fragment naming an Isseu, hermit of the holy well above the Grwyne, who, before the Norman descent, had cured a pilgrim of leprosy with its cool sacred water. He had been left a hat full of gold to build a church in thanksgiving.

It was the usual doubtful account of an origin, except for the addition: that Isseu was later murdered at his well. So there was both a well and a murder, at Merthyr Issui as more famously at Merthyr Clitauc. Yet the strange names, Isseu or Issui, might be threads into that much older labyrinth, where pagan and Christian walked side by side in the shadows. Isseu, Issui, Esus. Esus was the name that should not be spoken, that most powerful of the Gods who was also, in the Fourth Branch, Math.

Conan came, still stooping, into the bright sunlight. He was of middle height and broad shouldered. His lustrous, curling black hair had only recently changed to a pure white. Eirwen immediately poured out her story. Sir Roger Picard, still in the assembly at Pipton, had sent back his sergeant with orders for twenty more bowmen. Rhodri and Hywel, as soon as they heard, had offered to go. So Conan must now stop them, forbid it. As the son of a clerk Rhodri had no obligation. And it was a campaign into England, far England, that the lords were preparing. Conan must tell him at once to forget the whole idea.

Conan put his arm over Eirwen's shoulders, comforting her. He looked across the stretch of grass at the boys. Each was just nineteen. Boys, bowmen. All the complexities of generation seemed to dance in the sunlight. He was a man of fifty-nine with a wife of thirty-seven and a son of nineteen. At Pipton, across the mountains, a king of fifty-eight was said in effect to be senile. Holding that third Henry was a man a year younger, Simon of Montfort, who was said to be offering a transformation of the realm. Conflicting, stubborn wills of these men in their late fifties, and then bowmen, restless boys, called up to resolve them.

A conflicting will here also: Eirwen's fierce, loving care for her son. That was entirely natural, but Conan still found it hard to see the larger choices as real. How could any honest man connect with these struggles, endless but invariably promising an end: this last effort, this decisive victory? It was turbulent to re-enter them from the recorded, alternative world of Genillin and Issui or Isseu. But it was an entry he now had to make, as an advising, a deciding father.

Rhodri was standing awkwardly, with that familiar adolescent bend of one knee. His face was lowered but his eyes were looking up. His arms were loose and uncertain.

Conan left Eirwen and walked across to him. 'What was the actual message?' he asked authoritatively.

'That twenty more bowmen should join the troop.'

It was Hywel who replied. Rhodri only looked anxiously into his father's face.

'But there are plenty of trained men. Neither of you is bound to arms.'

'The sergeant says the bound men are all trying to get out of it, saying they have the shearing and dipping of the sheep, and the calves' weaning.'

'Yes, it is what gets overridden,' Conan said.

'What do you mean, father?'

'I do not mean the obvious end of that argument,' Conan said, carefully. 'For then you, without flock or herd, would consider yourselves free. Yet you are free only in that absence. The military service is still not your duty.'

Rhodri shifted his feet. 'Father, you can always spin your arguments,' he said, his face reddening. 'But to us it's very simple. Are we to stay here all our lives, in this back of beyond? Shall we never get a chance to go out and see the world?'

'Do you think it's the world you'd be seeing, Rhodri?'

'It would be a change, anyway, from being shut up in Tretwr. Staring at the same old mountains, watching the years going past like empty clouds.'

Conan looked away. 'Your mother does not want you to go.'

'Of course. But I'm not a child.'

'She's afraid for your life. Can't you see that?'

'If we don't take a chance we shan't have any life.'

'Are these battles the only life then? Prince Llewellyn and Baron Simon, and lords and knights on this side or that?'

'They've got King Henry as a captive,' Hywel said excitedly, 'and they've put Prince Edward in gaol in Hereford. They say they're going to free the whole country.'

Conan looked sadly back at them. Eirwen had come close beside him, and was holding his arm.

'I cannot put you in gaol,' he said sternly to Rhodri. 'But I give you no permission. I forbid you to go.'

Rhodri stepped back. 'That's easy for you, isn't it? You just stand there and give out your orders. But it's the lord who's asking for men. And when it happened for you, you chose your own way.'

'That was different, Rhodri,' Eirwen said, intervening.

'Not so different, Mam. He wanted to change his life and he did it. He took his own responsibility. Now he won't let me take mine.'

Conan stared between his feet at the pale, warm grass. His mother and father had been drowned, off Quiberon, when he was nine years old. His mother's brother Alain, a Black Canon, was about to travel to Wales, to join a house where new preachers were urgently needed. With consent from his order he took the orphaned boy with him, to Llanthony.

Conan grew up in the priory within a single future, of joining the order himself. Alain taught him to read and write, and he had added spoken and written Welsh to his native Breton and church Latin. The library of the priory had a large collection of church and secular documents, as well as several books. Much of Conan's boyhood and adolescence was spent in the library and the muniments room. His ambition settled to becoming *scholasticus*, when he was old enough to take his vows.

The man now looked back at this studious boy as at another life: one which had realised its future, but in ways then unforeseen.

He had taken his vows and joined the preaching community of the priory. It was a time of great activity. The buildings of the new establishment were rising on all sides. The original settlement of William and Ernisius, so prosperous and fashionable in its first thirty years, had declined after the fighting of the 1130s when Richard de Clare was killed by the Welsh on the mountain above. A daughter settlement, Llanthony Secunda, was established near Gloucester. It flourished while its mother continued to decline. In the end only the old and the incompetent were sent to the remote upland valley. They were so poor that they were often short of clothes and even food, while the daughter house was still rich.

Then at last there was a revival. The rich Walter de Lacy, lord of

Ewyas among many other lands, extended his father's patronage of the remote Llanthony Prima. New buildings began to be raised. To the revenues from Lacy estates in Ireland were added the tithes of the whole Honddu valley in which the priory stood. There were added also the holdings of Oldcastle, Walterstone and Newton; the fishing of Lake Syfaddon and the pannage of distant Maescoed; the rectories of Llancillo and of Merthyr Clitauc. Rights of management and of justice passed from the lord to the priory. Llanthony acquired its own court of law, with jurisdiction in all offences of murder, assault and breach of the peace, of rape, arson and theft, and of illegal native hunting. It had its own coat of arms, of three oak branches stemmed on a rose between two pinks. From the gathered tithes and fines came the finest new priory buildings. It had its own gallows.

It was the year 1215 when Alain brought Conan to Llanthony. By 1230 the modern priory was complete. In the final phase they built slype, chapterhouse and prior's lodge. Conan grew up among the scaffolding and the hammering of masons. He became an Austin Canon but he did not become *scholasticus*. Though the buildings were fine, the number of canons was small and declining. As well as regular preaching service, they undertook the many new duties of landlordship and management and law. For the old hostility of their native tenants, free and customary, had never died down. There were endless, even daily, disputes about stolen animals and shifted boundaries.

Conan was now generally known by his adopted religious name Teilo. His choice had been questioned, but he had argued that the name of the Welsh saint who had long ago sailed to Brittany was appropriate to a Breton canon now serving in Wales.

After his uncle Alain's death, Teilo was increasingly turned to as interpreter and mediator in disputes and trials. He was the only canon with command of colloquial Welsh. Thus, instead of the life he had foreseen, in library and muniment room, he became in effect a bailiff, sent here and there on the priory's business. There would be a disputed weir or disputed measures at a mill. There were counts of flocks and controversial diversions of streams. There was management of the retting of flax downriver.

He took on this daily work in God's name and in the trust of his House. But his qualification for it – that he could speak easily and freely with the people – was also, through the years, the source of growing doubts. After an especially tangled and bitter dispute at the mill at Cwmyoy he asked the Prior to allow him to resign this work. He wished to return to reading and contemplation within the priory walls. His request was refused. But a year later, in 1235, when he was just twenty-nine, he was sent as resident priest to the church of Merthyr Clitauc, across the mountain in the valley of Mynwy. This had been, unexpectedly, the decisive move of his life.

'Father Teilo, look!'

The high, sharp call was like the cry of a bird. Conan, who had been lying on the grass in the warm sun, rose quickly on his elbows. Eirwen was standing to her waist in the pool above the weir, lifting a dripping sticknet above her shoulders. Two large brown trout were twisting and thrashing inside it. The water that still streamed from the net was bright and dazzling in the sunlight. Eirwen swung the net, and her loose red hair swung in the same movement. Conan stared, unable to speak.

The weir, with its rush of water, was just below the church. Beyond the quiet brown pool the oaks of Fyrddin rose steeply. Over the pool itself, with its broad flat sandstone edges, alder and hazel dipped to the water, past a haze of flies. The steady rhythmic swish of the weir and Eirwen's sudden sharp cry were isolated sounds within a deep well of quiet. Conan could not speak, but his whole spirit was smiling.

'Ei,' Eirwen screamed.

Conan was on his feet and running as her first slip on the mossy wet stone turned to a tumbling fall. He was in the water and wading against its cold resistance as she threw out her loose arm, struggling to right herself. The fish were still in the net. He reached her and caught her shoulders. With more force than he intended he lifted her clear of the pool. He kept her in his arms as he walked with short steps, his soaked tunic dragging at his legs, to the grassy bank by the old martyr's stone.

He put her down and sat beside her. He could still find no words. Though she was soaked, in her linen tunic, and even her hair was wet, her first thought was still of the fish. She leaned forward and raised the net. Conan, watching her closely, saw that the usual light red of her hair had darkened in the wetting. It was like the building stone in this valley, which darkened with rain. Her skin was very pale, even paler than usual. The freckles on her forehead stood out more clearly. Her mouth was open and breathlessly laughing.

'Thank you, Father,' she said, and quickly kissed him on the cheek. He sat very still, quite bewildered. He saw her get up with the net and take the fish to the stone by the bank and kill them. He saw her take a brown trout in each hand, leaving the net on the grass. It was as if he was watching another life, from some hiding place in the wood. Or as if no knowing watcher, no self, was present, but only the being he now watched.

A constriction stabbed in his chest. He had been holding his breath.

'Well, tell me,' she said, coming back and standing above him, 'tell me how lovely they are.'

He looked up. Some words came.

'What?' she asked, still smiling and asking for praise. It was only then that he realised that he had spoken in Breton. But he was glad it had been so.

'Father Teilo,' Eirwen said, picking up his confusion and demanding attention.

'Forgive me,' he said, quietly.

'Forgive you? What for? When you just pulled me out of the river?'

'You are soaking wet, Eirwen. You should go in and change.'

'No, I'm not going to. I'm going to let the sun dry me.'

He looked at his own black gown, which was wet from the waist. 'There's a mess we've both made,' he said, looking up at her.

'No mess,' she said, holding his look.

He looked away. There were jackdaws chattering on the high tower of the church.

'Your old black stuff is so thick,' she said, kneeling by his legs and twisting the hem of the gown to wring out the water.

He watched her, meaning to stop her. But she seemed unaware of him, intent only on squeezing the cloth. He breathed deeply and forced himself up. She pulled her hands away.

'I'm sorry,' he said. 'I was speaking in Breton.'

'What's that?'

'I was born in Brittany. In the Montagnes Noires, before I came to these Black Mountains. My name then was Conan.'

'Before you were a priest?'

'I wasn't born a priest.'

He had recovered himself now. He looked down the river beyond the weir, to the ford, the well and the millstream beyond them. He saw the three small wooden houses by the track from the ford: his own priest's house, the huntsman's house, and the house of the weirkeeper Olen, Eirwen's father. It was into this small settlement, with the miller's house only fifty yards away, that he had come to serve God. And he had not lived, since the death of his parents, in any mixed human family of men, women and children.

As resident priest for the priory he had more than his religious duties. It was his task to supervise the mill, the weir and the hunting. He must count the flocks and crops of all the priory tenants in the lands of the old gift, from the ridge of Cwrwm and the brooks of Trineint across Olchon and Mynwy to the summit pool of Fyrddin. When he first came to Merthyr Clitauc his neighbour's child Eirwen was a little girl of seven. She played in and out of his house, and he took her fishing and for walks. He was now thirty-eight and Eirwen was sixteen. He was a priest and she was a daughter of his family in God.

'Are you still called Conan then?' Eirwen asked, looking into his face.

'No, we take a new name under God, in submission to His service.'

'But if you were just walking through the ford and I shouted out "Conan!" would you look round and know who I meant?'

'Perhaps I would. If it was you calling.'

She went very quiet. He wished he could drag back his words. He dared not look at her.

'It isn't the name,' she at last said.

'No. Of course.'

She was again very quiet. He moved forward, looking down at his wet gown. When he was some paces away she called suddenly after him.

'I'll bring you in a trout when I've cooked it.'

'No, don't . . .' he said anxiously, turning.

Against the sunlight her wet tunic clung closely to her body. He stared at her breasts and her thighs.

'Why not?' she asked, simply.

'I don't know,' he said, and hurried to his house.

From that day above the weir Conan knew that his life had changed. He found it easier now to remember that long awakening of his body. It had been a slow redirection of his senses beyond himself, where there had always been intensity, to a being so different, so apart, yet in the end so reachable, so touchable and so completing.

At the time he was more aware of the opposite movement: a relentless, often desperate, application of physical control; a submission to discipline and to redirecting prayer; an ashamed struggle with a renewed and still secret shame. Yet the outcome was certain long before events finally forced it. The worst pain of the first struggle was his presumption of selfishness, unbearable desire. No girl of sixteen could desire so much older a man, let alone a priest. Yet that was at last put to open test. Continuing to seek out his company, she was noticed and understood by her mother. In the end, in great embarrassment, Olen Cored, her father, asked to speak with him.

'She is troubling you, Father.'

'No. Not troubling.'

'You are a priest. She is a girl. She doesn't think.'

'I always remember I am a priest, Olen.'

'I know, Father. But it is Eirwen I worry about. If this silly idea gets fixed in her head.'

'What silly idea?'

'That you could be a man to her, Father.'

Conan checked his answer. Then he said, impulsively:

'I am sure, Olen, that she thinks nothing of the kind. If you think so, let us ask her. Let this come out in the open.'

Of the many things which had then caused shame, it was the memory of these words which stung most sharply. For the recommended openness was a fraud. He was grasping, desperately, for what, still unacknowledged, he most needed to know. Yet Olen had simply agreed. They stood together with Eirwen and her mother under the low smoke-stained ceiling of the weirman's house. It was Olen who put the question, as bluntly as before.

Eirwen went very pale. She looked away from her father into Conan's face. He then knew from the look that he had betrayed her.

'He is Father Teilo,' she said, very quietly.

'That is what I mean, girl.'

'If he were not Father Teilo, yes, I would love him as a man.'

There was a shocked silence. Conan waited some moments and then left without speaking.

Late that evening, Olen came again. 'It is impossible now, Father. I cannot leave my work so it is for you to go and speak to the prior.'

'And what should I tell him?'

'You must tell him to take you away.'

'And if he will not?'

'Then I will go to him. You are a good man, but this has happened before. You are vowed to be celibate but each man's body has its powers. There are priests, bad priests, who take women into their houses and father children on them. It is supposed to be secret, but everyone knows. I will never surrender Eirwen to that.'

'Nor will I,' Conan said.

Yet he waited some days before walking across the mountain to the prior. Since the crisis was open he was newly bewildered. While it had been a matter only of controlling his own desire it had been, for all its pain, a simpler problem. But what was now emerging was a much wider change. 'If he were not Father Teilo, yes, I would love him as a man.' In some ways that prospect was simple, but since he was a boy of nine he had lived inside an order whose rules were exclusive and permanent. Any idea of moving beyond it had been literally unthinkable. And he knew already what the Prior would say.

It went as he had expected. He had already sinned, gravely, and must undergo penance and punishment. After a month's solitary enclosure he must return, barefoot, to Merthyr Clitauc. He must express his sorrow and regret to the wronged parents. He must then return to the priory, for duties within its walls.

On his penitential return from the priory, Conan paused on the ridge of Hateral. He looked out at the great wooded plain beyond the mountains. The sweet air of gorse and bracken touched and stroked his face. A hundred years before, as he had read in Wycombe's book, Prior Robert of Bethune called unwillingly from Llanthony to be Bishop of Hereford, had stood on this same ridge, 'feeling like Adam of old, being driven from paradise into exile'.

Conan's thinking now was different, but the feeling connected. He suddenly shouted a great 'No', and turned away from the track to the Mynwy. Hurrying, almost running, he made his way north. Soon the priory was below him in its clearing by the Honddu. From this height the imposing buildings were an isolated patch in the valley. It was strange that for thirty years it had been his whole world.

Looking out the other way he saw the small clearing of Merthyr Clitauc, a grey stone in the deep green pool of the oaks. Only the high stone tower of the church stood out clearly. Further up the Mynwy valley the tower of Ewyas Lacy castle jutted high on its mound, commanding and dominating the widening vale of the Olchon. That secular tower was now a factor in his decision.

The estates of the Lacys had long included Ewyas. But Lord Walter had come to regard the remote mountain lordship, poor in yield by comparison with his many richer lands, as, in effect, a religious retreat. As well as his many gifts to Llanthony he had endowed a small Grandmontin abbey in the far uplands of Craswall. He had also decided to be buried there, and the body of this blind old man had been brought to Ewyas Lacy castle, just three years ago. There was a long funeral procession up the difficult packhorse track above the Mynwy. All the neighbouring lords and clergy, and the freeman tenants, walked behind the black cart. At Craswall they passed the old British church, in its circular enclosure on the isolated spur, named for Saint Wynac, but now rebuilt and renamed for Saint Mary. Beyond it was the little Grandmontin abbey, in Cwm y Canddo under the Cefn.

The French monks of Craswell were a wholly enclosed community. They grew no crops and kept no herds. Lay brothers managed all their dealings with the world. Their only immediate resource was their colony of bees: the only creatures, they believed, who could not harm or deprive their neighbours.

They would bury Lord Walter, but they did not appear at the procession. The cart with the body was left at the door of their chapel and the mourners withdrew. Conan, walking back with the others, found himself step by step with Sir Roger Picard of Tretwr.

'A burial in age is now not so common,' Picard said, cheerfully.

'Yet the sense is the same,' Conan carefully replied.

'You think so, monk? I have seen too many young men killed. Yet this burial of Lord Walter is at least a change from his father's.'

'What was that, my Lord?'

Picard laughed loudly. In the shared silence of the mourners, even on this return journey, the noise of the laugh was magnified. Several men looked round indignantly.

'You mustn't believe all you hear, monk. It was a sad death, they say, of Lord Walter's father Lord Hugh, on his estates in Meath in Ireland. He was showing an Irish peasant how to use a pickaxe. When the peasant swung it, as instructed, he cleaved Lord Hugh's skull.'

Conan stared at the stones on the track. He did not trust himself to speak. When Picard, untroubled, again laughed, it was as much as Conan could do to keep his own face straight.

'These accidents!' Picard said, and put his arm, easily, across Conan's shoulders.

They walked in silence for some time, in a sudden sympathy. When they were in sight of Ewyas Lacy, Conan broke the silence by asking of Picard's lineage. He had remembered a document, read many years back at Llanthony, of a Miles de Picarde and a disputed mill at Felindre.

'Aye, one of us,' Picard said, jovially.

'There are so many old records,' Conan said, 'It's hard to know what to do with them.'

'I know. They're still littered and rotting in Tretwr. Nobody has the time to go through them all. Or wit, for that matter.'

'The titles and lineages are always preserved.'

'Yes, if there's a challenge, but we do better to look to our swords. Still, when the cases come, a few might be useful. You should get your Prior to send you over to us, Teilo. Someone like you would understand them.'

'No, my lord, he wouldn't allow that. It's beyond our territory.'

'Yes, monks keep territories too. You're not all fixed on heaven. But I'm telling you now, if you ever see a chance, you know where we are. Just come, we'd make you welcome.'

It was this invitation, which Picard had probably at once forgotten, that rose in Conan's mind, as he stared down at the jutting tower of Ewyas Lacy. When he thought it through it seemed the only solution, short of renouncing his love of Eirwen. And in the delight of the sweet air he knew, with every step, that any such renunciation had become impossible. What he desired had come late in his life, by any ordinary reckoning. But it was the more intense, the more overwhelming, in this very delay. It was a discovery of a life which had been locked inside him since the numbing death of his parents and his removal to the caring weight of the priory. He could not renounce this discovery and continue living.

Yet no other solution was possible. His conscience was horrified by the convenient 'housekeeping' arrangements which he knew other priests had adopted. Any idea of seduction or elopement was equally alien. But there might be just this one chance. If Picard would give him employment – and he had wide experience, not only as a scholar, translator and interpreter, but also in the accounting and management of enterprises and lands – he could petition for release from his vows and withdraw from his order. He would then be free to marry honourably, and with means of support.

He reached the Pass and Twmpath and turned south for Tretwr. He was walking too fast for so long a journey. He was already breathless. In some corner of his mind he was no longer quite rational. He could hear himself explaining in detail, to the sceptical, narrowed prior, that the monks of the old British church, many in these same places, had been free to marry; indeed that their sons had often succeeded them. Within Christ every sacrament, and marriage as the sacrament of human love and generation, should be taken as holy.

Yet he knew as he thought this that it was stupid to suppose that any countervailing history, however persuasive, could shift or even touch minds locked in a present order. Moreover even these best arguments came limping behind. What came first, and what persuaded, was desire. He could rehearse intricate words to the prior, or to Picard, or to Olen. But only one kind of being was actually present: her pale face under the swinging light red hair; the curve of her arm as the net strained from the water and the sunlight shone in the stream. All that moved him was the voice and the body of Eirwen, her bright spirit gathered in that quiet declaration: 'if he were not Father Teilo, yes, I would love him as a man.'

He reached Pen Trumau, and now Tretwr was below him. It was as if there, by the bright Rhiangoll, Eirwen was already waiting for him. He heard her high, sharp call.

*

Rhodri and Hywel had stopped at Pen Trumau, waiting for Conan to come from the rhiw. They were swinging their legs as they sat on a jutting rock.

Conan pressed forward. He was fit enough, but he could not keep up with these strong young men. Yet he was bound to go on with them. If he and Eirwen had simply refused, they would have run away.

It had been finally settled that he would accompany them to Pipton and discover what was happening. The message from young Roger Picard, son of the old lord who had first employed him, had included no details of the proposed campaign. Conan doubted that he could say anything to dissuade them from enlisting, but for his own sake and for Eirwen's, and for their own young lives, he must seriously try.

'Not going too bad,' Rhodri called, jokingly, as he came up.

'It's a familiar track,' Conan said, out of breath. 'And if you have often done it the climb is that much easier.'

'It can't be,' Rhodri said.

'Have you never heard of the spirit?' Conan answered and laughed.

They let him rest for a while. They then all walked on to Waun Fach. On the gentler slope he kept pace with them. At their next rest he sat with his staff between his knees. Beyond them, from this height, the wide country around the mountains was spread out as in a great map. A lark was singing, high above them. The sweet summer air was still.

'When I was young,' Conan said, 'and sitting like this on the mountain, I had what I thought was a vision.'

'A vision from God?' Hywel asked.

'Perhaps, since He is in everything. Yet what I believed I saw was a vision of the world. I looked at these mountains, and they seemed like walls to protect a sweet holiness settled among them. In one of their valleys, my old priory of Llanthony. In the next, Merthyr Clitauc. In a third, Merthyr Issui. In the uplands running north, the quiet abbey of Craswall. Beyond it, beside the Dore, the great Cistercian abbey. It seemed then that this whole country was given to God. The mountains were sheltering His holy servants. Yet beyond them, on all sides, in that lower and easier country, the world's battles raged. Out there were the castles, the armed troops, the killings and the treacheries. Out there the unending struggle for power.'

'You say you only thought it was a vision?'

'It was clear and strong. And in a way it was true. But then I began seeing the connections between the one life and the other. It was from their bloody conquests that the lords endowed the religious. And beyond their own calling the religious repaid them, confirming and blessing their honour and power.'

Hywel said nothing. Rhodri, embarrassed, was looking away.

'What I thought I saw, my sons, was not a vision from God. It was an order of the world.'

'We all,' Rhodri said, 'have to live in the world.'

'Yet we still make our choices. What we see, if we choose, from this height, is neither an order nor a vision, but something more compelling. We see a history.'

Neither of the young men spoke. Conan stood, holding his staff. 'For look south by Cerrig Calch to Bergavenny. Though its castle is old in blood, I speak only of happenings during my own lifetime. Third Henry brought a subduing army. But within the same autumn old Llywelyn ap Iorwerth, called in Wales the Great, recaptured the castle. The lords of this region fought on each side, Marshall and Turbeville with Llywelyn, Clifford and Walter Lacy with Henry. An infant conceived at that time would grow to a man of thirty, and then again fighting would ravage his fields. An army of young Llywelyn was fought to a standstill by an army of Third Henry. In the low hills of Uwch Coed, the three castles, Grosmont, Skenfrith and Llanteiolo, passed in a bloody triangle from Braose to Burgh to the King. There was a dawn when Third Henry ran barefoot from Grosmont as Llywelyn and the barons assaulted it. Can you not see these shapes as you look at this land?'

Rhodri and Hywel did not answer.

'Or look west beyond Lake Syfaddon to Brecon. In 1217, when I was a boy learning Welsh in the priory, a hundred marks were paid to old Llywelyn that he should not burn the town. But in 1231 and again in 1233 he burned it, for it was a French and English colony in old Welsh land. In that last year, in this broad Wye valley below us, Third Henry captured castles to punish one of his French lords, Clifford. For Clifford had forced the king's messenger to kneel and eat the very paper of the royal command. Can you still not see these shapes? On those hills beyond the Wye old Pain's castle was besieged, overwhelmed, reoccupied, rebuilt. The castle of Radnor was burned and the town was destroyed. In 1231, Hay town was burned. Third Henry and Burgh were defeated when a monk of Cwmhir found a stratagem for the Welsh. But within two more years Henry was marching his army through these mountains to an assault at Bergavenny. Now again, in these past months, Third Henry's army has retaken Hay castle and occupied Brycheiniog. And Prince Llywelyn and Baron Simon have brought new armies and taken them back. Thus old battles lead to new battles. The bloody chain is endless.'

Rhodri and Hywel sat silently, with their heads down. Conan waited, and then moved, pointing his staff to the horizon and describing a great circle.

'We see, but yet cannot see a history. The dead are buried. The burned timbers are consumed. New honours are built, awaiting the next destruction. A man who survived the fierce battles of the Thirties has a son grown ready for the fiercer battles of the Sixties. At every point around us, in any direction, we look at these strongholds of blood. Yet the lands between them, the woods and the fields still lie peacefully below us. Through a lifetime I might sit on this mountain, and in every direction, as in a single moment, see the fires of these battles staining the sky. I would hear the loud shouts of the angry assaults. Yet still below me this other land extends. Ravaged and requisitioned, roughly marched through this way and that with the contending banners brushing the branches, with the arrogant standards stuck in its red earth, the living greens still spread their sweetness. Is this then the otherworld of the old fathers? Look well and it is rather our native world. It is only the rushing blood that is alien. The old island is overridden by a devilish history. A sweet country, raped by armies, now groans and labours and delivers new armies.' Conan lowered his staff. He closed his eyes. 'It is to some monstrous birth of this sort that you now hurry over your mountains.'

Rhodri got up. He did not look at his father. Hywel followed him, glancing back. Conan waited, and then opened his eyes, as slowly, as if from an ordinary rest, they walked steadily along the track. He moved quickly to overtake them. They moved for some distance in silence.

'It is strange,' Conan said, in a lower voice, 'but through all these times of battles the houses of the religious have been raising new buildings. After every victory and conquest a new edifice is offered to God. Yet do you think He can accept it?'

Neither of the young men replied. A wind from the northwest was now blowing in cloud. The track they were following was already overcast. In the wide green valley below them there was a constantly changing pattern of patches of sunlight and the rushing shadows of clouds.

'Look,' Conan said, pointing away to the east. Below a bank of dark cloud, sunlight was spreading in broad rays, lighting a distant place that lay golden among the shadows. 'It is how the City of God has been painted,' Conan said.

'Yes,' Hywel answered, 'I have seen that.'

Rhodri turned as Hywel spoke, and looked at his father.

'It is not the City of God,' Conan said. 'It is old Hereford, the place of the armies. There by the Wye, for many centuries, the forces of these wars have assembled. Under that golden light there is a cathedral of red stone. It is two years since the barons attacked it and imprisoned its bishop. Then the castle was captured by Prince Llywelyn and Baron Simon.'

'And Prince Edward our enemy is in prison down there,' Rhodri said, smiling and lifting his fist.

'Indeed he is,' Conan said, 'at the latest report. As still this history moves.'

Already, from the height of Rhos Dirion, the great assembly of Pipton could be clearly observed. As Rhodri, Hywel and Conan made their way down Rhiw Wen they were beginning to hear the sounds of the encampment. Past Tregoyd towards Aberllynfi they could see the many colours of the great forces that were gathered in the wide bend of the Wye.

Yet none of these distant views prepared them for the extraordinary energy of the huge encampment itself. Coming down from the quiet mountains, they were suddenly in a world where life had changed its dimensions.

The first camp, east of the Llynfi, was of the force of Baron Simon de Montfort. Between the long rows of brown tents, groups of men sat together, talking and laughing, their lances and swords on the grass beside them. Horses were grazing down to the river, and beyond them several men were in the water, splashing each other's naked bodies. A yellowing grass track led to the high square tents of the lords, with pennants of all colours strung from their poles. A juggler was performing before the largest tent, throwing and catching six pewter cups in a constant stream.

Beyond him, beside a plank bridge, a French minstrel was singing a chanson to a crowd of laughing soldiers.

> Ly eveske de Herefort
> Sout bien que ly quens fu fort
> Kant il prist l'affere;
> Devant ce esteit mult fer;
> Les Engleis quida touz manger;
> Mes ore ne set que fere.

There was a loud shout of applause.

'What's he saying?' Hywel asked Conan.

'It's when they chased the Bishop of Hereford out of his cathedral two years ago, and locked him up in Clifford's castle. I've heard this song before, and there was a verse about the brave Clifford. But he's changed sides since so I don't suppose we'll get that.'

'They change their songs according to the times, do they?'

'Of course. Listen.'

The minstrel strummed his Welsh crwth.

> Mout furent bons les barons
> Mes touz ne sai nomer lur noms
> Tant est grant la some.
> Pur ce revenk al quens Simon
> Pur dire interpretison
> Coment hom le nome.

> Il est apelé de Montfort.
> Il est el mond et si est fort
> Si ad grant chevalerie.
> Ce est voir et je m'acort
> Il eime dreit et het le tort
> Si avera la mestrie.

There was again a loud cheering. The soldiers took off their caps and shouted for Montfort. Hywel and Rhodri, not understanding them, stared round uneasily.

'These aren't our people,' Rhodri said.

'They are the allies of the Welsh,' Conan said.

Rhodri frowned and turned away. Hywel followed him. The minstrel was singing again.

> *El mond est vereement*
> *La ou la comun a ly concent*
> *D la terre loée . . .*

Conan hurried after Rhodri and Hywel.

'They're cheering their leader,' he said when he came up with them. 'Montfort, the song says, is strong in the world. He loves right and hates wrong. He will get the mastery and all the common people give him their consent.'

'In French,' Rhodri said, frowning.

'In French, English, Welsh, it's what we say we are,' Conan answered. 'That boy was singing in French about the Bishop of Hereford threatening to eat up all the English and then getting the surprise of his life. It's this name or that, a shout and at last a song. Any man here is lucky to know what he is and what he's fighting for.'

'We fight for our own homeland, our bro,' Hywel said.

'It is all against the Saxon,' Rhodri said, confidently.

They were walking along the bank of the Llynfi, where it made its last separate flow from Lake Syfaddon to the Wye. On the other side of the little river, and far out across the broad green flood meadows, were the big Welsh encampments, with their bright flags and standards. A group of barefoot archers was competing on a brown-and-white hide target set on posts on a mound, one of the graves of the Old Ones. The bowmen were shouting loudly as each hand of arrows flew, yet each shout, since they had entered the encampment, was only a momentary rise from the cries, the calls, the ordinary voices of the thousands of men now brought so closely together.

While Rhodri and Hywel watched the bowmen, Conan looked along the bank of the Llynfi to the tent he recognised as Roger Picard's. A big fire with a spitted lamb was burning near the tent, and Conan recognised several of the armed men sitting around it. He called Rhodri and Hywel, and they joined their own lordship. It was assuring to find a known place in the vast noisy camp.

Picard was standing hatless, in the opening of his tent. Conan went forward to him.

'My Lord, I . . .'

'Conan! Have you brought our reinforcements yourself?'

'Not exactly, my Lord. I have come to understand what is happening.'

'Then I wish you luck. The great ones are still at it, deciding. But there is no doubt at all that we have to march east. Young Gilbert de Clare has changed sides. He has released Prince Edward from prison in Hereford. Edward is now raising a King's army all along the Severn.'

'But the King himself is still held?'

'Oh yes, Montfort has him. Though the old devil is so confused he probably hardly knows where he is.'

'He's not the only one confused.'

'You're right, Conan. I can't tell myself which of our neighbours is with us or against us. All that's really certain, as you can see across the river, is that the Welsh are here and mean business.'

'Yet what business, my lord? Are they interested, would you say, in Montfort's parliament of the barons?'

'They are interested in Wales. If the English are divided they will join the closest party.'

'Perhaps. But then it is easy to understand why so many Marcher Lords are going back to the side of the King.'

'And why I should shift, Conan?'

'There is another cause. Not only Wales and England but Montfort's ideas of a parliament. An idea of laws to limit this absolute power.'

'Including the absolute power, in the March, of our greater Barons? For that would also happen.'

'In any case, my Lord, such a law would have to be welcomed.'

'And if so, to be fought for, Conan. But the causes are mixed. The Welsh fight for their own lands, yet Llywelyn and his princes are as fierce in their own privileges as any Englishman or Frenchman, offering the rest of us, mixed as we are, an idea of a new state.'

'A new justice, my Lord. Yet it is still a war of the barons. It is not a war for these barefoot boys.'

'They owe service, Conan. To their own due lords.'

'It is on that we differ, my Lord. To their own lands they owe service. But not to the quarrels of others.'

'That is a monk's view, Conan.'

'I could wish, my Lord, that it were.'

There was the sound of horns and trumpets on the far side of the river, among the Welsh camps. Men were running from all the tents towards a procession with fluttering pennants, which was riding in from the west.

'We had better go and see,' Picard said.

'Leave your lads here to get a meal with the others. That should be Llywelyn arriving.'

They crossed the plank bridge and joined the great company streaming across the meadows to the distant point of assembly. There was a loud cheering ahead of them, and the horns and trumpets were sounding continuously. Lance cavalry, barefoot bowmen, solid companies of footsoldiers pushed towards the centre of attention. Llywelyn ap Gruffydd, a small dark man of forty, mailed and helmeted, stayed on his big grey horse on the trampled grass before his tent. Other Welsh lords sat their horses and ponies in an arc beyond him. There were the senesgal Goronwy ap Ednyfed, Rhys Fychan of Dinefwr, Gruffydd of Powys, Owain ap Bleddyn of Edeyrnion.

'Honour to the High Prince of Wales,' Goronwy cried, and all the great company shouted and waved their caps. The trumpeters sounded a long fanfare.

'Lords and men of Wales,' Llywelyn called. His voice though deep was not carrying. There were shouts for silence.

'Lords and men of Wales, we stand armed and ready near the borders of the land of our fathers. What is still to redeem we stand ready to redeem. Our dear land, as the prophets have told us, will be again united and free.'

There was loud cheering even before he had finished his words. Goronwy shouted for silence.

'We are here beside our Wye,' Llywelyn continued, 'with others, French and English, who acknowledge our cause. They are in our country by our invitation and within our alliance. You need not fear that they will outstay their welcome. With their delicate stomachs, they do not favour our mountains. While we eat meat they pine only for bread. They want to return as soon as they can to the soft fat life of their lowlands. We wish them all Godspeed.'

The cheering rose again. Conan, standing beside Picard, who was forcing a smile, saw Llywelyn's enjoyment of the applause. He saw also the embarrassment of Goronwy the senesgal, which he was trying but failing to hide. As Llywelyn paused, Goronwy leaned across and spoke to him. Llywelyn nodded.

'They are our good friends, our allies,' he resumed. 'I can assure you of that. The French lord Simon of Montfort is our old and true friend. Third Henry, our old enemy, is within his power, and is at last learning wisdom. He now offers us a charter, confirming our titles and our lands. In return . . .' Llywelyn hesitated. The cheering had risen again. 'In return we acknowledge him. And we support the new state of Lord Simon against all and any of its enemies.'

There was little interest in this. The pressing Welsh forces had heard enough. But there were now shouts at the back of the crowd. From across the Llynfi another column was riding, with Montfort and a company of French and English knights at its head. The Welsh bowmen and footsoldiers fell back to let them ride through.

Conan looked up at Montfort. He was greyhaired and relaxed, his intelligent face so accustomed to command that he rode through the pressing soldiers without really looking at them.

He rode slowly up to Llywelyn. He extended his hand. As Llywelyn took it the attendant lords cheered, but most of the soldiers were silent.

Montfort raised his arm. He spoke in French to the Welsh lords, with his back to their soldiers. Conan and Picard followed his words.

'Honour to Llywelyn ap Gruffydd, lawful Prince of Wales, and to all his lords. The time has now come, honoured lords, to advance. The desertion of Clare must be severely punished. We will take his castles at Monmouth and Usk. We must then ride East, for his treachery has loosed Edward, and an army is gathering against us beyond the Severn. It is an army raised to defend injustice! An army raised to protect every arbitrary power! We will march and destroy them, not only in the name of Wales or of England, but in the great name of law.'

There was no cheering, but the Welsh lords, taking turns, rode forward and shook Montfort's hand. The Welsh troops only waited and watched.

Conan turned to go, and Picard followed him. As he left the assembly, Conan looked beyond the crowded meadows to the green heights of Twmpath and Pen y Beacon, on the edge of Ewyas. Near the bridge, ignoring the assembly around Llywelyn, a company of Ewyas bowmen sat close together beside the river. They looked up, but did not move, as the many strangers passed.

'Two accounts of the war,' Picard said.

'Yet which will it be?'

Conan did not answer. Seeing the Ewyas bowmen, his mind had gone back to the old time in Merthyr Clitauc. He saw the Mynwy again, and the weir, but remembered most the deep silence of the woods, and these hunters moving through them with their rough elm bows.

'I am committed,' Picard said. 'I shall march with Montfort.'

Conan said nothing. They were approaching the fire, where Rhodri and Hywel were sitting eating with the others. The young men did not get up when Picard and Conan reached them. Conan waited, and then moved to sit close by Rhodri.

'I have heard what they say. You should not go with them.'

'I shall go where my friends go,' Rhodri said, stubbornly.

'My son, a man may fight with his friends for his own land, his own family. But it is a different battle to assault the lands of others, under whatever title or cause.'

'We are all agreed here, father. We will fight for our prince and our people.'

'I can then only beg you yet again not to go on this adventure.'

'It is my own life, father. I have made my choice, as you once made yours.' As he spoke they heard new shouting in the meadows beyond the Llynfi. A troop of Welsh horsemen were galloping in a wild practice charge along the wide green bank of the river. Many horns and trumpets sounded again. The young men of Tretwr rose and looked excitedly across.

Conan leaned on the thick oak rail of the bridge at Tretwr. His eyes were tracing the tiny furrows in the weathered wood, but his mind was separate and elsewhere. There was a footstep behind him, and he felt Eirwen gripping his arm.

'Cariad,' he said, without turning.

'You must come in, Conan. You must eat.'

'No, my body still refuses what it knows it needs.'

Eirwen moved and clasped his hand. He turned and looked at her. The skin of her face was pale and the edges of the eyes were bruised and reddened. Yet her springing hair, under the broad white cap, was still a warm light red, and as she looked up at him she smiled.

'I should not have begun it,' he said. 'I should not have involved you.'

'But then there would have been no real life at all.' Her voice was high and sharp. He remembered her cry from the weir and her cry to the tower, and they were like a single lasting cry.

'Eirwen, I wish with all my heart . . .'

'As always,' she said, interrupting him.

He took the pressure of her hand. They turned together and walked into the castle. Roger Picard was not yet back. He had gone into England, under a pass of safe conduct, to make his peace with the King and Prince Edward. Others were making the same journey, after the killing of Montfort at Evesham.

'No, this wish . . .' Conan said, but she again interrupted him, holding tightly to his hand.

It was the end of August, more than three weeks after the battle, before Hywel had got back, bringing the news of Rhodri. The Welsh bowmen and footsoldiers, used to fighting in hills and forests, had been quickly broken and defeated in that open country by the Severn. Rhodri was cut down by a horseman's sword. Hywel stayed beside him until the next charge, but by then, with his eyes still open and staring, Rhodri was dead. Hywel had run to hide in an orchard. There were no Welsh princes to rally the survivors. The Welsh companies were all under Marcher Lord command.

Conan halted, looking up at the tower. He remembered that he had been reading the story of the martyr Issui or Isseu when Eirwen had called him to intercede with Rhodri. It was now unbelievably long ago.

'I wish with all my heart,' he said fiercely, 'that I had never at all understood this world.'

Eirwen released his hand and looked up at him. 'But it has been your whole life, understanding. As Father Teilo or as yourself, as Conan.'

'Yes, but I wish with all my heart that it had never been so. For then the blow falls twice. Once as it falls on all who are bereaved. But then again, as sharply, on those who have read the signs and understood them. That is the second blow, that we know such things must happen, while our world remains of this kind.'

Eirwen narrowed her eyes. 'You could not have known it would be Rhodri.'

'Yes, Rhodri. Or Hywel or Iago or Ieuan or Dafydd. The sons we raise in love that this cruel order destroys. And to understand that this is so is the final bereavement.'

Eirwen looked away. Conan saw the bitter turn of her shoulders. If he had understood too much he had also said too much. He heard briefly, from his lips, an inarticulate sound. As it came he reached out to her and held her closely in his arms.

Widows of the Welshry

$\blacklozenge$

Suddenly overnight the weather changed. After the weeks of heavy rain, since late summer, the autumn air was bright and clear. Sunlight shone on the drenched grass and on the still dripping leaves of the oaks. The sky above Wenallt was a pale washed blue.

Ieuan stretched his arms. He was not looking forward to the day. With so much of his own work waiting for an end to the rains, he had been impressed for carrying service, hauling timber for rebuilding the old mill at Llangwathau. As Ieuan ap Gruffydd, a freeman of the kin, he should not have been liable for hauling, which for time out of memory had been the work of bondmen.

It was one of many things which had changed since Humphrey de Bohun became Lord of Brecon and Hay. A morose, invalid bachelor, said to spend most of his time discussing the scriptures with Augustinian monks, Humphrey had twisted and broken many customs of the March. He had fined the kin of Talgarth for using their customary weights and measures. In a dispute with the tenants of Cantref Selyf he had imprisoned seventy men for six months without trial. He had suppressed the local court and confiscated the lands of Philip ap Rhys, lord of Bronllys. Freemen from the whole lordship had now to make regular suit in long journeys to Brecon, and the penalty for not appearing was a fullgrown cow or a fine of twelve shillings: a cowprice that by custom had been less than seven.

Yet, even from sick Bohun, this hauling service, imposed on freemen and bondmen alike, had still been a shock. The rhingyll himself, Owain Sais, had been embarrassed to pass on the order, although he had it directly from the Constable of the Castle, Sir Hugh Lloyd, who had it coldly and firmly from the wheezing but emphatic, rarely seen Bohun.

Ieuan looked beyond Wenallt to Pen y Beacon and Twmpath. The sheep of the kin were still up on the common grazing, for the grass even at those heights had grown strongly in the rains. If it were not for this damned hauling he would be up to look them over and make a start on cutting the bracken. So would others of the kin, from Wenallt and Cilgeufford and Maestorglwyd. But now he must wait for Idris the bondman to bring up his ox, to make a pair on Ieuan's waggon and haul the difficult trail to Llangwathau.

Ieuan went round to the front of the long house, to look out for Idris. But then he stopped, amazed. Beyond the familiar steep slope to Pantyfithel just below him, and the large open quilleted fields, worked in strips, towards Caenantmelyn and Danyfforest, it was as if the land had disappeared, had been swallowed up. He looked more closely. Across the whole valley of the Gwy lay a thick white mist.

It had settled like curded milk in a bowl. Its upper surface reflected light like a summer cloud. It seemed a lake of mist, a cloud fallen from the sky, lying settled in the valley. Its edges were distinct. It began below Tylau and Trewern, following almost exactly the boundary of the Welshry. Above it, in a great ring, were the green wooded heights of Wenallt and Feirig, and in the distance Cusop and Brilley and the hills above Clyro: all the lands of the Cymry from Euas to Elfael. Nothing could be seen through the thick white cloud. It was like heaped snow or blocked ice. Or it was an inverted world, in which a man looked down at the sky.

Ieuan released his breath. He knew well enough, from a lifetime, what lay under the thick mist. There were the broad, flat green meadows along the curve of the Gwy: the meadows of the lord's demesne and the Englishry. There was Hay itself, on its mound above the river, and its castle facing the mountains. On the towers hung the blue and yellow flags of the Bohuns, and on the high standard the embroidered Bohun swan. Around the castle, huddled close, were the burgages of the English settlers, the tradesmen and dealers. The demesne of the Englishry ran to the first pitch, near Llanigon, of the steep slopes towards the mountains. It was as if the white mist now insisted on the boundary between them.

The high fields of the Welshry were green among the oak woods: more than a hundred holdings of the kin: holdings the castle called tenantry, but the land was of the kin and was distributed by them. Bohun was no landlord but, as alien master, commanded the persons of kin and bondmen alike. The bond families, from the old taeogtrefi of Trefens and Llanigon, worked directly for the lord and his officials. But the freemen had commuted their service to silver and to the commorth or kallamay – the render of seven cows – every second spring. Below the green pastures there was arable land, growing oats and barley and wheat. The kin had held its own until this latest Bohun had near throttled them. It must still somehow hold its own. If indeed that cloud had fallen, and castle and town had been smothered, the kin on native land in the mountains would breathe only their own sweet air.

There was a call from inside the house. Ieuan went in to find Mair making butter. She had a bowl of buttermilk and a piece of oatcake ready for him. He went to kiss her forehead, but she pulled away. Her mouth was small and moist. There was a thin smear of butter on her lower lip, where she had been tasting. She was heavily pregnant, in her last month. At eighteen she was eight years younger than Ieuan, but he had waited for her since he had first seen her at Blaendigedi Uchaf, a lively blackhaired girl with pale clear skin and bright red cheeks. It would be time, when this hauling was done, to fetch her sister down to help her.

'He's not come, old Idris?' Mair asked.

'There's a very heavy mist down below.'

'He should send his Olen. That's a strong one, the ugly great thing.'

'It isn't his Olen. Idris only married Nest after Olen was born.'

'That old rape, was it?'

'Aye, proved on Henry Bailey, but Hywel Fychan protected him.'

'Poor old Nest!'

'Aye, but she don't let Olen forget it, and Idris works his guts trying to keep the peace.'

Mair stared down at her butter. Ieuan moved quickly behind her and put his arms around her waist. She hesitated, but then leaned slowly back against him. He moved his hands and spread his fingers over the rounding of the child. They rocked slowly in silence.

'Bleddyn's quiet,' Ieuan said.

'What do you expect?'

'Last night he was kicking.'

Mair eased herself forward. She looked round into Ieuan's face. 'Suppose it's a girl?'

'No, I've felt him. He's Bleddyn all right.'

'It isn't like feeling a lamb.'

Ieuan laughed and moved his fingers over her tight tunic. He moved his hands and slowly lifted the rough woollen cloth. His fingers moved, gently, over her warm skin.

'All you want, you men, is a boy.'

'For the kin I want a boy.'

'For there to be a kin you need both.'

'The kin needs a boy for the land. Now you are carrying him for me. I always knew you would carry him.'

'If I can give him to you, Ieuan, I will. But would you still love our little girl?'

'I love you, don't I?'

Mair turned and laughed. She pulled free from his hands and let her tunic fall back into place.

'I only saw Bleddyn once. He had his bow and his helmet. He was marching down to Bronllys for the muster.'

'He marched as far as Crecy and that was the end of it. I am last in my own blood until this one is born.'

Mair smiled. She reached up and touched his hair. She lifted her lips and kissed him. He held her close, but was looking away. 'I'd better go. For sick Bohun!' he said, abruptly.

He went out into the yard. Almost at once he saw Idris leading his ox up the pitch from Pantyfithel. He waved and went to lead his own ox to the waggon.

The cut oak was lying ready for them, on a steep slope below Feirig. That had been a performance in itself: not only Owain rhingyll but Richard the forester and Jac the carpenter of the castle and Huw the second miller, pacing the thickgrowing oaks on the scarp below the rock outcrop on Feirig, choosing exactly what they wanted – for all trees even on kin land belonged to the lord – and the slaves behind them with their axes to do the felling and trimming. It was how these lords arranged things: not the varying work of freemen, but one for this, one for that, others for others. And at the end of the line, when the slaves had finished, stood a freeman and a bondman – no difference made between them, as the old law required – to haul for a mill which the lord would monopolise, allowing the kin no mills of their own, grasping yet another hold for payment and charge.

Idris came slowly up, prodding his old ox. They made a sad pair. In his late forties, Idris looked older, his grey head slightly bowed and his arms bent outwards, the thick fingers hanging loose. Yet his temper was sweet, and his singing voice was still fine. He had some of the oldest songs of the Welshry but he knew no stories. 'All that,' he once said, 'has gone dark.'

They walked together towards the scarp of Feirig. Ahead of them, isolated in a thorn fence, was a tall rowan, whose leaves had turned prematurely to dark brown, almost black, and now hung drooping from the branches. Yet all over the tree, blood-red berries were hanging in thick glistening clusters, like a flock of coloured birds, as if the tree had produced only them.

Ieuan waited as Idris stared up at the rowan. The old man's eyes had a blind look, staring but not seeing, the gaze turned inwards. Ieuan moved impatiently and Idris shifted and followed. The heavy oak trunks, cut into lengths, had been dragged to a bank by Penyrallt, where they could be loaded on the wagon.

'Three trips,' Idris said, looking over them.

'No, get on, we can do it in two.'

Idris looked from under his eyebrows. 'You reckon?'

'We'll have to. I've got my own work waiting.'

They backed the waggon close to the bank. Ieuan got ready to slide the first log, but Idris said the wheels must be chocked.

'We'll get some stone then.'

Just beyond the bank, overgrown with thorn and elder, was the place they both knew as the Cave of the Old Ones. From the track it looked just a heap of old stones, but on the other side there was a built entrance, with standing flat slabs and a huge capstone. Bones had been found beyond a litter of stones on one side. Ieuan walked to the loose stones, but Idris had gone in another direction.

'Better leave them lie,' Idris called as Ieuan turned.

'You don't believe the old tale that they can harm us?'

'Not harm us, no, but better leave them lie.'

Idris had found other stones. His brown hands moved over them, as if feeling their grain. There was dust from the stones in the lines of his wrinkled palms. He stooped and lifted and put in the first chock. Ieuan hurried to put in a second.

'It's slippy, this first bit,' Idris said, 'till we get to Pantyfithel, and then again by Llangwathau.'

'We won't do it by talking about it.'

Idris spat on his hands. They moved to the first log and slid it on to the waggon. It went easily and they moved to a second, which went in awkwardly.

'Two more then,' Ieuan said.

'No, one at the most.'

'I told you, I've got my work.'

They slid on a third, but Ieuan had to get in the waggon to drag it over the others. To get the fourth settled they had both to stand in the waggon and drag and roll. Idris unwound a long rope from his waist and tied it across. He was still looking unhappily at the excessive load.

They got the oxen together and roped them to the shafts.

'I'll lead,' Ieuan said. 'Put the chockstones on top, we might need them again for the pitches.'

Idris did what he was told. He had gone very quiet. Ieuan prodded the oxen and they set off across the grass to the lane. The big wheels dug into the sodden ground and Ieuan whipped the oxen to keep them moving. They were strange to each other, and also unmatched. At last they reached the lane: a deep hollow way between high wooded banks. The lane had been stoned, but in the heaviest rains floodwater had changed it to a stream-bed and its surface was very rough.

Ieuan was controlling the oxen now, steadying and slowing the pace. Then Idris's ox slipped, in a patch of sloping mud, and Ieuan shouted angrily to right him. As he heard the shout Idris saw a large projecting stone where the floodstream had loosened the earth. It was directly ahead of the right wheel, and the waggon was already tilting left. He shouted and ran forward, but the wheel struck and slid on the rock and suddenly the whole waggon was coming over.

Idris scrambled for a footing but slipped and the waggon fell over him. As it tipped the oxen went down and the uppermost log slid forward and hit Ieuan hard on the back of the neck. He screamed as he fell. Idris had fallen in the ditch. Only part of the weight was across him. But he could not move, and Ieuan was lying where he had fallen. Fighting for breath, Idris tried to release his leg, but the oxen were scrambling up again and with them the waggon moved and a log slid and fell heavily across his stomach and thighs.

Somewhere quite close a dog was barking. Idris heard it as a throbbing in his head.

Henry ap Rosser, senior cais of the Hay lordship, shook the boy's shoulders and shouted, 'Slow it down, slow it down.'

Madoc looked down at his dog. He was afraid that if the cais went on shaking him the dog would go for his leg, and then it would be all over. He was still shaking himself from his run to the castle. When he had found the overturned cart he had run for his father at Pantyfithel, and three other neighbours had been shouted across. They had found Ieuan dead, with dark blood from his mouth. Old Idris, though trapped, was still occasionally conscious. He had whispered what had happened. While the men untied the oxen and started moving the wagon and logs, Madoc was sent to run to the castle, for death and accident came under the castle's law and must always be immediately reported.

Scared of the castle, which he had never been inside, Madoc had approached an English boy who was playing with a hoop by the gateway. The boy did not understand what he was saying, but at last fetched the cais. After some more shaking, and slowly getting his breath back, he told what had happened.

'Trust them!' said Henry ap Rosser.

'Sir?'

'Give them the simplest job, and this is what they make of it.'

'But Ieuan is dead, sir.'

'Ieuan ap Gruffydd? I know him. A restless one. We've had trouble with him before. And old Idris, you say? That's a family. That Olen nearly ran off when he was sent driving Lord Humphrey's cattle to his estates in Essex. And that's a soft job if you like, driving the beasts after Calammay.'

'I don't think Olen did, sir.'

'You don't think what?'

'I don't think Olen went to Essex, sir. There was other men went.'

'What does that matter now, boy, with this accident you keep on about?'

'Sir, old Idris was alive when I left. My father said you would want his evidence.'

'Evidence? All right. You get back, I'll ride up.'

Madoc hurried away, calling his dog close. As he went down the narrow street to the wall three boys were standing at the open front of a skinner. As he passed they shouted, 'Welsh snot, Welsh snot.' He knew what they meant, though the words were meaningless. He stopped, and his dog growled, pointing them. As they hesitated, he walked on to the road through the demesne.

Henry ap Rosser, riding at ease, passed Madoc before he had reached Cae Nant Melyn. When Madoc at last reached the place of the accident the cais had taken charge. Ieuan was being laid on a hurdle, to be carried up to Penyrallt. Idris still lay in the ditch, and the cais was bent over him.

'He's gone,' the cais said. 'We'll have to take your word for it, Morgan.'

'I know what he said,' Madoc's father replied.

'Then see to him. Get that Olen to fetch him. I must go on up and see Mair.'

When Henry ap Rosser arrived at Penyrallt, reining in his cob and looking carefully around at the woodpile, the midden, the haystack and the poultry yard, there was already the sound of women's voices from the longroom of the low wooden house. He dismounted slowly and approached the open door. Mair was lying on the bed, covered with brown blankets. Two neighbour women stayed close to her. The half-finished butter stood on the long ash trestle. The cais went to the bowl and dipped his finger to taste. Then he walked slowly towards the bed. The women watched him anxiously. Mair's eyes were closed. He reached under the blanket for her right hand. She started and looked up at him.

'Ieuan is dead,' he said slowly and clearly. Mair looked into his eyes. 'He was your husband by law?' the cais asked.

Mair did not answer. One of the neighbour women intervened.

'It is not yet a year. We were both witnesses.'

The cais continued to hold Mair's hand. To his surprise she now grasped his fingers tightly and continued to press them. He nodded.

There was a voice from the doorway.

'They are bringing up the body,' the cais said.

Rhys ap Hywel looked up at him. He did not come to Henry's shoulder. His lean face and hands were covered with large brown spots over pale white skin. His thin hair was grey, but his small moustache was sandy.

'Get the winter curtain,' Rhys said, turning away to the women.

'Clear the trestle and set it in the corner. Hang the curtain to cover it.'

The women moved at once. Rhys walked on into the yard. 'A bad accident,' he said, to the cais who was following him.

'Yes, it seems to be an accident. The coroner will decide it.'

'The bondman Idris gave his witness to Morgan.'

'It will be thoroughly tested. But I have seen the stone. And also that they overloaded the waggon.'

'There will be no fine for that. If there was a fault they have paid.'

'There will be ebediw, death fine, to the lord. For he has lost a man who owed service.'

'Of course, ebediw. In our last case, for the status of Ieuan, the ebediw was nine shillings.'

'You will find that it has risen. It is now ten.'

Rhys walked to the woodpile. He picked up a block of pine which had been half split.

'It is a hand always tightening on our throat,' he said, looking round at the cais.

'It is the law,' the cais replied.

'Is it your law, Henry ap Rosser? Ten shillings is the price of two hundred and forty days' reaping.'

'You have it very exact.'

'I have to know it. Just as I know there is never that much reaping, in all the lord's fields by the Gwy. It is not in silver but in beasts we shall pay.'

'There are beasts.'

'For how much longer, cais? It is not only our old dues. In the time of Lord Humphrey there is as much in fines and in gifts. At his entry we were cut to the bone. As the flesh was growing again, there was the gift for the expedition to France; and when it again grew, the gift for new work on the priory. It is all we can now do to pay what is foreseen, between lord and man. But surprise no longer surprises. In all seasons and all conditions that sick cupped hand is held out.'

'Be careful of your words, Rhys. And be glad it is a friend who is hearing them.'

Rhys threw down the block. 'You have to make show as a friend. But this is the time of y dreth fawr, the great tax, and old friendships soon wither.'

The cais looked away as he replied. 'A lot will depend, in fact, on the coroner's view of the accident. Was it the fault of the men? Or was it an act of God and subject to deodand?'

Rhys clenched his fists. 'It is new again with Lord Humphrey, this using of deodand. But in this it cannot apply.'

'It may indeed apply. I will give you two cases. A man on the Usk by Talybont was carrying stone in his boat for a weir. It was overloaded and it sank. The man was drowned. The finding was that the water, the stones and the boat caused death, and thus were forfeit to the lord.'

'A sunken boat and welcome!'

'It is the law of skilled men. For in the second case a candle fell on a bed and the woman sleeping in it burned to her death. The candle and the bed were the causes, but since both were consumed no forfeit was recoverable.'

'These have nothing to do with this accident.'

'You speak knowing nothing of the law. For it could be said, here, that the oxen, the cart, the stone and the logs caused death, and then by deodand are forfeit to the lord.'

Rhys spat on the ground. Past the yard fence, along the track from the Cave of the Old Ones, four men were carrying Ieuan's body on a hurdle. As they came near the doorway the cais stepped forward and looked down at the face. It was peaceful, the eyes closed under the curling dark-brown hair, but there was still dried blood around the mouth. The cais spat on his palm and rubbed it over the mouth. He had to spit and rub again to get it clean.

'Now return him to his home,' he said, formally.

The bearers carried the body in their arms and laid it on the trestle. Rhys and the women stood between the carrying and Mair. One of the women went to the body and began to undress it. Rhys and Henry ap Rosser went again to the yard.

'Mair is pregnant,' the cais said.

'Yes, in her last weeks.'

'That makes a difference.'

'To you, cais, no.'

'Are you sure, Rhys? For if Ieuan's land falls in without male heir, it could be subject to escheat by the lord.'

'This is land of the gwely. It passes only in ach ac edryf, kin and descent.'

'Until there are no male heirs.'

'There are heirs as far as third cousins, within the kin.'

'Yet are there cousins? Ieuan's elder brother Bleddyn is long dead, and he did not marry.'

Rhys looked back at the house. 'Cais, the kin lives. Yes, Bleddyn was killed, a bowman soldier who followed the Lord William to the battle across the sea.'

'The battle of Crecy, Rhys. It was a great victory.'

'Bleddyn was killed. He had served for twopence a day. But in the kin there are the brothers of his father and the sons of those brothers.'

'I know of none, Rhys.'

'You know better than I do the lines of our kin? Is that what you are saying?'

'I am saying you need a male heir.'

'Mair is carrying an infant. The infant may be a boy. She will stay in this house, not only the nine days that are allowed by law but until the child is born. It is in any case not right to move her. Her sister will come.'

'And if the child is not a boy?'

'You keep the peace, cais. I will keep the kin.'

Henry nodded. He put out his arm and patted Rhys's shoulder. Rhys pulled it away.

'She will then go back to her father at Blaendigedi Uchaf?'

'Of course. And before your Lord's ebediw she will take what is hers: her argyfrau, the marriage portion she brought, which was two milking cows; her cowyll, Ieuan's morning gift after wedding, which was eight yearling sheep; her personal goods and her share of the common goods.'

The cais looked around. 'Then part of the ebediw will fall on the whole kin.'

'It is how it is done, for we live by rights and obligations in common.'

'Within the lord's law.'

'Under the lord's law.'

The cais smiled. He looked in the house again and then went for his cob. 'I'll be getting down to the Pant. That Olen, if they've found him, should have carried Idris home. But that is the difference, Rhys, you see. I go to the house of the bondman, bringing the lord's law. And you, Pencenedl, do not.'

'Idris was an honest man but was not of our stock.'

'Yes. A man without ancestors. Isn't that what he'd be called?'

'It is only the truth. He is without lineage.'

'Yet was he an alien? Was he from elsewhere?'

'No, he was born here.'

'And his father and fathers before him?'

'It may be so. Nativi caeth are not recorded within a kin's memory.'

'As I said, Rhys, that is the difference.'

Rhys spat towards the rick. 'A difference indeed. Without obligations, without care of each other.'

'He was known as a kind man.'

'It is more than personal kindness. It is the duties and right of a kin.'

'We shall see, perhaps, how that Olen manages it.'

'And your lord,' Rhys shouted, waving his finger. 'For your lord, depend on it, will have his hand cupped there too.'

The cais smiled and saluted. He rode slowly out of the yard.

Olen, hurriedly fetched from his work, dredging the stream at the mill, carried Idris's body home on Idris's ox. He did not stay to talk to the men who were at the place of the accident, working to clear the fallen logs. His mother Nest had been told of the death, and was standing at the door of their hut, watching Olen and the ox cross their meadow. Within his bond holding Idris had this one acre, the property of the lord. It had been worked before him by Nest's father Mared.

Nest did not look at Olen when he reached the doorway. She went to the side of the ox and lifted Idris's grey head. With thumb and finger she pinched the lean cheeks. Then she walked around the ox, looking down at its legs and hooves. The hair was caked with red mud.

'You can carry him in, can you?' she said, not looking at Olen.

He hesitated. The twin boys, Adaf and Llew, had come to the doorway and were watching them.

'Where do you want him?'

'On his bed.'

'It is your bed too.'

'Must I carry him myself? Or ask these boys?'

Olen looked away. 'He is a man I loved. I would carry him anywhere.'

'Because he was soft with you. A father would not have been so soft.'

'It was not that. He was a man everyone loved.'

'Loved! To hear you say that.'

Olen looked past his mother to Adaf and Llew. 'Give us a hand,' he called. 'We'll carry him decently.'

The boys, gravefaced, came forward. Olen lifted Idris's shoulders and each of the boys took a leg at the knee.

'Turn,' Olen said.

They walked in so that the head, resting on Olen's stomach, entered last. Nest followed them, and when they had laid the body on the bed ordered them out. Adaf and Llew stood close, wanting to ask Olen about the accident, but Nest reappeared and called them.

'Go now, as I told you, to Dore. Go by the Cefn ridgeway. Ask at the lodge for my brother Elidyr.'

'You said Brother Joseph,' Adaf said.

'It is what he is called, in the abbey. They will know him by both names.'

The boys turned to go.

'Keep together,' Nest called. 'And don't come back on your own. Do what your uncle tells you.'

The boys shouted and ran off.

'You're sending for him to arrange things, are you?' Olen asked, doubtfully.

'Yes, I am. I don't intend to be cheated.'

'Who'd cheat you?'

Nest looked at him contemptuously, and went back into the hut.

Olen stood for some time, then went to the ox and led it through to the brook. As it stood in the water he looked across the meadow. Idris had said, often, that when the time came he would speak for Olen at the castle, so that he could carry on the holding. But with this sudden death nothing would have been said, and in any case, without Idris, he was not sure that he wanted to stay here. The problem was who to ask, with Idris gone.

There were many stories of opportunities elsewhere, since the deaths of the Black Plague. Seven years ago, in 1349, many thousands had died along the Severn Sea, and as far north through

Gwent as Abergavenny. Only a few isolated outbreaks had come this side of the mountain, but in those other lands, south and east, there was ground untilled, farms deserted, even flocks abandoned. A pedlar had said in Hay that the Lord Humphrey's lands by the Severn, at Caldicote, were especially hard hit, but that few could be persuaded to go there, for fear of the plague coming again. Yet could the son of a bondwoman get permission to go? Might he even be ordered down there? Idris would have advised him, though he knew little of the law. But now that real father, that man better than a father, was beyond all reach.

There was a shout from behind him. The cais, on his cob, was riding into the meadow. Olen walked across.

'You got the old man back then?'

'Aye. And the ox.'

'I suppose you think the ox is yours.'

'Well he isn't theirs, up Penyrallt.'

The cais rode on. 'She's got him inside, I suppose?'

'Aye.'

'I'm sorry about it. He was a fair old chap.'

'He was more than that.'

The cais looked down at him, frowning. 'Aye, better for you if you had been his son.'

'I was his son, how he treated me.'

'And her?'

Olen looked away.

As they approached the hut, Nest came out and stood facing them, folding her arms. She was a short, broad-bodied woman; worn at thirty-five, but strong and determined. Her face was broad, with a small thin mouth. Her black hair was braided under a white cap. She had tied a sacking apron over her long brown tunic. The edges of the apron were dark with water that had splashed when she was washing Idris's body.

'What are you here for?' she called to the cais.

'By the law, woman. There is a man dead.'

'Have you trotted your cob to tell me that, when I've hardly finished washing his body?'

'There are things to arrange.'

'Not with you, cais. I've lost my man, but I shall see I'm not cheated. I've sent for my brother to come.'

'From the abbey?'

'He'll be here soon enough. There'll be no cheating then.'

'Nobody's trying to cheat you. In a day or two, perhaps, the reeve will come up and see what you've got.'

'He'll see it. It's little enough.'

'Whatever it is, it belongs to the lord. But the reeve will see you all right. He'll let you stay, and this one can help you.' He pointed down at Olen.

'Him!' Nest said.

'He's your son, isn't he?'

Nest turned and went back into the hut. The cais dismounted and walked across to the pig yard. Most of Idris's small holding, below the thick oakforest, had depended on his pigs. With pannage in the woods, he had developed a herd which was admired by all his neighbours and was well known in the castle and the town, where most of it went in his bond render to the lord. The cais looked round when he had reached the yard, and beckoned Olen across.

'I expect she's loosed half of them to the forest, before they can be reckoned.'

'No,' Olen said.

'You think I don't know my own people?'

'Are we your own people?'

'Well, she's a widow woman, and she had her misfortune before. Nobody's going to be too hard.'

'What hard? You won't take more because Idris is dead?'

'It all belongs to the lord, boy. It'll be for the reeve to say what you can keep.'

'But the land?'

'No, the land stays with her, while she works it. That'll be your job now, I expect.'

'I don't know,' Olen said.

The cais looked at him closely and then walked back towards the hut. Olen followed.

'I see it's cleared down below,' the cais said, pleasantly. 'It was bad this morning when I got the call.'

Olen shook his head. He found it hard to follow what the cais was saying. Then the connection came, and he looked down at the castle and the town on its mound. They were shining in the sunlight. He could see the spots of colour on the flags of the towers. The long reaches of the river also shone in the sun, and the fields along its banks – some green with floodgrass, some brown and yellow with stubble from the reaped grain, some pink and red in turned fallow earth – were a bright patchwork. He remembered the thick white mist of the morning, as he had walked to the mill. Idris had pointed down at it, when he was fetching the ox. It was sometimes the other way round, with low cloud on the mountain and clear sunlight in the valley.

'Look after your mother,' the cais called from his cob.

Olen lifted his arm.

'And keep out of trouble yourself, mind.'

Olen turned away.

Olen was at the brook with the ox when he swung round and saw his mother close behind him. She had taken off the sacking apron, but her face was flushed.

'Doing nothing as usual?'

'I'll do what I have to.'

'And what do you have to, now my man has gone?'

'I'll do the work, Mam.'

'Aye, so you say. But all I can think of is when I had you to look after, and it was that good man saved me.'

'He was always a good man.'

'Not that he didn't gain himself, coming here and marrying me. The lord put him in after my father and he had something for a change. Before that he was on the roads, though he always wanted land and animals.'

'He was good with animals.'

'All he got was through me. There was good stock and chattels. And if he had to take you, still there was the price I had for you.'

'Yes Mam, the price.'

'A steer they gave me, and silver for five years.'

'Yes Mam, you said.'

'Five years. But we've kept you nineteen.'

'I know, Mam. That's why I must work.'

'I was cheated at the court. They were all in it, that lot with Hywel Fychan. They stood together there watching, because he was one of their own.'

'He?'

'Henry Bailey. Your father.'

'But they found him guilty, Mam.'

'He was a follower of Hywel Fychan, a no-good bit of a soldier. And Hywel Fychan protected him.'

'I know, Mam. You said.'

'I said? I've said nothing. While my man was alive I was careful to say nothing.'

'I don't understand.'

'No, you don't understand. That long devil riding, with his sandy hair and moustaches, and his great ugly nose and teeth. I was fifteen, walking the ewes from Feirig. He rode his horse beside me. He kept asking me my name. And then he was down all over me.'

Olen looked away. 'Mam, you know I'm sorry.'

'You say you're sorry. But what I'm telling you, I still see his face, working at me.'

'You wouldn't forget it.'

'You tell me I wouldn't forget it. But have you ever known why? Have I ever told you why?'

'I don't know, Mam, really.'

'Because it's your face. Your face. You've grown exactly like him.'

'If he was my father . . .'

'Yes. If they'd watched you grow they'd have had no need of a court. That same colouring, that same nose. And when you got your second teeth, that was the very worst of it. You had that same gap between your two front teeth. Go on, feel it. That proves you're the son of your father.'

'Well I know I am, Mam.'

'You say you know. And now anybody could see it. But that wasn't enough when they cheated me at the court.'

'Mam, how did they cheat you?'

'I should have had more for the price. It was that Hywel Fychan protecting him. They speak for their own.'

'They still found him guilty.'

Nest turned away. She walked to the edge of the brook and patted the ox. Olen waited, not daring to speak.

'I was raped at fifteen,' Nest said, quietly. 'You'd think that was enough, and there was no doubt about the man. But they took me into that court, in the castle, and when they'd heard the story they fetched a box with a holy relic: a fingerbone of Igon. They made me hold the box in my right hand and then they told me to hold him. Hold his thing.'

Olen stared at the ground.

'His thing! His prick. I had to hold it in my hand, and the holy relic in the other, and say: "with this I now hold he penetrated my body, and from this I now hold came my child."'

Olen rubbed at his face.

'Mam,' he said hoarsely.

'Mam indeed!' Nest cried. 'As if I ever wanted you! As if all you are isn't that rape, and then me standing there, shamed beyond a shame.'

Olen was silent for some time. Nest also did not move, but then suddenly picked up a stick and prodded the ox from the brook.

'Now this one has killed my good man,' Nest cried, and hit the ox across its face.

The ox stumbled at the bank, but then moved away to the meadow.

'Are you saying you want me to go, Mam?' Olen at last asked.

'You would have gone before if that Idris had not protected you!'

'Protected me from my mother? A son who could never choose how he came to be born?'

Nest turned and looked up at him. Then she turned away and spat. 'You know nothing about any of it. You are a man like him. You will never understand it.'

Nest's brother Elidyr arrived late that night, with Adaf and Llew. The hut was very crowded, and Olen slept outside. When he smelled bacon in the morning he made no move to go in, but at last Elidyr came out and greeted him.

'A very sad time for your mother, Olen.'

'Yes, and for us all.'

'I will see to all the affairs. I have experience of the world.'

Olen did not answer. He barely knew Elidyr, who had gone as a lay brother, a conversus, to Abbey Dore before Olen was born. As Brother Joseph, working for the prosperous abbey, he had been given increasing responsibilities. Olen had seen most of him when he was only six or seven, when, as Brother Joseph, Elidyr had been sent to work on the abbey's big sheep grange at Gwenddwr, up the Gwy towards Buellt. On his journeys between the grange and the abbey he had often called in to see his sister. He had then been moved to other granges, in the Dore Valley and across the Mynwy in North Gwent. He had called in once after a journey with wool to Bristol, where the abbey loaded ships for export. He had many stories of the strange foreign men he had met in the port, and of the reputation of Abbey Dore's wool, fetching the highest price in all Europe. In his sister's, once his father's, hut on the mountain he spoke with ease of this wider world.

'You have had nothing to eat, boy.'

'I'm not hungry.'

'In the abbey we learn to be abstemious. Before I was your age I could always control hunger.'

'There was bacon, was there?' Olen said, looking up at him.

'It is different here.'

Olen made to move away, but Elidyr called him back. He was short and very broad, like his sister. He wore a good brown gown and new-looking leather sandals. There was a leather purse at his belt.

'Your mother will need all your help, Olen.'

'Yes, but we'll manage.'

'Adaf and Llew are good boys, but at thirteen they have still a year or two to go.'

'They work well enough.'

'Yes, but they'll need watching, until they're old enough to take over.'

'Take over?'

'Yes, in their bond. It is how the reeve will arrange it.'

'And I am not in the bond?'

Elidyr moved away. He fingered his purse. 'The crime committed on your mother . . .' he began, but then stopped.

'I know,' Olen said.

'Nothing, nothing, can make up to her for that.'

'Idris treated me as a son. I will work, if only for him.'

'Yes, but the crime . . . Have you never been told this?'

'I have indeed been told.'

'Then you should stay, for her sake, until Adaf and Llew are just that bit older.'

'And then go, you mean?'

'But obviously you will go. You could go today.'

'I don't understand. Would the reeve order me?'

'The reeve has nothing to do with you.'

'But we all take his orders. We work where he sets us.'

'The others, yes. But not you.'

'How am I supposed to be different?'

'Because of the crime committed on your mother.'

'That is supposed to make me worse than others?'

Elidyr closed his eyes. He stayed thinking for some time. 'I should not have spoken,' he said at last. 'Yet sooner or later you would be bound to hear it. You are of free blood from your father. In marriage or in rape, still the blood counts. Henry Bailey was a freeman and so you are free as his son.'

'Free to do what?'

'Free to move, as we who are unfree are not. Free to take tenancy of land. Free to be smith or priest. Free to fight and bear arms. Free in any service to your lord.'

Olen was too amazed to speak. He looked from Elidyr to the hut, and then across the meadow and beyond the pig yard to the forest. The sun was shining on Wenallt and some metal was catching its lights and reflecting it.

'You moved,' he said, looking back at Elidyr.

'That was in the time of the old lord, Lord John. In piety he allowed three of us to go to Dore as conversi. He could have levied chevage, which any unfree man must pay if he lives beyond the lordship, but this too he released.'

'Would it have been so different if you had been free?'

'In the end, perhaps not. But if I had been of free blood I would have taken my vows as a monk. It was the same call of faith, but I served it differently.'

Olen looked at the hut. Adaf and Llew had come to the doorway. He smiled and waved at them. They ran out across the meadow, and as he followed their run he saw two horsemen, turning in from the track above Llangwathau. He shaded his eyes and saw the cais and the reeve.

'Now it will all be settled,' Elidyr said, watching the horsemen. 'But be careful, Olen. Leave all the talking to me.'

Olen watched the reeve, Gilbert Lewis, as he dismounted. He was a man in his fifties, finely dressed and wearing his chain of office, but overweight and short of breath. The skin of his face was red mottled, more from drink than from weather. He was not an unkind man, but it was generally believed that he knew everything – at least everything to do with land and animals. A man nobody in his senses would ever imagine he could cheat.

'You're the holy brother, I suppose,' he said to Elidyr.

'Sir, I am Brother Joseph of Dore.'

'That thieving pile, is it? Is that Robert Wroth still the Abbot?'

'Sir, our abbey under him is holy and hard-working, as it has always been.'

'Then why do none of its neighbours believe you? How can you explain that?'

'There are many lies told against us, sir. They are told in envy.'

'Envy, is it? Because you've got control of the wool trade?'

'Sir, but for the Cistercian order there would be no wool trade.'

'You think so? You'll be telling me next your White Monks invented the sheep.'

'No, sir. But we learned how to manage large flocks, and then we took wool beyond local dealing and into large-scale trade.'

The reeve dismounted. He was breathing heavily and seemed genuinely angry. 'I'll tell you, Brother Joseph, what your order actually did. Under the cover of your Charter of Charity, which commanded only labour and poverty, you brought a new spirit to this land, a mean and grasping spirit. Given estates in piety, often poor or forested land, your White Brothers thought of nothing but squeezing a profit. You enclosed and tilled, you cleared woods by assart. You, I say, Brother Joseph, but I am talking of your masters, for simple men like you were their tools – unpaid and well-disciplined labour under a cover as conversi, lay brothers. From Dore they suppressed parish churches – Bacton was the first – and appropriated their tithes. They haunted the beds of the dying, to give them the cowl and get their property. At Dore, it is known they tonsured two rich dying women. In this endless grasping they gained seventeen granges, beyond their own immediate land. They could then keep large flocks, with each grange as an enterprise, and you conversi its unpaid servants. After that came the tax gathering, devolved to their abbots, and there was always money in their hands to bank and trade with. Buildings and wayleaves given in piety became a network of trade. In a port you would have a hospice, but also warehouses and ships, and as a religious order you were made free of tolls. So to Flanders and Italy you took not charity but dealing, not faith but gain. And now, misers as you are, you plead poverty to escape your obligations. But still, only and always, you accumulate wealth.'

Elidyr stared at Gilbert Lewis through this long denunciation. If he was surprised by the onslaught he did not show it. His hands were loosely clasped, his lips steady and slightly open, as if for a word or even a smile.

'I am sorry these lies have been told, sir,' he now said, quietly.

'Lies!' the reeve echoed, throwing out his arm as if in appeal to the cais. 'I'll tell you what is no lie. You worked, did you not, on the grange at Gwenddwr?'

'Yes, for many years.'

'And do you know what has happened to it now? It has passed from Dore Abbey to a company, of two of your monks and three laymen. And this though the Charter of Charity expressly forbids joint dealings with all beyond the Order.'

'I cannot believe it, sir.'

'Because they would not tell you. But I know it is true. My brother is one of the five.'

Elidyr looked away. The cais, who was becoming impatient, stepped forward and spoke to the reeve.

'Shall I fetch the woman, sir?'

'Yes. Fetch her. Now that I have tamed this holy brother.'

'Sir,' Elidyr said, 'my sister's needs are my . . .'

'Be silent,' the reeve shouted, his breath almost choked.

'As you wish, sir, but allow me to say that if even half the stories you tell about the Order were true, there might still be found more charity than in a cruel and grasping lordship.'

'You dare say that to me! Cais! . . .'

'I dare, sir, because I live in the Lord Christ.'

The reeve shouted again for Henry ap Rosser, but the cais was seeming not to hear and was already at the doorway of the hut, calling Nest outside. She came slowly, her face downcast. She walked to the reeve and went at once on her knees before him.

'Sir, in my great trouble, you are my only protector.'

'Nest, get up,' the reeve said impatiently.

'Sir, my good man is gone, and I . . .'

'Get up, I say. You are a hard woman. Don't play this girl's game with me.'

Nest hesitated, then got to her feet.

'I heard you discussing with my brother, sir. It is a comfort . . .'

'Leave your brother out of it. It is all very simple. I am sorry about Idris. I would not find a better pigman if I rode between Severn and Wye. He cannot be replaced but . . .'

'Sir, sir, I must tell you. Every day, these eighteen years, I have worked with my good man. I made fire, I nursed them, I nursed a litter like human babies.'

'All right, Nest, all right. And you can go on doing it. I want the pig herd kept up, and you and your sons will manage it.'

'Sir, thank you, and for my two sons. But Idris's chattels, sir . . .'

'I'm leaving everything in the hut. And you can keep that old ox. All I shall take, now, is your last litter.'

'The last! But sir, if . . .'

'Nest, you are getting off lightly, so don't . . .'

Elidyr stepped forward.

'To take a whole litter from a woman just widowed . . .' he began, but now the cais went across to him, seized his arm and hurried him away.

Nest watched them go. Then she looked back at the reeve. 'It's not a good litter, sir, the last. There might be . . .'

'Nest, I know pigs. I shall look for myself.'

Nest smiled and curtseyed. The reeve looked round and saw Olen, who through all the talking had kept back out of sight.

'You! Olen, is it? Take me to the pigs.'

Olen hurried forward. They walked up together.

'I was just remembering,' Gilbert Lewis said. 'Your mother thanked me for herself and for her two sons. But there are twin boys, aren't there, younger than you?'

'Yes, sir, Adaf and Llew.'

'Then why did she say two sons?'

'Sir, I was not the son of Idris.'

Gilbert Lewis stopped. He put his hand on Olen's shoulder and pulled him round to look into his face.

'Of course! I should have remembered. The rape!'

Olen did not answer.

'Yet you are Nest's son all the same.'

'I am, sir, but she thinks of me as the son of a crime against her, and she has forgiven neither of us.'

'I'll say nothing about that. But your natural father, one of Hywel Fychan's men . . .'

'Henry Bailey, sir. A freeman.'

The reeve nodded and smiled.

'I see. So that's how the land lies?'

'Is it true, sir,' Olen asked nervously, 'that by my father's blood I am myself free?'

'Yes, Olen, you are.'

'But then why was I not told it? Why did she not tell me, if she hated me so much? Or why did Idris not tell me, since he loved me?'

'He brought you up. You were a son to him.'

'Yes, but now that he has gone?'

'I know. It's difficult. But let's just look over the pigs.'

They reached the pig yard. They walked together round the pens, and the reeve spoke again of Idris and of his great skill with the herd. He also counted the youngest litter and ordered Olen to bring them next day to the castle.

'Come yourself.'

'Yes, sir.'

'You are free, Olen, but not of this kin, this gwely. There could be no land for you here.'

'But I can move, sir, can't I?'

'I'll make some enquiries. I'll send you on to whoever can help you. That is, if you're certain you want to leave your mother.'

'You heard her, sir. My two sons.'

'They are young, but perhaps they can manage. I'll see.'

'I'd stay for a time, sir, if . . .'

'Yes, it will take some time. There will be formalities and so on, the old records of the case.'

'I've heard that at Caldicote . . .'

The reeve stopped and looked hard into Olen's face. 'It's a story for you, I suppose. The Black Plague, people die, there is free land.'

'No, sir, but . . .'

'It was no ordinary plague, Olen. It was the worst ever known, and though the first peak passed they are still getting cases. If it breaks out again, as it did in '49 and '50, it could be almost the end of us.'

'It didn't reach here, sir.'

'Yes, in fact, several cases. They were burned and kept quiet.'

Olen looked away. The reeve walked a few paces and then turned. His mottled face was grave. 'You heard what I said to your uncle about the White Monks. It was all true. In his defence he spoke back about the cruelties of a lordship. Some of that may also be true. There is greed and cruelty in the hearts of many men. But listen, Olen, for I know the workings of life. Nothing that has been done, nothing that could be done, is as cruel, as insistent and as arbitrary as these devilish buboes, this evil black death. It is no excuse for any of our human cruelties, but this is a power beyond us, a power within life itself, which now perversely carries death. So far our mountains have saved us. May they long save us, and may we long save them!'

Olen looked up. By the hut the cais had remounted and was leading the reeve's horse. Elidyr stood free, close to Nest. Adaf and Llew, shouting as they played, were running home across the meadow.

For Mair's labour, her sister Elen had come. Her father and elder brother were in close discussion with all the kin about the future of the holding. Several elders from the nine centres of the Welshry came and walked the land at Penyrallt, to prepare for the decison of tenancy. There could be descent of rights to land only through the male line. In the earth itself there was no property, for land and kin were inseparable; the one was the other.

It was finally agreed that Ieuan's nearest male relative, a third cousin with a holding at Maesygarn, but also working two quillets in the big open field at Caenantmelyn, should receive two further quillets now worked by Morgan of Pantyfithel. He, in return, would get the working of Penyrallt, which adjoined his own holding. Meanwhile Mair's animals by the customs of argyfrau and cowyll, her dowry and wedding gift, were removed to Blaendigedi Uchaf, where she would live again in her father's house. Her personal goods and her share of the common chattels were also carted up over the mountain, on the old track past Cilonw and Maescoch. The kin had been wounded, but now the kin healed.

Mair, though young and strong, was almost broken by Ieuan's death. In the last days of labour Elen was so worried for her that she sent for the wise woman Gwen of Plascelyn. When the birth was close Mair's mother, who was crippled, was brought in a cart to be close to her. Rhys ap Hywel, the pencenedl, also came for the birth.

It was a painful but short labour. The child was a boy. Mair's mother held him, and Rhys ap Hywel knelt and kissed his forehead.

'He is Bleddyn ap Ieuan, Bleddyn of the kin,' he said, formally. 'He is born to his rights in our land.'

The women were impatient, and he quickly went out. He stood talking with Morgan of Pantyfithel by the large woodpile, and later Mair's father joined them.

Nine days after the birth, and on the seventeenth day after Ieuan and Idris were killed, Mair's brother Ifor fetched the ox and harnessed it to the repaired waggon. Mair walked out, carrying her baby. Elen followed with clothes, bedclothes and pans. The waggon was loaded.

Mair looked down the steep slope towards Hay and the Gwy. The weather had changed again. The sky was grey and the north wind was sharp. She got into the waggon, with Elen beside her. Ifor prodded the ox forward, on the long track over the mountain.

GLYN TO ELIS: 13

◆

The sky was clearing in the west, but now the wind was rising – a cold searching air from the north. Glyn huddled closer under the bank. As so often, on these mountains, the sharp edge of the wind seemed to be carrying but not yet forming rain.

Centuries earlier, on a chill day in late October, below Rhos Dirion, Henry Earl of Derby, newly Duke of Hereford, rode to inspect his inherited lordship of Brecon. A retinue of forty horsemen surrounded him. Fourteen horses drew waggons laden with the goods he had collected on the earlier part of his triumphal journey. The tenants of these mountain lordships had been summoned to attend him in his court. They would celebrate the joyful accession with a gift to the Duke of two thousand marks.

The same edge of wind, blowing across the exacting procession. Endlessly, into these mountains and valleys, alien lords had ridden for tribute. Yet the dominant direction was now changing. A new earl would ride in to collect his birthright, but many more processions were riding the other way. The noisy trampling of four hundred head of cattle, setting out one cold autumn morning for the Bohun estates in distant Essex, along the first drovers' roads, but not, as later, for sale; simply the methodical annual transfer of what Bohun took as surplus from his lordships of the March. Livestock, wealth on the hoof. An endless unpaid export of cattle raised on this grass. And not only living creatures were driven from these mountains, but also the new computation, the more effective and portable transfer of money. On a bitter December day, in 1387, a troop of archers drawn from the fighting men of the border rode to escort the treasure carts filled with bullion from the Mortimer estates, including Ewyas and Blaenllynfi, to proud and distant London. No longer the fierce moments of battle and seizure, of looting and devastating, *vastatio*. A new caste in a new function: not warlords but regular and ruthless exploiters. A whole century, the fourteenth, belonging to these Lords of the March.

Clare and Braose, Fitzherbert and Tony, Lacy, Clifford and Cantelupe: the old arrogant names. But now rising names: de Burgh and de Bohun; Stafford, Hastings and Beauchamp; Montague and Despenser. Above even these, along the length of the March, Fitzalan and Mortimer: Mortimer owning sixteen lordships and controlling two others. A concentration, consolidation of power. Nine of the seventeen Earls of England are Marcher Lords. Combining or contending in England, using profit drained from this border country, they assert absolute autonomy within the March itself. 'The March was never a parcel of the realm of England.'

But then a parcel of what? The old Principality of Wales, centred on Gwynedd, had passed from Welsh hands with the killing of Llywelyn ap Gruffydd – Y Llyw Olaf, the Last Prince – in 1282. Until that distant redoubt fell, the lordships of the March were open to Welsh challenge. But now, in those terms, there was peace. The Lords of the March were neither threatened by rival Welsh lords, nor, within their lands, subject to the English King. The liberty of the March was their absolute licence, in life and death, in law and taxation. Intriguing and intermarrying, accumulating and purchasing, they met on their own frontiers for what they called Love Days, attended by officials and *fideles*, negotiating disputes, disposing of runaways and criminals, each asserting an autonomy within a corporate autonomy.

Along a border country still by reputation wild and lawless, yet for the first time in many centuries free of contending armies, they ruled from or visited their ninety castles, massive stone centres of administration and legal suit. In the boroughs protected by their castles English immigrants and settlers purchased rights of trade now forbidden to the Welsh. From the uplands above, the Welsh, free and unfree, in surviving traditional groups, looked down on the centres of power which, practically, looked down on them.

The first wealth of a lordship was its subjects, especially men. But the full wealth was whatever the lord deemed his own, in what the land bore, but also, more profitably, in all actual social relationships, where the lord was a party to all things. Yet, within this ubiquitous imposition, the basic economy was changing. A general market, in corn and wool and in beef, was gaining ascendancy over local subsistence and render. In the same way, the old communal renders of traditional communities to their native lords, were, against generations of habit and resistance, being remorselessly pressed into individual economic relationships, bypassing those older formations in which social and economic identities, even within exploitation, coincided. These transformations were still immature, but they were steadily, even irresistibly maturing.

Corn was already a large market, mainly from the arable land of the manors in the valleys, Usk and Wye, which surrounded the mountains. On the uplands, without manors, the system was different. The lord had absolute property in arable, meadow, pasture, forest and waste; in all birds and beasts; in all fisheries, mills and ferries. The great increase in profit came from this. Timber and charcoal from the forests were directly sold. Tenants had no right to cut even dead trees on the land they worked, though some concessions were made for seasonal building. Hunting in the forest was strictly controlled and the ownership of dogs forbidden. In a Bohun lordship the penalty for being found in a forest was forfeiture of all goods or the loss – severing – of a foot. Fishing, similarly, was heavily penalised, especially with nets. To gain land from the waste required a paid licence. But above all, in this pastoral country, the old grazing commons were made subject to toll, typically a cyfrif of two capons and two hens for each beast entering the pasture. The digging of fuel peat was forbidden or charged.

The ancient pastures of these families now saw a concentrated development of cattle for export and, especially, a market in wool. The national and international market developed by the Cistercians passed, in large part, to the lords, who held huge flocks under professional stockmen. Despite recurrent disease, management was easier and the profits direct. In the second half of the century local demesne production was steadily abandoned in favour of lease, rent and farm by increasingly absent landlords. Hunting parks, on the other hand, were jealously marked and guarded; the famous park at Grosmont was a favourite of the House of Lancaster.

Into this system, through the century, came the terrible Black Death. The severe pestilence of 1349 raged through Gwent into Abergavenny, killing many and reducing the profits of lordship. The exploitation of what remained was redoubled, but the plague came again in 1361, 1362 and 1366. In 1369 it leaped the mountains, and there was heavy death and loss in Hay, Talgarth and Brecon, and in the inner valleys. Still the money exactions continued, though there were fewer to pay and some land was going out of use.

The crop that could always be raised was the special crop of lordship: the administration of law. To be born, marry or to die was to pay money to the lord. To pay damages to another was also to pay them to the lord. To have acted beyond his law was to pay heavy redress, with long suit and attendance at court. For convenience, as it was described, penalties that had been incurred or that might have been incurred (a question requiring long argument and attendance) were consolidated as a redemption, and a communal pardon. The redemption – the Great Tax, Y Dreth Fawr – became a regular source of lordly income.

Where armies had ravaged for more than a millennium in this disputed border country, bubonic plague and Marcher Lords now ravaged in their turn. The March was racially complex, with many local hatreds. The men of Glyn Bwch, the old Maenhebog, marched to Clifford and burned two hundred houses; the records do not say why, but the time tells us. For this was a land of two peoples, with two underlying social and legal systems. The English of the towns were privileged in office, in trade and in law, though they still complained bitterly of the wild, devious and thieving Welsh. The complexities of intermarriage and of landholding and inheritance were endless grounds of dispute. Often the facts of the society did not fit the simple perceptions of an opposition of two races: the richer Welsh, allied with Norman and English families, went to court and university in England and sought and gained some official positions. But in the mountains the perceptions were harder, and the system which exploited them so efficient that it would have been hated even without its racial definitions.

There were local risings, like the burning of Clifford. But towards 1400 a new and more widespread feeling awoke. The poets wrote of a coming Mab y Darogan, a Son of Destiny. At the start of the new century, after a military rising in the north of the March, the English parliament passed a whole series of laws against the Welsh. No public assembly was allowed except in the presence of the lord's officers. No Welshman could be admitted to public office. No arms could be borne by Welshmen in highway or town. 'No waster, rhymer, minstrel or vagabond' could go to the common people of Wales for maintenance. English strangers to each district were to be moved into castles and walled towns as garrisons. Meanwhile, Welsh labourers in England left their work and returned to their homelands. Welsh students in Oxford and Cambridge came back to their own country. New and bloody lines were being drawn.

Glyn turned his face to the still rising wind. He closed his eyes. He thought again of those passing processions: the Welsh cattle out along the drovers' roads to the English estates; the groaning treasure train of the incoming Duke of Hereford; the cartloads of bullion on their way to distant London. There was another kind of procession, the fighting men, who were levied for wars in Scotland and Ireland, in France and Flanders. Three thousand five hundred men went out from the March to the English victory at Crecy.

These were the ultimate profits of lordship, to crop armed men in the battles of lordship elsewhere. But what would happen if these men, seasoned in arms, turned to fight on their own account? The wind was now forming and driving a cold rain.

'Taid, Taid,' Glyn called against the storm.

The Abergavenny Rising

♦

Hooves struck sharp stones on the pitch from Honddu to Crucornau. Within the steep canter the prisoners were running, tied together by ropes on their wrists and waists. All were breathless. The two older men were swaying from side to side as they ran. The horse troop halted at the inn yard.

'That's Edric,' the ostler shouted. He was peering at one of the men who had dropped, exhausted, on the cobbles of the yard.

'And Rosser and young Saunder,' his brother exclaimed. He moved closer until a warning sword barred his way.

The leader of the horse troop, a tall man of thirty in a light golden cloak, called down to the ostler. 'Find your reeve Gwatkin and tell him Sir William Lucy wishes to see him at once.'

'Sir! Lord! The reeve is not here. He left early for the castle!'

'For Bergavenny?'

'Yes, lord.'

Lucy looked around. Many men had left their work and were gathering, looking down on the prisoners. He dismounted and called for ale from the inn. He ordered the horses to be watered. The prisoners were closely guarded by the soldiers, with drawn swords.

Iorworth ap Rhys, whose land bordered the inn, stood forward and called to the brothers Edric and Rosser.

'Why are you taken like this?'

'It is a mistake,' Edric called back.

'Or a lie,' Rosser added.

'You must tell us what has happened.'

Edric struggled to his feet. The soldiers did not interfere.

'Yesterday, brothers, after noon, a gentleman from the castle came to our reeve Gwatkin and told him to find three men to fetch cattle from Garway. Gwatkin called Rosser and myself, and we called our nephew Saunder. We were to be at Talyram below Elchon before dark last night and to report to Grono Sais. He would deliver us nineteen bullocks, and at dawn we were to drive them to the manor of Lanbedr. We were shown the cattle, and this morning we set off. But as we were crossing Mynwy ford, this lord the sheriff and his men rode down on us. They said we were stealing the cattle. We explained our orders and Grono Sais was fetched to get at the truth of it. Brothers, he denied that he knew us or that he had given us the cattle. Yet hours before he had been with us when we penned them from the herd. Now the lord sheriff is taking us to the castle as thieves, which as you who know us will realise, is false.'

Iorworth waited, and then stood closer.

'This Grono Sais? What is he?'

'He is bailiff, we were told, to the lord at Garway.'

'And was there payment for the cattle?'

'None from us. Our work was to drive.'

'Who was the gentleman from the castle?'

'I did not know him. He did not speak to us. Only Gwatkin dealt with us, but the gentleman was standing near by.'

There was a long silence. Then Iorworth approached Sir William Lucy. 'My lord, believe me, we know these men. They are honest men. What they have told you must be the truth.'

'Must be, fellow? When they were taken red-handed and when their feeble story collapsed with the first witness?'

'There must be some mistake or some falsehood in others. These men would not go from their village and steal.'

'All Welshmen steal,' Lucy said. 'Mount up.'

The troop reassembled. Rosser and Saunder got to their feet.

'Ride,' Lucy called, and at a brisk trot the party rode towards Abergavenny, with Edric, Rosser and Saunder running tied among them.

Lady Joan, daughter of the Earl of Arundel and wife of Sir William Beauchamp Lord of Bergavenny, was in the castle solar with her Receiver John Churcher, when the sheriff of Hereford rode in with his prisoners. They went together to the hall to receive him and to hear his account of their capture. When the poor excuse they had to offer was mentioned, Lady Joan asked Churcher to find Reeve Gwatkin. He returned explaining that he had been unable to find him, but that he had sent others to make sure of his attendance.

'It is, in any case, an obvious lie,' Lady Joan said. 'How could cattle be honestly brought overnight from another territory?'

'Indeed, my Lady,' Sir William Lucy said. 'It is the very form of a Welsh lie.'

'I will try them first thing in the morning,' Lady Joan announced, 'for my lord will not return from Pembroke for some days at best. If you will stay, Sir William, I shall be glad to entertain you and see justice done.'

The sheriff accepted the invitation, and Lady Joan called a servant to see him properly lodged.

When they were again alone Lady Joan and Churcher withdrew to the solar. She closed the door and turned to him.

'You looked hard for this Gwatkin?'

He smiled. He was three years younger than his lady, handsome and finely dressed in a short houppelande. His grey eyes were large and amused. He stood with one hand on the table behind him, lightly crossing his legs. 'With my usual devotion,' he replied.

'And must I look hard for the young gentleman from the castle?'

'That is your privilege, lady.'

'You must not trifle with me, John. If you arranged this it was madness to steal from Hereford. If William Lucy gets hold of you, even I cannot save you.'

'There is no danger,' Churcher replied easily. 'Gwatkin will say whatever I tell him to say.'

'But why take such risks? Is what I give you not enough?'

Churcher walked towards her and took her hands. 'You know I have my manor to stock,' he said earnestly. 'I have no wealth from birth. There is no real risk. The Welsh steal our cattle so often that they are always there to be blamed. This Gwatkin and his fellow Grono Sais of Garway have played this trick for many years. When I caught Gwatkin at it there seemed no reason why I should not turn the trick for myself. And if he does not support me he knows I have evidence to hang him.'

She pulled her hands away. 'You would say the same of me I suppose?' she said angrily.

'Of you, my lady? Your life is an open book.'

'Which you would teach my husband to read I suppose?'

'Indeed not. It has never been part of my duty.'

She moved away and looked from the window at the bustle in the courtyard. 'One thing is certain at least, John. These Welsh villeins must have no chance of seeing you.'

'But that is easily arranged. And Gwatkin is already well rehearsed.'

'The risk is still there. The whole thing must be done quickly. They must be hanged by noon tomorrow.'

'It will be Ascension Day.'

'None of that matters. For them it will be ascension to the gallows.'

After a brief trial in the first hour after dawn, Edric, Rosser and young Saunder were condemned. Sir William Lucy sat at Lady Joan's right hand, and, with her permission, questioned Gwatkin closely. But he was firm in his denial that he had given any such order for cattle to be moved. Gwatkin added that he was surprised that they now told such a lie, for he had always known them as honest and faithful villeins.

It was decided that the men should be hanged at once. The sheriff and his posse led the three prisoners to the gallows outside the main gate. They were surprised to find an unusually large crowd of villeins gathered there, men from the eight manors of the lordship.

When Lady Joan left the great hall she hurried to the southwest tower to overlook the executions. She ascended the narrow spiral staircase. Her right hand lifted her crimson houppelande to its high embroidered girdle. The other rested on the rough stones of the tower wall. With each pointed step her sleeve trailed the dusty tread. As she neared the top, she caught the scent of hawthorn from the trees below the castle mound. Early bees were gathering oily honey from their blossom. The morning sun lit the blunt crescent of the Blorenge hillside, and the Usk as it curved through the wide flood plain between the hills and the castle. The pasture, watered by the willow-lined streams, supported a herd of summer cattle.

Emerging from the stairway her horned head-dress and veil were seen above the battlements by the waiting villeins.

'It's the Devil himself ascending on this holy day,' a voice cried. The three prisoners and their guards turned to stare at the woman on the tower.

Then another voice cried, 'Jezebel! Jezebel!'

More voices joined the chant. A flight of arrows fell on the guards, one fatally piercing the sheriff of Hereford through the neck. He fell, crushed beneath the trampling feet of the villeins surging through the castle gates.

The three prisoners were pushed towards the back of the crowd, where a boy stood holding three mountain ponies on a rope.

'Edric! Rosser! Saunder!' he called.

When the men approached, he cut their bonds. Each grasped the mane of a pony and jumped on its back. The boy gave them a sharp slap on the rump, and, crouching low, they set off northwards towards the Black Mountains.

The men at arms withdrew inside to defend Lady Joan, who now became a virtual prisoner in the castle of her absent lord. The sheriff of Hereford lay dead, and suddenly the serfs were in complete control. Their rising caught up the more general grievances in the manors, and soon the whole lordship was in rebellion. This in turn became part of more widespread disturbances in Wales as a whole. At the end of August two years later, as the Welsh Annals tell us, Abergavenny was burned to the ground. Then the lord, William Beauchamp, wrote from Hereford to King Henry at Woodstock appealing for help to restore order, saying that he was all but ruined. In mid-September the king and a royal company arrived in Hereford, and set out to subdue south Wales: among these troops was an especially able and trusted knight, Sir John Oldcastle.

Thus a small local rising, starting out as a protest against the desecration of a holy day, grew into and merged with that general rebellion of the Principality, which found a figurehead in Owain Glyndŵr.

The Comet

◆

Edric stood on the ridge of Finnon y Parc. A cold north wind was blowing from the oak forests beyond the Wye valley. Lower down, green bracken shoots were pushing up through last year's flattened litter. A red kite, so close in colour to the dead fronds that only its white head was visible, sailed past him on a rising current. The man coming up the grass track by Wern Ferig must be Bleddyn ap Ieuan from Penyrallt farm. He waved his shepherd's staff and called sharply to the young dog that was circling among the gorse bushes to come to heel. Edric hurried down the zigzag sheep track to meet him.

Over the past year the two men had grown to trust one another, and though the life of a villein on the arable lowlands of the Bergavenny manors was alien to the free kinsman of the Welshry, need had drawn them together. The three fugitives gave Bleddyn help on the farm, haymaking, shearing, and especially looking for lost sheep on the mountains, and he repaid with gifts of food, and shelter among his cattle in the hardest weather.

'The women have sent you some bread and salt meat,' said Bleddyn, holding out a linen sack.

'My thanks to your wife and mother Mair. I found a few grouse eggs among the heather on the tops.' In his pouch were three red-brown eggs with specks and blotches of a darker red-brown. 'The others are mending the roof. Rain got in during the night. Rosser patches while the young one fetches turves and heather. Do the mountain people use these round hollows for shelters?'

'The summer shepherds may have, but not in my time.' He found a flat boulder to sit on. The dog was running to and fro again among the gorse as Edric put his eggs down carefully on the grass.

'I have a favour to ask you,' Bleddyn said.

'We are more in your debt than we can repay.'

'You know I am pencenedl. As head of my kin group, I have been asked to give a sign to the men of these mountains.'

'This headman is a lord? He is powerful?'

'Not a lord, the senior landholder of his kin. He makes some decisions, like the one that brought me back to the farm where I was born, and where my father had farmed, twenty years after his death.'

'What do you want me to do?'

'Will you light a fire, the day after tomorrow at the top of Pen y Beacon? By day it should be fed with damp wood to give smoke, and at nightfall with dry wood and gorse to give a blaze that will guide our people here. It must be big enough to be seen from the lordships of Ewas, Hay, Ystradwy, and Blaen Lynfi. The men will come up the valleys and over the pass to gather by the Stones of the Old People. Then the bards will come.'

'This is important?'

'It is said that the bards are travelling through the land with a message and a prophecy.'

Two days later men began to gather at the stone circle below the beacon hill, where the tall stone marked the line to the midwinter sunset over the western hills. As it was getting dark a line of torches was seen coming up from Penyrallt to the open plain of Caer Bwld. At the head of the procession strode a tall man wearing a long blue cloak over his white robe. Behind him, carrying his staff, came a younger man, the second bard. The crowd moved towards them.

'It is Iolo,' a voice shouted.

The bards crossed the Field of the Bull and mounted the round burial mound of Twyn y Beddau. Surrounded by torches, Iolo stood with arms uplifted, his russet hair blowing back from his pale face till the crowd was silent.

'My friends,' he said, 'people of the Black Mountains, I bring you joyful news. The great star, which you have seen appear in the sky these last months, has moved northward to settle over Gwynedd. It is a sign from heaven. It is the third great star of history. The first foretold the coming of Christ, that was the Star of Bethlehem. The second foretold the birth of Uther pen Dragon, father of Arthur who drove the Saxons from our land. Now our star has risen. Another Son of Destiny has arrived. Owain Glendŵr is to lead us. He is already fighting to drive out the Saxons. At Ruthin and Myndd Hyddgant he has won great victories. He has sacked Montgomery and the Cistercian house of Cwm Hir. Owain is a learned man. He has written from his court, in the French language, to King Robert of Scotland, to remind him of their common ancestor Brutus, from whom Great Britain is named. He recalled that Brutus had three sons, Albanact, who founded the royal house of Scotland, Locrine of Britain, and Camber, his own ancestor through Cadwallader. He has asked for his help to fulfil the prophecy, that together with the Scots we would be delivered from the Saxons, freed from their tyranny and bondage. Our Prince Owain has written to the princes of Ireland, asking them, in the Latin tongue, to come to his aid. Now he asks you also, men of the Black Mountains, in our own native tongue, to join the struggle, and fight to fulfil the prophecy!'

A murmur went through the crowd, which surged towards the bard, but he again raised his arms and continued: 'The barbarous Bolingbroke, who comes against us, is a godless man. He has raided our churches, even Strata Florida, and tethered his horses at our altars. He has laid waste our land, and carried off one thousand of our children to be slaves in England. Here, boy!' He turned and beckoned to the group around him. A small boy of ten years or so stepped forward. He was thin, barefoot, and roughly dressed in a short tunic. 'Show yourself to these good people. Tell them how you were rounded up and driven like cattle by the Saxon soldiers, your parents slain, your home burned. Tell them how you fell by the wayside, on the long cold march, and were left to die, a prey to hunger and the wolves!' The bard opened his arms wide in a gesture which embraced the crowd. 'My friends, shall we allow these outrages to continue? Or will you take up your bows and arrows and join our prince to purify the land?'

A great shout followed his speech. It was now very dark, blotting out everything but the circle of torches around the mound. As the comet appeared in the northern sky, the young bard came forward. He asked all the men who were ready for battle to kneel before him and swear an oath on the comet to fight with the Son of Destiny, Owain Glyndŵr. Young Saunder was one of the first to swear.

In the year that followed, news of the fighting came to Rosser and Edric in the mountains, but nothing of their nephew. In the summer, as they were shearing sheep with Bleddyn, they heard of the Welsh attack on Brecon castle, then in August women gathering whin-berries on the Hateral saw smoke from the burning priory of Bergavenny. News came up the valley that their former lord, William Beauchamp, had appealed, from his refuge in Hereford, to the king, saying that he was all but ruined from the disturbances in his lands.

'If his wife had had her way we should have been ruined two years ago,' said Rosser.

In September, a friar travelling from Hereford reported that King Henry was gathering an army there to put down the risings and that his three castles, Grosmont, Skenfrith, and White Castle, were preparing for siege. Then shepherds from Pen Cerrig Calch saw similar preparations at Crykheoll castle in the keeping of John Pauncefoot. Ewyas Lacy, held by the widow Constance le Despencer, was also making ready.

A few weeks later they saw the English troops, under the royal banner, come up the valley of the Usk to Henry's castle of Brecon, held from his first wife Mary Bohun. Soon the lordships of the north and west parts of the Black Mountains were brought under control.

The Welsh who could, escaped back to their homes. The formal submissions of the lordships of Brecon, Builth, Cantref Self, Hay, Bwch and Dinas, were made to Henry's trusted knight Sir John Oldcastle and his two supporters, canon Fairford and John ap Henry, the steward of Dinas. These lordships were then received into the king's grace, and for them the war was over. But still young Saunder did not come back.

'We shall not see him again, unless he is wounded and on the run,' said Rosser.

The following summer, Saunder, his arm covered with a blood-stained rag, appeared one evening as the brothers were cooking a wild duck over the fire outside their hut.

'I thought you would be back one of these days,' said Rosser. 'Did the Sais chase you off?'

'We had a defeat over at Campston hill. Our prince's banner was captured. A fine white banner with a golden dragon on it. We tried to get it back. We chased the Sais from cover down the Trothy all the way to Monmouth. That's the way for us to fight. We can never win the pitched battles. We caught up with them in the end on Craig y Dorth, and fought till they hid inside the castle walls.'

Rosser gave a sharp laugh, and took the roasted bird off the spit. 'So now you have come back with a gammy arm and no banner,' he said.

'It's not the end. My arm will mend. Prince Owain will get a new banner.'

Rosser laughed again.

'He will lead us to victory. He is a magician. He appears everywhere there is fighting.'

'Have you seen this magician?' Rosser asked.

'No. But I have seen his banner.'

Saunder's arm was slow to mend. He spent the winter with the brothers in the mountains, going down to the farm every few days to have his wound tended by Mair. She was skilled in the use of herbs for healing, and gave him draughts of elderberry cordial to keep out the cold. By spring of the next year he was ready to rejoin the fighting, and set off one cold March morning with a full quiver of new arrows and a restrung bow. The high walls of the pass sheltered him from the east wind. A few mountain ponies, still in their rough winter coats, were cropping the short grass. Down the Honddu valley the boulders and stunted blackthorn trees gave place to thick oak forests. The priory of Llanthony stood empty and neglected, its store rooms broken open. The monks no longer felt safe among their Welsh tenants, and had withdrawn to Hereford. Below a mountain stream, their retting mill had fallen into disrepair. The dried shocks of flax, pulled each day by the abbey's labourers, stood abandoned, their blue, white and pink flowers long withered. Sheep grazed above the empty abbey, and across the river over the slopes towards the Coed y Dial.

When he reached the inn at Crucornau he ordered ale and asked the landlord for news. The landlord looked at the longbow resting against the wall, and the full quiver of arrows at Saunder's feet.

'News of the fighting you mean?'

'Aye. I have been living in the mountains till my wounds were healed. I last saw the Sais retreating into Monmouth castle. We chased them down the Trothy valley, and won a fine victory at Craig y Dorth.'

'They say it was their victory. But I seem to know you. Have you been here before?'

Saunder smiled, and looked up at the smoke-blackened beams where two iron hooks were fixed.

'I was one of the three prisoners who halted here four years ago with Sheriff Lucy, on our way to be hanged at Bergavenny.'

'You are looking well for a hanged man. The folk in London call us "Welch doggis" and pass new laws against us. But they have found that dogs can bite.'

'Where can I find Prince Owain's men?'

'He is not in these parts, but you will find Rhys Gethin, with eight thousand men, on his way to Grosmont vill. The English prince is there in the castle. They mean to capture him.'

'Then I will join Rhys Gethin, and trust he's as fierce as his name. If we capture young Harry, the war will soon be over.'

Saunder did not return to the mountains till after May. By then the people of the south and east of the Black Mountains had made mass submission to the young Prince Henry of Monmouth, all the districts of Hothenay, Slad, Ffwothog, Y Glyn, Olghan and Stradewy.

'Lost any more banners?' asked Rosser. 'I see you have brought back both your arms.'

'We could have won a great victory at Grosmont if Rhys Gethin had attacked the castle right away. Instead he let his men burn and pillage the town. The king's troops arrived from Hereford, and we were unprepared. We were sure the Welsh bowmen would join us, but this time they stayed with the Sais, and we were overwhelmed. The young prince and his knights came riding out of the castle, Talbot, Newport, and Grendor, all veterans. It was all over for us. They know war. We only know how to fight.'

'How did you get away?' asked Edric.

Saunder was sitting slumped on the grass, poking the wood embers with a stick. Behind him a crow drifted down and settled on the wall of the sheepfold.

'Some of us escaped, and moved south with Prince Owain's son Gruffydd, to Bryn Buga. We attacked the castle they call Usk, but we could not take it, and they defeated us again at the hill of Pwl Melyn. May it was when we fought at the Yellow Pool, just four years after you and I were condemned to death at Bergavenny, so I was not afraid to die. I thought, I have had four more years of life since that morning, and killed many Sais, I am ready for whatever happens to me. Not everyone felt like that. There was a friar who preached to us before the battle. He told us not to fear death, but to remember that all who fell in battle would sup that night in heaven. When the battle turned against us, we saw him slipping away from the field. The soldiers taunted him, and one said, "Why aren't you waiting with us to share the heavenly banquet?" He said, "My sons, this is one of my fast days, so I must deny myself the pleasure," and ran off!'

'A wise man,' said Rosser. 'I warrant he is eating well enough now.'

Saunder threw his stick away angrily.

'Many of our soldiers will never eat again unless it is in heaven!' he said. 'Our army was chased through the river Usk to the great forest of Monkswood. Some escaped, but they say that fifteen hundred were killed in battle that day, and three hundred prisoners were taken and put to the sword before the castle. Owain's brother Tudor was slain, and his son Gruffydd was taken to London a prisoner. I think this is the end of our struggle.'

The three men sat around the fire saying nothing. The scent of hawthorn mixed with the stronger scents of bracken and woodsmoke.

'This lot here have turned Sais,' said Rosser.

'But not Glyndŵr,' said Edric. 'He will never make his submission.'

Oldcastle in Olchon

◆

Caradoc crossed his yard to the grassy mound, which his father had told him held the bones and stones of the Old Ones. From the top of the mound the dark figure of the lone horseman along the ridge of Cwrwm from Hateral stood out even more sharply against the silvery autumn sky. The proportions of horse and rider seemed strange. The legs of the horse were unusually long, as if it were a colt. The body of the rider seemed exceptionally tall. Caradoc had noticed this effect before in a figure outlined on the ridge. What now most concerned him was who this rider might be. None of his own people were on the mountain that day, and all those who lived down the valley and had business to transact or visits to make would travel along the roads halfway up the slopes beside the springs and the sources.

Caradoc fetched his sword and bow. He hurried to the copse at the foot of the track which led down from the ridge, in case the rider came that way. As he approached he heard women's voices, and saw old Megan, whose mother had been one of the last slaves in these mountains, with her widowed niece Elen. Her husband Ifor had been killed while serving with Prince Owain: controversially, since it was claimed that he had been killed after the Defynnog submission to the English captains.

Caradoc moved forward to the women, and said in a low voice: 'There is a stranger coming, say nothing. Be quiet for I want to surprise him in a challenge.' The women, turning their faces under their stiff white caps, nodded and continued their gathering of blackberries into the bright yellow osier baskets.

Caradoc found the screen of a bush from which he could command the track and waited. It was a long wait, yet he had some sense, some inner sense, that this stranger would come.

At last he heard the sound of the horse on the loose stones of the track and he drew his bow. The rider came into view through the arch of trees. He was indeed tall in the saddle. He wore the hat of an English soldier, but the cloak of a Welshman. He was a man of middle age, with heavy moustache and long fair hair. Caradoc drew his bow tighter and aimed at the stranger's heart.

'Halt!' he shouted. 'Halt!'

The stranger looked around, his hand going to his hip.

'Halt and state your name and purpose,' Caradoc shouted.

The stranger looked up.

Caradoc remained concealed.

'I am Oldcastle,' the stranger called, in a deep strong voice.

'Oldcastle? What is that?' Caradoc called.

'John Oldcastle,' the stranger said. 'John Oldcastle knight of Almeley in the shire of Hereford.'

'An English Captain!' Caradoc exclaimed.

'Indeed, I have been my king's captain,' Oldfield replied. 'But I come now on a different business. What this business is I will not say until I know to whom I am speaking.' The stranger's Welsh was fluent, but with a Saxon edge.

Caradoc waited for some moments. 'I am Caradoc ap Haddon,' he called, 'of this valley of Olchon. Now tell me your business.'

'That is easy,' Oldcastle replied, 'since it is you, Caradoc ap Haddon, that I have come to see. For I was given your name in Hereford by one pure in the faith.'

'Which man gave you my name?' Caradoc called, warily.

'It was Thomas Skinner the elder; one of many in that city brought to the light by the good William Swinderby who had fled to this shire from his own persecutors.'

'I know nothing of this Swinderby, but I know this Thomas from the markets. He has an honest reputation.'

'It is now more than his honesty. For when we met and were secret he told me that you and he had spoken very earnestly of the Antichrist.'

'I do not know of the Antichrist. But I remember speaking with him of the grasping ways of these neighbouring houses that pretend to the name of religion. I mean the Abbey of Dore and the Priory of Llanthony, whose hands have been heavy on the people of these mountains. We had among us a third house in the uplands of

Craswall whose members lived indeed in the manner of holy men observing their vows of poverty and giving no annoyance to their neighbours. Yet that peaceful house was suppressed, while the grasping houses have continued to flourish.'

'Indeed,' Oldcastle cried, 'for they are limbs of the great body of Antichrist, and all who oppose them are called heretics or traitors.'

Caradoc took his arrow from his bow and scrambled down to the track.

'Dismount, sir, if you please,' he called.

Oldcastle jumped down from his horse.

'Lay your sword on the ground before you,' Caradoc ordered.

Oldcastle hesitated, but then smiled and obeyed.

'What you say of these houses is true,' Caradoc began, 'yet the real question is otherwise. You speak against the ungodly, but you are still John Oldcastle. You are an English captain who fought against our liberty in the wars. The houses of the monks are our enemies, but then so are you.'

'I have not concealed it,' Oldcastle replied. 'I deal with all men honestly. I am an English knight and I fought for my prince and my race against all who opposed them, not only in your Wales but in far Scotland and Flanders. In my whole life I have never done less than my duty.'

'I know nothing of those distant wars. But you came in arms among our mountains. You took the submission of our men of the west at Defynnog.'

'It was an honourable submission.'

'There are many who doubt that. There were lives lost.'

'Not by my command. In all my life I have observed the laws of war.'

'Yet the question remains between us. What welcome can you suppose in these places you have harried?'

'My friend, I do not suppose it. But in all honesty I ask for it. Not by the custom of hospitality, but by what with me is even stronger, our common life in the faith.'

'We would expect you to look for that, not here among your enemies but among your own people.'

'My own people? Who are now my own people? For in the plotting and corruption of that great Antichrist I am hunted for my life.'

'Why for your life?'

Oldcastle reached inside his tunic and took out a small leather book. He held it in front of his face and then reverently kissed it.

'This that I hold is my life, for it is the word of God in his Holy Testament. Yet my life is at stake because its words are those of my own mother tongue. English words. The Antichrist is content with its Latin Scriptures for then the people cannot understand them and perceive the distance between Christ and its own vicious life. In the last year by an act of the king in Parliament at Leicester it was ordered that whoever should read the Scriptures in the mother tongue should forfeit land, cattle, body, life and goods, and should be allowed no sanctuary, though sanctuary may still be given to the worst thieves and murderers. If any man persists in reading the word of God in his own language he will first be hanged for treason against the king, and then be burned for heresy against God. It is from these penalties that I now ride into your mountains.'

Caradoc was silent for some time. He stared closely into the knight's face. Above the heavy moustache, the skin of the cheeks was a bright red with broken veins at the cheekbones. The eyes, which looked steadily back at him, were a clear blue. At the angle of the left jaw was a long pale scar.

'These are distant quarrels,' he said at last. 'You hold the holy book in your own tongue, but it is not our tongue.'

'It can be brought to your tongue by your own learned men so that all may read and find grace.'

'It is not then an English cause you pursue?'

'No, friend. It is God's cause.'

Caradoc again waited, then turned on his heel. 'Follow to my house,' he said quickly. 'You shall at least in God's name have rest and food.'

As Oldcastle took his horse and followed him up the lane, the women Megan and Elen came from behind the brambles where they had been listening to the men speaking and watched them out of sight.

'It was him at Defynnog,' Elen said excitedly.

'We know nothing of it,' old Megan replied, 'but he speaks like a godly man.'

'It was no godly man made me a widow,' Elen answered sharply, and went back to the bush, where she picked hurriedly at a fresh crop of berries, looking down at her red stained hands.

That evening, after a supper of mutton and cheese served by Caradoc's wife Olwen, Oldcastle moved from his stool and stretched his cloak on the rushes by the fire in the centre of the long room. The cattle were not yet housed in their stalls beyond the central passageway, since there had been a good late growth of grass, and they could stay some weeks longer in the fields. Only half the flock of sheep had as yet been brought down from the mountain. After a while Olwen climbed the ladder to the sleeping loft at the eastern end of the room, where the children were already asleep. Caradoc stared down at Oldcastle's long body as he lay stretched by the fire gazing into the red embers.

'You are tired. Shall I leave you to sleep?' he asked.

'I am tired but I shall not easily sleep,' Oldcastle replied. 'For in these last months even my days have been a nightmare, and all my dreams are strange to me.'

'Yet you have ridden far, and your body will force you to rest.'

Oldcastle raised himself on his elbow.

'Did you ever see,' he asked, 'Prince Henry, now Fifth Henry King of England?'

'Indeed,' Caradoc replied, 'for we of these southern and eastern valleys made our submission to him at Crucorney in 1405. He took little notice of us, for he was then not much more than a boy.'

'It was that boy I served with from his earliest years,' Oldcastle said sadly. 'We raised our swords together. We lay side by side in the fields. We were as close, it seemed, as brothers in all the trials of the wars.'

'And this is the king who now pursues you?'

'That is the nightmare. For I must tell you that several of his most loyal knights, who had carried the burden of the war against Glyndŵr, were men of true faith and of piety: Lewis Clifford, John Cheyne, Thomas Clanvow. Our devotion to the crown and to our religion was widely known, and blamed by no man. In our duty, after the worst of the fighting, we sustained many poor and godly preachers in our own districts. After my marriage I inherited the barony of Cobham in Kent and entered the House of Peers. Again, in my duty I supported more honest and godly preachers, and by this time there were writings of sermons and other addresses

prepared by those who had come to the true faith in the light of the
noble teaching of Master Wiclif. All this was our honest and godly
work. But when that same prince, whom I had served and loved,
came two years past to the throne on the death of his father, he was
at once surrounded by the greedy and worldly lords of the Church,
under their Archbishop Arundel. And he who had been brave and
hard in the field was now soft and supple in their hands. For they at
once moved against us who were a threat to their worldliness, and
we who had looked to our prince as a friend, were slandered and
cast off as if we were no more than the riotous companions of his
boyhood.'

Caradoc shifted on his stool. The knight, still gazing into the fire,
seemed to be talking more to the embers than to his actual listener.

'It is the way of some princes,' he said at last.

Oldcastle turned as if surprised, and sat up. Outside in the
darkness there was the bark of a fox, and Caradoc's chained dogs
began barking in reply.

'I was accused of heresy,' Oldcastle said, 'and called to be
examined by Arundel and his creatures. I refused to go. When I was
at last persuaded, at the insistence of the new king, I offered to
defend my true faith by law of arms against any champion they
might set against me. "It it not your sword but your soul that now
comes to trial," they contemptuously replied. I went away and
prepared a writing of my honest beliefs and of my submission to
Christ. I caused this writing to be sent to the king. He then called me
to him, and I went in gladness. This would be again my Hal, my
prince, my comrade of the wars. But he had scarcely looked at the
writing. He handed it at once to the lords of the Church who
surrounded him. Then, when we were alone, he urged me to submit
at once to the authority of the Church. I replied that I would always
obey him as king with all I have of fortune or nature. But I could not
and would not obey the Pope and his creatures, because I knew from
the Scriptures that the Pope is the great Antichrist and the open
adversary of God.' Oldcastle paused, and then stood abruptly. He
walked restlessly around the fire. He pushed in with his boot a half
burned ash branch. 'When the King heard these words he was
angry. "How can you, John, speak this treason to my face?" "It is
no treason, my lord," I replied. "It is open treason," he shouted, "for
the authority of the crown and of the Church are as one. It is your

way of rousing conspirators, you false, and treacherous Lollards, who now challenge the one with the other." "The word Lollard," I replied, "is but the mumbling cant of these vicious lords of the Church. We are all honest knights and in our religion serve only the written and revealed word of God." "It is no word of God," he cried, "to say the Pope is the Antichrist." "I will prove it to you, my lord," I replied calmly, "for Christ was meek and merciful, the Pope is rich and a most cruel manslayer, as his daily acts prove." But at this, finally, the young king was beside himself. He said he would speak no more with me. He called in the Archbishop and gave him full authority to proceed against me for heresy. I looked very openly at the boy with whom I had fought in the field, but he only turned his back. I was taken at once to the Tower, and then my examination would begin.'

Caradoc got up and stretched his arms.

'You are tired, my friend,' Oldcastle said. 'You must go to your bed. I will speak more of this tomorrow.'

Next morning, early, when Caradoc came down from the loft, Oldcastle was already gone from his place by the fire, though his sword still lay on his cloak by the white ashes. He hurried out to the yard and saw the tall figure of the knight on top of the grassy mound looking down the valley to the south. Caradoc called and went up to him.

'This is a fine valley,' Oldcastle said, 'for you get the best warmth of the sun, and your mountain shelters you from the heaviest of the winds. Though the sides are so steep, you have good pasture I see beside your river.' They looked down together where the cattle were grazing in a meadow beside the wooded stream.

'What is that sharp rockfall, below your western ridge?'

'There are two,' Caradoc replied, 'the Red Darren and the Black.'

'And there, beyond the mists in the valley? Is that the Castle of Ewyas Lacy?'

'It is, my lord. You can see how bluntly it watches over and guards us.'

'You hold your land from that lordship?'

'Indeed no. For this is the Welshry, and our own land, though we must pay commorth to the constable.'

'There is only a constable? Does no lord live there?'

'It is not explained to us, my lord. The constable was appointed by the Lady Despenser, whom none of us have seen.'

'Then it will be held by the Mortimers,' Oldcastle said confidently, 'whatever names may be used.'

'It is the same commorth whatever the name.'

'Of course, but some lords may harass you, and others deal honestly.'

Caradoc looked away. "Many things,' he said, 'were done in the war.'

Oldcastle nodded. He was looking up at a buzzard, which was circling above the pastures. They heard its sharp, thin cry.

'Yet you now live well here, my friend. I have seen your cattle and your sheep, the bees in your orchard. You have geese and pigs in plenty.'

'The bees are now flying to the heather on the mountain. It will be our best honey.'

'It is a life to be envied if left undisturbed.'

'Yet that, my lord,' Caradoc said sharply, 'it has never been.'

Oldcastle smiled and looked down at the orchard, where Megan and Elen and two men of the household were picking apples.

'Are those for cider?'

'Yes, what they are taking now.'

'I walked among them. You make perry also?'

'A little. We have only the small pears.'

'I saw them. They are little better than wild. We have much finer pears at Almeley.'

'Is it your home, Almeley?' Caradoc asked.

'Yes, I was born at Almeley, to the north beyond the Wye. When I was a boy in my father's house I could look every day at your mountains. That strange black wall attracted me, and I had dreams of making discoveries beyond it. When I asked my elders they said only that it was a place of magic and danger. Even my father, who was never fanciful, said he saw it always as a storm cloud, which would one day break upon us.'

'You were looking from a distance and without knowing.'

'It may be so, yet when Glyndŵr rose against us we all believed he was a magician, and had spirits in his power.'

'We saw none,' Caradoc replied.

'Of course, when it came to fighting it was only man to man. Yet many still say that he is in truth a magician, for he has disappeared, though many have looked for him.'

Caradoc did not answer.

'There is rumour,' Oldcastle persisted, 'that he is at Monnington in the Dore valley with his daughter. Yet none have seen him there, and the people speak only of a strange old man whom they call John of Kent.'

'John of Kent is of Grosmont,' Caradoc said shortly.

'I am not pressing you, my friend, yet I think through the surprising changes of fortune. Glyndŵr the great enemy is now pardoned by the king. Many search, but none can find him, as if he had vanished from the earth; yet I, John Oldcastle, the Prince's captain, am condemned and hunted and from day to day almost taken.'

'Our Prince is among his own people,' Caradoc said.

Oldcastle looked away, northward.

They went back to the house and ate oatcake and drank buttermilk. John Oldcastle had fallen silent. When he got up again restlessly, he turned on Caradoc.

'Your words search my heart. Who are now my own people. In my own shire where I lived in honour, where I was even sheriff and member of Parliament I am denounced from every pulpit, and my excommunication declared among the people. It is by the order of the bishop of Hereford, a canting Carmelite friar Robert Mascall. And though they will not let the people read the word of God in their own mother tongue, yet this declaration is ordered to be in English, for of course they will speak plainly when it suits their purposes.'

Caradoc said nothing.

'I am safer in Wales,' Oldcastle said loudly, 'than in my own country.'

'Are you sure of that, my lord?'

'Nothing is any more sure. You say you submitted to my Prince after Grosmont?'

'Yes.'

'You had fought at Grosmont?'

'Yes.'

'You captured and burnt the town, but did not attack the castle, though the Prince himself was inside?'

'Yes.'

'Yet now the Welsh archers of these mountains are serving with King Henry in his campaign in France.'

'There was a levy of the younger men.'

'You were yourself an archer?'

'Yes.'

'I turn these matters all ways and a strange thought comes to me, which would indeed be a kind of heresy. We have fought, you and I, as Welshman and Englishman, yet in the way of the world such distinction is confused and at times altogether confounded. And then perhaps indeed it is a false distinction and the only division under Christ is between the ungodly and the godly.'

Caradoc hesitated. 'It may be both,' he said, but did not wish to continue the argument. He walked to the yard, and Oldcastle followed. One of the men came up from the orchard and Caradoc went down with him. The black cart was filled with the small shiny cider apples and a roan pony was being backed into the shafts. The group walked beside the cart to the cider press behind the house. The apples were unloaded into the stone trough and Caradoc adjusted the screw of the press. Busy with his work, he did not at first notice that Oldcastle had wandered away. When he left the press he heard the sound of chopping on the other side of the house, and walked through to find him at work on the woodpile. He had taken off his tunic, which lay neatly folded on the ground with his leather-bound Testament on top of it. As he finished work on a big cherry branch, he turned and saw Caradoc.

'It is not work I would expect you to be doing, my lord,' Caradoc said.

'In the field I lived hard,' Oldcastle replied, 'and it seemed to me that I might deserve in this way another night by your fire.'

'You are welcome without the work. It is a law among us Welsh that a soldier is given shelter.'

'Even an English soldier?'

'If he comes in peace.'

Oldcastle smiled and went on with his work. Caradoc went back to the cider press, and it was mid-afternoon before they met again.

They sat and drank cider together on the low stone wall which divided the yard from the orchard. The women, in their white head dresses, were again picking apples to refill the cart. The sun was moving lower above the high wall of Cwrwm, which was already black in shadow. On the crib the green grass and the yellowing bracken were still bright in the sun.

'I have been looking at the tracks you make to the ridges,' Oldcastle said. 'They surprised me by turning so often at such narrow angles.'

'The pitch is too steep for any other way,' Caradoc replied.

'I am sure you are right, but it is strange. In these mountains there are hardly any direct ways.'

'They are old beyond memory,' Caradoc said. 'Always we follow the steps of our fathers.'

'Is there no fast track from this valley?'

'Indeed,' Caradoc said, 'for if you follow the river to its source there is a narrow track over the pass. It is littered with loose stones, and the ponies often slip there. But when you are beyond the pass there is good riding to the Beacon and the Hay.'

The sun was now touching the black wall of Cwrwm. Oldcastle took his Testament from his tunic and laid it between them.

'You have heard the words of Christ preached, but have you read them for yourself?'

'I do not read, my lord, and my English is only the daily words of the market.'

'Yet you have learnt the full difference between true religion and false?'

'I cannot say. I take mass from an honest priest, and I try to live honestly. I know the greed and tricks of the Abbey of Dore, yet as to true and false I am not fitted to judge.'

Oldcastle put his hand on the Testament. 'With these words of God all men are fitted to judge. This is why I have supported honest preachers who can bring the words to those not yet able to read.'

'Yet you were blamed for this?' Caradoc asked frowning.

'All are blamed who would spread the word of God beyond the licence of the lords of the Church.'

'And for this you were condemned?'

'I was condemned for what they call heresy. I will tell you the words which I used at my trial: "Anyone who rebukes your vicious living you say must be a heretic, and you set your doctors to prove that there are no Scriptures to support. This is a venom shed into the

Church." The Archbishop at once asked me, "What is that venom?" I replied: "Your possessions and lordships."'

Caradoc lifted himself from the wall. He was silent for some time.

'You do not follow my meaning?' Oldcastle asked.

'There are possessions and lordships everywhere,' Caradoc replied.

'Indeed, yet by the word of Christ the clergy should be secluded from all worldliness, and live in single poverty. If they live otherwise, as so many now do, we knights are bound by law of office to compel them to change their ways, just as we are bound by law to preserve the common people from oppression and tyrants and thieves. What then are we to do when we find the very Church oppressing and stealing?'

Caradoc turned and looked shrewdly into Oldcastle's open face.

'I begin to understand,' he said quietly.

'I am glad,' Oldcastle continued, barely noticing the look, 'for I could prove it on them. They draw money from their shrivings and confessions and from their feigned absolutions and pardons. The pilgrimages they promote, for people to gaze on idols, are conceived only for profit. With all these practices they are drawing to themselves the substance and wealth of the kingdom. Against this we say that the true use of wealth is to serve the people, to found hospitals and universities and to endow those landless knights on whom the safety of the realm must depend.'

'The course is familiar,' Caradoc replied, 'for it was these aims that Prince Owain Glyndŵr came among us to accomplish when we had lifted the Saxon yoke.'

The women had left the orchard and were driving the cows up for milking. Olwen brought bread and meat on a large wooden platter and placed it on the wall. Oldcastle reached out his hand for the bread and was lifting it to his mouth when he suddenly spoke again.

'They could not answer me on that,' he said excitedly, 'but instead they set me a trap on the nature of the blessed Sacrament, for I had affirmed that in the Sacrament we eat the very body of Christ in the form that he lived on this earth. This is the word of Scripture, but it was not enough for them. "You say," they asked, "that it is the body of Christ, yet is it also when blessed still bread?" "Certainly it is bread," I replied, "for this is the truth of his word. Just as when he lived on earth he was seen as a man, and his Godhead was visible only in faith, so this that we see is and remains true bread, but in its blessing as a sacrament is the body of Christ." At this they all shouted. There were now not only the three who first examined me, but a great company they had assembled in the Friary in Ludgate, priors and doctors, priests and monks, canons, friars and clerks, even bellringers and pardoners. "You are condemned from your own mouth," one of the doctors pronounced. "In no way," I replied, "for this is the case, that in my frail youth I offended God most grievously. I hurt many men in my anger and committed many other terrible sins, yet for this breaking of God's laws you crowd of Churchmen never yet cursed me. It is only when your own authority is challenged from the very word of the scriptures that you condemn and cruelly use me."'

The cattle were crossing the yard with Elen walking behind them.

'This now,' Oldcastle shouted, 'is the evil of Holy Church. For they still urged idols against me. "Will you not worship," they asked, "the very cross of Christ?" "Where is it?" I replied.'

Oldcastle stood on the low wall and extended his arms to make a cross. The last rays of the setting sun seemed to surround him.

'"Should I worship this?" I asked them. "Christ's cross figure was of wood," they replied. "Then should we worship that wood as an idol?" I challenged them, "for by the word of Scripture our salvation is not in the cross but in him that died on it."'

Elen had stopped in the yard as Oldcastle's loud voice continued. She was staring fixedly at him. There was a shout along the track and Caradoc's neighbour Morgan of Turnant rode his grey pony across to them.

'Caradoc!' he shouted. 'There are soldiers coming armed from the castle.'

Oldcastle turned at once and jumped from the wall.

'They hunt me,' he shouted.

Caradoc moved quickly.

'Get your sword and your cloak. I will go for your horse.'

Oldcastle ran into the house. Caradoc hurried to saddle Oldcastle's big horse. As he was leading it to the yard Oldcastle was hurrying from the house. Olwen was thrusting a bag of food into his hand. Then Elen cried and ran forward. She was carrying her milking stool. As Oldcastle was passing her she threw the stool between his legs and he fell heavily.

'What are you doing, woman?' Caradoc shouted.

'He killed Ifor in his wars,' Elen cried, 'and now in this place he speaks of Holy Church as evil, and with his own body mocks the death of Our Saviour.'

'You understand nothing,' Caradoc shouted distractedly.

Oldcastle still lay on the ground. He was badly winded by the fall. Morgan went and helped him to his feet, but he was still dazed.

'Mount!' Caradoc shouted, and they helped him to the saddle. As he settled there the Testament slipped from his cloak to the ground. Caradoc picked it up.

'Now ride,' he ordered. 'By the river, as I told you, to the pass.'

He slapped the horse's rump, and it galloped away.

They watched horse and rider disappear among the oaks toward the stones of the source.

Caradoc never saw John Oldcastle again, but it is known that he remained at liberty in different parts of Wales for a further two years. He was then at first betrayed, and, after a fight, captured in 1417 near Welshpool. He was sent to the Tower of London, and condemned again for heresy and treason. With his arms bound behind him he was drawn on a hurdle to a gallows in Saint Giles's Field. He was then hung in chains above a slow fire in which he burned alive. This was in the fifth year of the reign of the Fifth Henry: a year now famous for the victory of Agincourt, the battle in which Welsh archers from these mountains were fighting in the very month when Oldcastle came to Olchon.

Last

———◆———

*P*ress your fingers close on this lichened sandstone. With this
stone and this grass, with this red earth, this place was received
and made and remade. Its generations are distinct, but all suddenly
present.

Postscript

◆

My husband Raymond Williams died before *People of the Black Mountains* was finished. He designed the book to be read as a whole, and many of the earlier themes were to be picked up again in the later stories. He left two versions of his plan for the rest of the book, which varied slightly, and, as these notes were skeletal, I have also drawn on memories of conversations; for example, the plan marked 'provisional' contains things not in the later version, though he talked of including them, in particular the Wars of the Roses, and the Rebecca Riots. No doubt there would have been some changes when the detailed work had been done, but the following outline is the nearest I can get to the stories he was going to write and the subject of the link passages, as he called the sections entitled 'Glyn to Elis'.

By the thirteenth 'Glyn to Elis', Glyn has reached the Old Quarries, Chwarel y Fan. The thirteenth sequence now contains only the 'Abergavenny Rising', 'The Comet' and 'Oldcastle in Olchon'. So his novel ends in the place where it began almost 25,000 years before, Little Stone Valley where the hunter Marod and his band finally trapped the horse herd. Here too we see new lines being drawn up as national rivalries give place to religious alliances. The power of the crown extends into the Marcher lands as heresy is identified with treason: both peoples are now pawns in the central games of Church and state. This would have been followed by a story of how the people of the Black Mountains survived the Wars of the Roses by moving their cattle from one rival lordship to another to escape the plundering armies. The next story was to have been about the effects of the Acts of Union of England and Wales, after the Tudor victory, on the life of a farming family, and the growth of the wool trade.

He planned to follow this with a story set in the valley of the river Dore. A young girl who had been in London as a maid to Blanche Parry of New Court was to return home with stories of the very different life of the royal court. Blanche Parry was lady in waiting all her life, to Elizabeth I, and sponsored her great nephew Roland Vaughan at court. Roland later went to Ireland, where he contracted an illness referred to as 'the country disease', and came back to the Golden Valley to develop an ideal community in 'the Paradice of the backside of the Principallitie'. He proposed to irrigate the valley with the help of four thousand 'mechanicalls', to improve the land and relieve poverty. In his proposal published in 1610, he referred to them as 'Jovialists' and proposed they should all wear 'Scarlet Cappes'. The scheme ended in failure.

The final story in this section was to be about a small Baptist community in the Olchon Valley, one of the first: the publication of a Bible and prayer book in Welsh towards the end of the sixteenth century fostered the growth of Protestant sects in a mainly Catholic Wales.

The link passage, 'Glyn to Elis: 14', would have been on the mountain above the wooded ridge of Ewyas, 'Cefn Coed Euas'. This was to be about the idea of 'Britain'. With the arrival of the Tudor dynasty on the English throne in 1485, the Welsh felt they had reconquered England, and many of the nobility moved to the English court. John Dee, the mathematician and philosopher, related to Blanche Parry and many other border families, was established at the court of Edward VI by 1551. An interpreter and populariser of science, he survived the persecutions of Mary's reign, and became a consultant on state affairs to Elizabeth I. He wrote, in a series of *Titles*, now lost, of his concept of a British Empire which could claim Scandinavia, the Arctic, and islands to the west, conquered, he believed, by King Arthur. He also laid claim to the whole of the New World for Elizabeth, on the basis of the story of the twelfth century Welsh explorer Madoc.

Section 14 was planned to contain stories from the period 1640 to 1800. The first would follow the occupation of Elchon, or Ewyas Harold, by the Scots army in 1645, during the Civil War, with possibly some reference to the poet and physician Henry Vaughan who came from Scethrog in the Usk valley and was the grandson of

William Vaughan of Tretower. (Like most people of the area he was a Royalist.)

The next story would describe the martyrdom of a Roman Catholic priest, David Lewis, a native of Abergavenny, who held services in a chapel on the summit of Great Skirrid, also called Holy Mountain. The owner of Llanvihangle Court, whose family had also acquired the Priory and lands of Llanthony on the dissolution of the monasteries, was the local Justice of the Peace and Member of Parliament John Arnold. He accused, arrested and brought to trial the priest whom people called 'The Father of the Poor', in 1678, in the panic following the popish plot of Titus Oates. David Lewis was accused of treason and put to death at Usk. Accounts of his trial and address from the scaffold still exist.

The Skirrid Inn was the scene of the next story. Following the Monmouth Rebellion Judge Jeffreys held court there in the 'bloody assizes' of 1685. Some local people were sentenced to be hanged, and many more were transported to slavery in the colonies.

Howell Harris, a leader of the Methodist revival, known as the greatest Welshman of his century, was to be the central figure of the next story. In 1735, while a schoolmaster at Llangorse, he became converted and started working as a lay preacher. Later, travelling with Madam Sidney Griffiths, he 'collected' converts into societies and associations. Twenty years later he had gathered a 'Family' from all over Wales, who formed themselves into an almost self-sufficient community at Trefeca, which later became a college. Harris also became a founder member of the Brecknockshire Agricultural Society and attempted to combine community living with learning, religion and improved agriculture.

The link section 'Glyn to Elis: 15' was to show Glyn's reflections as he reached the high point of Bal Mawr, on the part played by religion in the history of the mountains.

The fifteenth sequence was intended to cover the period from 1800 to 1910. The first story was of the move of a farming family uphill to new land during the agricultural prosperity of the Napoleonic Wars. This expansion to marginal land could not be maintained when prices fell again with the end of the war. The family was forced to break up, and one brother, Bleddyn, to emigrate to the United States.

During the nineteenth century there was a revival of the eisteddfod as a serious activity, intended both as a gathering of poets, and a more general celebration for cultural activities and competitions. The story of an eisteddfod in Abergavenny in the middle of the century would have recalled its early traditions, and in particular the meeting of 1176 at Cardigan held by the Lord Rhys, Rhys ap Gruffydd, just after the Abergavenny Massacre.

In one plan, a story about the Rebecca Riots was intended next. Agrarian poverty, increased tithe charges and the Poor Law Amendment Act of 1834, contributed to riots especially against charges at tollgates on the public roads in the early 1840s. Men on horseback dressed as women, burned the gates and tollbooths, taking their motto from the book of Genesis, 'And they blessed Rebekah and said unto her "may your descendants possess the gate of those who hate them".'

The final story of this sequence was to centre on the funeral of a man on a small mountain farm. Two brothers of the widow attend the funeral. One, a miner, has come from the coalpits of South Wales, the other, Rhodri, is a soldier on leave from the South Wales Borderers. He was to tell of the part his regiment played in the Zulu Wars of 1879, and their decimation in the defence of Rorkes Drift. The central event of this episode was to be the arrival of the 'sin eater', a custom which still existed in the mountains into the nineteenth century. After the funeral meal had been served to the mourners, the coffin was closed and a glass of wine placed on it. The sin eater was usually a poor man who travelled around to funerals for this purpose. He would drink the wine and so take on the sins of the dead. The mourners also followed an old custom known as 'the last sacrament'. Cake and wine were offered them as they stood around the coffin, handed round from east to west, the way of the sun.

Glyn had reached the Tower and Garn Wen, the sacred stone circle, by 'Glyn to Elis: 16'. This section was to have been about language. In this border country English is now most commonly spoken, having been the official language of law courts and public life since the Acts of Union in the middle sixteenth century. Welsh, the language of family and home for many people, was saved from extinction by the publication of the Welsh Bible and prayer book a generation later. This had preserved the literary language and kept the spoken language as a unit.

The stories in the sixteenth sequence were to cover the period from the First War to 1942, during the Second War. The first story was of the son of the soldier Rhodri, who had left the army to marry and settle in the Black Mountains. The son was to grow up there till the First War, then volunteer and join the South Wales Borderers, (as Raymond's father had done) to be wounded and return home to meet and marry the girl who later became the mother of Elis, and thus Glyn's great-grandmother.

I believe, though it is not in either of the plans, that there would have been a story in this section about the construction of a new road to the Black Mountains, for the building of a reservoir in the Valley of the Grwyne Vechan, supplying water to the mining valleys of South Wales. A large settlement of construction workers lived there during the work in the very places where the hunters of Maenhebog had once found refuge.

The next story, based on a true episode, would have concerned the discovery made by a farmer in the 1930s while ploughing up a field in the Olchon Valley. He uncovered what turned out to be a double cist grave. One cist contained the body of a woman, the other, better preserved, of a young man, wounded in the head. Buried alongside him were barbed and tanged arrow-heads, a wrist-guard, some round stone discs, and a bell-shaped beaker.

During the war an American aeroplane, returning from a mission, crashed in the Black Mountains. The next story was the discovery of the pilot's body with the name Bleddyn on his identity disk: but no one would have recognised him as the descendant of the Bleddyn mentioned in the earlier story who had emigrated to the States from a nearby upland farm a century before.

The last story was to be of Elis's boyhood and youth in the mountains, and his call-up during the war to the Royal Corps of Signals. (Raymond himself joined the Signals during the war, but soon moved to the Guards Armoured Brigade.)

Glyn was finally to find his grandfather Elis with an injured foot, inside the stone circle of Garn Wen, and take him, with the help of the Mountain Rescue team, to the local hospital. A word which it is difficult to decipher follows. I think it must be Nemeton, a name which the Celts had used for a sacred place, some of which were places of healing. (Burros, in the story of Bibra, goes to the temple of healing at Nemetobala to be cured.)

There are a few notes about the final section. It would have been about 'the connection of memory through remembered generations', and also of 'memory across a place'. Another note just says 'Learning'. There was certainly to have been a discussion with Elis about the 'neolithic hippies' he had met and argued with at their camp on Twyn y Beddau. I believe that Elis's argument was to have been that the way the hippies used the place as a parking-lot and source of liberty cap mushrooms, while drawing their means of life from the whole society, was quite unlike the life of the neolithic people who had lived there, and that their lifestyle was a misuse of the land and a form of exploitation of the settled workers who were committed to the place for their livelihood, and that of their descendants. The neolithic people had lived in the Black Mountains within the limits of their own resources, with full awareness, from the experience of many generations, of what they could do to nature and what nature could do to them. Elis would have argued that people can only survive if they live in harmony with each other and with their land, as Karan had said to the Wise One, 'for the sweetness of the place'.

Joy Williams, 1990

Place Names

Abisso Aberllynfi settlement, Gwernyfed
Alaron Longtown
Arcala settlement near Monmouth
Bald Hills Malverns
Banavint Pen Twyn hill fort, ancient Bentelim
Bear Mountain Myndd Eppynt
Bodosa settlement in the Dore Valley
Burro Burrium, Usk
Cala a cave
Cambo settlement where the Monnow bends to flow east
Cara a stone
Carvon Carfan, Alcarfan, Skenfrith
Caeriddon Credenhill Camp
Cicucio Roman fort at Brecon
Claerion Clyro
Cornio Twyn y Gaer hill fort
Cross Valley Vale of Ewyas, Valley of the Honddu
Crouco Crucio, Crugader, Crug Hywel, Crickhowell
Dun Rignan Dinas Rhiangoll, Dunon Osniu, Castel Dinas
Elchon Ewyas Harold
Elfael region north of the River Wye
Erdyl Ercing, Erging, Archenfield
Ferdun Ferddin, Mynydd Merddin
Glaura settlement by Lake Llangorse
Glevum Gloucester
Gobanio Gofanio, Bergavenny, Abergavenny, Y Fenni
Gofyf iron works at Gwernyfed
Grain Valley Valley of the River Dore
Guenta Venta, Gwent

Guerinou   River Grwyne Fawr
Guuy   River Wye
Hawkstone   Maenhebog, Menhebog, Glan Bwch, Twmpath
High Buck   Bocalt, ridge from Pen y Beacon to Gospel Pass
Hodoni   South River, River Ondi, Honddu
Horn Point   Crib y Garth, Cat's Back
Isca   Caerleon
Iuas   Euas, Ewyas
Iupania   settlement on Severn Estuary, near mouth of Wye
Lanoluc   settlement under Pen y Beacon, Maes Goch longhouse
Leucara   Lake Locara, Ara, Syfaddon, Llangorse
Little Mountain River   Upper Monnow
Little Stone Valley   Olchon Valley
Look Hill   Little Doward
Madrun   settlement near Talgarth
Mamcala   Home Cave, King Arthur's Cave (Paviland cave is also referred to as Mamcala)
Masona   Telim, Satelim, Altyrynys
Menvandir   Durrington Walls and the round houses on Salisbury Plain
Myngui   River Mynwy, Monnow
Riverjoin   junction of River Monnow and River Dore
Sacred Circle   Garn Wen
Salmon River   Uisc, Usk
Satelin   Telim, valley settlement at join of River Monno and Honddu
Seariver   Hsabren, Severn
Skirrid   Broken Mountain, Isgirit, Skirrid Fawr
South River   River Honddu
Stream of Birds   River Rhiangol
Telim   Altyrynys
Uroicaissa   'place of heather', upland from Cusop Hill to Urishay Common
Venta Silurum   Caerwent
White Cap   Pen Cerrig Calch
White Land   Southern England
Wolfhead   Mynndd Llangorse
Yellow Hills   Cotswolds

Book List

◆

Since the first part of *People of the Black Mountains* was published many readers have said that they would like to learn more
about the history of the region, so we have provided a short list of
the books and periodicals which proved most useful in researching
the background to the novel. They are listed in chronological order
of the general periods to which they refer.

People have also asked how true the stories are. All the stories
were invented, but the settings are as authentic as possible, and the
later ones are based on known historical events, such as the Viking
raids, and the killing of Richard de Clare. Other stories are based on
archaeological finds – for example one can see a reproduction of the
Olchon cist where the character Anailos (who appears in Part I) is
buried, in Hereford Museum. The body of an elderly woman,
deformed in exactly the same way as Bibra, was actually found at
Kentchester, known as 'Magnis'.

Colin Renfrew (ed) *British Prehistory* (Duckworth 1974)
J. G. Evans *The Environment of Early Man in the British Isles*
(University of California Press 1975)
Colin A. Lewis (ed) *The Glaciation of Wales and Adjoining Regions*
(Longman 1970)
D. Garrod *The Upper Paleolithic Age in Britain* (Clarendon Press,
Oxford 1926)
G. C. Boon and J. M. Lewis *Welsh Antiquity* (National Muse·.m of
Wales 1976)
R. B. Lee and I. Devore *Man the Hunter* (Aldine Publishing Co.
1968)
John G. D. Clark *Prehistoric England* (Batsford 1940)

John G. D. Clark *The Stone Age Hunters* (Thames & Hudson 1967)

K. Branigan *Prehistoric Britain* (Spurbooks 1976)

John G. D. Clark *Prehistoric Europe: The Economic Basis* (Methuen 1952)

Lynch and Burgess (eds) *Prehistoric Man in Wales and the West* (Bath 1972)

I. W. Cornwall *Prehistoric Animals and Their Hunters* (Faber 1968)

S. C. Stanford *The Archaeology of the Welsh Marches* (Collins 1980)

John G. D. Clark *The Mesolithic Age in Britain* (Cambridge University Press 1932)

M. D. Sahlins *Stone Age Economics* (Routledge 1989)

S. Piggot *Neolithic Cultures of the British Isles* (Cambridge University Press 1954)

E. W. Mackie *Science and Society in Prehistoric Britain* (P. Elek 1977)

D. D. A. Simpson (ed) *Economy and Settlement in Neolithic and Early Bronze Age Britain and Europe* (Leicester University Press 1971)

P. D. Webley *The Neolithic Colonisation of the Black Mountains* (B. B. Celtic Studies No. 18)

F. E. Zeuner *A History of Domesticated Animals* (Hutchinson 1963)

W. Ridgeway *The Origins and Influence of the Thoroughbred Horse* (Cambridge University Press 1905)

C. Fox *Life and Death in the Bronze Age* (Routledge 1959)

H. N. Savory *The Late Bronze Age in Wales* (in *Archaeologia Cambrensis* 1958)

H. N. Savory, in I. Foster and L. Alcock (eds) *The Southern Marches of Wales in the Neolithic and Early Bronze Age* (Routledge 1963)

I. Foster and L. Alcock (eds) *Culture and Environment* (Routledge 1963)

R. Ewart Oakeshott *The Archaeology of Weapons* (Lutterworth 1960)

B. W. Cunliffe *Iron Age Communities in Britain* (Routledge 1978)

Nora K. Chadwick *Celtic Britain* (Thames & Hudson 1963)

Henri P. E. Hubert *The Greatness and Decline of the Celts* (Constable 1987)

Anne Ross *Pagan Celts* (Routledge 1967)

Anne Ross *Everyday Life of the Pagan Celts* (Batsford 1970)

K. H. Jackson *Language and History in Early Britain* (Edinburgh University 1953)

A. L. F. Rivet and Colin Smith *The Place Names of Roman Britain* (Batsford 1979)

V. E. Nash-Williams *The Roman Frontier in Wales* (University of Wales 1969)

Grace Simpson *Britons and the Roman Army* (Gregg International 1964)

Julius Caesar *Gallic War V*

Tacitus *Life of Agricola, Annals*

Peter Salway *The Frontier People of Roman Britain* (Cambridge University Press 1965)

P. A. Holder *The Roman Army in Britain* (Batsford 1982)

E. Birley *Roman Britain and the Roman Army* (Titus Williams 1953)

S. Frere *Britannia* (Routledge 1987)

A. H. M. Jones (ed) *A History of Rome Through the Fifth Century* (Harper & Row 1968)

G. R. Jones *Post-Roman Wales*, in *The Agrarian History of England and Wales*, ed H. P. R. Finberg (Cambridge 1972)

J. E. Lloyd *A History of Wales* (2 vols, Longmans 1911)

John Morris *The Age of Arthur* (Weidenfeld 1975)

Gildas (ed M. Winterbottom) *The Ruin of Britain* (Phillimore, Chichester 1978)

Nennius (ed John Morris) *The History of the Britons* (Church History Society 1938)

Nennius (ed and trans. John Morris) *The Welsh Annals* (Phillimore, Chichester 1980)

N. K. Chadwick *Celt and Saxon* (Cambridge University Press 1963)

P. Hunter Blair *Roman Britain and Early England* (Thomas Nelson 1963)

Gwyn A. Williams *When Was Wales?* (Black Raven 1985)

Wendy Davies *Wales in the Early Middle Ages* (Leicester University Press 1982)

Wendy Davies *An Early Welsh Microcosm* (Royal Historical Society 1978)

Wendy Davies (ed) *The Llandaff Charters* (National Library of Wales 1979)

H. P. R. Finberg *The Formation of England 550–1042* (Hart-Davis, MacGibbon 1974)

P. H. Sawyer *The Age of the Vikings* (Edward Arnold 1962)

H. R. Loyn *The Vikings in Wales* (Viking Society for Northern Research for University College London 1976)

B. G. Charles *Old Norse Relations with Wales* (University of Wales Press Board 1934)

E. N. Dumbleton *Llangorse Crannog* (in *Archaeologia Cambrensis* 1870)

Thomas Jones (trans.) *The Chronicle of the Princes* (*The Red Book of Hergest*) (University of Wales 1973)

The Mabinogion (trans. G. and T. Jones, Dent 1949)

D. Walker *The Norman Conquerors* (Swansea 1977)

H. C. Darby and I. B. Terrett (eds) *Domesday Geography of Midland England* (Cambridge 1971)

A. T. Bannister *The History of Ewias Harold* (Jakeman & Carver, Hereford 1902)

A. T. Bannister *Place Names of Herefordshire* (Cambridge 1916)

Geoffrey of Monmouth *History of the Kings of Britain*

Walter Map *De nugis curialium* (ed and trans. M. R. Jones, Clarendon Press, Oxford 1983)

Giraldus Cambrensis *The Journey Through Wales* (Penguin 1978)

Giraldus Cambrensis *Description of Wales* (Penguin 1978)

Gerard J. Brault *Early Blazon* (Clarendon Press, Oxford 1972)

Isabel S. T. Aspin (ed) *Anglo-Norman Political Songs* (Blackwell 1953)

R. Millward and A. Robinson *The Welsh Borders* (Methuen 1978)

David H. Williams *The Welsh Cistercians* (Hughes & Son, Griffin Press, Pontypool 1970)

William J. Rees *South Wales and the March 1284–1415* (Chivers Press 1974)

F. G. Llewellin *The History of St Clodock* (John Heywood, Manchester 1919)

Geoffrey L. Fairs *A History of the Hay* (Phillimore, Chichester 1972)

D. Sylvester *The Rural Landscape of the Welsh Borderland* (Macmillan 1969)

William Rees *The Mediaeval Lordship of Brecon* (Brecknock Museum 1968)

R. R. Davies *Lordship and Society in the March of Wales 1282–1400* (Clarendon Press, Oxford 1978)

D. Jenkins and M. Owen (eds) *The Welsh Law of Women* (University of Wales Press 1980)

J. D. Griffith Davies *Owen Glyn Dŵr* (Eric Partridge 1934)

J. E. Lloyd *Owen Glyn Dŵr* (Clarendon Press 1931)

Adam of Usk *Chronicon*

Select Works of Bishop Bale (ed H. Christmas, Cambridge 1849)

Periodicals

Antiquity
Archaeologia Cambrensis
Brycheiniog
Bulletin of the Board of Celtic Studies
The Monmouthshire Antiquary
Proceedings of the Prehistoric Society
Transactions of the Woolhope Naturalists' Field Club